THE
NUMBERED
ACCOUNT

BLOOMSBURY READER

Discover books by Ann Bridge published by
Bloomsbury Reader at
www.bloomsbury.com/AnnBridge

THE
NUMBERED
ACCOUNT

ANN BRIDGE

BLOOMSBURY READER
LONDON · NEW DELHI · NEW YORK · SYDNEY

This edition published in 2013 by Bloomsbury Reader

Bloomsbury Reader is a division of Bloomsbury Publishing Plc,

50 Bedford Square, London WC1B 3DP

ISBN: 978 1 4482 0495 3
eISBN: 978 1 4482 0451 9

Visit www.bloomsbury.com to find out more about our authors and their books
You will find extracts, author interviews, author events and you can sign up for
newsletters to be the first to hear about our latest releases and special offers

Contents

Chapter 1

Glentoran

The red-funnelled *Flora Macdonald* sidled skilfully alongside the grey wet quay of the small West Highland port, watched by Edina Reeder, who also scanned the passengers waiting above the gangway; when she saw among them a tall elegant figure with a tawny-gold head she smiled and waved. Presently a porter in a seaman's jersey carried the luggage out and stowed it in a brandnew Land-Rover, while the two cousins kissed and exchanged greetings.

'Philip and I thought you were never coming back to Glentoran,' Mrs Reeder said. 'You haven't been up since our wedding, and that's nearly two years ago.'

'I know. I was such ages in Portugal—both times. But it's heavenly to be back now.' As the car shot off from the harbour— 'This is a terrific machine,' Julia Probyn said. 'Philip, I suppose?'

'Oh yes, everything is Philip. You won't know Glentoran!' Edina replied. 'When we got married Mother, in her most Early Christian Martyr way, suggested withdrawing to the little dower-house, but of course we didn't allow that—she's in the west wing. Philip has turned it into a self-contained flat, with a sub-flat for Forbes, horrid old creature! And we raked up Joanna—do you remember?—housemaid ages ago—to be cook; she makes just the sort of horrible food Mother likes, so it's all perfect.'

'I thought the west wing used to be damp,' Julia said.

'Ah, but not any more. Central heating throughout! I expect it's very bad for one, softening, and all that—but I must say it's exceedingly comfortable to be warm everywhere, after those awful wood fires. And Olimpia adores it, salamander that she is.'

'Oh, you've still got Olimpia?'

'Yes indeed. Between having a boiling hot bed-sitting-room, and Philip to talk Spanish to her every day, I think she's settled for life—and of course her food is better than ever.'

'It couldn't be *better*—it was always divine.'

'Well it still is; more divine. Colin's here,' Mrs. Reeder then said. 'He was delighted when you rang up to say that you were coming, because he's going off again fairly soon to the Middle East, or one of those troublesome places.'

'Oh I *am* glad. What luck! Dear Colin.' Miss Probyn was devoted to her other cousin, Edina Reeder's young brother. 'How is he?'

'I fancy he's got something on his mind,' Edina said, slinging the Land-Rover round the curves of a steep hill under huge overhanging beeches, 'but he hasn't uttered. I daresay he'll tell you.' As they reached the top of the hill and emerged into open country—

'Goodness! You've ploughed that slope above Lagganna-Geoich!' Miss Probyn exclaimed. 'It used to be all rushes. What *can* grow there?'

'Winter wheat. It's all been drained—with the government grant, of course—and fenced, as you see.'

Indeed as they now entered on the Glentoran estate, evidences of prosperity and good husbandry appeared on all sides: strong pig-wire fences, Dutch barns, new iron gates painted red; so different from the beloved but rather derelict Glentoran that she had known all her life that Julia fairly gasped. 'I can't think how you've got it all done in the time,' she said, after being shown three or four silage-pits, and a herd of pedigree Ayrshire cows.

'Oh, Philip works all day and most of the night, and adores it. But I must say it's very nice to have some money to come and go on, and be able to treat the land properly. Wait till you see the hill-pastures, limed and re-seeded and all! Of course the subsidies don't nearly cover it, one has to dip into one's pocket all the time—but Philip says he'll be able to bring out a terrific, and quite true, loss on the property for income-tax for this year and next.'

Julia laughed, and returned to the subject of her cousin Colin.

'What makes you think he has something on his mind?'

'He mopes, and jerks his thumb.'

Many of the Monro family had the hereditary peculiarity of double-jointed thumbs, enabling them to turn that member downwards in a spectacular and quite horrible fashion; the operation made an audible creaking sound which was curiously sickening. Edina used this peculiar gift sparingly, being a calm person; but Julia was intensely familiar with it in Colin Monro, as a symptom of nervousness or worry.

However, he showed no sign of either at luncheon, which took place rather late. In spite of all the external improvements, Glentoran within was its old shabby self, rather to Julia's relief—except for the genial all-pervading warmth from the central heating, and a newly-installed fitted basin with scalding hot water in her bedroom. Clearly Philip Reeder believed in spending his good money on useful, practical things rather than on aesthetic amenities; the drawing-room, to which she presently went down, had its old worn and hideous carpet, and the familiar faded cretonne covers. Here Philip gave her a stiff gin, and here also she encountered Colin and old Mrs. Monro, his and Edina's mother.

'How nice to see you, Aunt Ellen,' Julia said, kissing her, and holding out a casual hand to Colin.

'I can't think why you haven't been near us for so long,' Mrs. Monro said fretfully.

'I've been abroad, you know.'

'Everyone will go abroad—I can't think why. Mary Hathaway has gone abroad, when she might just as well have been here,' Mrs. Monro pursued, in a complaining tone. 'She's gone to Switzerland, of all places.'

'To stay with an old flame,' Edina put in. 'Really old—about 80! He lives in Gersau, wherever that is.'

'On the Lake of Lucerne,' Colin said.

'Oh, you know-all! Mother, if you've finished your sherry let's go in, shall we? Julia, bring in your drink.'

Julia, instead, downed it. 'I hate spirits at table.'

Over the meal Mrs. Monro resumed her grumbles.

'I can't think why Mary should have wanted to go to Switzerland. I went there once, and I thought it a most horrid place—all mountains, really there's nowhere to walk on the flat. They took me into an ice-grotto, in some glacier, and it dripped down my neck. I think all that ice and snow about is most unhealthy.'

4

Philip Reeder, laughing, reminded his mother-in-law that large parts of Switzerland were far from any ice or snow, and really not much more mountainous than Argyll—round Lake Neuchâtel, for instance. Julia noticed a certain preoccupation in Colin's expression while the talk was of Switzerland, which left it when they turned to discussing local affairs; presently he addressed her in Gaelic, still spoken here and there in the district; they had both picked it up as children from the keepers and the boatmen, and he gave his rather high-pitched giggle of pleasure when, after a second's hesitation, she replied in the same archaic tongue. After that they talked in Gaelic across the table; this irritated old Mrs. Monro, who eventually protested—'I was brought up to think it very ill-bred to talk in a language that others present cannot understand.'

'They're not ill-bred, Mother; they're merely good linguists,' Edina told her mother. 'So was father, he spoke Gaelic perfectly, the old people always tell me—"He had the Gahlic" is their phrase. You and I aren't linguists, worse luck for us; if we were, we could have learnt it.'

'My dear, I never wished to learn such a useless language,' said old Mrs. Monro, with the complete finality of the rather stupid person.

After lunch Colin determinedly took Julia out to stroll in the garden; Philip went off to the farm and Edina, after returning her mother to the west-wing flat, settled down to some overdue correspondence about Girl Guides. Julia was struck afresh by what a little money—Philip's money—was doing to Glentoran: the lawns close-mown; the strangling brambles cut down from the immense species rhododendrons (brought back as seeds by Hooker himself from the Himalayas) along the banks of the burn; all the deadly growth of sycamore seedlings cleared out from between the rare shrubs along the upper avenue.

'Goodness, it is lovely to see this place being put to rights again,' she said.

'Yes, I suppose so.' Colin sounded *distrait*, as though the improvement in what was really his own estate meant very little to him. Presently he stood still.

'Julia'—he paused.

'Yes?'

'I know it's none of my business, but I'm so fond of him that it worries me—' he paused again, in obvious embarrassment.

'Well?' Julia asked, guessing what was coming.

'Well, how *do* things stand between you and Hugh?'

'They don't stand at all,' Julia said, quite unembarrassed. 'He asked me to marry him in Portugal, and I said NO.'

'Why on earth? He's such a splendid person.'

'I just couldn't feel it the right thing to do—somehow he didn't seem the same in Portugal as he did in Tangier.'

'What do you mean?'

'What I say—and more than that I won't say, because I couldn't explain properly. I'm sorry about it, very, but there it is.'

'Don't you think it's about time you stopped amusing yourself with men, and then turning them down?' Colin said crossly. 'First it was that wretched Consett, though I admit he was a bit of a wet, and now it's Hugh—who certainly isn't wet.'

'No, of course he isn't,' Julia said, with perfect good-temper. 'But I can't marry him because he's your boss, and you're fond of him. I must want *badly* to marry the person I do marry; it wouldn't be fair to them, otherwise—in fact much more unfair than rubbing them off in good time.'

Colin laughed, rather unwillingly, at the flat way in which Julia brought out this piece of wisdom. Suddenly he gave her a kiss.

'Oh well, you're not actually a hag yet,' he said, 'even if you are rather a monster! I daresay you'll find a man you badly want to marry one of these days. Don't leave it too late, though.'

'Try not to, darling,' Julia said, returning his kiss.

Julia wondered after this conversation whether Colin's gloom had been about her and Hugh Torrens, his chief in the Secret Service, and hoped that having said his piece, the young man might feel better. But he continued abstracted.

The whole party foregathered for tea in the diningroom, which, Julia observed with nostalgic satisfaction, was as gloomy, shabby, and ugly as ever—woodlice still crawled, and died, between the outer panes and the hideous stained glass which defaced the upper half of the windows; the log fire still spat and fizzled ineffectually—though, thanks to the central heating, this made no difference to anyone's comfort. Half-way through the deleteriously ample Scottish meal of two kinds of scone, four different cakes, assorted jams and jellies and honey in the comb, the telephone rang. Philip Reeder had installed an extension in every sitting-room in the house, as well as in his own and Edina's bedroom, instead of the single inconviently-placed instrument in the chilly cloak-room near the front door; he rose from the table and answered the call.

'Telegram for you, Julia,' he said, and held out the receiver.

Besides putting in all these telephones, that practical man Philip Reeder insisted that there should always be a writing-block and a pencil beside each machine—woe betide his wife if either were ever missing. Both pad and pencil were in place when Julia went over to the table under the woodlice-laden window; she listened, wrote down, questioned, scribbled again—finally she tore the top sheet off the block, and returned to the table.

'So sorry, Edina. It's from Mrs. H.'

'Why does Mary Hathaway need to send you such a huge long telegram?' old Mrs. Monro asked.

'She's ill, Aunt Ellen, and she wants Watkins to go out and look after her; she's afraid of being a trouble to this old Mr. Waechter and his servants.'

'I'm sorry to hear that,' Philip Reeder said—he had soon come to share the Monro family's affection for Mrs. Hathaway, always their prop and stay in any trouble. 'What's wrong with her?'

'Congestion of the lungs.'

'There! What did I say?' old Mrs. Monro exclaimed triumphantly. 'Switzerland *is* unhealthy. I expect poor Mary went into an ice-grotto!'

'There are no glaciers within forty miles of Gersau, Mother,' Colin put in.

'Then I expect old Mr. Waechter, who I believe is extremely rich, drove her to one,' his mother said obstinately. Philip put a more practical question to his guest.

'Why does she wire to you, Julia? Can't Watkins just take a ticket, and go?'

'Oh no,' his wife hastily told him. 'Watkins can't bear travelling abroad—that's why Mrs. H. didn't take her along. Julia, I suppose this means that you've got to drag that spoilt old creature out in person, doesn't it? Oh what misery!—when you've only just come. I can't think why anyone has a lady's-maid!'

'My dear, when they existed they were a great convenience,' her husband told her—'though this Watkins person sounds rather an unsuitable type, I must say.'

'Watkins has been with Mary Hathaway for twentyfive years, Philip,' his mother-in-law pronounced—'and she is a most faithful and excellent servant.'

'Well, have you got to go out and take her, Julia?' Colin asked—rather to his cousin's surprise.

'Yes, I'm afraid I must do just that,' Julia said. 'Edina, I am so sorry. Philip, may I send a telegram? I ought to do it after tea.'

'Of course. But send it N.L.T., at half the day price,' her host said, with his usual practicality.

'Fine. I must wire to old Watkins too, and tell her to pack her traps and be ready to start when I come. Oh yes, and I must book a flight from Renfrew. What a bore! I was so happy to be up here again!'

'I suppose you'll fly?' her host said. 'Shouldn't you book plane seats to Switzerland too?'

'Oh no; Watkins will never fly—we must go by train. Yes, of course we must get sleepers.'

'Where to?' Reeder asked.

'Berne,' Colin pronounced suddenly. 'You change there for Lucerne, and then take a steamer on to Gersau.'

'How do you know all this?' his sister asked him. The young man jerked his thumb out of joint as he replied—'I just *do* know.'

'Next assignment Switzerland?' his brother-in-law asked. 'Sounds as if you'd been mugging it up.'

'It's coming in very handy for me,' Julia said, as Colin merely shook his head, frowning at this attempt at humour.

After tea much telephoning and sending of telegrams took place: a flight was booked from Renfrew for the following after-noon, Cook's promised sleepers from Calais to Berne two days later; Julia just caught her bank manager and organised travel-ler's cheques. During all this fuss Colin hung about, silent and preoccupied; when Julia said—'Well, that's that'—after talking to the bank, he put in a word.

'What about Watkins's passport?'

'Oh Lord!—I never thought of that. I don't for a moment suppose she's got one. Will they be shut now? What are we to do? We shan't have much time to rake up a Minister of Religion or a Justice of the Peace to vouch for her.'

'I think I'd better ring up the office. They will probably be able to fix it.'

'Could you? Would they?' Julia said, immensely relieved. She was also happily surprised by Colin's helpfulness.

'I expect so. What's her Christian name?'

'No idea,' and 'May,' Julia and Edina said simultaneously.

'Just May? May Watkins? What a name for that old dragoon.'

'Yes, May,' Edina repeated firmly. 'Her mother doted on old Queen Mary. Endless girls in Watkins's generation were called after "Princess May".'

'All right—though it sounds pretty silly to me. Now you girls can clear out. I'll tell you what happens.'

Julia and Edina obediently removed themselves; they sat on a new teak seat on the terrace, in the westering sun, looking out over the drifts of daffodils in the rough grass round the lawn, where the pink candles on the great horse-chestnut were just coming into flame—its lower boughs drooped down to the ground.

'How funny that Colin should lend a hand like this,' Edina said, 'after being so sour when Philip ragged him about Switzerland.'

'I was just thinking the same thing,' Julia replied. 'But anyhow, what a boon! That office of his can fix anything. Still, I do wonder what's behind it—it isn't a bit like him.'

A window was thrown up behind them.

'Where shall May's passport be sent?' Colin's voice enquired.

'My flat. No, my club; of course the flat's shut.'

'That grisly place in Grosvenor Street?'

'Yes.' The window was slammed down again.

'Good for him,' Julia said.

Presently Colin appeared on the terrace.

'All fixed, darling?' Julia asked.

'Yes, darling darling.'

This was another piece of youthful nonsense, dating from the long happy holiday summers when Colin was at Eton, and Julia at a finishing school in Paris; they used the word 'darling' then as a sort of call-note, like a bird's special note of alarm, for any secret thing between them. This had irritated old Mrs. Monro even more than their speaking Gaelic at meals, but it warmed Julia to hear Colin use the old silly re-duplication now. And when he said, 'Come up to the azalea glen—they're all out, and you haven't been yet,' she agreed at once.

'She ought to pack,' Edina said.

'Oh, I'll pack tonight.' The two young people went off up the avenue, arm-in-arm.

The azalea glen at Glentoran when in flower is something to see. The banks of a narrow ravine, down which a small burn runs, were planted long ago with azaleas which have grown to an immense size; the great rounded bushes overhang the water, sprawl above the path, below the path, and even encumber the small wooden bridges which here and there span the glen—fallen blossoms are carried away by the clear noisy water. It is a most beautiful place, full of all shades of colour from cream to coral; the scent, with its hint of incense, is almost overpowering. And here, on a rather decrepit wooden seat—Philip Reeder had not yet extended his new teak benches as far as the glen—Colin and Julia sat and talked; and what Julia privately expressed as 'the nub' emerged.

'If you're really going to Switzerland anyhow, darling, I thought you mightn't mind doing something.'

'For you?'

'Well yes, in a way.' His horrible thumb shot out.

'Tell,' Julia said comfortably.

'Yes, I will. It's about Aglaia Armitage. Her father's dead and her mother's no good—she ran off to the Argentine with a Dago tenor even before poor Armitage died, four years ago.'

'Is Aglaia in Switzerland?' Julia had visions of a girls' school near Lausanne or Ouchy.

'Oh no. But her grandfather died the other day.'

'Was he looking after her?'

'Not much, no—she lived with an aunt in London, her father's sister. But'—Colin paused, and his thumb jerked out again. 'He left her quite a lot of money, and she ought to be sure of getting it,' he said.

'Well, can't the will simply be proved, if he left it to her?' Julia asked, puzzled by Colin's obvious anxiety.

'The money isn't in a will. It's in Switzerland.' He stuck again.

'Darling, do be a little more clear. Why no will?'

'Oh, there's a will all right, and she's his heir. But—did you ever hear of numbered accounts?'

'No. What are they?'

'Well people all over the world, if they want to have some of their funds safe and sure, put them in Swiss Banks.'

'Oh, funk-money. Yes, very sensible. I expect masses of Levantines and Armenians and rich ones from those unreliable South American republics have millions stowed away there. But what are these numbered accounts?'

'Accounts with a number, but no name. Anonymous, you see.'

'No I don't, quite. Unless somebody in the Bank knows which name is attached to what number, how does Mr. Sophocles Euripides or Senhor Vasco da Gama get his money out when he wants it?'

Colin laughed.

'I don't know the exact mechanism, but there's some sort of secret record, or code, and the owner can touch his cash in need. Only it's not quite so easy when the person who made the deposit is dead, and that's the case with Aglaia's fortune.'

'What was her grandfather's name? Armitage? The English do this too, do they?'

'I wouldn't know. He wasn't English, and his name wasn't Armitage; that was her father.'

'Then what was the grandfather's name?'

Colin hesitated; he gave a curious youthful giggle of embarrassment before he said—'Thalassides; Orestes Thalassides.'

'Oh Lord, not the old shipowner? He must have been worth a packet.'

'Yes he was. And he did make a will all right, with proper legacies—don't you remember, half a million to Cambridge alone for science fellowships?—and more to various Redbricks. But although the papers called her a great heiress, all that didn't leave an awful lot for Aglaia except this Swiss money. And—' again he checked—'you see he may not have told the Swiss Bank that she is his heiress.'

'Won't the will show that?'

'We hope so, but it isn't dead certain.'

'If the will makes her his residuary legatee, or whatever they call it, surely she's on velvet?—except for death duties.'

'That's just the point. The lawyers seem to think that the will may have been left a bit vague for that very reason.'

13

'Oh, these smart foreigners! Here are all our own Dukes and peers selling their family portraits to pay those revolting death-duties, and Mr. What's-it-ides puts his dough in a foreign bank to escape paying.'

'Don't be nasty, J.,' the young man said, mildly and rather sadly.

'Sorry—no, I won't.' She considered. 'But Aglaia knows this money has been left to her?'

'Yes.'

'And told you?'

'Yes,' Colin said again, blushing.

Julia pounced, so to speak, on the blush.

'Colin, are you engaged to Aglaia?'

'M'm'm—after a fashion.'

'Is she sweet?' Julia asked, with warm interest.

'Yes, incredibly sweet. I want to marry her, if only to get her away from this dim aunt she lives with since her mother ran away. Well not 'if only'—I long to marry her.'

'Where did you meet her?'

'Oh, in London, like one does. She knows some cousins of the Macdonalds.' He paused. 'But you see I've really nothing to marry *on.*'

'Well I suppose you really have Glentoran—though of course you don't want to call that in, with Philip and Edina so blissfully happy here, and making such a go of it.'

'No, of course I don't, and anyhow I want to go on working. But that doesn't bring in much.'

'Does that matter, if Aglaia's got plenty?'

'Only that everyone will think I'm marrying her for her money—which I'm not. I'd marry her if she hadn't a single Swiss centime, if I could support her. And she wants to marry me,'

Colin added guilelessly, 'so she might just as well have her own cash, since it's there. But you do see, darling, that all that is just why I should like someone like you to go and *aborder* the Swiss Bank. I mean, you know I'm not after her money.'

'Of course, darling.' Julia reflected for a moment, sniffing at a spray of azalea which she had picked off the nearest bush. 'What I don't quite see,' she said then, 'is why your Aglaia can't simply go out with a copy of the will in her hand, walk into the Bank, give the secret number, and get the cash. How much is it, by the way?'

'About half a billion dollars, I believe.'

'That says nothing to me,' Julia stated airily. 'I never can remember if a billion is a hundred million, or a thousand million, or a million million. And anyhow I can't really think in dollars— 'divide by three' is what I say when I place an article in America. But it sounds quite a nice little lump sum, whichever it is! Well, why can't she do what I say?—just go and collect herself?'

'Well for one thing she's a minor, under 21; and for another, she doesn't know the account number.'

'How ridiculous! Who does? Don't the lawyers or the executors?'

'No. It seems these things are kept pretty dark—no one in London has the faintest idea. But there is someone out there who quite certainly does know; her godfather, a Swiss Pastor, who is also her guardian.'

'Why a Swiss godfather? Oh well, never mind; no odder than a Greek grandfather—all international! Well, can't she go and get it from him?'

'Not at the moment, no. For one thing her mother has just sent for her to go and pay a dutiful visit in the Argentine—she's sailing this week.'

'Colin, what nonsense! Why must she go to her unpleasant mother?'

Colin hesitated. 'Well, it might be a wise move. The lawyers think her mother may have an idea that the numbered account exists—Aglaia has told them, of course—and that if she goes out there it might put the mother and her Dago husband off the scent, and prevent them from trying to get hold of the money. The lawyers have been wondering, and so has Aglaia, how to set things in train in Switzerland in the meantime, very discreetly and quietly, of course—and now that you're actually going to be out there, it struck me at once that you could have a try. Your lovely silly face is such a help!'

'Beastly child!'

'Well, would you?'

'I don't see why not, when I've got Mrs. H. all settled. It might be rather fun, really—and in Morocco I seemed to have quite a light hand with bankers, like some women have for pastry. Have you got the guardian's address, who has the essential number?'

'I can get that for you.'

A huge sound of a distant bell resounded through the glen. Julia sprang up.

'The dressing-bell! We must fly.'

'We don't dress,' Colin said, following her down the path between the mountains of blossom.

'No, but we clean ourselves. And Ronan and his mamma are coming to supper, so I must tidy up a bit.' She ran on.

Out in the avenue—'I shall have to have a copy of the will, you know, Colin, or the bank certainly won't play; and some *pièces justificatives* for the godfather, or he won't either,' Julia said.

'Yes, of course. I'll get you all that—I shall have to come South and see that you're properly briefed, now that you've agreed to take it on. Darling, I *am* glad that you will.' He gave her a quick light kiss. 'I needn't tell you to keep it all utterly dark.'

'Hardly!' Julia said, with good-tempered sarcasm.

Colin's remarks the previous day about her throwing men over had rather upset Julia—until all the business about Mrs. Hathaway broke they had been wriggling about at the back of her mind like small ugly worms; she had remembered poor Steve in Morocco, whom Colin didn't know about. He made a third. While she quickly changed into a short dress for dinner she thought with discomfort about Ronan Macdonald, and wished he weren't coming; on some earlier visits to Glentoran he had obviously been attracted by her, and she had flirted with him a little, gaily and un-seriously. She hoped he wouldn't start all that up again, under Colin's very nose.

He did, however. Julia Probyn's unusual lion-tawny blonde-ness and great grey eyes were something men readily fell for, and did not soon forget—after nearly two years Ronan Macdonald had evidently not forgotten them, and tried to begin again where, he hoped, they had left off, when he found himself sitting beside her at dinner. Julia was markedly cool to him, both then, and afterwards in the drawing-room—he finally withdrew, hurt, and devoted his attention to his hostess. After the guests had gone Julia stated her intention of going upstairs at once and breaking the back of her packing before she went to bed; Glentoran is a long way from Renfrew, and she would have to make an early start. However, she was extremely disconcerted when Edina, who had come up with her, and sat in an armchair while Julia rapidly and skilfully folded suits and dresses and stowed them in suitcases, tackled her on the subject. After accusing her of being 'beastly' to Ronan all the evening she said—'You and he had such a carry-on round the time of our wedding that I thought he might be the reason why you turned that Torrens person down—Colin's boss.'

'Colin shouldn't gossip' Julia said vexedly, snapping a suit-case to and laying it on the floor. 'Certainly that had nothing to do with Ronan.'

'I've sometimes wondered if you cared for Colin,' Colin's sister pursued.

'Wrong again!' Julia said, putting another suit-case on the bed, on which she had carefully spread her bath-towel to protect the quilt. 'I adore Colin, but there never has been, and never will be, any question of our marrying.' Her voice was severe and cold. 'Really, you might have realised that, Edina—you're his sister.'

'I'm sorry—I expect I've been sticking my neck out. But you do rather go on and on, don't you?'

'All you young married women think of nothing but making matches for your friends!' Julia said, not without justice. 'However, I won't hold it against you—I know you can't help it!' Edina laughed, and kissed her Goodnight.

But flying South from Renfrew next day, in between thinking about Colin and his Aglaia, and the general danger of marrying too much money, the worms—added to by Edina—wriggled in Julia's mind more actively than ever. Was there really something wrong with her and her behaviour? Was she a *belle bitch sans merci?* She laughed her gurgling laugh at her own phrase, but she was troubled all the same. Ought she, next time, to let the thing rip, whatever happened? She continued to brood on this idea till rage at the behaviour of the staff at London Airport mastered all other feelings.

Chapter 2

Gersau

'There,' Julia said, returning from the bookstall at Victoria to the carriage where she and Watkins were installed, and throwing a batch of illustrated weeklies and the livelier dailies down on the seat. 'Now we shall have something to read. I know you like *The Queen*, Watkins.'

'Oh, thank you, Miss. I do indeed. But I'll save that for a bit later on. Do you want the *Mirror*?'

Julia didn't; but before starting on *The Times* she glanced through the *Express* and the *Daily Sketch*. She was a little startled to find, in both, numbers of photographs of Aglaia Armitage, with flaring headlines: 'Millionaire's Heiress goes to join her Mother'—'Richest Girl in Europe sails for South America'; the *Mirror*, she saw, struck a characteristic note—'So beautiful, so small, and so RICH!' She examined all the pictures of Colin's girl with the deepest interest. Aglaia Armitage was indeed tiny, seen in relation to gangways, police, and bystanders; she could hardly be much over five feet. But she was beautifully made,

19

with lovely feet and ankles, and her face in the studio photographs was attractive and intelligent, as well as undeniably pretty. Fascinated on Colin's account, Julia read the reporters' descriptions—things which normally she execrated. Miss Armitage, she learned, besides being 'petite' was ash-blonde, but with dark eyes—'an unusual combination.' True enough—and on the whole she liked the look of the girl her dear Colin loved.

Her study of the papers was interrupted by Watkins.

'Do look at that man, Miss—the tall one, talking to the Inspector on the platform. Do you think he can be a detective? He keeps walking up and down, up and down, watching the passengers.'

Julia and Watkins had arrived early, and so had plenty of time for staring out of the carriage window, as everyone does at Victoria, besides reading the papers. Julia now looked obediently where Watkins directed. She saw a tall man, lightly built, with a curious sharply-chiselled face (the word 'gothic' sprang into her mind) which besides intelligence showed an amusing quizzical quality; she thought he looked what she called 'fun.' He was strolling up and down beside the Inspector, casting rather sardonic glances at the passengers for the Golden Arrow who passed, accompanied by porters wheeling their luggage.

'Don't you think he must be one, Miss?' Watkins pursued. 'He's been doing that for ever so long.'

'Shall I ask him if he is?' Julia said, on a gay impulse—going abroad always went to her head far more directly than any alcohol.

'Well, why not, Miss?' Watkins said, with a discreet giggle.

Julia slipped along the corridor, stepped down from the train, and went over to the tall man; the Inspector tactfully moved away.

'I beg your pardon, but are you a detective?' she asked, hardily. The man put a finger to his lip.

'No. On business,' he said with a faint smile—his voice and accent were as attractive as his appearance; the small episode seemed to amuse him.

'Oh I see. You behave so like one! Please excuse me for asking.'

'A pleasure,' the man said, smiling more broadly; Julia, feeling a little foolish, went back into the train. 'He says he isn't,' she told Watkins, and started on *The Times*. But soon she was again interrupted by the maid.

'Do look at that young lady coming along, Miss! Isn't she the proper ditto of that girl in the papers? Can she be going to South America this way?'

'No, not possibly—she sailed yesterday, you know,' Julia said, before she even looked out of the window. When she did she was startled. Walking along the platform between two men was a girl whose resemblance to the photographs she had just been studying was quite astonishing. She was minute, her hair was the palest blonde possible, and when she turned her head in their direction to speak to one of the men with her, Julia could see that she had dark eyes and eyebrows. How very peculiar! The occurrence was so surprising as to cause Julia a sudden faint sense of unease. She looked carefully at the girl's two companions. One was a tall, dark, handsome young man, slender but athletically built, and distinctly un-English in appearance; the other was shorter, broadly-built with grey hair and a bushy grey beard—he too didn't look entirely English, nor did he walk like an old man. Julia glanced round to see what had become of the detective—she still thought of him as that, in spite of his denial. Yes, there he was, chatting to the Inspector, and apparently paying no attention to these late arrivals, who so surprised her. She sat back as they passed out of sight.

Presently a whistle blew, and the train pulled out. Julia was so intrigued by the resemblance of the girl on the platform to Aglaia Armitage that as the Boat Express shook and rattled through the suburbs she walked along the corridor to find where the party was sitting. They were in the second coach ahead; she took a good look at all three. Yes, the girl really had dark-brown eyes, and dark eyelashes too; and the older man's grey beard was slightly parted in the middle, she now saw. She went back to her carriage.

Soon a hand-bell, rung along the corridor by a white-coated steward, announced lunch. Julia had frugally brought sandwiches for herself and Watkins for this first meal; they would have to pay a fortune for dinner and breakfast on the other side of the Channel. But she didn't suggest eating at once—she gave it ten minutes, and then again walked forward down the train, hoping to find that the party which interested her had gone to eat, so that she could examine the labels on their hand-luggage. They had gone to eat, right enough, leaving overcoats on their seats—but there was no hand-luggage! Feeling fooled, and foolish, Julia went back and ate sandwiches with Watkins.

Every time she sat down Julia Probyn was conscious of an unwonted weight against the front of her thighs. This was caused by the 'coffre-fort,' that old ingenious American device by means of which the most careless ladies can carry currency about in almost perfect safety—a small canvas wallet with two or three compartments, slung on webbing straps from a belt round the waist and worn under the skirt; the slapping against the legs affords comforting evidence that one's money is still there, and the thing can hardly be removed short of an attempt at rape. Mrs. Hathaway, Julia knew, possessed several of these objects, and she had caused Watkins to produce the largest of them 'for our money'; but in fact it contained a copy of the late Mr. Thalassides' will, and signed authorisations by Aglaia's lawyers and bankers in London to the Swiss Bank 'to give full information to Miss Julia Probyn' concerning the moneys in the numbered account. There was also a scrawl in Colin's rather crabbed writing giving the name and address of the guardian-godfather who knew the number of the account—La Cure, Bellardon—and a cautiously-worded note from the lawyers, suggesting that the Pastor of Bellardon also should give 'all facil-ities' to Miss Probyn.

Colin had flown South from Glentoran on the plane after Julia's, the first on which he could get a seat; he had brought all these documents round to her club, and they went through them together—the other occupants of the half-empty room appeared mostly to be deaf or blind, or both. Julia read through the papers carefully. They were addressed to *Messieurs les Directeurs* of the Banque Républicaine in Geneva.

'Oh, so they do at least know the name of the bank,' she said, folding them up and putting them in her handbag. 'Only a photostat of the will. I see.'

'Yes, but you also see that Judkins and Judkins have had it attested by a Commissioner for Oaths. Honestly, I think you've got everything you need now, bar the actual number, which old de Ritter, the guardian, will give you.'

'Let's hope he will,' Julia had said.

Experienced passengers on cross-Channel steamers book a steward the moment they get on board to take their luggage ashore on the further side, and see them through the *Douane* and into their sleepers; Julia, who usually flew to France, failed to do this till too late. Her French porter, in spite of bribes and adjurings, as usual collected eight other people's luggage beside hers, and kept her and Watkins waiting for more than twenty minutes in the Customs shed before he appeared, behind a barrow piled nearly as high as Mont Blanc. This *contretemps* prevented Julia from checking on the movements of the girl with the extraordinary resemblance to Aglaia; through the dusty, dirty windows she thought she caught a glimpse of her boarding the Paris train, but she could not be sure. Oh well, it was probably just a coincidence. For the rest of the evening she was diverted by Watkins's reactions to foreign food, and to adjusting her undressing to a sleeper.

The Swiss Customs examination on trains from Calais now takes place at Berne; sleepy, hungry, and feeling generally dishevelled, Julia secured a porter, a tall fair middle-aged man, for their hand-luggage, and deposited this, with Watkins, in the pleasant station restaurant—then she went off to the Customs. Another *contretemps*—their registered luggage had not arrived. Julia, indignant, insisted coolly but persistently in her rather moderate German on being taken to see someone in authority, and was eventually led by the tall porter to a small office adjoining that of the station-master; here she made her complaint to two well-educated, civil-spoken men, who took down all details and asked where she was going?

'To Gersau—and the luggage must come on at once, *frei*,' Julia said firmly.

Oh the delightful helpful Swiss, so unlike surly French official-dom, she thought, as her address in Gersau was noted, and she was promised that the missing luggage would be sent on as soon as it arrived in Berne. 'This must have happened in France—in France *anything* can happen!' one of the officials said. 'We regret the inconvenience to the Fräulein.' Julia laughed, thanked him, and went back to the restaurant to tuck into coffee and rolls-and-butter with Watkins.

Emerging some two hours later from the high airy station at Lucerne and crossing the open space outside it to the quay, the lovely heat hit them—blazing sun, brilliant sky, the cobbles and tarmac almost incandescent. 'My word, Miss, I shall be glad to get into a cotton dress,' Watkins observed. 'But this is a clean, pretty place,' the English maid added, casting an approving glance at the trim beds full of bright flowers. 'This seems a clean country—I noticed the fields and gardens as we came along. That last train was clean, too. I do like things clean!'

Watkins's desire for a cotton frock diminished on the lake steamer, whose swift passage over the blue-green waters made sitting on the deck quite chilly. They retreated into the saloon, where Watkins gazed out through the windows, and continued her comments.

'My goodness me, Miss, do look at that! Is there any reason for a hill to stick up into the sky like a power-station chimney?' (This was Watkins's reaction to the Bürgenstock, seen end on.)

'Switzerland *is* like that, Watkins,' Julia replied, laughing. 'The whole place is up on end.'

But though Julia was more familiar than Watkins with the power-station-chimney aspect of Switzerland, since she had twice spent three weeks ski-ing at Zermatt, she knew nothing whatever of the country beyond what could be seen from trains or ski-slopes, or learned from how its hotels are run; of the industrial and commercial, let alone the private life of its inhabitants she was completely ignorant, as most tourists are. Her enlightenment began at once, at Gersau.

This whole small place is compressed into a fold between two of the steep green ridges running down from the Rigi. Along the lake front is a fringe of hotels, restaurants, gardens, and filling-stations, Gersau's public face; but up behind are large unsuspected houses in shady gardens, giving onto narrow quiet streets with occasional small shops, which supply the needs of the inhabitants rather than souvenirs for the tourist.

A tall stately old gentleman in a Panama hat was standing on the little quay, attended by a manservant in a red-and-black silk jacket; as Julia and Watkins stepped off the boat he raised his panama and said, 'Is it Miss Probyn? I am Rudolf Waechter,' in perfect English, and then greeted Watkins—'Your mistress will be very pleased to see you.' Julia was surprised to see no sign of a car or even a taxi, but none was necessary; their luggage was placed on a hand-barrow by the manservant and they walked, slightly uphill, barely two hundred yards before reaching a large plastered house with deep overhanging eaves, and passed through a heavy old door of carved walnut into a cool hall. Within, the staircase had walnut banisters, and there was old walnut panelling everywhere; Persian rugs and carpets covered the floors and even the stairs, and on the walls modern French paintings were skilfully juxtaposed with some lovely Primitives which, Julia later learned, were early Rhenish, something in which her host specialised.

'You will want to see Mrs. Hathaway,' he said, as he took her upstairs. 'Luncheon will be at 1.30, so you have time—Anna will show you your room, and then take you to her. It is very good of you to come yourself to bring her maid—and I am, of course, delighted to have you here.'

On an upper landing Anna, a neat elderly maid, was waiting, and took Julia to her room, Watkins following. 'Room' was an understatement; Julia had been given a suite consisting of a large bedroom, a sitting-room, and a bathroom. Bedroom and sitting-room both opened onto a deep balcony, set with luxuriously comfortable *chaises longues* and small tables, an extra room in itself. The bathroom, like all the rest, was of a *recherché* perfection—the whole thing was so exquisite that Julia almost gasped. She threw her hat on the bed, and then asked Anna where 'Miss Watkins's' room was? Anna, beaming, led them out onto the wide landing again—more superb rugs, Julia noticed—and opened the door of a pleasant bed-sitting-room, also with an adjoining bathroom.

'Well, you will be quite comfy here, Watkins, won't you?' Julia asked.

'Provided the water's *hot,*' Watkins replied, turning on the tap in the basin. A cloud of steam answered her incredulity; a little abashed, she turned off the tap. 'Yes, Miss; it's a pretty room—and quite clean, too.' Julia was satisfied; if Watkins passed the Waechter house as clean, she would give no trouble. She asked Anna to take them to Frau Hathaway.

Watkins had been put in a room next door to her mistress, who was housed in another lovely suite. Julia studied her old friend's appearance anxiously when Anna ushered them in, but it was clear that Mrs. Hathaway was, as she pronounced herself to be, very much better; her colour was quite good, and her voice as firm as ever when she gave directions to her maid.

'I'm glad to see you, Watkins—I hope you had a good journey. Now go and unpack and get yourself straight, while I talk to Miss Julia. They will bring you some lunch in about half an hour; after that you must rest, and then learn your way about the house; and later you can make my tea, and do some washing for me.' Watkins obediently made her exit.

'My dear child, this is so good of you,' Mrs. Hathaway said. 'I'm sure Edina was furious at having you reft away the moment you got to Glentoran, after so long. But Herr Waechter wouldn't hear of my going to a hospital, and he hasn't a large staff, admirable as they are; I really felt I couldn't impose the strain of having me waited on a moment longer than was necessary.'

Julia said it was fun coming—'and what a marvellous house.'

'Oh yes, it's bursting with treasures—partly inherited, of course, and then he has this passion for Rhenish Primitives and Persian rugs; he has spent a lifetime, and a fortune, collecting them. He only took a fancy to French painting much later—but just in time to get some good things. He has *three* Blue Picassos.'

'Golly! But where did he get his money?' Julia asked, with her usual frankness.

'Oh, fine optical glass for precision instruments—Waechters are known all over the world for that. Oddly enough, since the War they get that mineral they use for it, the stuff which looks like flour, from a place not so very far from Glentoran—it's three or four per cent purer than anything they can mine even in Czechoslovakia. I wish I could remember its name,' Mrs. Hathaway said, rather wistfully, 'but at the moment I can't.'

'Never mind. And does Herr Waechter still work at this glass performance?'

'Oh no—he only goes to Board meetings occasionally. A nephew runs it now.'

'What are the inherited treasures?' Julia asked, surprised, in her English ignorance, that Swiss manufacturers should inherit any heirlooms.

'Oh, the furniture—a lot of it is beyond price; you must get him to show you—and some of the Primitives. His father collected those, and started his interest in them. And of course the house itself, which is over 200 years old; that came from his grandmother, who was a Carmenzind.'

28

'I saw that name on a shop as we walked up,' Julia said. 'I thought it so queer, and pretty.'

'Yes, the place is full of them; it's a great Gersau name.' Mrs. Hathaway paused, and looked with shrewd amusement at her young friend. 'I don't want to bore you; I don't think I shall, you being you—but did you ever realise that Gersau was an independent Republic, within the Swiss Confederation, till 1818, or thereabouts?'

'No—and it seems impossible! This tiny place a Republic? Like San Marino?'

'Yes, only perhaps even smaller. Don't go by size for values! And its last President before it was absorbed—even the Swiss absorb, sooner or later,' Mrs. Hathaway reflected sadly—'was a Carmenzind; Rudolf Waechter's great-grandfather.'

Anna at this point brought in a tray with Cinzano, ice, and slices of orange. 'Will the ladies please serve themselves?' she said, and retired. Julia poured out for both, and sat down again.

'This is all quite fascinating,' she said. 'I had no idea that Switzerland was like this.'

'Of course not, dear child. The English always think of the Swiss purely as a race of hotel-keepers, with a few hardy peasant guides thrown in—and, of course, as makers of cuckoo-clocks. Well they are hotel-keepers, though that is really our fault; it was the English who invented and patented Switzerland as the Playground of Europe. Even dear Rudolf Waechter, besides his glass business, has a controlling interest in three or four of the major hotels. But they have this private life as well, which has been going quietly on for centuries—and it is a very civilised life, as you will see in this house.'

'I am seeing,' Julia said.

'It can be combined with hotel-keeping, too,' Mrs. Hathaway

pursued. 'Othmar Schoeck's parents—you know, the great composer, who died not so long ago—kept a delightful hotel in Brunnen, quite near here; I knew him well as a girl. Old Papa Schoeck was an artist. I didn't much care for his pictures, too Landseer-ish, all chamois and eagles. But there he was, painting away in his studio on the top floor in his spare time, while his sons went to the University in Zürich, or became great musicians. I don't know who started the idea that hotel-keeping is a low, deadening trade. Can it have been the Americans?'

Julia was just saying that she didn't know any American hotel-keepers, but that so many English hotels were deadly as to suggest that the theory had its origin in England, when Anna again appeared, summoning her to luncheon, and bringing a tray for Mrs. Hathaway. 'From now on, Miss Watkins will bring up all my trays,' Mrs. Hathaway told the Swiss maid firmly in German. 'For this the Fräulein has brought her here.' Anna smirked and nodded, and led Julia down to the first floor, on which were both the drawing-room and the dining-room.

The latter, where they ate a delicious lunch at an early walnut refectory table, was panelled throughout in the same wood; Julia, by way of making conversation, observed that it was odd to her to see such an ancient table made of anything but oak.

'Ah, but you see the walnut has always been our principal furniture tree, not the oak; and since we are not a maritime nation, we seldom imported mahogany.' Her host drew her attention to the old carved dresser and other pieces in the room, including a near-Biedermeier tall-boy between the high windows. 'You will notice that it is not pure Biedermeier—and that is precisely what gives it its value. Here, from the eigh-teenth century, we copied foreign styles, but always with slight differences; if anyone shows you a piece of antique Swiss furniture which is correct Empire, or correct Biedermeier, you may be sure that it is a fake.'

Julia was delighted with her host. Over coffee in the drawing-room, which also had a broad balcony, she felt secure enough to ask him how he had come to know Mrs. Hathaway?—explaining that she looked on her almost as a mother. She was touched by the way he told the story. Mrs. Hathaway, as a girl, had come with her parents to stay at one of the family hotels in Lugano—'I was the receptionist then; we must all learn our trade, from the bottom up! But there were dances on Thursday and Sunday evenings, when I danced with her—and fell a little in love with her.' Julia loved the gentle reminiscent smile with which the old man said that. 'We both married,' he pursued, more briskly. 'She had sons, I had no children. But our friendship we have kept.'

Julia, entranced by this glimpse into the past, asked what her beloved Mrs. Hathaway had been like as a girl.

'Plain,' Herr Waechter said flatly; 'and her mother did not dress her well. But she had a merry laugh, and great intelligence; also she was always what now I believe you call "tough", though the word was unknown then.'

'And was it her toughness you fell in love with?' Julia asked, absorbed by these revelations.

The old man laughed.

'Miss Probyn, you are rather clever! I never phrased it to myself in this way, but in fact I believe that was what I fell in love with.'

Their heavy luggage arrived about 4 p.m.; a telephone call from the quay announced its arrival, and the manservant went down with the hand-cart to fetch it. There was nothing to pay, since the railway was at fault. Again Julia blessed the Swiss.

Mrs. Hathaway had to keep her bed for several days, but once Watkins had got the hang of the house, and could wait on her, Julia was fairly free, and her host insisted on taking her out with him in the car, which a chauffeur drove, when he had to go anywhere. The first of these occasions was a visit to his wine-merchant in Brunnen; Julia in her ignorance was astonished at every meal by the excellence of the Swiss wines she drank, and was delighted at the idea. She was even more delighted by the reality. Accustomed to the urban precincts of Messrs. Berry Brothers or the Wine Society, she was startled to drive into a cobbled yard flanked by a low line of buildings backed up against a steep wooded hill-side; when Herr Waechter, escorted by the foreman, walked all through the sheds, piled high with crates and barrels, to inspect the bottling of some wine in which he was particularly interested, she found it fascinating to see ferns and hazel-boughs poking in at the barred windows. Out of curiosity she enquired about the price of whisky, and was led into a cupboardlike room on whose high shelves were ranged whiskies of every conceivable sort. The well-known brands, owing to the low excise duty, were about the same price as in England, in spite of the high Swiss rate of exchange; but unheard-of varieties were priced at as little as twenty-four shillings.

'Can one drink this stuff?' she asked, holding out a bottle labelled *Bonnie Bluebell* to Herr Waechter.

'That, no. But this, and this'—he reached two bottles down off the shelves—'are quite good. Do you drink whisky? I have plenty.'

'Yes, I do—and when we leave you I shall want some; Mrs. Hathaway likes it, too. I'd like to buy a little, as I'm here, and with you to help.' She left with five bottles of *Claonaig Cream*, which cost her only six pounds and proved to be a very tolerable whisky indeed.

They drove on to Schwyz, where Herr Waechter said he must see a cousin who made cement—'I have a small interest in the firm. And you should see Schwyz; it was the birthplace of the Confederation, and it is a charming town. I ought also to call on two of my sisters-in-law, widows, and not very interesting; but their houses are pretty.' Indeed as they drove across the flat plain towards the twin peaks of the Grosse and Kleine Mythen, which stand up like two gigantic stone axe-heads above the small town, they could see the cement-factory away to their left, its buildings all floury with grey dust. 'It is rather a defacement,' Herr Waechter said regretfully; 'but it gives employment, and brings in money. We seem compelled, today, to live in an increasingly ugly world.'

But there was nothing ugly about the world into which he soon introduced her—the old Swiss families in the old town of Schwyz. They lived in large houses in big high-walled gardens, full of flowers and fruit-trees; the houses themselves were as stuffed with walnut panelling and period furniture as his own, though without the rugs and French pictures—and they all, it seemed, were related to endless other families alike engaged in industry. Julia got that afternoon, and on subsequent occasions when the calls were returned in Gersau, an unusually intimate picture of the *original* European democracy—since the Greek and Italian republics have not survived. All these people kept hotels, or made watches or machinery, or precision instruments; but their homes were in these ancient houses, full of inherited treasures, and they could trace their ancestry back four or five hundred years.

A couple of days later they drove to Zurich. Herr Waechter was writing a history of Gersau, and had already completed a rather learned book on Swiss furniture, now in the press; he wished to discuss these with his publishers there. They lunched at the Baur au Lac (one of the best hotels in the world) in the glass-enclosed outside restaurant between the green-flowing river on one side and the great garden, brilliant with flowers, on the other. The restaurant was full of people, all apparently Germans or Swiss—it was early in the season for Americans; Julia commented on the fact that there seemed to be no English. 'I have so often heard people at home speak of the Baur au Lac.'

'Oh, the English can't afford to come here any more,' her host said, matter-of-factly. 'Not with this quite ridiculous travel allowance, for which there is really no excuse at all! The pound stands well; this limit of £100 is purely a bureaucratic *idée fixe*. And it does harm to England's reputation.' He paused, and sipped his wine. 'In Switzerland,' he went on, 'we know a good deal about the standing of all currencies, and we regret this folly very much. The Germans, whom you defeated, can come here and spend as they please; so can the Belgians, who surrendered and left you *plaqués* outside Dunkirk; so can the French, who ran away. It is only the English, who stood alone for a year and a half defending European freedom, who may not travel in comfort on the continent they—and they *alone*—saved!' The old gentleman spoke the last words with savage severity.

'Good for you, Herr Waechter!' Julia said with warmth. 'I couldn't agree more. I wish you'd write a letter to *The Times* about it.'

'Perhaps I shall, one day. Here in Switzerland we feel deeply about this. We have not forgotten that our tourist and hotel industry, which is of great importance to our economy, was in effect started by the English—the mountaineers who came to climb, who also really created our corps of guides. Hence our first hotels—and we do not like, now, that English visitors should be forced to stay in second-class places.'

Julia was moved by this, remembering Mrs. Hathaway's remarks a few days earlier.

The offices of Herr Waechter's publishers were as much of a surprise to her as his wine-merchant's. She had once or twice been taken to cocktail-parties given by London firms, in stately premises in Albemarle Street, or more functional ones nearer the Strand, and expected something of the same sort. Not at all. The car bore them up to a hillside suburb overlooking the city, where lilacs and laburnums bloomed along shady streets, and stopped outside a modern villa, with a plate on its gatepost bearing the words 'Eden-Verlag'. Herr Schmidt, the principal, a middle-aged man with a clever face, greeted her host with respectful warmth and bore him off upstairs, first installing Julia in a sunny room full of flowers and armchairs, and inviting her to amuse herself with the books which lined the walls—'We do some fine illustrated books.' He laid several on a centre table. While Julia was examining these the door opened and a rather shaky little old man, with tufts of grey hair round his baldish skull, came in and introduced himself in rather bad French as Herr Schmidt's partner; he proceeded to lead her round the shelves, pointing out various books, including several translations into German of novels by well-known English writers. Julia's inveterate curiosity suddenly moved her to ask him whether any of these people used numbered accounts? The question produced an extraordinary outburst.

'Numbered accounts!' He almost spat out the words. 'Oh yes,

often we are asked to pay royalties into numbered accounts by people who do not wish to pay taxes at home! They come here and spend it on winter-sport. But *these* can get their money when they want it—unlike the heirs of the wretched Jews and Poles and Hungarians, to whom it was refused by the banks.' Again he almost spat the last word, his face twisted with a sort of despairing anger.

'Refused? But why on earth?' Julia asked.

'Because death certificates shall be produced before the bank will pay! And how many death certificates were given of those who perished in the gas-chambers at Oswieczim' he used the Polish name for Auschwitz—'or were beaten to death at Mauthausen, or died of starvation in Belsen and Buchenwald? So those who looked ahead and sought to make some provision for their children used their prudence in vain; those of the younger generation who escaped were denied their heritage.'

'How ghastly,' Julia said; though she was horrified, the little old man was so wrought up, and the story sounded so extraordinary, that she wasn't sure if she quite believed it. 'It sounds impossible,' she added.

'Oh, everything is possible! There was more than that,' Herr Schmidt's partner went on. 'The Lüblin Government, the Communist clique forced on us by the Russians, asked the Swiss Government to pay to them 300 million dollars of Polish money, deposited in Switzerland. The Swiss Government paid—I leave you to guess from where they got the money!'

'Good God! That really was too much,' Julia exclaimed.

'Quite so.' Her agreement seemed to soothe the little man; he went on rather more calmly. 'This created a certain scandal; now the Government here are more discreet—other requests of the same nature have been refused. But all over Switzerland these banks are putting up wonderful new buildings—with the money of the dead, while their heirs starve!'

Julia was distinctly relieved that at this point Herr Waechter reappeared, and took her away. What she had heard disturbed and worried her; she wondered if it could be true, and longed to ask her host, but for some time she refrained, assuming that a man of 80 would be tired after such an expedition. But quite the contrary; the old gentleman seemed so brisk and spry, quite cheered up by his outing, that eventually Julia asked him what truth there was in the story of the death certificates?

He frowned.

'The old Petrus will have told you this, of course. It is true that payments are withheld unless a death certificate is produced; this is perfectly natural, and correct; otherwise the door would be open to every sort of fraud. And latterly matters have been arranged better, at least as far as Germans—Jews mostly, of course—are concerned; the German Government is very liberal about granting death certificates to those presumed dead, and also the United Nations circulates lists of names, partly from the very ill-kept records of the prison-camps, asking whether there is any evidence as to the life or death of those so listed—if there is no evidence that they are alive a death certificate is granted. But this was not the case in the first years after the war; the machinery had not been established, so the banks were helpless—they had to abide by their rules.'

'Of course—I see that,' Julia said. Then she asked about the payment to the Polish Government?

'Oh, everyone has heard this story!' Waechter exclaimed—'and here also the thing is complicated. No bank may pay out the money of a private individual to anyone but that individual or his legal heirs; that is why the private fortune of the late Czar of Russia is still lying in your banks in London, in spite of repeated requests from the Bolshevik Russian Government that it should be handed over to them. Government money is a different matter; one government may, quite reasonably, hand this over to the established successor of a previous government in a foreign country. What became of those lorry-loads of gold bars which the Polish Government sent down through Rumania to Constanza when the German invasion threatened? You should know—your own Consul helped to carry them on board ship!'

Julia didn't know; she had never heard of this episode and enjoyed visualising a sweating Consul humping gold bricks up a gangway in a hot Black Sea port.

'I've no idea,' she said. 'Do you know where it is now?'

'No. It has been suggested that it came here—we are such a repository! If it did, our Government would have been perfectly within their rights in handing it over to the Polish Government. But though there has been endless talk about this payment, there is no evidence that it was really made—and never will be!' he added with finality.

Julia was fascinated by these glimpses of international finance, about which, like most people, she knew nothing. Herr Waechter obviously knew a good deal, and she decided to try to clear up the substance of another of the old publisher's complaints while the going was so exceptionally good—she asked if it was true that the splendid new bank buildings in Switzerland were really being paid for out of 'the money of the dead,' as old Dr. Petrus had said.

Herr Waechter fairly exploded.

'This is complete rubbish! and libellous rubbish too! I have already told you that machinery is now in operation to clear the accounts of those who died in the prison-camps; but in any case our banks have no need of such moneys. When German shares and Mark obligations were far down, after the War, our banks bought them up—to the great relief of the holders—and since Germany's wonderful recovery these have enormously increased in value; so much so that our banks hardly know what to do with their money. Very sensibly, they are using it to bring their premises up to date; this gives employment, and helps our young cement industry.'

Suddenly the old man did look tired, Julia saw with compunction.

'I'm sorry I bothered you with all this,' she said. 'But I was upset by what that old man told me.'

'Of course you were, and rightly. Justice and injustice, and human suffering are things about which *all* must be upset.' He spoke with emphasis. 'But may I ask you a question?' he went on. 'How come you to know about numbered Kontos? From Dr. Petrus also? For the English public, I understand, has hardly heard of them, though many English, even in official positions, are now using them.'

Julia concealed wariness by laughter.

'Are they really? Oh, what fun!' She thought quickly, and decided to use Paddy Lynch. 'I have a banker friend who told me about them; that's why I asked Dr. Petrus whether any of his English authors used them—and uncovered all this story.'

'A banker in London?'

'No no—in Casablanca.'

'Oh, Casablanca!'

Julia laughed again, and broke off with an enquiry about a church they happened to be passing; Herr Waechter's historical enthusiasm deflected him, as she had hoped, from the matter of numbered Kontos. But all the way back to Gersau, through orchards that were pink drifts of blossom, she was worrying about one thing. Colin had said she had everything she needed to deal with Aglaia's numbered account; but she hadn't got the death certificate of Mr. Thalassides. And quite clearly, from what she had heard today, that was essential.

Chapter 3

Bellardon

On their return Julia was met on the upper landing by Watkins, who followed her into her room.

'Mr. Colin was on the telephone for you at lunch-time, Miss. He seemed very much put about that you was out.'

'Where from, Watkins?'

'London, Miss. He gave me a message, and said you was to have it the moment you came in.'

'Well what was it, Watkins?' Julia asked impatiently. What could Colin want to ring her up for?

'He said—"Tell Miss Julia to get on with the job I gave her as fast as ever she can". Really, Master Colin has a cheek, to be giving *you* jobs!—but that's what he said, and what's more he made me repeat it,' Watkins said indignantly. (She had dandled Colin as an infant, and still could not take him very seriously.)

'Anything else?'

'Oh yes—he gave his orders as cool as anything! You was to stay here till you get a letter from him, but to be making arrangements meantime to go and see the clergyman. He said you'd know who he meant. And he kept on saying—"Tell her to hurry; it's urgent". Three times, he said that.'

'Thank you, Watkins. Tell Mrs. Hathaway I'll come along to her in a minute or two.'

As she washed and put on powder Julia considered. Mrs. Hathaway really was much better. The doctor, who had been the evening before, had said that in a week or ten days she would be fit to move; he recommended that she should go to Beatenberg, above the Lake of Thun, for two or three weeks—the air there was peculiarly beneficial. Watkins had by now come to terms with Anna and the rest of the staff, so clearly dear Mrs. H. could safely be left for the moment. And after supper she asked her host if she might make a telephone call.

'Of course. To England?'

'No—to a place called Bellardon.'

'Is that in the Canton de Vaud or the Canton de Fribourg? I know it is in one or the other, but they are so intertwined that it is a little confusing.'

'I haven't a clue,' Julia said airily. 'Does it matter which Canton Bellardon is in?'

'Yes, certainly. You see here we have an automatic telephone system, with a different call-number for each canton—you dial that, and then the number you want in the canton.'

'Oh, not by towns? How odd! Well how am I to find out which canton Bellardon is in?'

'The telephone book will tell us that.' It did—Bellardon was in the Canton de Fribourg, whose call-number was 037. (They all begin with an o.) Julia looked through the two or three pages of the Bellardon section, searching for the name de Ritter; it was not under R, nor under D.

42

'I can't find him!' she exclaimed.

'Whom do you seek?' Herr Waechter asked.

'A Monsieur de Ritter, at Bellardon.'

'Oh, the Pastor—yes, such a brilliant man. Look under Pasteur, and you will find him.' And among the Ps, sure enough, Julia found the entry—'*Pasteur de l' Église Nationale, J.-P. de Ritter, La Cure, Bellardon.*' She dialled the two numbers, and was through in about fifteen seconds—the Swiss automatic telephone system works like magic—and the Pastor himself answered. Julia gave her name and said, a little deprecatingly and quite untruly, that she was a friend of his god-daughter's, and wanted to come and see him.

'Dear Mademoiselle, I have nearly 150 god-daughters!' the rich voice answered gaily.

'All English?' Julia asked.

'Ah no! Only two English ones.'

'Well, Aglaia is the one, of those two, that I speak of.' (In spite of the automatic telephone, Julia's instinct for caution made her reluctant to use the surname.) 'But look, I want to come very soon, probably the day after tomorrow.'

'Come from where?'

'Gersau.'

'Then you must stay the night.'

'Yes, but I don't want to be a bother. If you would just book me a room in the hotel I can come in and see you.'

A loud, very engaging laugh came ringing down the line.

'Leave all that to me. Just come!—telephone your train, and we will meet you at the station. *Au revoir.*' He rang off.

'He sounds frightfully nice,' Julia said to her host.

'Jean-Pierre de Ritter? He is one of the world's charmers. So was his father, whom I knew very well indeed. They are an old

Berne family.' There followed details of inter-marriages with Waechters and Carmenzinds.

Julia waited anxiously for Colin's letter next day. It didn't come by the first post, but she took occasion to tell Mrs. Hathaway that she would probably have to go away for a day or two, on a job for Colin—she knew that Watkins would have reported his telephone call to her mistress.

'More Secret Service work?' Mrs. Hathaway asked. 'You know, my dear child, I do think they ought soon to start *paying* you for what you do. It all comes out of the Estimates, after all—which means out of our pockets—and I don't see why the Government should have your services free.'

'Oh, this is a private thing of Colin's,' Julia assured her blithely. 'Nothing to do with the Secret Service at all.'

But Colin's letter, which arrived by the second post, promptly disillusioned her on that score.

'This business is turning out much more serious and more tiresome than I thought when I asked you to take it on,' he wrote. 'It seems that the old boy, along with his money, deposited some rather hideously important papers. I only heard this when I was having supper with H. last night. He's in rather a flap about it, as indeed everyone is, because we've heard that some *most* undesirable characters are onto this too, and may be taking rapid action of some sort about it. I didn't gather exactly what, but it is quite menacing. And when I mentioned that you were actually going to see you-know-who, H. begged me to lay you on and get you to function as quickly as possible. (He doesn't care to write to you himself, naturally.) But he laid it on me to tell you that it is really vital, repeat vital, that you should get these papers away from where they are and into your own keeping as fast as you possibly can.

'So please get cracking, darling. Wire me when you are going, darling darling. Endless love, C.'

Julia sat on her pretty shaded balcony looking out at the silver gleam of late spring snow on the mountains across the lake, and frowned over this missive. Hugh again! How tedious to be mixed up in yet another of his jobs. But neither she nor Colin had ever used their call-note 'darling darling' to the other in vain; if she couldn't help Colin without helping Hugh, so much the worse— but she would help Colin, come Hell and high water. She went and procured a couple of telegraph forms from old Herr Waechter—she guessed, rightly, that he was a person who still kept telegraph forms in his house—and presently took a tele- gram, neatly printed in block capitals, down to the small post-office. She was careful to use Colin's home address. The message read: 'Yes I will darling but how tiresome stop Starting tomorrow. Love.' She signed it 'Darling'. The fatherly old man in the post-office put on his spectacles to spell all this out. 'Darling shall mean *Liebchen*, not?' he asked smiling—and Julia, smiling too, said '*Jawohl*'.

She refused a drive with Herr Waechter because she wanted to catch the afternoon post with a letter by air to Colin—sitting in her little *salon* she wrote hurriedly that she was going next day to see 'the parson person'; it was all laid on, and she would do her best. In view of what both Petrus and Herr Waechter had said she added: 'What I haven't got, and *must have*, is a death certificate—they won't play without. You must take my word for this; I learned it quite by accident, but I *know*. If you can get it in twenty-four hours, post to the Parsonage; if it takes longer than that, probably better send here.'

She paused at that point, and read Colin's letter through again. The passage about the 'most undesirable characters' taking rapid action made her wonder if she ought to mention the curious episode of the girl at Victoria, but when she looked at her watch she decided that there wasn't time; she closed her letter and ran down, hatless, with it to the post-office.

On the way back she slipped into one of the lake-side hotels, borrowed a time-table from the porter, and looked out the trains to Bellardon. It meant an early start, and she did most of her packing before she went to sit with Mrs. Hathaway before dinner; even before doing that, and while Herr Waechter was still out, she put through a call to La Cure giving the time of her train, blessing the anonymity of the Swiss automatic exchanges. If this sort of thing was going on, one couldn't be too careful.

She was off next morning on the first boat to Lucerne, and continued by train to Berne, where she had to change. Her luggage there was carried by the same tall porter; looking from her carriage window Julia caught sight of the detective!—also seeing his luggage aboard the train for Geneva. Julia saw him first, and watched him furtively; this time he appeared to be much more definitely on the look-out for someone than he had been at Victoria. She studied his face again, and found it more attractive than ever. 'Gothic' was undoubtedly the word for its rather harsh angles and deeply-incised lines; it was also intelligent, and the expression at once sardonic and gay. It was curious, seeing him again like this; she wondered what he was up to. Could *he* be one of Colin's undesirable characters?

Julia had time in hand, and she was hungry after a 7 a.m. breakfast; when the detective had entered his train she got out and went in search of a sandwich and a newspaper. Returning with both, hurrying through the subway which at Berne Haupt-Bahnhof connects all the platforms, she ran slap into him, coming down the steps. He stared—then gave his twisted grin, and half-lifted his hat. Clearly he remembered her. Slightly disconcerted, Julia regained her carriage.

The lowland agricultural cantons of Switzerland, like Vaud and Fribourg, are little visited by foreign tourists, and were as unexpected by Julia as Herr Waechter's house. Sitting in the train, thankfully munching her *Schinken-Brötchen*, she noted with a country-woman's interest the methods of the Swiss farmers: the fresh grass being mown by hand in narrow strips and carted off to feed the stalled cows; the early hay hung on wooden or metal triangles to be dried by air as well as sun; the intense neatness of the gardens round the houses, with rows of lettuces and shallots, and a single stick to support the French beans, at present only a green clump of leaves at its foot. The houses themselves surprised her; she had imagined all the Swiss to live in wooden chalets, but here the houses, though deep-eaved, seemed to be much more plaster than timber. Now and again, towards the end of her journey, on her right she caught glimpses of a lake which a fellow-passenger told her was Neuchâtel; and on the horizon hung the blue shadow of the Jura.

She did not stay in the hotel at Bellardon, for the excellent reason that there is none. It is a tiny place, where tourists are unknown. At the station, where she was the only passenger to alight, Julia was met by a small dark-haired woman, rather beautiful, who said, 'You will be Miss Probyn? I am Germaine de Ritter.' Mme de Ritter caused the stationmaster, the sole railway employee of Bellardon, to pile Julia's luggage onto a small hand-cart with a long handle, the exact duplicate of that used by Herr Waechter's manservant at Gersau; this she pulled after her out into a small sunny street, saying easily—'My husband had to take the car, but it is only two instants to the house. We are so glad that you have come to us; we are devoted to Aglaia'—which made Julia feel fraudulent. They passed along one side of a grassy open space, closed at the further end by the whitewashed bulk of a church with a tall bell-tower. 'We think our church beautiful,' Germaine de Ritter said; in fact, in its solid simplicity, beautiful it was.

La Cure, the Pastor's dwelling, was a very large eighteenth-century house with painted panelling in all the rooms, and gleaming parquet floors—everything spotlessly clean. Mme de Ritter drew the hand-cart into the small front garden, saying, 'Jean-Pierre will bring your luggage up when he returns for *déjeuner*—is this sufficient for now?' and as she spoke lifted Julia's dressing-case off the cart. She carried it herself up the broad staircase with its wide shallow treads and polished beech planks, and showed her guest first her pretty bedroom—slightly defaced by a tall cylindrical black-iron stove for heating—and then, across a wide landing, a bathroom with basin and lavatory.

'It is a little inconvenient, only to have one bathroom, especially when the children are at home,' she observed; 'but you see this house is Church property, so it is not easy to have alterations made.'

Julia asked about the children. There were eight, all grown-up except Marcel, aged 15, who went daily to a *Lycée* in Lausanne; five were married, and living near by; two others were in jobs in Geneva, but already *fiancés*. 'Our children come to see us frequently—I hope you will meet them all while you are here,' Mme de Ritter said, and then excused herself. 'I have to see to the *déjeuner;* it will be at 1.30, as my husband is late today. When you are ready, do sit in the *salon* or the garden; make yourself at home.' It was borne in on Julia that her pretty hostess, so girlish-looking that seven adult children seemed an impossibility, probably had to do the cooking—she learned later that she did the entire work of the house.

Julia unpacked her dressing-case, installed herself, and then went down to the garden. Here she found a curious mixture of beauty and utility. Fine fruit-trees bordered a well-kept lawn, there were seats and wicker chairs on a flagged space under some pleached limes, and beyond these a kitchen-garden, well stocked with asparagus, lettuces, spinach and young beans, and new potatoes. But the flower-borders along the paths beside the kitchen-garden were rather neglected, and clothes-lines, from which hung an array of snowy sheets, ran down two sides of the lawn. Julia went across and felt these; they were perfectly dry. She went back to the house and found her way to the kitchen, where Mme de Ritter was busy with pots and pans on a huge stove.

'The sheets are quite dry—shall I bring them in?' she asked.

'Oh, how kind you are! Yes, do. The linen-basket is in there'— she gestured with her head towards a door—'and the bag for the pegs.' Julia went into what had obviously once been a scullery, but now housed a vast white-enamelled washing-machine, some wooden towel-horses, and several old-fashioned wicker linen-baskets; she gathered up one of these and the peg-bag, and went out again to the garden, where in the warm sunshine she took down the sheets from the lines, folded them, and laid them in the basket. As she was carrying this load back into the house she encountered her host.

'Ah, Miss Probyn! You are very welcome. Please let me take that—Germaine has already set you to work, I see.'

'No, I set myself,' Julia replied, surrendering the basket, which the Pastor carried through into the wash-house.

'*Ma chère*, is luncheon ready?' he asked. 'I must be off again rather soon.'

'In five minutes, Jean-Pierre. You said 1.30, and at 1.30 you will be served.' His wife was perfectly tranquil, and equally firm.

Laughing, the Pastor led Julia into the big cool *solon*, where the numerous chairs and settees were all stiff and rather upright—there was nothing to lounge in. On the walls were some rather attractive portraits in pretty old frames, covering, Julia guessed, at least the last three hundred years—several of them bore a striking resemblance to her host. Jean-Pierre de Ritter was a man of medium height, but he gave the impression of being small, partly because he was so excessively lightly built, with very fine narrow feet and hands; partly because of the squirrel-like rapidity of all his movements. He was handsome; clean-shaven, with merry brilliantly-blue eyes under a massive forehead, the only big thing about him; and this peculiar combination of figure and feature was repeated all round the room, on the panelled white-painted walls, looking out from dimly gilt frames in a variety of dress that spanned the centuries.

'We will not talk about my god-daughter until this evening,' he said at once. 'I have to go the moment after *déjeuner* to the Court at Lausanne, to give evidence in a most distressing case—probably murder, a thing so rare with us.'

Julia of course said the evening would do perfectly. She looked hopefully round for drinks, after her early start; but none were in evidence, and none were offered. Her host asked suddenly—'Do you speak French? Easily?'

'Yes, very easily.'

'Then we shall speak French. It is simpler for me, and even more so for Germaine; she is French, a French Protestant from the Loire valley, where as you probably know there are a number of Protestant communities.'

Julia didn't know—however, French they talked at lunch, to the manifest relief of her hostess. It was all highly political and intellectual, and Julia was quite unable to answer many of her host's questions on what the English thought about the raid on the Rumanian Legation in Berne, the suicide of the Swiss Chief of Police, Dr. Adenauer's attitude to NATO, and the value of the activities of Moral Rearmament in Morocco. His own remarks on these and other subjects were shrewd, witty, and at the same time restrained—Julia remembered that Herr Waechter had called him a brilliant man. When he left at the end of the brief meal he already commanded Julia's respect.

In the afternoon Henriette, one of the married daughters, arrived in a station-wagon with the whole of her weekly wash, to be done in the vast *Pharos* in the ex-scullery. In theory she merely used her mother's washing-machine; in fact Germaine did all the actual work, pouring in the soap-powder and bestowing the linen; then rinsing and taking-out while Henriette, in the garden, kept a maternal eye on her two pretty little girls and her toddler son of 2, and did a little desultory weeding. She too talked, endlessly and very well, to Julia, who had undertaken to pick the spinach for supper; crouched over the hot crumbly earth between the rows of succulent green plants, Miss Probyn tried to make reasonably intelligent responses about the works of Kafka and Romain Rolland, and Gonzague de Reynolde's *Qu'est-ce que l'Europe?* This last she had read—and praised, throwing leaves into a basket as she spoke; Henriette was pleased.

'Oh, I am glad!—for really he was a formidable writer. But later he became rather Fascist, and I think annoyed the English.'

'Yes—I remember that he wrote some terrible nonsense about the Italians and *Mare Nostrum* and all that,' Julia said, rising to her feet and moving two steps further along the green rows. 'But that didn't prevent *Qu'est-ce que l'Europe?* from being a splendid book.'

Henriette, much encouraged, asked if Miss Probyn admired

Rilke? 'You know that his *belle amie* lived at Sierre, and he visited her daily?'

Julia didn't know—she felt rather out of her depth in the rarefied intellectual atmosphere of La Cure. She had always imagined Calvinists—surely the Swiss National Church was Calvinist?—to be terrific theologians, but completely *bornés* and inhibited otherwise; and here she was, being utterly stumped on politics and literature by these same supposedly rigid people. Having piled her basket with spinach, she took it in to Germaine. In the wash-house were two more of the big linen-baskets, full of clean wet sheets and towels. 'Are these to go out?' she asked.

'Yes—but I will take them,' her hostess replied.

'What rubbish!' Julia exclaimed. 'Henriette!' she called through the window, 'Come and help me out with your *linge*!' Turning, she surprised a rather startled and happy smile on her hostess's face. When Henriette came in they carried out the two heavy baskets, and pegged the wet linen in the sun and breeze along the lines beside the lawn.

'Rilke my elbow!' Julia thought to herself. 'Why not do one's own *work*?' She was becoming quite a partisan of her beautiful hostess. Henriette, as they stretched out sheets, continued to talk, now about her family, and from her lively chatter Julia learned yet other aspects of Swiss life. The Iron-workers' Guild in Berne had given Henriette a small *dot* when she married, and were going to do the same presently for Marguerite, who was already *fiancée;* and they were helping to pay for Marcel's education, as they had done for that of his two elder brothers. Julia was much more interested in this than in Rilke. Were there still Guilds in Switzerland? she wanted to know. Henriette was a little vague.

'Well at least there were, and there are funds still existing, to help those whose families have always belonged to the Guild. It is an hereditary thing—for of course Papa is not an iron-worker,' Henriette said, with a disarming girlish giggle. 'But he is really a Bernois, and his family have belonged to this Guild for—oh, for centuries; so they help with the boys' education, and our dowries. It is very convenient, *en tout cas*, for we are so many, and Papa and Maman are not rich.'

However, there was Kirsch, locally made and excellent, with the coffee after supper, before the Pastor bore Julia off to his study, where a business-like desk with a typewriter and two shabby leather armchairs were looked down upon by shelves-ful of books going up to the ceiling: masses of theology, but also plenty of modern stuff in French and German, and in English too—Winston Churchill, Osbert Sitwell, Virginia Woolf, and of course Galsworthy, for whom Continentals have such a surprising enthusiasm. 'But this Miss Burnett—why has she such *réclame?*' the Pastor enquired, fingering a row of modern novels. 'Clever dialogue, yes; but it is needlessly confusing if one does not know who speaks. And it seems to me that she has little to say except that children often disagree with their parents, and that governesses may be more intelligent than their employers! This last the Brontës told us long ago, and with greater simplicity— and genius.'

Julia already delighted in the Pastor, and would have asked nothing better than to spend the evening discussing books with him, but the urgency of Colin's letter was strong on her; also she had been greatly struck by the welcome and hospitality so freely shown her, without any explanation of her presence being given. She agreed hastily about Miss Burnett, and then pulled out of her bag the copy of Mr. Thalassides' will, and the letters from Aglaia's lawyers and bankers. 'As she is still technically "an infant", and as I was coming out to Switzerland anyhow, I was asked to look into it,' she said, realising how lame the words sounded even as she spoke them.

M. de Ritter drew up one of the old armchairs for her; then he spread the papers out on his desk, and studied them.

'The authorisations are quite adequate,' he said at length. 'But I am a little surprised that my god-daughter's lawyers did not come to deal with this matter themselves.' He looked up at her, with a shrewd gaze.

'For one thing, I'm not sure that they even knew of the existence of this numbered Konto till they were told,' Julia said bluntly.

'Who told them, then?' he asked quickly.

'Aglaia, I imagine.'

He tapped on the table, thinking; then he gave a sudden laugh.

'And if they do not know, how do *you* know? And why did they authorise you?'

Julia laughed too—she liked him so much. But as she laughed she was thinking. Yes, obviously she must come out into the open—nothing could be done without him.

'Oh, why indeed?' she said cheerfully. 'Monsieur de Ritter, it's no good my fencing with you. In fact there is more to this than Aglaia's fortune.'

'The oil question, I suppose?' he said. 'Oh dear yes, that was bound to come up. But again'—he looked at her, in her cool summer frock of lime-green silk, sitting so beautiful and relaxed in the shabby leather chair—'Why you? Are you a very close friend of Aglaia's?'

'No. I told you a lie about that—I'm sorry. I've never even met her,' Julia said candidly.

'*Tiens! De plus en plus drôle!* Well, there must be a reason—even for your telling a lie! What is it?'

'Her fiancé is a cousin of mine, and as I was coming out here, he asked me to undertake this errand.'

The Pastor pounced on the fiancé aspect.

'Your cousin, you say, is her fiancé? What is he like? Is he well-off?—rich?'

'Yes, he's quite well-off; he has a very large property in Scotland. He doesn't need Aglaia's money in the least, Monsieur de Ritter,' Julia said crisply.

He smiled at her disarmingly.

'*Très-bien!* You see I have to make these enquiries; there is now no one but myself to guard the interests of this child—the aunt she lives with, her poor father's sister, is a kind woman, but *peu capable*. And your cousin directs his *bien*, his property, himself, as my sons-in-law do?'

'No, not at the moment. His sister and her husband are running it for him.'

'Oh? *Pourquoi?*'

'Because he has a job that keeps him abroad a good deal of the time,' Julia said carefully.

The Pastor considered, again tapping the table; then he gave her a look so shrewd as to be almost sly.

'Abroad. And you say he assigned this task to you? Including the oil affair?' Julia nodded—but the Pastor's next remark came like a bomb-shell. 'Is your cousin by any chance an agent of your Government?'

Julia had to take a lightning decision. She had seen enough of Colin and Hugh Torrens to know that in their job Rule I is never to admit to Secret Service activities, if it is at all possible to avoid this. But here speed was essential, and de Ritter was the key to the whole thing; she was really at the point of no return. To cover her hesitation she laughed.

'Monsieur de Ritter, what a man you are!'

'Yes, but is he?' the Pastor insisted. 'You see, when Aglaia was staying here last year she confided to my daughter Marguerite that she had recently met a young man who acted as a British Government agent, and that they were much drawn to one another. So naturally I am wondering; is this individual and your cousin the same person?'

'Yes, undoubtedly,' Julia said, thinking what a clot Aglaia must be to have spilt these particular beans, and what an even greater clot Colin was not to have told her not to! 'But to put your mind at rest, my cousin Colin is much more worried about the official side of this affair than about your god-daughter's fortune.' She carefully added a little praise of Colin—his simplicity, his charm, his conscientiousness, his enthusiasm for his work.

'Has he any head for *les affaires?*' her host asked, practically.

'For money? No, very little, I think. You and the bankers will have to occupy yourselves with all these billions—money isn't his line at all; it doesn't interest him much. He could look after Glentoran—his place in Scotland—all right, when he retires. But Monsieur le Pasteur, since you've guessed what Colin is, and what is at issue, will you let me explain the whole thing?'

He was so elegant about this.

'Do not let me press you—only tell me what I need to hear. But I should know this—are you, yourself, of the same profession as your cousin?'

'No. That is, not officially—I have, accidentally, helped him and his friends once or twice; that's all. I retain my amateur status!' she said smiling.

'Well now, tell me just as much as you please. You have satisfied me in regard to the personal aspect, which is the important one.'

Julia liked him very much for saying that—it fitted in so completely with the whole atmosphere of La Cure; the austerity, the elegance, the hard work cheerfully done; the affection, and the preoccupation with the things of the mind. Calvinists or no, these people lived in a wonderful world and one seldom met with in the greedy materialistic twentieth century—the word 'rat-race' simply had no meaning at Bellardon! Much more at ease, she explained that initially Colin had only asked her to look into the matter of the inheritance—but then had come the telephone call, and the letter explaining that important documents had been deposited along with the money, which should be secured as quickly as possible. In fact, what she wanted was the number of Mr. Thalassides' account.

'You do not know me in the least,' she ended, opening her bag—'but you have those letters from Aglaia's lawyers, and here is my passport.'

He waved it aside. 'A very poor likeness. Why must you hurry so much? We should enjoy a longer visit—my wife has lost her heart to you! The papers and the money are safe enough in the bank.'

'Monsieur de Ritter, that is just what my cousin's colleagues fear they may not be. They believe that other people are after them. That is why I have come here so suddenly—they say the matter is *de toute urgence.*'

'Who seeks them?'

'I have no idea—I wasn't told, except that it is the documents they are after.'

He frowned. 'It would be.' He looked again at the papers on his desk. 'But you have no death certificate for the old Greek! You can do nothing without that.'

'I know. I wrote to my cousin yesterday to ask for it. I told him if he could get it at once to post it to me here.'

'How can he get it at once? Thalassides died in Instan-bul, in the Park Hotel! And in addition, to satisfy the Bank the copy must be stamped and attested by the British Consulate. Latterly he held an English passport.'

'Oh glory!' Julia exclaimed in English. 'But all that will take ages!'

'At least it will take several days,' de Ritter said. 'So you see that you will have to prolong your visit! Germaine will be enchanted—and so shall I.'

Julia didn't respond very adequately to this pretty speech, because she was doing some of her usual practical thinking.

'I wonder if they know in London where he died,' she said. 'Oh, sorry—how sweet of you. Yes, I love being here, only it's an awful imposition on your wife. But I think I must let Colin know about Istanbul.'

'We will telegraph tomorrow, early,' the Pastor said.

Germaine presently took Julia up to her room.

'At what hour would you like your *petit déjeuner?*' she asked.

'Oh, whenever you all have yours,' Julia said, anxious to be accommodating.

'We breakfast at a quarter past six,' her hostess said. 'You see Marcel has to catch an early train to Lausanne for his school, and Jean-Pierre likes to be in the church at least by a quarter to seven, to have an hour to say his prayers in peace before the day's work begins. But this is early for you—I can bring you a tray in the *salle à manger* at any time. Just name the hour.'

'Golly!' Julia muttered—and named the hour of 8.30. What people! she thought, just before falling asleep in the narrow but gloriously comfortable Swiss bed, with the smell of lilac coming in at the window.

Chapter 4

Geneva

Julia gave careful thought to the wording of her telegram the moment she awoke, and went down to breakfast with it written out on a sheet of paper.

'See my letter stop Grandpa died in Constantinople and paper I asked for must be stamped and verified by our consulate there stop staying here pro tem stop hurry repeat hurry.'

She signed it 'Darling'.

The Pastor read this through carefully when she handed it to him.

'You have put "stop" three times, when really the sense is quite clear without,' he said, pulling out the pen clipped into his breast-pocket. Julia snatched at his hand.

'No, leave it. It's the way they telegraph. Is it all right otherwise? I don't think it gives much away, do you?'

'No. Why'—he turned his blue eyes, usually so dancingly gay, onto her with a certain severity as he asked—'Why do you sign it "Darling"?'

59

'Oh, that's a code word. It just means urgency, between Colin and me,' Julia said airily. As he continued to regard her a little seriously she turned her doves' eyes onto him. 'Dear Monsieur de Ritter, do take this from me' she said in English. 'Would I be busting myself to secure Aglaia's fortune for her, if Colin was really a "darling" to me?'

His expression relaxed.

'Very well—yes, I accept what you say. But a telegram should be signed with a name, here.'

'Well Darling is a name. There was Grace Darling, the girl in the life-boat,' Julia replied promptly.

He laughed loudly.

'All right. So now I take this to the Bureau de Poste, and meanwhile you stay with us. How nice!'

When a telegram like this of Julia's reaches a certain headquarters in London it sets all sorts of activities in motion. Tall men, with rather dead-pan faces, reach for their desk telephones and talk to one another, or walk along corridors to other rooms for conversations face to face; small men, usually in brown felt hats, scurry unobtrusively about Whitehall and the purlieus of the Strand. In this particular case, in a matter of hours, men in rather loud check caps were hurrying through the steep narrow streets of Istanbul, and returning, frustrated by the innate Turkish passion for stalling, to their superiors. Ultimately there were even telephone calls between London and Ankara. And it all took quite a long time, as everything to do with Turkey does.

Meanwhile Julia, when she had breakfasted, asked to be allowed to ring up Gersau; she spoke to Herr Waechter, enquired after Mrs. Hathaway, and learning that she was going on well explained that she, Julia, would not be returning for a few days. 'Please be sure to telephone if she gets worse, or wants

60

me,' the girl said earnestly. 'But I feel sure that in your house, and with Watkins to harry, she will be perfectly all right unless she has a relapse. And I should really stay here—she will understand.'

She heard his dry old-man's laugh when she spoke of Mrs. Hathaway harrying Watkins, but he promised to do as she wished.

Julia spent the next five days very happily at La Cure, taking part in a form of life completely new to her, which she both admired and enjoyed. She got quite accustomed, when she went to the bathroom at 7 a.m., to seeing her hostess, in an enveloping check overall, with a cotton kerchief framing her beautiful face, pushing one of those heavy lead-weighted polishing pads on a long handle to and fro across the broad beechen planks on the wide landing, or rubbing up the walnut table and the other pretty pieces of old furniture which ornamented it with real beeswax, mixed with turpentine in a small earthenware jar; the same of course went on downstairs in the hall, the *salon*, the *salle à manger* and the Pastor's study—and later in the bedrooms: theirs, hers, Marcel's. In the house-work—which was usually finished soon after ten—Julia was never allowed to take any part except to make her own bed, and this only under protest; but in other ways she did what she could to help Germaine. She took plates and cups out of the Swiss version of the Dish-Master and stowed them in cupboards; she picked peas and shelled them, sitting under the arbour of pleached limes in the garden, and did the same for the broad beans; she gathered the first strawberries, weeded the borders, and propped up with twigs gathered from the rubbish-heap the superb white peonies which filled them. Sometimes, if she was in time, she laid the table for lunch.

But these were morning occupations; in the afternoons the

Pastor, whenever he could, took her out on his rounds to show her the country-side. This was green and gently rolling, with cherries ripening in the orchards and along the road-sides, and the usual Swiss air of good cultivation and prosperity; here and there were small blue lakes. The villages were often charming, as well as spotlessly clean, and one or two of the old towns— like Murtag, with its broad street of lovely arcaded buildings—beautiful to a degree. Julia felt ignorant and foolish, in that she had never heard of Murtag; nor had she realised that half the Canton was Protestant and half Catholic, as the Pastor now told her, pointing out the different churches in place after place—sometimes both in one village, more often a differ-ent form of worship in each settlement.

But most of all she was interested by her host's conversation. As with literature, where his work was concerned he was both intensely practical, and rather original in his views. His parish was vast and straggling, eighteen miles one way by twenty or more the other, and he scorched about it in a big Frégate. So Julia was surprised to hear him say one day, when they were discussing the problems confronting the modern world, that he regarded *l'auto* as the enemy of the good life.

'I should have thought a car was essential for you, simply to cover the ground,' she protested.

'It depends on how usefully I cover it,' he said. 'When I walked, or even bicycled thirty kilometres to reason with my parishioners about their misdeeds, or to pray with them, they listened to me, for they felt that I had taken some trouble on their account; when I drive up in a car they do not pay half as much attention, and will almost interrupt my exhortations to ask what she will do at full stretch! It has completely altered their attitude, and our relationship.'

'Well, couldn't you still bicycle about?'

'Miss Probyn, I am 60 years old—and the work grows from year to year, as the State impinges more and more on individual lives. I spend half my day now at my desk, *tracassé* by filling in forms, or helping others to fill in their forms, when thirty years ago I could spend all my time on my proper task, that of a shepherd of souls. *Les paperasses* are even more of an enemy of the good life than *l'auto!*'

But on the whole Jean-Pierre de Ritter was optimistic about the present, and the future, of religion.

'The eruption of evil in the world which the last twenty-five years have witnessed—first Hitler's Germany, then the Communists and their prison-camps—has finally shut the mouths of those who formerly derided the idea of Original Sin, and equally of the deluded people who used to believe in human progress by purely human effort. Who now pays the smallest attention to Bernard Shaw or Bertrand Russell?—or the poor Webbs? Certainly none who have seen the photographs of what the Allied forces found in Belsen, or who have encountered Polish girls with big numbers tattoed in blue ink on their forearms in Auschwitz—or even who have read *Darkness at Noon*. No!' de Ritter exclaimed, standing on the accelerator in his eager emphasis—'The modern world has met Evil face to face, in Europe at least; and whoever has truly seen Evil is ready, is eager, to look for salvation, redemption. And the only Saviour, the one Redeemer, is Christ.'

He shot past a line of farm carts, slewing dangerously over onto the wrong side of the road; braked to avoid an oncoming lorry, and then proceeded at a more reasonable speed.

'It is to this that I attribute the quite remarkable resurgence of religion in Europe recently,' he went on. 'We have it here; in

France it is mainly Catholic, and most remarkable—the *Jacistes*, the *Jocistes*, the *Prêtres Ouvriers;* and look at those amazing Whitsuntide pilgrimages from Paris to Chartres, three thousand or more young people marching, praying, and hearing Mass, over the whole week-end of Pentecost.' He passed a tractor drawing a trailer laden with farm implements. 'How is it in England?' he went on. 'Have you the same thing?'

As so often while staying at La Cure, Julia found herself rather out of her depth. She had read *Darkness at Noon*, and she had heard of the French Worker-Priests, but she had no idea what *Jacistes* or *Jocistes* were, nor had she seen much sign of a religious revival in England, bar an article in some paper about a great increase in the number of Catholics recently. The poor old C. of E., judging by the attendance at village churches when she spent week-ends in the country, was far from being on the up-grade, and rather gloomily she told her host so. 'Of course there's been Billy Graham,' she added.

'Oh, emotional Revivalism!' he said, in rather crushing tones. 'But does that last?—do you know at all?'

And Julia had to confess that she didn't know.

In the evenings she met the family: Gisèle and her husband came to dine one evening, Henriette and hers another; Antoine and his wife on a third occasion—in each case one or two neighbours were asked as well. Both the girls had some of their mother's rather delicate beauty, while Antoine was the spit and image of the Pastor. He worked at a rayon factory not far off; the two sons-in-law were 'working farmers' (with the accent on working) living on land they owned—what the Scotch used to call 'bonnet lairds'. But Lucien and Armand, though they might have been forking dung or filling silage-pits since 5 a.m., could talk about Galsworthy or Rilke with the best—could, and insisted on doing so, and on kindred topics. How was Auden regarded as a poet in England? Had the curious preoccupation of the not-so-young intellectuals with the Spanish Civil War died a natural death?

'Surely,' Armand exploded—he was a blond giant of a man—'Surely even Spender must realise by now that this all arose from an attempt to create a Communist enclave in the extreme West of Europe, outflanking England and France?' And Julia, once again, had to confess that she had no idea what Spender now realised or didn't realise.

At last the death certificate arrived, direct by air-mail from the Consulate-General in Istanbul; the combination of the Turkish postage-stamp and the Lion-and-Unicorn embossed on the flap of the envelope aroused the highest interest in the village *facteur* who brought the letters, rather to Julia's annoyance; it might, she thought, have been sent more anonymously. The Pastor was already out on his rounds in the parish, and till he returned for the *déjeuner* she had to pacify herself, and help her hostess, by cutting asparagus and also lettuce for the salad—in Fribourg they sow lettuces thick and cut them like hay, to save the bother of transplanting; Julia was by now familiar with this curious trick. She was laying the table for luncheon when she heard her host's step in the hall; she hastened out to him.

'It's come!' she said. 'So I must be off as soon as possible.'

Jean-Pierre took this announcement, as he took everything, very easily.

'*Quel dommage!* It has been such a happiness to have you with us—Germaine will be lost without her under-gardener! However, after supper we will arrange everything.'

'Can't I go this afternoon? Colin said it was urgent,' Julia protested.

'There is no train that will get you to Geneva before the banks close. No—we will deal with it tonight. Now come and eat, and enjoy your lunch.'

They dealt with it that evening in his study. Julia again brought down her papers, together with the copy of the late Mr. Thalassides' death certificate, plastered with English and Turkish official stampings, the Turkish in ugly violet ink. The Pastor once more examined them all, then pushed them aside, drew forward a sheet of headed paper, and wrote rapidly; folded the sheet and put it in an envelope which he handed to her.

'This is the authorisation which I, as Aglaia Armitage's guardian, give you to collect the documents; it is incontestable. It gives the account *numéro*. I have told them that the money will not be taken away at this stage; her lawyers or her bankers can do that later—it is their affair. But I have instructed them to show you, if you wish, the certificates which give the extent of her fortune.' He paused, took a card out of his pocket-book, and scribbled on it. 'Do not show the authorisation I have given you until you are in conversation with one of these two gentlemen,' he said, handing her the card. 'They are two of the directors of the Banque Républicaine who know me well. If possible speak with Dutour; Chambertin is sometimes *un peu difficile.*'

Julia read the card. It said—*'Je recommande chaleureusement Mademoiselle Julia Probyn, de Londres, qui voudra discuter des affaires bancaires.'* As she put the card away in her bag along with the other papers de Ritter chuckled.

'They will think you want to open a numbered account,' he said. Then—'Where do you stay in Geneva?' he asked.

'I hadn't thought. What's a good hotel?'

'How are you arranged for currency?' he enquired.

'Oh, plenty. I get a journalist's allowance—I write for some of the weeklies, when I feel like it.'

'Then do write about the Canton de Fribourg! Come back to us, and learn more! However, if you are not short of money you had better stay at the Bergues; it is delightful.' He went out into the hall and there and then booked her a room. And the following morning her beautiful hostess once again dragged Julia's luggage down to the station on the hand-cart, and she set out for Geneva and the bank.

Julia, unlike many English people, was always ready to talk in trains. After changing for Geneva at Lausanne she found herself seated opposite a neat little man with a large brief-case, on which he was scribbling notes on narrow sheets of typed paper that looked like invoices. Julia's appearance of course produced its usual impact; he offered to put out his cheroot if she disliked the smell, enquired whether she wished the window up or down, and promised to show her Mont Blanc when it should come in sight. Soon they were in cheerful conversation—and it proved much more amusing to Julia than most casual conversations in trains. The neat little man presently explained that he held the Swiss agency for an English firm, who made surgical stays in a special air-light elastic weave—'Corsette-Air' was the trade name—and in Switzerland they had an immense sale; he named a figure for the firm's annual turnover which astonished Julia. She was even more astonished to learn that he had never been to England, and had never met any of the directors of the Yorkshire firm who manufactured 'Corsette-Air'—all had been arranged by corre-spondence, through people who vouched for him. More peculiar still, he could not really speak English, but he could read it suffi-ciently well to understand the letters from Yorkshire.

'And do you reply in English,' Julia asked, fascinated by this odd set-up.

Ah no, he always replied in German. 'They send my letters to Birmingham to be translated, and then reply to me in English.'

To Julia it all sounded quite crazy; but if the sums he had named to her were accurate, obviously it worked. And the little man himself was so eager, so energetic and enthusiastic that she could credit his making a go of anything. In his excitement over telling her about his work he quite forgot to show her Mont Blanc at the place whence it is visible—'*Ah, quel dommage!*' he exclaimed. 'From Geneva one seldom sees it; in fact you may say never.' Like so many Swiss he was bilingual; he told Julia in French how he wrote to his English employers in German, and how—he glowed with pride as he spoke—'Sometimes we even touch La Haute Finance; foreign business—not English, I mean; international. We are much used, because we are most discreet.'

'How thrilling!' Julia said, with her customary easy warmth, which really meant nothing.

'Is it not? I see that Mademoiselle comprehends. Listen to this—only the other day I, Kaufmann, was called upon to act as intermediary between very important *agences* belonging to two different nations, and pass informations from one to the other!' The little man was quite carried away, between Julia and his own enthusiasms; the girl could not help smiling at his idea of discretion, but merely said, as warmly as before, that this was *formidable*, that he must lead a passionately interesting life—to which he agreed eagerly. Then, as the train began to slow down at the outskirts of Geneva, suddenly he became cautious.

'This is of course most confidential, what I have told Mademoiselle,' he said rather nervously.

'But naturally. I am discretion itself!' Julia said soothingly. 'And I am grateful to you for having made my journey so interesting.' Whereupon the little man insisted on giving her one of his trade cards, and urged her to come and see him if she should be in his neighbourhood. The card depicted on one side a rather fully-formed lady wearing a Corsette-Air, and on the other bore his name and address:

Herr Viktor Kaufmann,
Villa Victoria,
Merligen-am-Thunersee,
B.O.

Julia suppressed a giggle at the letters 'B.O.'—she already knew that in Switzerland they stand for 'Berner Oberland'—not their usual English significance; she thanked the little man, put the card in a side pocket of her bag, and promptly forgot all about him.

The Hotel des Bergues at Geneva is indeed a delightful place; the Pastor had been quite right, Julia decided within the first five minutes. It is quiet, unobtrusively high-class, with excellent well-mannered service; it stands on the embankment beside the huge glass-green Rhône, close to where the river debouches from the lake, and exactly opposite the Île Rousseau, set with Claude-like trees. Upstream, on the lake shore, rises that exotic—and therefore so un-Swiss—fantasy, the only fountain in Europe which springs a clear three hundred feet into the air in a snowy jet which sways like a reed or a poplar in the breeze, glittering most beautifully in the sun against the distant blue shores. In theory the whiteness of the fountain's spray should be a *pendant* to that of the summit of Mont Blanc; in fact that tedious mountain seldom shows itself to Geneva.

She unpacked first, as was her habit, and then tried to telephone to the Banque Républicaine—it was already closed, the porter told her politely. So she went downstairs and strolled across the bridge spanning the Rhône to the Île Rousseau, where she observed with interest the wired enclosure reserved for the black swans, tufted ducks, and other varieties; and laughed at the typically Swiss notice about feeding the sixty-odd ordinary swans who hung expectantly in the strong current below the footbridge leading to the island: 'Please give your bread to the keeper; he will arrange it suitably to feed the birds'. She walked on to the farther side of the river, and strolled about a little; the whole place enchanted her, a city grey in tone, with an austere elegance combined with a certain simplicity. On returning to the Bergues she found that it had a tea-room close to the front hall; many people were having tea and cakes at small tables on the pavement outside, and Julia did the same, enjoying the warmth, the soft light, the shifting tops of the poplars on the island, the grey profile of the other half of the city beyond the river, and idly amused by the sight of the passers-by on the pavement beside her. One of these, a tall lanky man in a light suit of rather foreign cut suddenly checked, started, and came up to her, raising his hat—she recognised him as a man called Nethersole, whom she had occasionally met in London with her old admirer Geoffrey Consett.

Mr. Nethersole greeted her with the enthusiasm with which men usually greeted Julia, and sat down at her table. 'What in the world are you doing here?' he asked.

'Oh, just sight-seeing. I'd never been to Geneva before. How beautiful it is.'

'Yes, isn't it? I adore it. But have you seen the oddest sight of all?'

'No, I've only just arrived. What is the odd sight?'

'Oh my dear, the Palais des Nations! Well you'd better come

70

and have lunch with me there tomorrow; I work there. Will you? One o'clock, in the restaurant. Oh, what a piece of luck this is!'

Julia accepted this invitation, mentally praising Mr. Nethersole's tact in not asking if she had seen anything of Geoffrey lately. (Anyhow it is always nice to be invited somewhere in a strange place.) Nethersole soon flitted off, and Julia decided to go up to her room and write a full account of La Cure to Mrs. Hathaway before dinner; between helping Germaine and talking with the Pastor, she had only sent her old friend the scrappiest of notes. In the corridor beyond the main hall the lift doors were just closing; the lift-man politely opened them again for her, and she stepped in, saying '*Troisième*'. Three other people were already in the lift; one of them was the detective.

This time he grinned very broadly indeed, and murmured, 'How we do keep on meeting!' Julia put on her haughtiest expression, and made no response; she got out at the third floor, while he was borne upwards. This encounter disturbed her a little; if he really was one of Colin's *mauvais sujets*, it was rather tiresome that he should be staying in the same hotel. And half-way through her letter she went down again to the hall and procured from the concierge a small plan of the city; back in her room she looked out the Avenue de la République. It was only a short distance away, across the bridge by the island. Fine, she would walk there tomorrow, and give no address to a taxi to be overheard by bell-hops, hovering for a tip.

She woke next morning in good spirits; Julia had the priceless gift of sound sleep. Leaning from her window—she had no idea of her good fortune in being given a front room at the Bergues at twenty-four hours' notice, nor that she owed this entirely to Jean-Pierre—she first looked entranced at the fountain, profiled golden-white in the sunshine against the blue lake. But what was

71

that, looming mistily and incredibly high into the sky?—also golden-white, and immense? It could only be Mont Blanc; it was just where the chambermaid had told her to look for it the evening before. Utterly satisfied, Julia rang for her breakfast, which she ate at her window; then, in high heart, she set out on foot for the bank.

The Avenue de la République is full of banks, all enormous, many of them new. The Banque Républicaine was one of the most grandiose of all; when she stepped onto a door-mat ten feet long, huge bronze and glass doors opened of themselves; within, marble pilasters flanked the doors opening off lobbies— there was no human being in sight. She pushed on through this mausoleum-like splendour into a vast central hall, rising to a height of three or four storeys, and furnished with armchairs and sofas; there was no sign of banking whatever except for a few clerks behind glass walls round the sides. There was, however, a single desk at which sat a pimply youth, curiously inadequate to all this pomp and dignity; to him Julia handed M. de Ritter's card, and asked if she could see M. Dutour or M. Chambertin? The youth glanced at the card and went away, taking it with him—why not telephone, Julia thought, since there were two instruments on the desk. A long pause ensued—long enough to make her, at last, a little nervous. Eventually the youth reappeared accompanied by an older man, who led her to a lift and wafted her up to what he described as the *salle d'attente*.

The waiting-room was as rich as all the rest—a big desk, heavy leather armchairs, a deep pile carpet, some quite tolerable modern paintings on the walls. But the sun struck full into the room, and it was hot and stuffy; Julia went over and threw open a glass door onto a balcony. This was surrounded by window-boxes full of petunias and godetias—she was thinking how early it was for these to be in bloom when the door opened, and a man came in, holding de Ritter's card in his hand.

'I am Monsieur Chambertin,' he said. 'What can I do for you?'

Julia took against Chambertin from the start. He was a short man; younger than she had expected, but somehow with an elderly expression, suspicious and slightly sour. As he seated himself behind the desk she decided that this was going to be a sticky interview; and sticky indeed it proved.

She began confidently enough, however.

'You are doubtless aware that Monsieur le Pasteur de Ritter is the *parrain* and also the guardian of Mademoiselle Aglaia Armitage?'

'*Certainement,*' he said very coldly—indeed he seemed to stiffen a little at the girl's name.

'I come on her behalf—with Monsieur de Ritter's authority, as you see.'

'Mademoiselle, I do *not* see. This card refers only to *"des affaires bancaires"*, not to Mademoiselle Armitage at all.'

Julia apologised and handed over the Pastor's letter. 'I have other authorities also—pray have the goodness to regard them.' She opened her large lizard bag and drew out the documents from England, which she laid before him on the desk: the copy of Thalassides' will, attested by his lawyers; the authorisations from Aglaia's bank and lawyers to hand over any or all of the property to Miss Julia Probyn, if so requested; finally the photostat of the death certificate, so liberally covered with official stamps. M. Chambertin, adjusting a pair of pince-nez, began to look at them, at first with a rather contemptuous air; but as he read through paper after paper his expression changed from contempt to one of bewildered consternation. *'Mais c'est impossible, cela!'* he muttered to himself; then he rounded quickly on Julia.

'Might I see your passport, Mademoiselle?' he asked. For the first time there was nothing disagreeable in his manner, only what she recognised as genuine concern. She handed over her passport—he studied it, looked at the photograph, looked at Julia, and then raised his hands in a helpless gesture of despair.

'This is all completely incomprehensible!' he said.

'Why?' Julia asked. 'Surely these papers are incontestably in order? What is the difficulty?'

'Simply that Mademoiselle Armitage called here in person last week, and took reception of the money in the account.'

'And took the'—Julia checked herself in time. 'Took *everything* that you held in Monsieur Thalassides' numbered Konto?'

'Yes—all.'

Julia stood up. She was tall; at that moment she was menacing.

'Monsieur Chambertin, you have been duped! Miss Armitage sailed for the Argentine to visit her mother on the 14th of May, the day before I left for Switzerland myself.'

'How do you know this?'

'It was in all the English papers. As Monsieur Thalassides' heiress, whatever she does is news.'

'*La presse* can make mistakes,' Chambertin said, with the air of a man clutching at a straw.

'Hardly, in such a case. But in any event her fiancé would not; and he is my cousin.' She paused, thinking with intensity of the girl Watkins had noticed at Victoria, and of her two companions. 'Did Mademoiselle Armitage come alone?' she asked, sitting down again.

'But naturally not—she is not of age. Her guardian was with

her, and gave the authorisation.'

Julia was a little shaken by this.

'Do you mean Monsieur le Pasteur de Ritter?' she asked incredulously. 'Did you see him? He says he knows you.'

'No—I myself did not,' Chambertin replied, a little unhappily.

'Then who did? I can't believe it was Monsieur Dutour; he is a personal friend of the Pastor's too.'

M. Chambertin looked more unhappy than ever.

'No. It was Monsieur de Kessler, another of our directors, who conducted this interview.'

'Does he know Monsieur Jean-Pierre de Ritter personally?' Julia asked sharply.

'No, he does not.' M. Chambertin's unhappiness was now marked.

'Ah. I expect these people carefully asked to see *him*, instead of you or Monsieur Dutour,' Julia said. 'They are probably very well-informed.' Her confidence mounted with her anger. 'Monsieur Chambertin, I think we had better see Monsieur de Kessler.'

'So do I,' he agreed uncomfortably, and spoke into the desk telephone. He turned back to Julia. 'I can assure you that Mademoiselle Armitage and her party produced correct documents. We are extremely particular in these matters.'

'Oh, I am sure you are.' But she pounced on the word 'party'. 'There was a third?'

'I understood that the fiancé of Mademoiselle Armitage was also present.'

'Nonsense! Her fiancé is in London. I have been speaking to him there on the telephone. And you should perhaps know that I came to Geneva yesterday from La Cure at Bellardon, where I have been staying for the last week; therefore *I* know perfectly well that *Monsieur de Ritter* knows perfectly well that Mademoiselle Aglaia Armitage, for the past fortnight, has been on a steamer on her way to the Argentine. Certainly her guardian never came here last week. Would he have given me this letter of authorisation if he had?'

Before Chambertin could answer the door opened and a white-haired man with a pleasant pink face walked in; he was really old, without any doubt.

'Ah, *mon cher de Kessler*, how good of you to come up,' Chambertin said respectfully, rising as he spoke—it was evident that de Kessler was very senior among the directors. 'May I present you to Mademoiselle Probyn?'

De Kessler beamed on Julia as he bowed to her, and then asked Chambertin, rather bluntly, what he wanted?

'A little more information about Mademoiselle Armitage's fortune. Mademoiselle Probyn has been spending the past week at La Cure at Bellardon, and brings me now a letter from Monsieur le Pasteur de Ritter, in a handwriting which I recognise well, giving the number of the late Monsieur Thalassides' Konto and requesting me to hand everything over to her, Miss Probyn. But I understand that you have already dealt with this matter yourself.'

'Certainly—the account has been closed. Mademoiselle Armitage came in person—a charming young lady.' He still only looked a little puzzled, and definitely repressive to his junior colleague.

'You saw her passport?' Chambertin asked.
'But naturally.'
'And made a note of the number?'
'Certainly.'

'She provided you with *des pièces justificatives* which satisfied you?'

'My good Chambertin, for what do you take me? I work in this bank for forty-five years! What is all this? Why these questions?'

'I too come on behalf of Mademoiselle Armitage,' Julia put in, 'and I fear very much that something may have gone wrong— some confusion have occurred. As you know, Mademoiselle Armitage is not of age, and cannot yet take control of her fortune.'

'*Bien entendu*, Mademoiselle. But there was no confusion; she was accompanied by her guardian, who signed all the receipts.' He looked more puzzled, now, and turned to Chambertin. 'You know Monsieur le Pasteur de Ritter? A man of a very old and respected Bernois family.'

Again Julia spoke before Chambertin could reply.

'But you, yourself, are not personally acquainted with Monsieur de Ritter?'

'Till last week, no—only by reputation.'

Chambertin made to speak; Julia gestured him to silence.

'Monsieur de Kessler, this guardian who signed the receipts— was he tallish, rather stout, and with an iron-grey beard slightly parted in the middle?'

'*Exactement*, Mademoiselle,' de Kessler said, looking relieved. Julia quickly put a term to his relief.

'Monsieur Chambertin, would you be so good as to describe your old friend Monsieur de Ritter to your colleague? He is more likely to believe you than me.'

In pitiable embarrassment, but firmly, Chambertin said— '*Mon cher*, the Pasteur de Ritter, whom I have known for thirty years, is a short man, and noticeably slender.'

'Clean-shaven, also, *n'est-ce-pas?*' Julia added.

'Yes—certainly.' While de Kessler gaped Chambertin turned to Julia and asked—'How comes it that you know so well the appearance of—of the man who came and signed the receipts?'

'The impostor, you mean? Oh, I happened to see him, and the girl who was impersonating Miss Armitage, on my way here; they travelled to Calais on the same train.'

De Kessler, now quite bewildered, said irritably—'Mademoiselle, what is all this talk of impostors and impersonators?'

Instead of answering him, Julia turned to his colleague.

'Monsieur Chambertin, wouldn't it be as well to let Monsieur de Kessler see the documents *I* have brought?'

'Certainly. *Les voici, mon cher.*'

De Kessler went round behind the desk, put on his glasses, and studied Julia's papers, muttering to himself as he did so:— 'The bankers, yes, and the lawyers; the executors, yes; and the British Consul-General in Istanbul has *gestempelt* the death certificate.' Last of all he read de Ritter's letter; then turned back and read the date aloud—'*C'est hier!*' Now thoroughly upset, he turned to Chambertin. 'But this is impossible!'

'Oh no, Monsieur de Kessler—unfortunately it's all too possible,' Julia said. 'You have been tricked by a gang of crooks.'

The old man drew himself up (to Julia it was the most pitiable thing of all) and said:

'Mademoiselle, this does not happen with la Banque Républicaine!'

'Well, it has happened this time,' Julia said crisply; she was sorry for the old man, but more important things than his feelings were at stake. She turned to Chambertin. 'Do ring up Monsieur de Ritter now, and ask him if he really came in last week and signed Miss Armitage's fortune away? That will settle it. I know he didn't; but it may satisfy Monsieur de Kessler.'

'Mademoiselle, I accept *no* statements made over the telephone,' de Kessler said angrily.

'Oh very well—then we must drag the wretched man down here.'

Chambertin was fluttering the telephone book. 'Fribourg is 037,' Julia told him, 'and La Cure is 1101.' When the call came through she firmly took the receiver. *'Allo? Ah, c'est toi, Germaine. Ici Julia. Est-ce que Jean-Pierre est là? Ah, très-bien—j'attends.'* She noted the effect of all these Christian names on the two bankers while she waited, receiver in hand. When Jean-Pierre came to the telephone she spoke rapidly in English. 'Listen, I am at the bank. There has been a complete disaster, which I would rather not discuss on the telephone. Is there the least possibility that you could come down—this afternoon?'

'Only with great difficulty? Why?—what is happening?'

'We have been too slow. Those I spoke of have been ahead of us, and have gone off with everything. Someone else signed for them in your name.'

'But this could not happen! Both the men whose names I gave you know me perfectly well.'

'Of course they do. But unfortunately these persons must have known this too, and were sharp enough to ask for another director—*un charmant vieux monsieur qui ignorait les faits essentiels, et s'est laissé duper.'* Julia said the last words in French, deliberately—she saw that cheerful pink face become crimson.

'Le vieux de Kessler?' came down the line.

'Exactement. And he now refuses to accept any statement on the telephone—that is why I must put you to this trouble. I do apologise; it is not my fault.'

79

There was a pause. At last—'Yes, very well,' the Pastor said. 'Who received you?'

'Monsieur Chambertin.'

'Then please tell him I will be with him at half past four o'clock, *à peu près*'

'I would rather you told him yourself'—and she handed the receiver over.

The Pastor had a very resonant voice, and Julia could just hear his words. *'Mon cher Alcide*, what are your co-directors up to? This is frightful, what has taken place. I shall be with you between four and half past, and please arrange for your colleague to be present, and see that we are given admittance. Tell Mademoiselle that I will call for her at her hotel on the way.'

Chambertin transmitted both these messages, adding afterwards to de Kessler—'*C'est bien Jean-Pierre*—I cannot mistake his voice.'

Julia had been thinking as well as overhearing.

'Monsieur Chambertin, surely these people ought to be traced, if possible. Did they give Monsieur de Kessler any address?'

De Kessler said only La Cure at Bellardon, and for the *demoiselle* an address in London. '*Chez une certaine Madame Conway, à Kensington.*'

'That's Aglaia's aunt, of course—that's no help. They gave no indication of their movements?' she asked de Kessler.

'*La demoiselle* spoke of visiting Interlaken, to see the Jungfrau; nothing more. The *fiancé* spoke of making some ascensions.'

'Ah yes, the *fiancé*. Was he tall, dark, with a markedly olive complexion, and the figure of an athlete?' Julia enquired.

'*C'est exacte*, Mademoiselle,' the old man said.

Chambertin had a question to put.

'On which day did they come? Six days ago, you say? We must

alert Interpol, and also the *Fremden-Polizei*, the Security Police. It is possible that they have not yet left the country.'

'Wouldn't it be better to leave the police till Monsieur de Ritter has been,' Julia counselled. She was thinking that she must try to ring up Colin from the Palais des Nations at lunch-time.

'Mademoiselle, the reputation of the Banque Républicaine is at stake! There is not a moment to lose.'

Julia refrained from pointing out that the bank had already lost six days.

'As Monsieur de Kessler has their passport numbers, would there be any means of checking at the frontiers whether they have left or not?' she asked. 'No. I expect not—those men in uniform just open your passport, take a good stare at you, snap it shut and hand it back. They couldn't possibly keep a record.'

Chambertin smiled a little at this description.

'No, Mademoiselle, they do not. But they are quite observant, and this party of three, whom you seem to have observed very closely, might well be noticed. How was the aspect of the young girl, by the way?'

'Ask Monsieur de Kessler,' Julia said.

'She was blonde,' de Kessler said, hesitantly.

'Yes, but her eyes—the colour—and tall or short?' Chambertin asked impatiently.

'She was petite—and *très jolie*,' de Kessler said. Chambertin turned to Julia.

'Mademoiselle, can you help us?'

'Yes,' Julia said. 'This girl was certainly most carefully chosen as a double of Miss Armitage—needlessly, since the personnel of the bank failed to notice her appearance.' She could not resist that crack. 'She is very short indeed, very slender, with tiny hands and feet, and though she is—or has been made to

81

appear—ash-blonde, her eyes are dark brown.'

Chambertin was scribbling.

'Perfect,' he said. 'And her clothes—did you observe these also?'

'Yes. A pale cream suit, a little blouse to match, a light brown overcoat—and a hat of cream Bangkok straw, trimmed with brown nylon lace to match the overcoat. Shoes and hand-bag of brown crocodile.'

Chambertin went on scribbling. 'Miss Probyn, you would be worth a fortune as a detective,' he exclaimed.

'I want to be worth Miss Armitage's fortune, Monsieur Chambertin!' She looked at her watch—nearly twelve. 'Could someone call me a taxi?' She wanted to tidy up at the hotel before going out to lunch.

She did not, however, let the taxi take her to the Bergues; she got out at the foot-bridge leading to the Île Rousseau, and then walked to the hotel. These types seemed to be up to everything; one couldn't be too careful. And there was that damned detective, too, actually staying in the hotel. What on earth was he up to?

In her room she changed into a thinner frock—Geneva heats up in the middle of the day—and looked in the back of her engagement-book to make sure that she had got Colin's office number. She had, and she would just have to risk telephoning there from the Palais des Nations after lunch; surely it ought to be one of the safest places. Anyhow Colin was usually pretty quick at picking up what she was driving at, either in their 'darling-darling' language or, at the worst, in Gaelic. But oh, why hadn't she written to him about the girl at Victoria? 'Because one's afraid of looking a fool one goes and *is* a fool,' she muttered, as she put on scent and lipstick. She telephoned down for a taxi, which was waiting when she reached the hall; as she drove off along the *quai* beside the lovely green river, in spite of her frustration and worry she began to enjoy herself, and to look forward with pleasure to her luncheon with Nethersole. He was a curious learned creature, but with an amusing outlook on life; what his precise function with UNO—or whatever now used the Palais des Nations—might be she didn't know, but he had many forms of strange knowledge, any one of which could make him valuable to these international organisations.

Chapter 5

Geneva—the Palais des Nations

The Palais des Nations at Geneva is a very large, completely expressionless building. It isn't ugly, it isn't beautiful; it is just pale in colour, and *big*, with a lot of flags fluttering in front of it from tall pale poles. It stands in spacious green grounds, with a parking-space for cars all down the right-hand side of the broad entrance-drive. Within, the bigness and the functional lack of expression are even more marked. An immense hall stretches to right and left inside the door, with racks full of folders, with polyglot girls in light overalls standing behind counters, casually and chipperly answering the questions of even more polyglot enquirers. The enquirers are not only polyglot but polychrome; every shade of colour that the skin of the human race can take on, from splendid deep black to a pinkness like that of M. de Kessler's, were exhibited to Julia's fascinated gaze, standing in chattering knots on the wide marble floor, as she made her way to one of the counters, and asked where the restaurant was?

'Lift to the twelfth floor; over there,' a chipper girl said, without giving any indication of the direction.

'Over where?' Julia asked coldly. 'Could you take me, if you can't show me?'

'Oh sorry—on the right, round the corner,' the girl said carelessly. 'Lots of lifts.'

Julia walked to the right-hand end of the huge lobby and went round the corner, where there were a great many very large lifts. The lift-men were much more polite than the girl—as indeed men usually are more polite than the teen-age chits who answer so many of the world's telephones, and thus and otherwise conduct so much of the world's business; perhaps one day the world will get round to teaching them that good manners are a key to efficiency. Julia was wafted to the twelfth floor in an outsize lift which opened into the restaurant itself; an elderly waiter came up to her politely, and asked her pleasure.

'Monsieur Nethersole.'

'Par ici, Madame'—and he led her out onto a broad balcony, where Nethersole and another man were sitting having drinks. They both rose as she came up to the table; the second man was the detective.

'Ah, excellent!' Nethersole exclaimed. 'How good to see you— and how good you look! I couldn't collect a party for you in the time, but here is John Antrobus, who says he doesn't know you, unhappy creature! John, let me complete your education by introducing you to Miss Julia Probyn.'

Julia, already sufficiently disconcerted by her morning at the bank, felt that this was the last straw. For once she was grateful to Nethersole for his elaborations, which usually rather bored her; they gave her time to pull herself together, and when she held out her hand to Antrobus she said coolly—'So now we really *do* meet.'

'Why, have you met before un-really?' Nethersole enquired.

'Oh yes—Mr. Antrobus infests platforms! We bump into one another everywhere—and in lifts, too. He seems to cover the whole of Europe.'

'This is most interesting. But first, what will you drink?'

'A Martini, like you. I'm dying for a drink.' Nethersole ordered another double Martini, which was brought very quickly—but not more quickly than Julia was thinking. How could she best turn this meeting to account? Was it a coincidence? Was the detective in with the crooks, or on her and Colin's side? She wished passionately that she had bothered in London to learn more from Geoffrey Consett about what Nethersole really did; UNO—if UNO was what he was in—was of course liberally bespattered with fellow-travellers. But it was nice up there on the balcony; the air was sunny and warm, the green gardens below were pleasant, blue mountains rose in the distance. After a sip of her cocktail she decided to relax, and pick up what she could while she enjoyed herself.

Once his guest was supplied with a drink, Nethersole returned to the subject of her earlier encounters with Antrobus.

'Oh, I was very forward at Victoria; I went up and spoke to him,' Julia said airily.

'She asked me if I was a detective!' Antrobus interjected.

'Oh did you? Why? Do you think he looks like one?' Nethersole asked.

Julia profited by this excuse to examine that amusing face openly and deliberately.

'Yes, I think so. Detective-Inspector Alleyne might look very like him, don't you think? And he was behaving like one, too.'

Nethersole laughed.

'How do detectives behave?'

'Well, he was hanging about.'

'Loitering with intent, did you think?' Antrobus asked.

'Well really it was the maid I was taking out who thought it.'

'Goodness, Julia, do you still travel with a maid?' Nethersole asked, with intense interest.

'No, not still, nor ever!—I was taking her out to an old friend, who has fallen ill out here. But Watkins is very shrewd, and she's been at endless weddings—always plastered with detectives to guard the presents. She was positive that Mr. Antrobus was one.'

Both men laughed.

When they went indoors to lunch, in a long restaurant with big plate-glass windows giving onto the balcony, Julia deliberately abandoned that topic, and started another.

'Richard, what do you do in this peculiar place? Tell them about the Arabs, or the Walls of Jericho?'

'That sort of thing.'

Antrobus supplemented this uninformative remark.

'Richard is a tremendous Arabic scholar, you know. Since Sir Denison Ross died, he has no peer.'

'Oh, does UNO go in for scholarship? That's quite a new idea.'

Again the two men laughed, and Antrobus said 'Specialised knowledge generally comes in usefully, even here.'

Julia took him up on that instantly.

'Do you work here too, Mr. Antrobus?'

Did he hesitate? Barely.

'No, not really.'

'At Victoria I remember you said that you were on business.'

'How inquisitive you are! That was to put you off.'

'And are you still putting me off? How does one work for UNO un-really—as you and I met?'

This time there was no doubt about it; though Antrobus laughed, Nethersole at least was plainly embarrassed.

'Julia, I can't allow you to cross-examine anyone at lunch! Have some more smoked salmon.'

So there it was! Some form of secrecy going on—and she didn't even know Nethersole well enough to be able to get the truth out of him later. 'Oh yes, please,' she said; 'I really like to make a meal off smoked salmon.' As she helped herself she said cheerfully to Antrobus—'I'll apologise if you'd like me to; but like all women, since Fatima, inquisitiveness is my middle name.'

'Oh don't apologise,' the man said. 'If we ever get onto Christian—or Mahomedan-name terms, I shall call you Fatima!'

Julia was unexpectedly pleased at the idea of being called Fatima by Antrobus. The luncheon passed very pleasantly indeed; both men were amusing and talked well—Antrobus in particular had a caustic vein which amused Julia, and a free and completely natural approach to any subject—she had never yet met a man so disengaged, or so totally devoid of self-importance. Long before the meal was over she had become far more inter-ested in him as a person than in what he did, conscious though she was of her need, indeed her duty, to learn this—more than ever after Nethersole had so openly shut her up.

At one point the talk turned on the great variety of Swiss trades; Julia, by nature so open, just stopped herself in time from telling how the Iron-workers Guild in Berne paid for the de Ritter boys' education, and quite casually substituted the little agent for 'Corsette-Air'. She made a funny story of it, with the letters in German going to Birmingham to be translated; Nethersole laughed heartily; Antrobus smiled too, but after a half-second's pause—was there a flicker of surprise, of some extra interest, in the grey eyes under those sculptured triangular lids? Almost certainly Yes, for after a moment he asked—'Where do you say you encountered this entertaining individual?'

'Oh, in the train—just a pick-up,' Julia replied airily. 'You should know that I go in for picking people up.'

But in spite of her growing pleasure in Antrobus's company, when over coffee he offered to drive her back to the Bergues she refused firmly. 'I'll make my own way back—I might like to walk. Besides, I hope Richard is going to show me the whole of this lunatic place. Isn't there a sort of Chamber of Babel, where they all shout at one another through microphones which translate as they go along?' Laughing, Antrobus was nevertheless a little insistent—it was a long way, it was very hot, she would be exhausted, etc. Julia was pleased by his persistence, but couldn't help wondering whether possibly *he* wasn't as anxious to know about her business as she was to learn about his? In any case she was firm, and the gothic-faced man left alone. When he had gone—'Would you really like to see the Salle des Nations?' Nethersole asked.

'Yes, if you can spare the time; I don't mind. But first I want to telephone.'

'Where to?'

'London.'

'What an idea! I never telephone if I can help it. However, I presume there is one up here.'

This was a mistaken presumption. They were sent down to the main hall, where Nethersole made enquiries of one of the chipper chits at the counters. Oh no—all extraterritorial calls had to be made from the third floor. 'Round the corner for the lifts.' Round the corner they went, and up to the third floor, where there was a whole array of telephone-boxes.

'I suppose this is where the Press worthies queue up to send their ghastly nonsense,' Nethersole said, regarding the glass cubicles with a cold eye.

'Oh, don't wait,' Julia said. 'Show me the Salle another day.' She was suddenly nervous, afraid of being overheard, afraid of almost everything. Nethersole was very quick at the uptake, and said nicely—

'I'll go and wait on the lawn outside. I'm in no hurry. But you really ought to see the Salle, it's so portentous.' He went off, and Julia hoped fervently that he supposed her to be ringing up Geoffrey Consett.

She delved into her bag for money, wondering how one said 'A. D. and C.' in Switzerland. However, the man—thank goodness—at the desk was both polite and intelligent; on his advice she made it a personal call, giving Colin's name and the office number. Then she sank down onto a bench, and waited. In no time at all the man called out—'*Le numéro onze, Mademoiselle*'; Julia bolted into box II, and there on the line, as clear as if they were in the same room, was Colin's voice—'Hullo? Who is it?'

'Me—don't use names.'

'Of course not, darling. What goes on?'

'Every sort of *desastre.*' She heard him giggle at the Spanish word. 'No. it isn't funny. They've been ahead of us.'

'What do you mean?'

'I'll tell you. Listen carefully; I'm going to talk Gaelic'

'Well speak very slowly, will you? Mine's got rather buried.'

Julia had been thinking up phrases during the brief moments while she sat waiting on the bench. She now said slowly, using the archaic expressions of that archaic tongue: 'To the House of Gold, in this city, came a maiden who pretended to be one that she was not; *agus* (and) a youth who said that he was her betrothed—tall, dark-skinned, with the aspect of one who comes

90

from the lands of the Sun's rising.' She paused. 'Got that?' she asked anxiously in English.

'I think so. D'you mean a Chink?'

'No—Middle-Eastern.'

'O.K.—go on.'

'With them came a *bodach* (old man) who pretended to be the guardian of the maiden.'

'Hold on—the *what* of the maiden?' Colin asked in English.

'Guardian.'

'Oh yes, I see. But do talk slower.'

'At the House of Gold these three spoke with another *bodach*, old and foolish, who believed their words, and gave them the parchments.'

Colin's command of Gaelic was less than Julia's. 'The *what*,' he asked in English again.

'Documents, dope.'

'Oh God! Oh, damn! Why were you so slow? I told you to hurry.'

'Yes, but you hadn't given me the one thing needful, stupid—I had to wait for that,' Julia said sharply. She switched to Gaelic again. 'Thus six days were lost; and six days since, these went and obtained possession of the parchments.'

'As near as that?' Colin asked miserably, again in English.

'Yes.'

There was a short pause. 'Look, I'm finding this lingo rather a strain,' Colin said. 'Can't we play our old game?'

'Better not—this is much safer. I'll talk very slowly.' She went on in Gaelic—'*Mo chridhe* (my heart) you should come to me at once.'

'And if I cannot?'

'You must.'

'To what place?'

'But to the city of the House of Gold! Take wings!'

She heard him chuckle at that—even in Gaelic there was a phrase for an aeroplane.

'But there, where do we meet, *m'eudail?*' (my jewel.)

Julia herself paused, thinking how to say, 'Ring up' in Gaelic.

'You speak on a long thin thread with a small bell; you speak with him who is really the guardian of your betrothed one. He will tell you where we can meet. Got that?' she asked smartly in English.

'Yes; clever girl! Can you give me the number?'

'Better not.' She switched back to Gaelic. 'His name is not inscribed; seek the word 'shepherd'. Got that?' she asked again.

'I think so. All-same Niemöller, yes—no?'

'Yes. Good for you! The canton is Fribourg,' she continued in English.

'Why that? I knew it.'

'You'll see why. And on what day?' she added, again in Gaelic.

'Very soon.'

'*No*, my heart. The day that follows. I beseech you!'

She heard Colin giggle again.

'Goodness, what a memory you've got! Very well—when you say. I'm sure they'll let me go.'

'Obviously they must. Till then.' She closed this peculiar and mixed conversation in Gaelic, 'Farewell, my heart'—to which Colin very modernly replied, 'Bye, darling darling.'

She paid the huge cost of a prolonged personal call from Geneva to London in the middle of the day, and then was lift-borne down three floors to where Nethersole was patiently patrolling the rather poor turf which surrounds the Palais des Nations. Abstractedly, she allowed herself to be shown the portentous Chamber, with its pallid meretricious symbolic bas-reliefs (so like the old Queen's Hall in London), its tables, desks, microphones, and press-galleries—all the elaborate paraphernalia for international propaganda, and the loud pretending that 'there is peace, where there is no peace'.

'Rather dim, isn't it?' Nethersole said.

'Not dim—lurid!' said Julia with vigour.

She had little more than half an hour, when a taxi had carried her back to the Bergues, to freshen up and be ready for the Pastor. She decided to wait for him at one of the pavement tables outside the tea-room, so that there would be no giving of names to the hall-porter; certainly Antrobus—she still thought of him as 'the detective'—knew that she was staying there, but since she had signally failed to learn what he was doing, there was no point in giving away gratuitous information about de Ritter. She ordered an iced *café-crème*, paid for it at once, and sat sipping it at a table close to the hotel entrance; the moment the big Frégate drew up she walked quickly to it, and was getting in at one door before Jean-Pierre had time to get out at the other.

'*Tiens!* You are remarkably prompt! How are you?' he said, as he swung left over the Pont des Bergues.

'Distracted, of course,' Julia said. She looked calm and beautiful, which is a very good thing to do if one is distracted, though few achieve it—de Ritter glanced at her and smiled his shrewd smile.

'Distracted?'

'Yes. Aren't you? This old clot de Kessler has let these crooks carry off all Aglaia's money, and the oil papers, whatever they are.'

'It is serious,' he agreed, as he pulled up outside the over-magnificent portals of the Banque Républicaine.

The door-mat didn't let them in at this hour, but a uniformed porter, hovering behind the bronze and glass, did so at once, and took them, not to the *salle d'attente* with the petunia window-boxes, but to a much more severe apartment, where Chambertin and de Kessler awaited them.

Julia enormously enjoyed listening to Jean-Pierre's dealings with the two bankers—he tore them to shreds with the most urbane skill. Chambertin presently said that enquiries had been sent out by telephone, and that so far as could be ascertained, no such party had crossed the frontier, outward-bound, in the last six days.

'Then they must be waiting here—probably to meet someone; some emissary. *Écoutez, mon cher Alcide*, surely you realise that for the present any general alert, above all any publicity, is most undesirable? I imagine you must inform Interpol, but do urge discretion on everyone. You understand, of course, that since the passports *ces types* used to perpetrate their fraud on the bank were quite certainly forged, they may well use others for their departure. So the passport number may be of little relevance.'

Chambertin agreed to this last point, but he was terribly worried; the bank, he pointed out, was in a frightful position—he threw a baleful glance at de Kessler as he spoke.

'What I would suggest, if I may,' Jean-Pierre went on, 'is that a description of these three persons should be circulated to the Swiss police, with instructions to make enquiries—it goes without saying with the utmost discretion—at all hotels in *le pays*. Monsieur de Kessler can probably furnish a description?'

'Mademoiselle Probyn can furnish a much better one,' Chambertin said acidly.

'But how?'

'Oh never mind how! I happened to see all these crooks when

I was coming out,' Julia said—'the luckiest chance.' And presently she was dictating in French to an elderly male stenographer the best description she could give of the party she had seen at Victoria. 'If only I'd kept the papers!' she exclaimed at the end. 'They were full of pictures of Aglaia, and a photograph is worth *pages* of description.'

'Why were they full of Mademoiselle Armitage's pictures?' Jean-Pierre enquired.

'Because "Richest Girl in Europe" had just sailed for the Argentine. Of course she isn't that any more, unless these people are caught.'

'You, yourself, have no photograph of her?' Chambertin enquired.

'No.'

'In any case, must they not sign a *fiche* when they arrive at an hotel?' de Ritter asked.

'Yes, they must—but in what name will they sign?' Chambertin replied. 'It all turns on whether they are using one set of passports or two. Naturally the *fiche* must match the passport. If only we had a photograph!'

De Ritter turned to Julia.

'Et le cousin germain?' Might he—'

Julia interrupted him brusquely, 'Let us leave that for later.' She turned to Chambertin, 'If I can produce a photograph, you shall have it.'

Outside, in the car, Julia said, 'If you can spare another half-hour, let us go somewhere where we can talk.'

'Then to your hotel.'

'Oh no—hotel walls have longer ears than any others!'

He laughed. 'Then where?'

'Let's go and sit on the Île Rousseau—I love it.'

95

There they went, the Pastor parking his car on the farther side of the Pont des Bergues. Seated at a table under the trees by the river, looking upstream towards the lake, the lofty snowy fountain, and the blue mountains beyond, Julia spoke in English.

'Colin is coming out tomorrow. I telephoned to him at lunchtime from the Palais des Nations.'

'Telephoned to *Londres?*'

'Yes, certainly.'

'But this must cost a fortune!' the Pastor said, looking quite shocked.

'A fortune is at stake,' Julia said—'and a good deal more, too. But the question is, where can he and I meet? I thought you might know of some modest pension here where he could stay. I don't want him to come to the Bergues.'

'Why not?'

'Because there's a suspicious character staying there. I saw him on the platform in London when I saw those three, and he travelled out on the same train—and now here he is again. So I'd rather Colin stayed somewhere else.'

'At what hour does your cousin arrive tomorrow?'

'I haven't the faintest idea!—and he wouldn't have told me over the telephone, of course.'

'Why not?'

'Oh my dear Monsieur de Ritter, people in his job don't *advertise* their movements, especially when something like this is going on.'

'How very interesting! But how then can we establish contact?'

'I told him to ring you up at Bellardon when he arrives, and that you would tell him where to go. So do you know of a small, obscure place?' Julia pressed him urgently.

De Ritter considered for a moment—then he laughed his loud delightful laugh.

'Indeed I do. Bellardon is very small, and most obscure. Let him come and stay at La Cure; and you, *chère Mademoiselle*, shall return to us—we shall rejoice to have you—and there you can concert your plans in peace.'

Julia considered in her turn—she hesitated so long that the Pastor was surprised, and asked—

'You do not wish to come back to us?'

'Oh, it's not that—I adore being at La Cure. Only it's rather an imposition on Germaine, and besides I'm just wondering whether we ought all to be under one hat.'

'*Plaît-il?*'

'All three of us under one roof, if anyone tried something on. I don't want to be alarmist, but one never knows.'

'I am not sure that I understand you.'

For answer, Julia pushed aside her tawny-gold hair and showed the Pastor a long white scar running down one side of her forehead.

'I got that from a bomb in Marrakesh. The people who threw it were trying to blow up Colin, but they got me instead.'

The Pastor looked at the scar in horrified amazement. '*C'est affreux!*' He reflected. 'Such things are quite outside my experience. Nevertheless, I think Bellardon a good *venue*, and I must confess that I should greatly like to meet Aglaia's fiancé. What do you say?'

On the whole Julia said Yes.

'Then can I not drive you out tonight? How long do you need to *faire vos malles?*'

'Oh, I can pack in half an hour. But you mustn't pick me up at the hotel—I'll come in a taxi and meet you, somewhere where you can park inconspicuously. What about the station? People putting luggage in and out of cars all the time.'

He laughed. 'This is quite amusing. I feel as if I were living in a *roman policier*! Very well—I will park in the courtyard, and will wait for you myself in that restaurant on the left of the station entrance, at one of the outside tables. This is extremely normal.'

'That's right—normal is the ticket,' Julia replied.

Julia walked across one side of the rectangled bridge to pack, the Pastor returned across the other to get his car. In the hall of the hotel the concierge handed Julia a letter—it was from Mrs. Hathaway.

'As soon as you conveniently can, I should like it if you could come back here, and take me to Beatenberg. I am quite fit to travel now, if I have a courier—and I think it would be well to give the staff here a rest. Herr Waechter has taken rooms for us at the Hotel Silberhorn.'

She thrust the letter into her bag, packed quickly, and went down. In the hall stood Antrobus.

'Oh, are you leaving already?' he asked.

'Yes—I must get back to Gersau, where I have a friend who isn't well,' Julia said deliberately.

He looked at his watch.

'You will miss the last boat from Lucerne to Gersau tonight,' he observed.

'No I shan't—I'm stopping the night with friends on the way.'

'In Berne?'

'Well if it *is* any business of yours, not in Berne,' Julia said tartly.

'Oh, excuse me. Berne is on the way, that's all. Anyhow *bon voyage*—I hope we meet again soon.'

Julia hoped this very much too, but merely said, 'On present form it seems almost inevitable, doesn't it?'

At that he laughed, and came out and handed her into her taxi. What a mercy they had settled to meet at the station, Julia thought, as she said *À la gare!*' to the porter. The Pastor had managed to park fairly near the open-air restaurant; he rose from one of the little tables, her luggage was transferred to the Frégate, and soon they were speeding along the superb Swiss roads, the gentle country-side all golden in the evening light. It was late when they got in, but Germaine was waiting, pretty and fresh; the warmth of her welcoming kiss gave Julia a happy sense of homecoming. Over the excellent supper Jean-Pierre, to Julia's professional dismay, insisted on putting his wife into the picture thoroughly—Germaine was all interest and sympathy, and delighted at the prospect of having another guest.

'Tomorrow? By then more asparagus will be ready,' she remarked. 'You can cut it, Julia.'

In fact it was just as well that Germaine had been told, for when Colin rang up next day the Pastor was out, and she answered the telephone. Recognising an English voice—though it spoke excellent French—Germaine, who was much more security-minded than her husband, asked at once, 'Would you care to speak with your cousin? She is here—Julie, I mean.'

'Yes, if you please.'

While Julia was telling Colin to come straight on to 'the house of Niemöller's colleague' Germaine was consulting the time-table. 'Tell him to take the train of 15 hours 55 minutes to Lausanne, and change there. He will get a connection in a few minutes, and we will meet him at the station.' When Julia had rung off she said, 'Even if he spoke from the airport he will have time to catch that train.' She brushed some fallen peony-petals off the table in the hall into her hand, adding, 'Quite so much discretion is really hardly necessary here for internal calls; since everything is automatic there are no operators to overhear. But discretion never does any harm.' She returned to her stove and Julia went out to cut the asparagus for supper, and get fresh flowers for the dining-room.

'Cut some roses for your cousin's room,' Germaine called through the kitchen window. 'They are just beginning.'

It was Julia who took the hand-cart down through the clean sunny little village to meet Colin; he gave his boyish giggle over this novel arrangement. 'Don't kiss me at La Cure,' Julia said, after his cousinly hug on the platform.

'Why ever not?'

'Jean-Pierre was a little suspicious because I signed that telegram "Darling". I told him it was just a code-word, but don't go and wreck it all.'

'Is he stuffy and portentous? How frightful.'

'No. You'll see.'

Colin saw, over a late tea in the arbour beside the lawn, now festooned with the washing of a daughter-in-law. The Pastor was obviously studying his ward's fiancé with the deepest interest, and when they repaired to the study to talk *les affaires*, Julia could see that he was favourably impressed by the young man's passionate concern over the loss of the documents, and complete indifference about the money—he never asked a single question about that.

De Ritter told Colin that the Swiss police, very discreetly, were on the look-out for the party, and asked if he could supply a photograph of his fiancée? Colin, jerking his thumb out, an obstinate look on his face, said that he couldn't. He however produced the information that in London it was thought improbable that the impostors had yet left Switzerland; it was considered more likely that they would wait in this ultra-neutral country to contact their principals and hand over their haul. The Pastor innocently asked who the principals were?—Julia laughed at him. 'He couldn't tell you even if he knew.'

It was settled that Colin should go on next day to Berne to see 'our people' there, and take them Julia's description of the party of three; Julia then explained that she ought to return to Gersau, to take Mrs. Hathaway to Beatenberg.

'But how you come and go!' de Ritter exclaimed regretfully. 'We like *long* visits.'

'Some time I'll come and pay you a proper one, and stay ages,' Julia told him, 'when the job's done'—and rang up Herr Waechter to announce her return next day to take Mrs. Hathaway to Beatenberg the day after.

Later the Pastor drew her aside. 'I approve,' he said. 'A little immature still in some ways, but time will remedy that. *C'est un charmant garçon*' Colin for his part, up in Julia's room, said, 'He is most frightfully nice, isn't he? As an in-law I can't imagine anyone I should like more.'

'He's only a god-in-law,' Julia said. 'But I agree.'

Though Colin was going to Berne and Julia had to pass through it, they carefully arranged to travel not only by different trains but by different routes, he by Neuchâtel, she via Lausanne— to the Pastor's incredulous amusement. 'But you are in Switzerland!' he said.

'So are some other people,' Colin replied.

At Gersau next day in the *salon* Julia, idly turning over the pages of a fortnight-old *Paris-Match*, came on a page devoted to Aglaia and her story; there was a full-length studio photograph and, as often with *Paris-Match*, a snapshot (probably bought from a servant) of Colin and Aglaia together, looking very lover-like, in the garden of some country-house. Julia was normally rather scrupulous about other people's newspapers, but in this instance she did not ask Herr Waechter's permission, but took the magazine up to her room and removed the whole page; she cut out the studio portrait, borrowed a large envelope, and posted it herself to M. Chambertin at the bank with a note clipped to it—'This is the likeness you require. J. P.' The snapshot she put in her note-case.

Chapter 6

Beatenberg and the Niederhorn

Beatenberg is a mountain village perched on a ledge facing South above the Lake of Thun; its chief claim to distinction, apart from its remarkably beneficent air, is the fact that it is over seven kilometres, or nearly five miles, long. A bus careers at fairly frequent intervals up and down the long straggling street, set with hotels, pensions, convalescent homes and shops, from Wahnegg, at the head of the road up from Interlaken at one end, to the top of the funicular railway going down to Beatenbucht to connect with the lake steamers at the other—there is no way up or down in between, only sheer cliff. The drive up from Interlaken in the Post-Auto is rather hair-raising: for much of the way the road is narrow, with blind hairpin bends, and the bus vast; it proclaims its advent by blaring out a pretty little tune on six notes, and cars squeeze into the rocky bush-grown banks to allow the great machine to edge past, its outer wheels horribly near the lip of the steep wooded slope. A notice in three languages at the front of the bus adjures passengers not to address the driver, but this is cheerfully ignored both by the local passengers and the driver himself—if a pretty young woman is on the front seat there is often practically a slap-and-tickle party the whole way.

By this route Mrs. Hathaway, Julia, and Watkins—Watkins audibly disapproving of the blond driver's goings-on with a black-haired girl—arrived at the Hotel Silberhorn, a medium-sized hotel three-quarters of the way along that endless village street. Since Herr Waechter, brought up in the hotel trade, had recommended the place they had expected something rather good, and were startled by the extreme smallness of the rooms: Mrs. Hathaway's, a double room with one bed taken out, and a cubby-hole of a private bathroom, was quite small enough; as for Julia's and Watkins's singles, they were like prison cells, though each had a minute balcony with a chair—and all alike shared the view: the whole Blümlisalp range stood up, white, glittering and glorious, across the lake. The keynote of the hotel was extreme simplicity—coconut matting along the corridors, the minimum of furniture in the rooms; but the food was excellent, served piping hot on plastic boxes with pierced metal tops, over night-lights. The huge plate-glass windows of the restaurant commanded the view too; waitresses in high-heeled sandals pattered to and fro across the parquet floor, their heels making a loud clacking noise; their activities were supervised by a grey-haired woman known as Fräulein Hanna, who appeared to be a sort of combination of house-keeper, head barmaid, and general organiser.

It was all rather scratch, but there were the essentials, as Mrs. Hathaway said: comfort, cleanliness, good food, and, from Fräulein Hanna especially, the utmost consideration. Like all English travellers in Switzerland today Mrs. Hathaway and her party liked to brew their own morning and afternoon tea in their bedrooms, partly because then it *was* tea, but also because these items were not included in the very high *prix fixe;* if one took both of them, and coffee after lunch and dinner as well, it added ten shillings a day to one's expenses. Mrs. Hathaway and Watkins both had small electric saucepans with long flexes which would plug in in place of any electric light bulb; on seeing these objects Fräulein Hanna, far from showing any resentment, enquired earnestly what their voltage was?—it proved to match that of the hotel, to her manifest satisfaction. All three of course used Mrs. Hathaway's private bathroom; the hotel bathrooms were kept locked, and a charge of five francs, or nearly ten shillings, made for a bath. Watkins was outraged by this. 'Well really! How do they expect people to keep clean? And with all that water running to waste down-hill all the time!' (This fantastic charge for baths is in fact a thing which the Swiss *hôteliers* would do well to remedy.)

For the next two days Julia and Mrs. Hathaway explored their end of the village. They found a nice little shop barely three hundred yards away, set in a grove of pine-trees, at which to buy their sugar and Nescafé; they walked gently up a fenced path between flowery meadows to the Parallel-Weg, a narrow road running parallel to, but a short distance above the village street, with seats at frequent intervals; they peered in at the open door of the cow-stable just opposite the hotel garden, and saw the huge cream-and-yellow Emmenthaler cows, still tied in their stalls, munching away at fresh-cut grass—out in the meadows the hotel cat, also white and yellow, sat at the edge of the high uncut grass in the evenings, watching for field-mice. Mrs. Hathaway delighted in the place: besides the exquisite view, here was peace, calm, and a native community leading its own pastoral life, untroubled by the tourists, who so early in the season were relatively few.

Colin rang up on the second evening to say that he was coming next day, and would Julia book him a room? He came up on the Post-Auto, which always pulled up opposite a petrol-pump next to the cow-stable; before dinner he and Julia strolled up the little path to the Parallel-Weg, and leaning back on one of the wooden seats, with not a soul in sight, he told her what he had learned in Berne. 'They' had quite definitely not left Switzerland; they were waiting there to make contact with their principals, who would be coming in from abroad—meanwhile the Swiss police were conducting enquiries at all hotels.

Julia told him about finding the photograph of Aglaia in *Paris-Match*, and how she had sent it to Chambertin.

'Oh well, I think that was quite all right—really rather useful,' Colin said.

'You'd got one all the time, hadn't you?' Julia asked.

'Yes, of course I had—but why should those bastards have it? If they'd had any wits they'd have looked at *Paris-Match* themselves.' He sniffed the sweet air, and gazed across at the Blümlisalp range, now turning to a pale rose as the sun sank. 'How nice it is here! Do let's relax for a few days till something happens. What's the food like at the pub?'

'Good,' Julia told him.

In fact something happened the very next day. Mrs. Hathaway had quite got over the journey from Gersau, and was perfectly happy either sitting in the garden, or pottering up and down the village street with Watkins, so Julia and Colin decided to go up the Niederhorn, the mountain immediately behind Beatenberg, in the Sessel-Bahn; see the view, and walk down.

The now universal practice of winter sports in Switzerland

has conferred one great benefit on travellers at all times of year. Every mountain with slopes suitable for skiing has been provided either with a funicular railway, or at least some form of ski-lift, by which the lazy modern skier can be carried to the summit without effort, shoot down, be carried up again, and shoot down once more—they function in the summer too, so that any tourist can reach the tops of the lesser mountains. The Niederhorn Sessel-Bahn is one of the more elegant of these contraptions, with twin seats (slung from a strong steel cable) complete with foot-board and a little sun-canopy overhead, into which an attendant clamps the passengers by a metal bar across their stomachs. Julia and Colin, so clamped, were wafted out of the small station and up through the tops of the pine-trees. It was delicious sailing through the sunny air; people on other seats coming down on the opposite cable, a few feet away, waved to them out of sheer *joie de vivre*. Colin pulled out a map and looked out the way down—he was very map-minded. One path was visible, zig-zagging through the trees close below them; the only other slanted across the upper slopes to descend at the far end of the village—sheer cliffs cut off the section in between.

Half-way up they swung into a large shed, where the seats were hitched onto an overhead rail and hauled by hand round a semi-circle, to be hooked onto another cable for the upper section of the journey; the sides of this shed were full of enormous white-metal milk-churns.

'What *can* those be for?' Julia speculated. 'The cows aren't up on the high pastures yet.'

'How do you know?'

'Because they're still down in the village in their stalls—I'll show you. They're only taken up when the lower grass is finished, and it has grown properly up on the alps—a peasant was telling Mrs. H. about it. You can see that there's hardly a bite up here yet,' Julia said, peering down; they were now above the tree-line and swinging up over open pastures, still pallid and brownish after the recently-departed snow. 'Oh, look!' the girl exclaimed—'Those must be gentians. We must pick some for Mrs. H., she's mad on wild-flowers.' Colin, also peering from his seat, saw some brilliant blue stars shining in the drab grass. 'Good idea,' he said.

But on arrival at the small summit station it was at once evident that picking gentians would be a very bad idea indeed. Large placards in four languages proclaimed that the whole *Niederhorn-Gebiet* was a *Natur-Reserve,* where the picking of any flowers was most strictly forbidden. 'Oh dear,' Julia regretted as they strolled up to the platform on the top, where a panorama of the visible mountains was spread out under a glass frame beside a large telescope. Both panorama and telescope were crowded with tourists, jostling one another for position; Julia and Colin left them alone, and went over and looked down on the farther side. Here the Niederhorn, sloping up easily from the South, ends in a series of vertical cliffs, dropping some hundreds of feet to steep slopes of grass and forest above the Justis-thal, a long narrow valley running in from the Lake of Thun to a grey scree-covered *col* at its head. The valley is bounded on the farther side by similar slopes and cliffs, and a thin white thread of road runs up through the flat green meadows along the valley-floor. Julia was rather startled by the Flüh, or cliff; she drew back her head. They left the platform and walked away from the tourists, east-wards along the ridge, till from a projecting buttress they again looked over into the valley.

'What's the little town down on the lake?' she asked.

'Merligen,' Colin said, without consulting his map.

'Merligen? I have an acquaintance there,' Julia said, remembering the little man from 'Corsette-Air'. 'Colin, wouldn't it be nice to take Mrs. H. to Merligen on the steamer and hire a car, and drive her up the Justis-Thal?—I call it a darling valley. Why Justice, by the way?'

'Two English missionaries, Justus and Beatus, originally converted this part of Switzerland to Christianity. 'Ence the word orse-'air,' Colin said, using an old Glentoran nonsense. 'Beatenberg, too. But one can't drive up the Justis-Thal; it's a military area, where no cars are allowed.'

Julia cautiously peered over into the green depths. 'It doesn't look very military,' she said. 'I don't see any barracks, or anything.'

'No, you don't; that's the point. The barracks are in the mountains. Those cliffs opposite, and these plumb under us here, are bung full of ammunition and guns and so forth—in some parts they even have military hospitals inside the mountains, so I heard in Berne. Terrific people, the Swiss.'

Julia sat down on the yellowish turf and lit a cigarette.

'I'm beginning to think so.'

Colin gestured back at the Lake of Thun, of which a segment was visible at the mouth of the valley.

'That's full of stores, too—years' and years' supply of butter and cheese and flour and corn, sunk in metal containers hundreds of feet down. These lakes are very deep.'

Julia was entranced by this.

'But doesn't it get stale?—especially the cheese and butter?'

'Oh, they howk up the containers every so often, and empty them and put in fresh. A Swiss I met was telling me about it. The butter they always get out while it's still usable; and if the cheese is a bit dry they grate it and sell it in bottles.'

They wandered on a little farther, and came on a patch of still unmelted snow, dirty and pock-marked; round its edges small white crocuses were springing from the brown sodden turf, making a new snowiness to replace the old. 'Oh, I wish I could take just one to Mrs. H.,' Julia said.

'Better not—they mean what they say about picking flowers, as about everything else,' Colin said. 'I saw a type in uniform wandering about near the station. Come back to the pub and have a beer before we go down.'

The pub was a long low building with a restaurant and a broad terrace outside, on which numerous people sat drinking beer or coffee at little tables; Colin and Julia sat there too and drank their beer in the sun. 'It's a nice clean wash-place,' Julia said; 'boiling hot water.'

'I wonder how they get their water up here,' Colin speculated. 'There's no sign of a spring.'

'Pumped, I suppose,' Julia replied indifferently.

They had strolled and idled so long on the top that Julia said they had better not walk down, or they would be madly late. 'Let's come up another day and walk right along and down to the village at the far end.' Colin agreed to this, and presently they were swinging down through the air again, over the high meadows.

Now on the Sessel-Bahn you can see passengers travelling in the opposite direction a hundred yards away or more; and coming up towards them Julia now saw the girl she had seen at Victoria, perched in a seat beside the dark young man. 'Colin, *look!*' she breathed.

Colin stared. 'It can't be!' he exclaimed.

'No, it isn't. It's her double. But look well at the man—it's them all right.'

Colin looked hard at the pair as they were borne past in the

110

air, only a few feet away; then he and Julia discussed rapidly what to do. They decided that Julia should get out at the half-way halt and return to the summit, to see what she could of the pair, while in case she was not in time to meet them, Colin should go on to the bottom and wait there; when they came down he would follow them, whether they took the bus to Interlaken, or the funicular to Beatenbucht and the lake. 'They certainly can't get away at the top,' Julia said, thinking of that dizzy range of limestone cliffs and buttresses.

'Unless they do what we were planning just now, and walk all the way across and down to Wahnegg.'

'Oh, she couldn't. She was wearing the silliest little high-heeled shoes. Here we are'—and as they swung into the shed she called to one of the men who were manoeuvring the seats round the circular rail leading to the lower section to unclamp her bar and let her out. '*Der Herr auch?*' the man asked.

'*Nein*, not the Herr.' She sprang out. 'Stick to them like *glue*,' she called to Colin as he swung out of the shed and off into space.

There was some difficulty about getting a seat up to the summit of the Niederhorn again; though an occasional passenger got off at the halt to walk up the last stretch over the alpine pastures far more, with return tickets, had walked down half-way, and wished to finish their descent airborne. Julia had a booklet of the invaluable *Ferien-Billets* (holiday tickets), which, issued to foreign tourists, enable them to make mountain excursions at half the official price; she produced this, and after some fuss a ticket was accepted—usually they were only taken at the top or the bottom, she was told. She had to wait some time for a seat, and employed this interval, as was her habit, in ingratiating herself with the people on the spot, men in blue dungarees who manipulated the seats at the halt; from them she enquired about the milk-churns. Oh, those were for water. There was no water at the summit; every drop had to be carried up in the evening after the Sessel-Bahn was closed to passengers, in the churns, and manhandled from the station some hundred yards to fill the cisterns of the restaurant. 'Both guests and *Geschirr*' (kitchen utensils) 'need water for washing,' an elderly man said, grinning.

At last she secured an empty half of one of the twin seats, and was again borne upwards. She was tremendously excited—the more so after the delay at the halt; by keeping a sharp eye on the descending seats she had established that the pair she sought had not yet come down, nor did they pass her in the air. 'Just keep your eyes open—that's all you can do,' she adjured herself as she got out at the summit and began to walk up towards the restaurant.

This activity brought an immediate reward. A little below the path she saw on the grassy slope the sham Aglaia, a bunch of *Gentiana verna* in her hand, being violently scolded by one of the Nature-Reserve wardens. She ran down to them. The girl was in tears; obviously she could not make out what it was all about. There was no sign of the dark young man.

'The Fräulein does not understand,' Julia told the official.

'The notice forbidding to pick flowers is also in English,' he said indignantly.

'*Jawohl*—but the Fräulein must not have looked—I think it is her first journey abroad. Is there some fine to pay?' she asked, opening her bag.

'*Nein*. But let *das Mädchen* not do this again.' He stumped off.

'Oh, thank you ever so! What did you say to him?' the girl asked Julia, as they began to walk up towards the restaurant. 'He was being as nasty as anything, and I couldn't understand

112

a single word!'

'He was scolding you for picking those flowers,' Julia said.

'Why ever?'

'Because this is a Nature-Reserve, like our National Parks, and picking flowers is forbidden; there's a big notice in English to say so, just by the station. But I told the man that you hadn't looked at it, because it was your first trip abroad. Is it?' Julia asked, with a friendly smile.

'Well yes, ackcherly. I don't like it much, either—the food's so funny, and I can't talk to people, except the porter in the hotel, silly old thing! He does talk English, though.'

The imitation Aglaia was obviously the commonest of little Londoners; too suburban for anything as genuine as a Cockney, and not very intelligent. Julia was thrilled by this piece of luck, but a little worried about the dark young man. She tried to play her hand carefully.

'Did you come up here alone?'

'Oh no. Mr. Wright'—she corrected herself hastily—'I mean Mr. Monro came up with me; but he likes climbing up things, and he's gone off. He said I was to stay on the terrace and look at the mountains—but I hate those old mountains, all snow and ice, and when I saw these little flowers in the grass I came down to pick some. I didn't know it was wrong. I 'spose I'd better throw them away, if there's all this trouble.'

'No, give them to me,' Julia said, and stowed *G. verna* in her capacious bag.

'Well, that's a good idea. Aoh!' The girl gave a little scream, and nearly fell—Julia put out a hand and caught her. One of her idiotic high heels had turned on a loose stone, wrenching her ankle; between pain and shock she could hardly walk. Julia, an arm round the tiny figure, dragged her up to the restaurant and sat her down on a stool in the wash-room; she borrowed a pantry-cloth from the cheerful Swiss maids and applied this as a cold compress, tying it in place with her own head-scarf.

'Is that any easier?' she asked.

'Yes, a bit.'

'Then let's go out and have some coffee on the terrace. Do you like coffee?'

'Not all that much—but the tea here is so lousy! You *are* being kind.'

Julia ordered coffee for two. Perhaps she was being kind; certainly she was enjoying a most blessed stroke of luck, and set about profiting by it. 'How long have you been in Switzerland?' she asked.

'Nearly three weeks. Mr. Borovali said it would be a nice holiday for me, but it isn't being, not so very—and now I've gone and hurt my foot.' She showed signs of tears starting afresh. 'I expect he'll be cross! They said at the Agency that he'd be so nice, and give me a lovely time, but he's very often cross.'

Julia was riveted by the word agency, and asked about it.

'Oh, the "Modern Face Agency", off Shaftesbury Avenue. I get my modelling jobs through them. Oh, not artists or the nude, or anything like that!—just modelling for the ads, you know. I tried for a mannequin, but I'm too small, even for Small Woman clothes. But I get a lot of quite good modelling jobs, shoes or jewellery, mostly—my feet are a treat for shoes. Oh, do you think this ankle will swell?' Tears again threatened. 'My feet are my fortune, as you might say'—half giggling.

Julia realised that the little thing really had had quite a shock, and while she tried to console her about her ankle she ordered Kirsch for them both. 'Put it in your coffee—it will do you good,' she said. She was beginning to see a flood of

114

light, and while the girl sipped, she thought hard about safe questions.

'Oh, that does taste funny! No, it's nice, really. Ta.'

'Does Mr. Borovali pay as well as the Agency?' Julia enquired.

'Not quite—only £6 a week; but of course I get my keep for the month, and I'm to keep my outfit.'

'Mr. Borovali has good taste, has he?'

'Oh, perfect. Some *exquisite* things I've got.' The pretty little thing looked dreamily out at the glorious forms of the Bernese Alps, shining under the sun like the ramparts of Heaven. *'Exquisite,'* she repeated rapturously—'Evening frocks and all. Mum wasn't so keen on my coming, just with two gentlemen, but really, the clothes alone have been worth it—and they've been quite all right,' she added confidentially. She paused, and sipped again at her coffee and Kirsch.

'Mum isn't all that keen on the modelling either,' she pursued, 'but a girl's got to live, hasn't she? I'm no good in shops, I simply can't get the bills right! And since Dad died I have to help Mum; I usually give her £3 a week.'

This was said proudly, but very nicely—Julia was rather touched. She asked what 'Dad' had done.

'Oh, in business.' This too was said rather proudly. 'Well ackcherly he was a traveller for a surgical equipment firm, really quite high-class. I sometimes wish he'd travelled in the garment trade; then Mum and I might have got things on the cheap.' She looked wistfully at Julia. 'That's a heavenly suit you've got on—d'you mind if I ask where you got it?'

Julia glanced down at her own soft, plainly-cut grey-green tweed. In the context she suddenly did mind telling this eager candid child its origin, but she couldn't think of a probable lie in time, and said 'Hartnell.'

'Never! Well, it looks it.' She figured the stuff almost reverently.

'Where did Mr. Borovali get your things?' Julia enquired hastily. 'That's such a pretty dress.'

'D'you really like it? I am glad. He got them at a very good wholesale place, only they all had to be taken in, of course. But by the way, I oughtn't to call him Mr. Borovali—Mister de Ritter he likes to be known as, on this trip—in case you should meet him.'

'I'll remember—though I don't expect I shall meet him.' She was thinking how to frame her next question.

'How shall you get back, with that foot?' she asked. 'Have you far to go?'

'Only down to Interlarken. The bus goes from the bottom of this swinging-boat affair—goodness, isn't it ghastly? As bad as the Wall of Death, *I* think. And from the bus-stop in Interlarken I s'pose Mr. Wright—sorry, I mean Mr. Monro—will just have to take a taxi to the hotel.'

'I'm sure he will. Is it a nice hotel?'

'The Flooss? Oh, not too bad. It's right on the river, and you can see the steamers coming up to the quay, and watch the people going on and off. But Flooss is ever such a silly name, don't you think?—makes one think of floosies.' She giggled.

From this description Julia surmised, rightly, that the party must be staying at the *Hotel zum Fluss* in Interlaken, much praised by Baedeker, and was delighted to have this concrete piece of information for Colin. She felt it safe to ask this obviously foolish child how long she was staying?

'Well I'm not sure. We should have been going home day after tomorrow, but some friends of Mr. Bor—I mean Mr. de Ritter's, that he wants to meet, haven't turned up, so we must stay on till they do.'

'Oh well, if you're staying on we might meet again,' Julia said brightly. 'I'm up here at Beatenberg, at the Hotel Silberhorn, but if I come down I might look you up, Miss—?' Her voice hung on the query.

'Phillips—June Phillips,' the girl said briskly. 'I'd love to see you again—you're so kind.' Then her face fell. 'Sorry—I am too silly, with this foot hurting so! June Phillips is just my trade name; only I get so accustomed to using it. My real name is Aglaia Armitage.'

'So if I came to the hotel I should ask for Miss Armitage?' Julia asked carefully. Presumably they were still using the forged passports, but she wanted to be sure.

'That's right.' Then the pretty face clouded again. 'D'you know, I'm not sure you'd better do that,' June Phillips said worriedly. 'Mr. B. doesn't seem to care for me to talk to people; there are some English people at the Flooss, but if they start talking to me, he makes some excuse to get me away. Oh, I am so dull!'

How right Mr. B. was, Julia thought—in the circumstances he could hardly do otherwise, saddled with this witless little creature. But she was sorry for poor June, wearing her pretty new clothes in vain. Before she had settled on some suitable response the girl pulled out an envelope with an English stamp on it.

'You write your name and address on that, do,' she urged. 'And your 'phone number. Then I could ring you up, if I was free any time.'

After a moment's hesitation Julia did as she was asked—after all it didn't involve Colin in the least. As June Phillips pocketed the envelope Julia put a further question. 'Surely Mr. Monro is a pleasant companion?'

'Well not all that much. He's all right, and of course he looks ever so distinguished; but if we come out like this he always wants to go off scrambling on rocks, or climbing up some mountain—which is no fun for *me*,' June said energetically. 'And the rest of the time he's generally binding away about a situation he lost in one of those Arab countries, and how unfair it was.' She paused, and then leaned confidentially across the table. 'I don't think he's really enjoying this job any more than I am, except the climbing—though he's paid much more than me.'

'Oh really?'

'Yes!—and I do think that's unfair, too. After all, he isn't like anyone.' She caught herself up, dismayed. 'Sorry—I didn't mean that. I'm just silly today!'

Julia hastened to help her out. 'Perhaps Mr. Monro is an expert about something,' she said.

'Oh I don't think so, really, or why was he fired? But he has lived in these outlandish countries, and I think he knows these people that Mr. de Ritter is waiting for.'

At this point the young man himself appeared on the path leading up to the restaurant; he was some hundred yards away. June Phillips gave a little gasp.

'Oh! There he is! D'you think you'd p'r'aps better go away? I mean, he mightn't like to see me talking to anyone. Only you've been so good.'

'No. I shan't go away,' Julia said firmly.

'Well, you explain, will you?—how we met, I mean,' the girl said nervously. 'And by the way, on this trip he's supposed to be my fiancé,' she added hurriedly. 'Oh, it is all so difficult.'

'Don't worry,' Julia just had time to say before the young man rounded the corner of the restaurant and saw them. He paused, scowled, and strode over to their table. Julia spoke before he could.

'Mr. Monro?' He nodded, his relief evident at once.

'Miss Armitage has had an accident,' Julia pursued blandly—'she has sprained her ankle rather badly. I happened to be close by, and did what I could for her, but I think she ought to get back to her hotel as soon as possible, and see a doctor.'

'Oh, thank you, Miss—?'

'Probyn,' Julia said, studying him. Probably a Greek or a Levantine or something like that, she thought, noting the weak mouth, the big melting eyes, the superb Greek-vase figure—a born gigolo. He thanked her again, rather curtly, and then rounded harshly on June Phillips.

'How did you come to have an accident? I told you to stay here on the terrace.' There was no accent, except that it was not a well-bred voice; a Levantine educated at a second-rate English school, perhaps.

Julia's presence gave the girl courage to defend herself.

'Yes, but you were away such ages—and you never gave me money to buy a morning coffee, or anything! So I went down and picked some flowers, and a man came after me, and was nasty, and this lady came and sent him off. And then I hurt my foot, and she looked after me. More than you were doing!' June said, with a small display of spirit, like a kitten spitting.

'Oh well'—as he paused, rather nonplussed, Julia beckoned up a waitress and paid the bill. 'Well, we'd better be getting back,' he said to June. 'Come on.'

'Try your foot,' Julia said to the girl. 'Can you stand on it?'

June Phillips tried, and cried out with pain. 'Aoh, it *does* hurt!'

'Damnation! What an idiotic thing to do!' the young man Wright exploded.

'Oh nonsense,' Julia said coolly. 'If one neglects people, anything can happen. It's not in the least her fault.' He stared at her. 'Let's get her down to the Bahn—if we each take an arm she needn't put any weight on her foot.'

'I'll carry her,' the young man said; 'she weighs nothing.' And disdaining Julia's help he threw June over his shoulder like a sack and carried her, giggling, down to the Sessel-Bahn and in at the entrance on the far side. As the seats came up, were vacated, and pulled round the curve for the descent Julia nipped smartly ahead of the other two, secured a place, and was fastened into it by the attendant; June and Mr. Wright got into the next one. There is usually an interval of fifty to one hundred metres between the dangling seats, so as not to put too great a weight on the cable, and Julia reckoned that she would just have time to get hold of Colin and send him away before Wright could see him; since there was no longer any need to tail the party, it seemed to her rather important to do this. Her seat was launched, and she spun down through the sunny air, over the high pastures, among the fragrant pines—down, down, down, above the flowery meadows and the Parallel-Weg to the little bottom station. The moment the attendant unclamped the bar and released her she sprang out, waved to June, whose seat was just coming in, ran down the cement steps and walked rapidly along the zig-zag path leading down to the road and the big lay-by where cars and buses wait. From above she saw that Colin was there all right, half-perched on the retaining wall, sweet with plants of thyme and wild phlox, at the bottom of the path; but he was not alone—perched beside him, smoking a pipe and obviously engaged in most cheerful conversation, was the detective.

Annoyance at this inopportune appearance quite overcame her pleasure at seeing Antrobus. What was he doing there, just at this moment? Her original decision to get Colin away before Wright saw him persisted; but as she walked down the path towards the two men it occurred to her that it might be quite useful if she, at least, stayed to watch the impact of the impostor party on Antrobus—she might learn something, or she might not; anyhow worth trying. She slackened her pace—this had got to be planned fast—and glanced up behind her; June and Wright had not yet emerged from the station. In the last twenty-five yards she cast about for an excuse and hit on a poor one—all the same, she must try it on. She rounded the last corner and approached the pair.

'Oh hullo, Mr. Antrobus—how nice to see you again.' She turned to Colin. 'Colin darling, I'm out of gaspers. They have those beastly squashy local ones in that little shop just up the road; do go and get me a hundred, darling—fast, so that we can catch the bus.'

'I've got quite a lot,' Colin said, looking surprised at her knowing Antrobus.

'Oh don't be a clot, darling! *I* haven't, though I've got everything else.' She hoped he would take this in. 'Do please go, darling darling.'

At this key phrase Colin obediently took himself off up the road—Julia was surprised to find that she minded a good deal being forced to use these exaggerated terms of endearment to Colin in front of Antrobus. However, she turned to him calmly.

'Are you staying in Beatenberg, Mr. Antrobus?'

'No—I came up to have a look round. It seems a cheerful little place.'

'Yes, I think it's delightful—so unspoilt. Where are you staying, then?'

'Interlaken—a most charming town.'

Dead-pan double-talk! Julia pushed ahead.

'So you know my cousin?'

'Who?—that beautiful young man? Your cousin, is he? No, we just fell into talk as we sat here—he said he was waiting for someone.'

'And are you waiting for someone?' Julia asked recklessly, still rather unnerved by his appearance at this critical moment. Why was he everywhere when the impersonators were about? She glanced up the zigzags behind her—at last Wright had appeared, poor June again slung over his shoulder. Antrobus's glance followed hers; June's pretty face was hidden, of course, but Wright's handsome Near-Eastern visage was clearly visible. The man turned back to her.

'No,' he said, looking her full in the face. 'I was simply idling—Fatima!'

The name that in Geneva she had looked forward to hearing from him came, now, like a blow. Wounded, Julia blushed—her apricot blush that was so beautiful under her lion-coloured hair. She was also at once angry and suspicious—was he lying, and trying to embarrass her because he was lying? She mastered her temper, and thought very fast; well before Wright and his burden had reached the bottom of the zigzags she had taken a decision—not to conceal her acquaintance with that pair. Two buses, already half-full of passengers, were drawn up in the lay-by across the road, one for Interlaken, one for the Beatenbucht funicular—as Wright reached the level she went straight up to him and June.

'Let me help you, Mr. Monro. The left-hand bus is the one for Interlaken.' Breathing rather heavily, the young man set June down; Julia took her arm. 'Miss Armitage, how do you feel now? Come on, we'll get you a seat close to the door.'

All this was well within earshot of Antrobus; in fact Julia spoke rather loudly, on purpose. She and Wright together supported the girl across the road to the lay-by, where Julia spoke in German to the flirtatious blond bus-driver. 'The Fräulein has had a *Fuss-Brechen* on the Niederhorn; she should have a seat by the door.' The driver hopped out, heaved June in, and placed her on the front seat. The little thing leaned forward from the door to speak to Julia.

'Oh Miss Probyn, you have been so kind! I'll never forget it—never! If there's ever anything I can do for you, just let me know, and I'll do it!'

'I'll remember,' Julia said. 'Goodbye, dear. Take care of yourself.' Impulsively, she mounted the step of the bus, leaned in, and gave the nice, silly little thing a kiss. Then she turned to Wright, who stood by with an open air of concentrated ill-temper not commonly seen outside Athens and the Middle East.

'Mr. Monro, do get a doctor to look at that ankle. I'm sure it ought to be seen to at once.'

'O.K.' Wright said sulkily. 'Mind you, it's all her own fault.'

'Oh don't be an *ass!*' Julia exclaimed angrily. 'It's entirely *your* fault for going off to amuse yourself, and leaving her alone. And is that the way to talk about your fiancée, anyhow?'

Wright crumbled at once.

'Sorry,' he said apologetically. 'Yes, I did go farther than I meant, and—and it's all been a bit upsetting. Of course I'll get a doctor to her the moment we get down. Goodbye—thanks for looking after her.' He got into the bus and sat beside June; the blond driver gave out tickets and collected cash in a leather wallet, and the huge vehicle pulled out into the road and rolled away.

Antrobus too had strolled across the road, and presumably overheard the whole interchange—his question as the bus rolled off suggested this.

'Friends of yours?' he asked expressionlessly.

'Which, the idiotic little girl or the revolting young man?' Julia asked rather sharply.

'Well really I meant both. They seemed rather a unit as they came down that path.'

Julia could not help laughing.

'I ran into the girl up on the mountain today, and succoured her when she sprained her ankle,' she said; for once the truth was completely non-committal. 'But I never met her before—Bluebeard!'

He laughed loudly.

'*Very* good! Only you see you kissed her just now, and then you addressed her rather dreadful escort as Mr. Monro. Your so infinitely more attractive cousin said his name was Monro, too.'

Julia was worried by all this, but tried not to show it.

'Monro is a fairly common name in Scotland, isn't it?' she said. 'Like Antrobus.'

He laughed again.

'Quite true. But that young man doesn't look enormously Scotch, would you say?'

Julia also laughed.

'No. But don't Jews often take Scotch names? They seem to have a penchant for them.'

'That young man isn't a Jew,' Antrobus said positively. 'A lot of other probables, but not that.'

'What are your probables?' she asked.

'Levantine; or English father and Syrian mother, or English mother and Greek father—almost any Middle-East permutation and combination. But definitely not a Jew.'

Odd that he should speculate like this to her, if he really was in with them, Julia thought—but perhaps it was just a blind.

Anyhow two could ask questions.

'And have you never seen them before?' she said, remembering with almost passionate vividness the passage of three people down the platform at Victoria, under his very nose.

Before Antrobus could answer Colin came hurrying up to them, a flowered-paper parcel in his hand.

'There you are!' he said, thrusting it at Julia. 'It wasn't just up the road, it was at least half a kilometre!' He saw that the Interlaken bus had gone, and looked at her enquiringly.

'Oh thank you, darling. Well look, we'd better hurry, or we shall miss our bus. Goodbye,' she said coolly to Antrobus.

Colin also made his farewell to the detective.

'Goodbye,' he said, much more warmly than Julia, and holding out his hand. 'You might do worse than come up here, if you want flowers and walks—I don't know about the birds yet. Let us know if you do—we're at the Silberhorn.'

'Right—I certainly will, if I do come up. And don't forget to take your old friend who's so keen on flowers up to see the Alpine Garden at the Schynige Platte—she would love it. I'm probably going there tomorrow myself.'

'Damn, there's our machine moving!' Julia exclaimed. 'Come on!'—and she and Colin, running, leapt aboard their bus.

Chapter 7

The Schynige Platte

'Why did you push me off?' Colin began at once. 'Did you see them up on the top?'

'Yes—and learned a whole bagful. Tell you when we get in— no, it must wait till after lunch; we're fearfully late. But I pushed you off because I didn't want them to see you—him, rather; she's just a little cipher.' She glanced round the bus. 'What's all this about the Schynige Platte?' she asked—an English couple were sitting close behind them.

'Oh, it's some place above Interlaken where they've made a rock-garden and naturalised the wild-flowers and put labels on them, so that you can see what everything is; and there are little paths to walk about, and seats. He's mad on wild-flowers—and birds—and when I mentioned that Mrs. H. was keen on flowers too he said we ought to take her up. I think she could go; there's a railway right up to it, and a restaurant at the top.'

'A good idea,' Julia said. But both she and Colin found it rather a trial to have to sit through lunch talking on indifferent matters, when she was bursting with her news, and he was impatient to hear it. The Schynige Platte seemed a useful topic with which to entertain Mrs. Hathaway, since neither of them could tell her much about the Niederhorn; that lady was charmed with the idea, and when she went to rest declared that she should read it up in Baedeker while she was lying down. Colin and Julia repaired to a field below the hotel garden and sat in the shade of a mountain ash—the walls of the Silberhorn bedrooms, like those of many Swiss mountain hotels, were about as sound-proof as paper.

'Well now, what?' Colin asked.

Julia recounted her rescue of June Phillips, and the silly child's revelations. 'Obviously Mr. Borovali, or whoever employs him, went round all these advertising agencies and flipped through their photographs of girls with Pekes or outside banks, till they had the luck to find one who was passably like Aglaia. Then they engaged her for a month, and fitted her out, and brought her along as a sort of corroborative dummy.'

'Wouldn't she have had to speak a part at the bank?'

'Not much, would she? Aglaia's a minor still. I expect they just coached her up a bit. Heiresses don't have to be clever!'

'And why do you suppose they picked on this Wright person? Is he like me?'

'Not in the least, except that he's tall and has black hair. I imagine,' Julia said, remembering June's words about Wright not being 'like anyone', and her vexation at his larger salary, 'that they routed round till they found someone with a knowledge of these oil countries; and as he's been fired from a job out there and has a chip on his shoulder, what could be better? I think June said something about his knowing these parties who are coming here to collect the blue-prints—that alone would be ample recommendation, wouldn't it? And he's just the sort of creature to be ready for any crookery, I should say; I feel sure he'd sell his mother's corpse before it was cold for her eyes, for that new operation.'

Colin laughed.

'But anyhow, now we know where they are,' Julia said. 'So what next?'

Colin considered.

'Could he have had the papers on him today?'

'Definitely not, coming down. Pale corduroy slacks, silk shirt, and a silk wind-cheater—with no bulges! But where could he put them up there, and why?'

'Only that he went off alone like that.'

'She says he always does—anyhow they've had a week to find a much better place to stow them in than the Niederhorn Ridge! How big would the papers be, by the way?'

'I've no idea, I should imagine a fair thickness, though.'

'And foolscap size.'

'Julia, I don't know.'

'Well do find out. You and your department and your imaginings!—I never heard of anything so amateurish. I expect Mister de Ritter-Borovali has them in a briefcase in the safe at the Fluss, along with Jewesses' better diamonds.'

Colin grinned, wryly. 'How could we have seen them? They've been locked up in this damned bank.'

'Oh well. Anyhow, hadn't you better ring up your firm in Berne, so that they can cause the appropriate department to pounce?'

'M'm. Yes—yes, I had. They may know more now about how long the delay is likely to be.'

'But why delay at all? Why not pounce tonight, or at least tomorrow?'

'It's not as simple as all that, in a foreign jurisdiction,' Colin said soberly, rather impressing Julia. 'However, I will get onto them.'

'Well when you do, do ask if they know anything about this Antrobus man. Have you ever met him before?'

'No—we just got talking.'

'He doesn't belong to your outfit?'

'Not to my knowledge. Why should he?'

'Only because he keeps on turning up whenever your sham fiancée is about.' She recounted the episode at Victoria; seeing him entrain at Berne for Geneva, 'on the very day, mark you, before these stooges went to the bank'; his presence at the Bergues, and also at Nethersole's luncheon. 'And now he turns up here, again on the very day that June and the emetic Wright go up to the Niederhorn. You'd think he was watching them; if he isn't, he must be watching out for them—keeping *cave*, as one used to say at school. Anyhow, I'd like to know where he stands.'

'It is all a bit odd,' Colin said thoughtfully. 'But he struck me as a very decent sort of man. He's a member of the Alpine Club.'

'Did he tell you that?'

'Well it emerged.'

'You could have that checked.'

'Yes, of course—I will.' He brooded. 'How well do you know this party who asked him to meet you in Geneva?'

'Not well at all—I met him a few times with Geoffrey. He's an archaeologist, when he isn't with UNO. And I remember that Antrobus said he was a tremendous Arabic scholar,' Julia said, trying to bring out all her few facts about Nethersole.

'Isn't he permanently with UNO?'

'I don't think so—no. They lay him on when they want him, I gathered, and he goes if he isn't too busy digging up Jericho, or

129

deciphering Qumran scrolls.'

'The Qumran scrolls aren't in Arabic,' Colin objected.

'Not? Oh well, anyhow he's in those parts a lot of the time.'

'Middle East again,' Colin said gloomily. 'And of course a UNO part-timer could really be anything. Yes, I expect we ought to keep an eye on Antrobus.'

'That shouldn't be difficult, as he seems to be keeping an eye on us,' Julia said briskly. 'But *ask*, Colin.'

'I will. I'll go and ring up now, and see what I get on him—and give them this Interlaken address. They ought to be pretty pleased, J. dear.' He strolled off up the steep field.

Julia remained under the mountain ash, looking across at the white peaks of the Blümlisalp range, glowing like praising souls under the sun; she felt relaxed and happy. Colin's 'they' certainly ought to be pleased at this windfall. Of course it was not due to any skill of hers, merely to Wright's lack of conscientiousness— well what could you expect, with that face?—and poor little June's incredibly low I.Q. (She hoped that bloody youth really had got a doctor to look at the sprained ankle.) But it was a scoop, all right—quite a major scoop.

Colin, sooner than she expected, came slouching down across the meadow.

'Were they pleased?' Julia asked as he came up.

'No—I mean neither of the two chaps was in. I shall go in myself; whatever you may say about the Swiss telephones, I don't care about that box here. The door won't shut, and there's always someone in the Bureau next door. It's only about three hours, anyhow, if I go down by the funicular and get a boat across to Spiez. I'll let you know what goes on—I don't imagine the Bureau-Fräulein speaks Gaelic!'

Mrs. Hathaway took Colin's sudden departure as calmly as

she took most things, when Julia told her of it over Cinzanos upstairs before supper. She had a corner room, with Watkins's cell next door, so the question of being overheard hardly arose; Watkins was getting a little deaf, and was totally incurious about 'Master Colin' and his affairs.

'How nice that his work should bring him here just now,' Mrs. Hathaway said as she sipped, gazing happily out of the window. 'The only thing that surprises me is that there should be anything for the Secret Service to bother with, here; the Swiss could hardly get into mischief, one would have thought, because they're so busy; over things like cleaning their cows.'

Julia enquired about this.

'Oh yes—a peasant we met on the road told me all about it, this morning. Have you noticed those iron rings in that high wall above the road, just beyond our little shop, next to the glen with the waterfall in it?'

Julia nodded.

'Well those are where they moor their young beasts, before they take them down to the market; they bring cloths, and buckets to fetch water from the glen, and slosh the creatures down, there on the road-side. Isn't it charming?'

Julia thought it was, and said so. But she had a notion of her own in her head.

'Did you read up about the Alpine Garden at the Schynige Platte? If it's fine tomorrow I thought we might go.'

'Indeed I did!—and it is something I really do want to see. Yes, do let us go tomorrow.'

'You're sure you're up to it?' Julia felt a little guilty over her own initiative about making this particular expedition.

'Well even if I do get a little tired, doing something I enjoy will do me good,' Mrs. Hathaway said. 'There are wise ways of

131

spending one's strength, just as there are of spending one's money—and really the art of living is to recognise both.'

The next day was superb, and they set out in good time, on the musical bus. The town of Interlaken, small as it is, possesses two railway-stations: the West-Bahnhof, whence one entrains for Spiez and Berne, and the Ost-Bahnhof, or East Station, which serves Meiringen, Grindelwald, and the Lauterbrunnen valley, including Wengen and Mürren. The Post-Autos all pull up in the big open *Platz* outside the West-Bahnhof, and trains flit fairly often from one station to the other, rattling across an open street and thundering, twice, over the milky-green Aar on iron bridges—Mrs. Hathaway, however, who knew her way about in Switzerland, insisted on taking an open horse-cab from one station to the other. A row of these ancient vehicles is always standing in the Platz, the equally ancient horses droop-ing their heads, the drivers smoking cheroots and gossiping; in one of them they clop-clopped along the main street between small expensive shops full of souvenirs and summer sportswear, and innumerable hotels, some also small, some large and rich-looking. But what startled and fascinated Julia about Interlaken was that the whole town was full of the scent of new-mown hay. The meadows are all round it, and here and there impinge on the streets, so that the fresh sweet country smell is every-where, in what is indubitably a town. Towards the end of their drive they passed a building with the words 'Hotel zum Fluss' across its façade; Julia gazed at it with deep interest. Beastly Wright, the enigmatic Mr. Borovali, and poor June were all housed behind that yellow front.

To reach the Schynige Platte one takes the train from the Ost-Bahnhof for Lauterbrunnen, but leaves it after a few minutes at Wilderswyl, a village at the farther side of the flat sedimentary plain between the lakes of Thun and Brienz—part of this plain is occupied by a military airfield, whose hangars are turfed over to look like grassy mounds. Julia observed them with amusement; apparently the Swiss hadn't yet got round to stowing their operational aircraft in the bowels of mountains or at the bottom of lakes. But she was really keeping an eye open for Antrobus; there had been no sign of him at the Ost-Bahnhof. What a bore if he didn't come, after all! But at Wilderswyl, where they got out and stood on the wide platform, waiting to be allowed to enter the funny little coaches with their red-and-white blinds which carry one up the mountain, there he was; and was introduced to Mrs. Hathaway. It was hot there in the sun, but when an official unlocked the doors of the small train he said—'Have you a wrap, Mrs. Hathaway? If so put it on—it's often fearfully cold going up.'

Watkins was carrying her mistress's wrap over her arm: that old-fashioned but delightful garment formerly known as an 'Inverness Cape'—a long coat with a cloak slung over it from the shoulders; Mrs. Hathaway's was in a discreet pepper-and-salt tweed, and looked immensely elegant when she put it on. Then they climbed in, and all sat together; Antrobus and Mrs. Hathaway got on like a house on fire, both staring out of the window on the watch for flowers, and pointing out to one another any treasure that they espied. 'Oh, there's *Astrantia major!* Mrs. Hathaway exclaimed in the lower meadows, 'and the purple columbine—do look!' Higher up in the beechwoods—'Oh, quickly, *Cephalanthera rubra!*' Antrobus said, pointing out some tall spikes of a reddish-pink orchis, just before the train plunged into a tunnel. The moment it emerged Antrobus's head was at the window again, indicating the Martagon Lily, in bud, on the bank.

Julia was more pleased with Antrobus than ever because of his niceness and considerateness with Mrs. Hathaway; after a brief halt at the small station of Breitlauenen ('the Broad Avalanches') it became really chilly in the draughty windowless little carriage. But still there was more to see, and the detective knew all about it.

'Come over to the other side, now,' he said. 'In a big stony valley we're just coming to on the right you might see a marmot.' They all moved across the carriage—the train was not very full—and there on the stone-flecked slopes they actually caught a glimpse of two marmots before they fled whistling into their burrows, frightened, idiotic creatures, by the familiar noise of the train.

'They look so like seals,' Mrs. Hathaway said, delighted.

At the top they went straight to the Alpine Garden; Antrobus was greeted warmly by the girl at the entrance who sold tickets. It is certainly a most charming place, the wild plants grouped in situations approximating to the natural habitat of each, and every group with a metal label bearing its name; little paths wander to and fro, up and down; at intervals there are seats on which to rest and admire the splendid view. Mrs. Hathaway moved slowly along the little paths, peering, examining, admiring. Presently they came on a girl in breeches and a blue gardener's apron who knelt beside a new bed, carefully arranging stones and setting in some tiny plants; she too recognised Antrobus and got up, wiping the earth off her hands, to greet him in German with a rueful grin.

'Ah, you caught us completely over *Petasites niveus var: paradoxus!* We learn from *you!*'

'That one is a paradox,' the man replied, smiling.

'Please send us some more—you make us *aufmerksam,*' the girl

134

said, and knelt down to her task again.

As they strolled on, Antrobus told Mrs. Hathaway about the two girls, youthful botanists from Zürich University, who took care of the garden; 'They share that house down by the entrance, and eat at the hotel. They have a laboratory and a library, and prepare specimens. I often send them plants to identify, and they are so helpful and enthusiastic, bless them.'

Mrs. Hathaway presently said that she would sit and rest for a little, and then make her way up to the restaurant. Antrobus instantly suggested that he and Julia should take a short walk outside the garden—'There's a gate at the top that one can get out by'—and return for lunch. Mrs. Hathaway openly applauded this idea; so, in her heart, did Julia.

The Schynige Platte garden lies at just over six thousand feet, facing South, on the top of a ridge running East and West above the Lake of Brienz; as with the Niederhorn, on the northern side this ridge falls away in vertical cliffs and buttresses; one or two tall rocky towers stand up from it. A path leads under the nearest of these, known as *Der Turm*, and Julia and Antrobus wandered along it across the open slopes. Here they were soon among the anemones, the white and the yellow—drifts of great sulphur and silvery-white stars nearly two inches across, flowering up out of the rough pale grass—Julia fairly gasped at the sight. Then they climbed by narrow zigzags to the crest of the ridge through a miniature forest of Alpenrosen, the Alpine rhododendron, not yet in bloom, and the dwarf juniper, *J. nanus;* none were as much as two feet high, but it was a true forest all the same, on this minute scale. There were flowers too: the strange-looking Cerinthe and the tiny leafless veronica, *V. apkylla,* carrying its minute blue heads on bare stalks among the white rocks— Antrobus named them all, as botanists do out of pure love; Julia picked one or two of everything for Mrs. Hathaway.

On the crest itself, where there is a small hut to shelter the wayfarer, with—so Swiss—a telephone, they sat on a sun-warmed rock, looking out in front of them at that splendid mountain group of Jungfrau, Mönch, and Eiger, all blazing and glittering under the sun. Up on the ridge there was nothing but 'the peaks and the sky, and the light and the silence'—Julia herself was silent, suddenly moved; they sat so for a long moment. Then Antrobus turned from the snowy Jungfrau in the distance to the tawny-gold Jungfrau seated beside him.

'I get the impression that this says something to you?' he said.

Julia didn't answer at once. Then—'I never realised that anything like it was possible,' she said, slowly.

'Those are almost exactly the words that Keyserling used about the Taj Mahal,' he said, looking pleased. 'But have you never been to Switzerland before?'

'Only in winter—Zermatt. I can't think why not, since it's like this.'

'Well when you've finished your cigarette we'll see more flowers; we're too high here for some things.'

Julia went off at a tangent.

'That's the Lake of Brienz down there behind us, isn't it?' she asked, looking over her shoulder. 'Is it true that it's full of stores, sunk on the bottom?'

'Yes, certainly. Who told you? Not that it isn't common knowledge; the very bus-drivers taking tourists over the Furka-Pass show them the entrances to the underground barracks and hospitals, and the embedded gun-emplacements. In some ways the Swiss are strangely casual about security; curious, because their military dispositions are some of the most complicated in the world.'

'Couldn't the metal containers with all that butter and cheese be spotted from the air?'Julia asked—'like those forts and circles that Crawford or someone used to photograph?'

'Not very well. It's much harder to photograph, or spot, objects under six hundred feet of water than under six feet, or a few inches, of soil. And strange planes cruising over these lakes would stir up a hornet's nest of Swiss fighters to buzz them. But who told you?' he persisted.

Julia regretted her careless question. She was in an idyll at the moment, and the need to mention Colin jerked her back to the world of reality, in which this delightful companion at her side might be an enemy—*the* enemy. The thought hurt her surprisingly.

'Oh, my cousin,' she said airily, to conceal her discomfort.

'The second Mr. Monro?'

'Or would you say the first?' she answered brusquely, turning to look him straight in the face.

He smiled his gothic smile at her, and moved one hand in a gesture of brushing something away.

'Forget it,' he said gently. 'I'm sorry I said that. Just for today can't we sink Fatima and Bluebeard to the bottom of the Lake of Brienz along with the butter and cheese, and simply enjoy ourselves?'

'I was enjoying myself,' Julia said plaintively.

'Well go on! Do please. I'm so sorry; this is all my fault. And by the way I think Julia a much prettier name than Fatima.'

She blushed at that—hard-boiled as she was in many ways, Julia could never control her blushes, and the man watched the apricots ripening in her cheeks.

'How did you know?' she asked rather defiantly. 'Oh, Nethersole of course.'

'Yes—don't you remember that he said you would complete my education?'

'At least you're continuing mine!—all these names of flowers.'

'Ah, they're my besetting sin—flowers, and birds. Now I want to show you some more—come on.'

They returned down the zigzags to the path below the Turm; there he stopped, and looked at her feet.

'What are your soles?—rubber or nails? Do you think you can manage this slope? It's much quicker than going round by the garden.'

Julia was wearing stout leather shoes with thick ridged rubber soles; she held one up for his inspection.

'Yes, those ought to be all right. Better take my hand, though; this top bit is fairly steep.' Without waiting for a reply he took her hand and led her down the rough grassy slope, tacking diagonally across and across it; he went rather fast and Julia, who had never acquired the mountaineers' trick of the loose-kneed descent—toes out, heels in, and practically sitting back on one's heels—found herself rather breathless when they reached the bottom. (Holding his hand was a faintly breathless affair, too.) Here in a grassy hollow stood three grey-shingled wooden sheds, long and low; these, Antrobus explained, were *Senn-Hütte*, the huts to which the peasants repaired when they brought their cows up to the high alpine pastures for the summer months—the great time for cheese-making. As they mounted up a rutted muddy track on the farther slope—'Oh, here they are!' he exclaimed. 'Coming up to get the place ready.'

Down the track towards them came several men, steadying two enormous wooden sledges, whose upcurved runners slithered in the greasy mud; the sledges were piled high with household and dairying effects—churns, cooking utensils, mattresses, blankets, tools, and topping all two wireless sets. These last made Julia laugh.

'Oh, that's the modern world,' Antrobus said. 'Today the radio is an essential, even for cheese-making.' As they stood aside to let the clumsy sledges pass he greeted the men in a language incomprehensible to Julia; they laughed cheerfully as they replied.

'What on earth were you talking to them?' the girl asked.

'Berner-Deutsch—their *patois*. It's really more a very archaic form of German than anything else: for instance, instead of *gewesen*, for 'been', they say *gesie,* taken direct from *sein,* the infinitive of "to be"—and they usually swallow the last consonant if they can. I rather love it—Germans think it hideous, of course.'

'How did you learn it?'

'I used to come here as a child—for "glands"—and played about with the peasant children. And I've gone on coming a good deal ever since.'

'Oh yes—you climb, don't you?' By now they had reached the lip of the grassy hollow, and were on the broad track leading to the Faulhorn, and the great range opposite was again visible, glittering under the noonday sun. 'Have you been up those?' she asked, gesturing at it.

'Several of them, yes. The Jungfrau three times, the Eiger twice, the Mönch only once. And the Morgenhorn—do you see that very silver one? It's the first to catch the sunlight in the morning as you look up from Interlaken; that's why they call it that.'

'Pretty,' Julia said. 'Any others?'

'Yes, the Lauterbrunnen Breithorn, right at the end of the row.'

'The one that looks like a neolithic axe-head, only white?'

He laughed.

'What a good comparison! Yes. I was only fifteen when I did that; it was my first real mountain.' He turned to her. 'You've never climbed?'

'No—it never came my way.'

'You should,' Antrobus said, displaying the missionary spirit which is so strong in mountaineers. 'I think you would—well, find the right things in it.'

They wandered slowly on along the Faulhorn path, talking as they went; crossing a low ridge they came suddenly on another of those patches of discoloured snow half-filling a grassy saucer, surrounded by the white crocuses as by a miniature snow-storm, held motionless three inches above the wintry turf.

'That's what I wanted you to see,' the man said.

'It's exquisite,' Julia responded. A little farther on they came to another hollow, whence the snow had altogether departed, but only recently; here the soldanellas were growing in hundreds, their foolish little fringed lilac bells, with such an odd look of tiny paper caps out of Christmas crackers, nodding over the brownish earth—Julia was enchanted. He told her then about the Faulhorn path—'It's so broad and firm because it's really an old mule-track, probably dating back to the Middle Ages, by which goods were carried from Interlaken over to the Grosse Scheidegg, and so down to Rosenlaui or Grindelwald; in either case it was a short-cut in the summer months—saved miles.' They were so happy and easy together, there on the sunny mountainside, that Julia at last had the confidence to ask him, outright, what he was really up to? She felt she had to know—one mustn't lose one's heart to an enemy.

But the attempt was a failure, lightly and gaily as she did it—'*Which* Mr. Monro are you really shadowing?' As he had done at Victoria he smiled, put a finger to his lip, and shook his head; then, serious all of a sudden, he took her hand and held it firmly. 'My dear, I can't tell you,' he said, very gently. 'Let it alone, please. I asked you just now, up there by the Turm, to sink Fatima and Bluebeard to the bottom of the lake. Whatever happens later, for this one day, this one lovely day, do let us just be Julia and John.'

Her failure and his tenderness together quite overset Julia. She turned aside—she could not walk on, for he was still holding her hand in a firm clasp—both to conceal an unexpected stinging of tears in her eyes, and to think of an answer and then control her voice for it. He pressed her hand, watching her averted head, and pursued—' Can't you just say—"Yes, John," and leave it at that?—for today?'

She took a moment or two over it—oh, how difficult! Her watch was on her free wrist, and she looked at it. Then she turned back to face him.

' "We maun totter down, John"—we shall be late else,' she said.

The man, in his turn, was plainly a little shaken by the quotation. 'Oh!' That was all he said, but he raised her hand to his lips and kissed it before he let it go. 'But really we maun totter up!— quite a long way,' he added, lightening the thing. 'We mustn't keep your delightful friend waiting. What a charmer she is.'

As they walked back along the mediaeval mule-track and then up a short steep ascent to the hotel, Antrobus pursued the subject of Mrs. Hathaway, who had evidently taken his fancy. 'Is she inquisitive too?' he presently asked.

'That's not fair,' Julia said. 'If I mayn't ask questions, nor may you!'

He laughed—'So sorry.' But during lunch in the sunny

glassed-in verandah of the hotel Julia got the impression that Antrobus was rather warily assessing Mrs. Hathaway. At one point she mentioned Gersau, and Herr Waechter.

'Oh, you know him?' the man said. 'Such a wonderful house— and what a patriarch!'

'Well, if that is how you describe a childless widower,' Mrs. Hathaway observed, ironically.

Antrobus laughed, and they went on to discuss that so essentially Swiss thing, the long bourgeois pedigrees and the continuing industry and wealth, in the same families. 'No "Death of a Class" here,' Antrobus said at length.

'No. But don't you have to take neutrality into consideration?' Mrs. Hathaway said. 'The Swiss have escaped two wars, and therefore the penal taxation resulting from those wars. But if others had not fought, and died, and then been taxed almost out of existence, would Switzerland still be free, and able to revel in her neutrality? I have often thought that neutrality, like patriotism, is really not quite enough.'

Julia, who knew that Mrs. Hathaway had lost two sons in their late teens in World War I watched with closest interest to see how Antrobus would deal with this.

'That is quite true,' he said carefully. 'I was oversimplifying. But I still think that the social structure has something to do with it. The Swiss really only have two classes: peasants—who as a class are always immortal—and the *bourgeoisie*. In England we have at least four: the aristocracy; the upper-middle and professional class; the artisans; and again the peasants—whom we call 'country-people'; and of these the first two are of course by far the most vulnerable.'

'And possible the most valuable,' Mrs. Hathaway said, a little sharply. 'No—of course true "peasants" always preserve their

142

precious country values, in spite of the wireless.' She considered. 'Perhaps a two-class society has a greater survival value,' she said slowly.

Julia put in her oar.

'But surely in Bolshevik Russia, where they aimed at a "class-less society", they're now busy creating a new aristocracy all over again, of technicians?'

'A technocracy,' Antrobus corrected her. 'Specialised knowledge has its uses, but there is nothing particularly good about it. The word *aristos* means "best", don't forget.' Mrs. Hathaway was pleased; she laughed.

Julia was keeping an eye on the time, and on Mrs. Hathaway for signs of fatigue; they finished their meal rather hurriedly, and caught an early train down. Antrobus went with them as far as Breitlauenen, where he got out to walk down to Wilderswyl, hunting for flowers in the beech forests on the way. 'I'll bring you anything amusing that I find,' he assured Mrs. Hathaway.

Julia had already procured, and carried round in her handbag, a time-table of the Beatenberg buses. This showed her that they would have nearly an hour's wait in Interlaken, and as the Hotel zum Fluss was quite close to the Ost-Bahnhof, curiosity prompted her to suggest that they should fill in the pause by having coffee there, and then drive down to the West-Bahnhof for their bus. Mrs. Hathaway of course agreed; she liked her coffee after lunch, and in their haste they had missed this up at the Schynige Platte—so to the Fluss they went.

This charming hotel has two rather distinctive features. Opposite the entrance, but separated from it by a road where cars can pull up, is a raised terrace or garden shaded by chestnut-trees and set with tables, where light meals are served; also, for the convenience of passengers boarding or leaving the Lake of

Brienz steamers, there is a side entrance giving access—as a discreet notice announces—to *Toiletten* for both ladies and gentlemen. Julia's party availed themselves of both; they ordered coffee on the terrace, visited the *Toiletten* while it was being made, and then returned to drink it. It was nice on the little terrace; even here the air was full of the scent of new-mown hay, and resounded with the song of blackbirds. (The Interlaken blackbirds sing more loudly and richly than any others in the world.) A steamer drew in to the quay, and as they watched the passengers disembark Julia thought of June, so lonely and 'dull'—impulsively, she decided to ask for her in the hotel, and went in.

As an excuse she first asked the hall porter—who was bearded, fatherly, and chatty, the Swiss hotel version of the English family butler—if he could order them a horse-cab to catch the Beatenberg bus?

'Yes, certainly'—in his rather peculiar brand of English. Then Julia asked if Miss Armitage was in?

The old man's expression changed instantly, and rather startlingly, to one of hostility and suspicion.

'No. They left this morning.'

'Oh, I am sorry. I'd hoped to see her. How was her foot? Any better?'

The old porter thawed a little at that.

'Are you the lady who helped her up on the Niederhorn, and bandaged her foot? She said if you came I was to give you this'— he grubbed in his desk and brought out Julia's head-scarf.

'Oh yes, that's mine. Thank you very much. But is her foot better?'

'*Ein wenig*, yes—she can walk a few steps, the poor child.' The porter's suspicion did not appear to attach to June, and Julia pursued this promising line. At that hour, in mid-afternoon, the

144

hall was practically empty, the guests being either out on expeditions or sleeping off their midday meal upstairs.

'I hope they did get a doctor to see her?' she said, putting anxiety into her voice. 'This young man seemed to me to take her injury rather lightly.'

The porter scowled, and muttered something about a *frecher, ekeliger Kerl* (an insolent disgusting fellow) into his beard; aloud, and in English, he said, 'Yes, Miss. The older gentleman told *me* to get a doctor, and I sent for Doktor Hertz; he is excellent; he has a fine Klinik in the town. I know everyone here; thirty years I am Portier in this hotel! So the Herr Doktor strapped up the foot, but he said she should use it as little as possible, and that he would look at it again tomorrow.'

The porter was now obviously in the full vein of gossip; Julia, delighted, continued to probe.

'But now they have left? Oh, what a pity, since Dr. Hertz is so good. Did they leave an address? Though I have only met Fräulein Armitage once, I should like to know how she gets on.'

'No, they left no address,' the porter said, scowling again. 'They left hurriedly—and with good reason! Oh, *das kleine Fräulein* is all right—she is simply an innocent. But the others!'—he shrugged, with an expression of ineffable contempt. 'Curious customers, if you ask me.'

Julia continued to pursue the June line.

'Really? I should be sorry to think that this young lady was not with nice people—she told me that she had never left England before, and she is so young. Her mother is a widow, too. Have you any idea why they left so hastily?'

The porter leant over his desk towards her, and spoke in a lowered tone.

'The police came to enquire about them!'

'No!' Julia professed the expected surprise.

'*Aber ja!* Of course they spoke with me,' the old man said importantly, 'and I showed them the register with the names, and said that, as always, the passports had been sent to the Polizei—this is done in all hotels here. But then the police brought out a photograph and asked if I recognised it as that of the Fräulein Armitage? This is most unusual; in thirty years such a thing has never happened to me.'

'And was it of her?' Julia asked, delighted at this evidence that her clipping from *Paris-Match* was being used.

'*Gewiss!* It was badly done, on shiny paper, but certainly it was this poor young lady's picture—though why the Polizei should seek *her*, I cannot understand. And while I was looking at it— here at this desk, where we stand—up comes Mister de Ritter himself to ask some question of me, and sees the photograph, and may have heard the questions asked by the police, for all I know.'

'Good heavens! So then what happened?'

The porter was enjoying his dramatic recital.

'Oh, I know my duties! It is not my business to give away our clients to the police, whatever I myself may think of them. *"Moment"* I say—and of Herr de Ritter I ask, "Yes, sir, what can I do for you?" He enquired of me then about the times of the steamer to Iseltwald, on the Brienzer-See; I gave them, and he wrote them down—ah, that is a cool one—while all the time the photograph of Miss Armitage lies on my desk, under his eyes. He looked well at it, and at the two police—though these were in *Zivil.*' (Julia knew that he meant plain clothes.) 'And he thanked me, and went away.'

One up to Mr. B., Julia thought; crook or no, he had good nerves. 'And after that?' she asked.

'Oh, the police went off—to make a report, I suppose!' the porter said, with some contempt—'being now satisfied that the Fräulein Armitage is here. But less than an hour later she is no longer here! Within thirty-five minutes the valet comes down with the luggage; they pack, pay their bill, and off! Would not anyone think this odd?'

'Very odd indeed,' Julia agreed. 'And the police made no attempt to hold them?'

'Ach nein!—the police had gone. And now the birds are flown.'

'Did they go to Iseltwald?' Julia asked.

'No. They simply went across to the Ost-Bahnhof. I told Johann, who took their luggage, to note where they booked to; but they had a *Carnet* of *Ost-West Billeten,* as all who are wise do in Interlaken, and they used those. So one knows nothing. From the West-Bahnhof one can travel to anywhere in Europe.'

'All most peculiar,' Julia said slowly. 'And did you tell the police they'd left?'

'Fräulein, guests are guests!' the porter said pompously. 'As I said before, it is no part of my duties to lay informations to the police. If they ask questions I answer them, as in the matter of the photograph—but that suffices.'

'How very right. If I ever marry a crook I shall come and stay at the Fluss!' Julia said, and went out to rejoin Mrs. Hathaway, leaving the porter bowing and laughing. 'Don't forget our cab,' she called over her shoulder.

'Dear child, how long you've been! Can they get us a cab?' that lady asked.

'Oh yes; all laid on. I'm sorry I was so slow; the porter was rather a gossipy old thing,' Julia said carelessly, and Mrs. Hathaway asked no further questions—she was tired as well as tactful. But all the way back to Beatenberg in the bus Julia was

147

distraite, and rather silent. The reference of the porter at the Fluss to June as 'an innocent' exactly matched her own impression of the pretty, silly, good-hearted little thing who proudly gave a lot of her wages to support 'Mum', now that 'Dad' was dead; and she was filled with a slow, cold anger that international crookery should get hold of such a helpless creature and use her simply as a commodity to serve their beastly purposes. 'Expendable!' she muttered angrily, thinking of June's boredom, and how she had now been reft away from the excellent Dr. Hertz, who would have seen to her ankle, her source of livelihood.

'What did you say, my dear?' Mrs. Hathaway asked.

'Oh sorry, Mrs. H.—I was talking to myself. I must be going round the bend!'

'Nonsense, dear. I think soliloquies aloud are a sign of intelligent emotion—after all, where would Shakespeare have been without them? But do look out on the right—oh no, now it's on the left; these awful hairpins!'—as the bus negotiated another, playing its little six-note tune. 'There! Do you see that Enchanter's Nightshade? Unmistakable—but it's practically blue.'

Julia tried to pick out the small dull plant which so excited Mrs. Hathaway from among the heaths, whortleberry bushes, ferns, and other greenery which clothed the bank above the terrifying road. 'Oh yes, so it is,' she said. 'How odd!' Then she returned to her private preoccupations. She was no longer so pleased at the use to which her clipping from *Paris-Match* had presumably been put. It was almost certainly her fault that June's ankle was now going to be neglected. But when she sent the photograph to Chambertin she hadn't met June.

148

Chapter 8

Merligen

Colin rang up after tea. 'Where on earth have you been all day? I tried to get you three times.'

'At the Schynige Platte.'

'Oh. Well something very boring has happened. I gave my friends here that address, but I think the locals must have been a bit slow off the mark—anyhow your new acquaintances have gone.'

'I know.'

'How do you know?'

'I just found out. And it was the locals who scared them off, bumble-footing round with a certain photograph, quite openly, silly clots.'

'Any idea where they've gone?'

'None—I couldn't learn that.'

'Well can't you learn it? Do try. It's too maddening their vanishing into thin air like this, just when we thought everything was taped. And now we've heard that their principals, who were delayed, are probably arriving by air within the next forty-eight hours.'

'Arriving where?'

'Well wherever my would-be bride and her escorts have stowed themselves.'

'Her beastly escorts,' Julia exclaimed bitterly. 'Much they care about her!'

Colin ignored this.

'Well, darling, you see it's pretty urgent. Do you think you can find out some more, as you're on the spot?'

'No, I don't see how I can, since they now know that the polus'—she carefully used the Highland word for the police—'are after them.'

'They do definitely know that?'

'Yes—I told you. That's why they left at half an hour's notice.'

'*How* boring. So we've absolutely no clue?'

'No. Oh by the way, what about the detective?'

'The who?'

'The man you met yesterday. Is anything known of him by your friends?'

'Damn! I forgot to ask.'

'Oh really, you are a tiresome child! I told you, twice, to get a line on him.'

'Sorry, darling. But does it really matter?'

'It could matter a lot.' Julia felt that it probably mattered most to her, but did not say so. 'Find out—don't forget again,' she adjured Colin. 'Are you coming back?'

'Don't know yet. We may have to be spread pretty thin at these air-ports. But do try to think something up, darling; because if they keep the girl under cover, as I imagine they will now, we really have no clue at all.'

150

'No clue at all.' Those last words of Colin's stuck in Julia's head all the evening, while she saw to Mrs. Hath-away's supper in bed, and straightened out some woe of Watkins's; it was with her as she stepped out onto her balcony last thing, sniffing the sweet air and the scent of the opening rowan-blossom from the tree in the meadow below, and looked across the darkling lake at the Blümlisalp white under the moon. Another phrase of Colin's nagged at her while she undressed—'if they keep the girl under cover'. She visualised June locked in her bedroom, starved, anything; people like Wright and Borovali could easily be remorseless, now that she had served their turn. She got into bed and switched off the light, but was too troubled to sleep. Suddenly there flashed into her mind the recollection of the Mass that Father Antal, the old Hungarian priest, had said in the private chapel at Gralheira, away in Portugal, on behalf of Hetta Páloczy, another girl in ruthless hands—and how by a miraculous coincidence Mrs. Hathaway had found and rescued her. Here there was no priest or chapel; the little Catholic church at a bend in the long road through the village only opened on Sundays for two Masses. But prayer was always prayer; Julia hopped out of bed, and kneeling on the scanty mat which covered the pine flooring beside it she prayed urgently for safety for June. Then she hopped in again, and slept soundly.

She woke in the morning with a bounce, as the young and healthy do; switched on her electric *bouilloir* for her morning tea, and went out in her nightgown onto the little balcony. The sun was striking across the white peaks of the Blümlisalp; she thought of Antrobus, and what he had told her about the Morgenhorn, invisible from Beatenberg. An early steamer was crossing the lake from Spiez towards Merligen, hidden behind a ridge running down from the Niederhorn; as Julia watched it, idly, an idea stole into her mind of itself, as ideas sometimes do. The little man from 'Corsette-Air' lived at Merligen—and hadn't he said that he had been asked recently to act as intermediary between *agences* of different nations, and pass information from one to the other? Had he said *agences* or *agents?* She couldn't be sure; she hadn't been paying much attention. But if there were people like him who did this sort of thing, might it not be just worth while to see him again, and try to find out a little more about the nature of the 'informations' he transmitted?—learn more of how these things were done? It didn't amount to a clue—but the idea of going to look him up, having come into her head, persisted. Merligen was so near—she would lose nothing by going. It was only the vaguest of hunches, it might be all a fantasy; but her hunches and fantasies had sometimes served well in the past. Had she still got that card? She routed in her bag—yes, there it was—

Herr Kaufmann,
Villa Victoria. Merligen.

Her *bouilloir* boiled, and she made her tea and drank a quick cup; had a bath in Mrs. Hathaway's cubicle of a bathroom, and dressed hastily. It was probably all a nonsense, but Colin, poor sweet, had been so urgent, and she had nothing to do—Mrs. H. ought to keep quiet today, after yesterday. On her way down to breakfast she looked in on that lady, and found her none the worse for her exertions; she had slept well. 'But I don't feel like being very energetic today.'

'Much better not—keep quiet and rest. I'm flipping off on a tiny expedition the moment after breakfast; with any luck I shall be back for lunch, but don't wait.'

Ninety-nine elderly ladies out of a hundred, in the circumstances, would have asked where her young friend was going? Mrs. Hathaway did not, which was one reason why everyone loved her.

'Very well, dear child, I won't. It's a lovely day for an *Ausflug.*'

Julia, as Colin had done two days before, went down in the funicular at the end of the village to Beatenbucht, and thence took a trolley-bus along the lake shore to Merligen, at the mouth of the forbidden Justis-Thal. This proved to be a sweet little place, dreamy and tranquil in the spring sunshine, looking across the lake to the shapely blue pyramid of the Niesen behind Spiez; there was a single large hotel on the shore, many old chalets, and an endless crop of small new villas, mostly on streets inland from the lake—but what startled and pleased Julia was that the whole little town was white and sweet as a bride's bouquet with bushes of syringa and *Spiraea canescens* flowering in every garden. After enquiries she made her way to the Villa Victoria, in one of the new streets; a neat paved path between the usual bridal bushes led up to the front door. Julia, wondering a good deal how she was to work this interview, rang the bell.

The door was opened by a rather sour-looking middle-aged woman in a spotted black-and-white apron, with her hair in a net. Julia asked if she could speak with Herr Kaufmann.

'I am Frau Kaufmann,' the woman said, not at all agreeably.

'Ah, good day. Is your husband at home? I come to enquire about surgical stays.'

Reluctantly, casting on Julia the suspicious glance that ugly women so often bestow on beautiful ones, the woman admitted her, and led her from the cramped little hall into a rather modest-sized room, obviously a sitting-room-cum-office: a huge safe stood against one wall, a very large desk heaped with files and papers under the window; a nouveau-art sofa and armchairs, covered with a pattern which suggested an electrical discharge, were grouped round a nouveau-art fireplace. Julia was enthralled by this fresh version of a Swiss interior—one in which, moreover, thousands of pounds worth of business was conducted annually.

'My husband is away,' the woman said then; 'he had to leave suddenly, for Lugano. I expect you know that his business is really wholesale? What firm do you represent?'

At this point piercing screams in a child's voice were heard from somewhere upstairs. '*Warte ein Augenblick, Franzi*', the woman called. But Franzi would not wait; he renewed his screaming. With a snort of exasperation and a hasty '*Entschuldigen Sie, bitte*' the woman left the room and could be heard stumping up the small narrow staircase, and speaking to a child in the room above.

Julia, without the smallest scruple, instantly went over to the outsize desk and began to examine the papers left strewn on it, clear evidence of the owner's hasty departure. There were some invoices, clipped together; several letters with the 'Corsette-Air' letter-head from the firm in Yorkshire, all in English—nothing to help her there. But tucked in under the blotting-pad, only one corner peeping out, she came, with her inveterate curiosity, on an open envelope; she drew out the letter and read it. It was in German, from a chemist in Berne, and read: 'Our client Herr B. left his recent address today. He may shortly be calling on you in person to deposit a valuable consignment of goods.' Julia looked quickly at the *date—yesterday!* H'm—her 'Herr B.' had undoubtedly changed his address yesterday! Could the Borovali outfit be one of the *agences*, or *agents*, for whom Herr Kaufmann had recently been asked to act as an intermediary, to receive and pass on 'informations'? 'Goods' might perfectly well mean blueprints—this letter could possibly mean something. Hastily she scribbled down the chemist's name and address in her diary; she just had time to put the envelope back under the blotter and sit down on one of the hideous chairs before Frau Kaufmann reappeared, with apologies. The little boy was ill, she said; he had measles, and the fever made him fretful. But now, about the Fräulein's firm?

Julia expressed sympathy about the child—'But I had better speak with Herr Kaufmann himself. When does he return?'

'I await him tomorrow, or even tonight. *Übermorgen* would be better for the Fräulein to come.'

'Then I will call again. It does not press,' Julia said.

The woman asked her name.

'That is unimportant—I will give it when I return.' Then she asked if she could take any message to the doctor, or the chemist, in the town?

'Thank you, no; I telephone,' the woman said, disagreeable to the last.

Walking down the sunny little side street between the snowy gardens, Julia wondered whether Franzi's screams were another wonderful stroke of luck, or whether the letter meant nothing? Anyhow, she thought, Colin ought to have that chemist's name and address, just in case. She decided to telephone from the big hotel by the lake; Berne is a longish call, and she knew from the Silberhorn that Swiss hotels have a little machine in the bureau which clocks up both time and price—but of course she had to risk giving the Bureau-Fräulein Colin's number in Berne.

Mr. Monro was out. When would he be in? 'No idea.' A cheerful English voice spoke.

'Well please ask him to ring up his cousin'—she gave the Silberhorn number—'as soon as he can; but only after 3.30.'

'O.K.—good,' the cheerful English voice replied. 'Have you got some news for us?'

Julia laughed. This might be half-clever, or too amateurish for words. But she did not want to lose time.

'Nothing hard,' she said down the telephone—'but there is an address that I think it *might* pay you to keep an eye on—round the clock.'

'Fine! I've got a pencil. Go ahead.'

Julia gave the chemist's address, and had it repeated. 'And the 'phone number?' the voice asked.

'Oh please look that up yourself!' Julia exclaimed—she wasn't going to say that she hadn't had time to write it down, over the telephone.

'O.K.,' the cheerful voice said again. 'That shall have attention. Thanks very much.'

Julia paid for her call, and then ordered an iced Cinzano, and sat on the terrace beside the lake—a drink was always cover of a sort. And while she drank she reflected. Yes, on balance she had probably done right to give the Berne chemist's address to an unknown voice—but still she was worried. Oughtn't the Villa Victoria to be watched too? If there was anything in her wild guess about the chemist's letter, Mr. Borovali might call at any moment to drop the papers, and that old sour-puss Frau Kaufmann would pop them in that huge combination safe, and then how could they be retrieved? She lit a cigarette and pondered, gazing at the Niesen—and finally came to another decision. Yes, she would chance her arm with the local police.

At the police-station she handed over her card and asked for the *Herr Chef*—she had no idea what the German for 'Superintendent' was. Rather to her surprise after a moment she was shown into an inner office, where a tall middle-aged man, with fair hair turning grey, courteously asked her her business.

Julia, in her very moderate German, enquired if he spoke English.—'I can express myself better in my own language.'

He smiled at her.

'Fortunately, Fräulein, it so happens that I do; I spent some time in England before joining the *Polizei.*'

'Oh, I am very glad.' Julia did not smile; she spoke slowly and seriously.

'All I ask of you is to listen to something I have to tell you. You do not know who I am, though here is my passport'—she gave it to him—'and I do not expect any response to what I tell you; that will be a matter for you and your superiors. Can you spare me five or six minutes?'

This rather portentous opening caused the official to assume the cautious non-committal mask of police all over Europe. 'Please speak,' he said.

'I believe the police in Switzerland have been circulated every-where with the photograph of a young English girl,' Julia said; 'a girl now accompanied by two men, one old and one young.' She opened her note-case and took out the small snap-shot of Colin and the real Aglaia which she had cut out of *Paris-Match* at Gersau, and handed it across the table. 'This is, I think, the same young lady.'

The official took up the photograph and examined it; then went to a cupboard, unlocked it, and took out and laid on the table a coarse photostat of the portrait of Aglaia which Julia had sent to Chambertin. He compared the two—then, completely po-faced, he turned to Julia.

'And so, Fräulein?'

'In this town there lives a certain Herr Kaufmann—at the Villa Victoria; an agent for "Corsette-Air", a foreign firm selling elastic stays. Probably you know his name.'

'*Natürlich*' the man, still po-faced, said.

Julia, feeling that she might be making a frightful fool of herself, nevertheless kept steadily on.

'I have reason to think it possible that the two men accompanying the young lady whose picture you have there—a Mr. Borovali, though his passport is made out in the name of de Ritter, and the young one, whose passport is in the name of Colin Monro—may possibly call at the Villa Victoria. If they do so, it would almost certainly be to dispose of some documents of the highest importance, which they obtained recently by fraud from the Banque Républicaine in Geneva. The photograph you have there'—she put a pink-tipped finger on the photostat—'has been circulated, I think, mainly with a view to the recovery of these documents.'

Still superbly po-faced—'And so, Fräulein?' the official asked again.

'Nothing, really,' Julia said coolly, 'except that it might assist your superiors, who took the trouble to send you that photograph, if a watch were kept on the Villa Victoria. I think you were also furnished with a description of the two men: the one elderly, grey-haired, with a grey forked beard, the younger very tall, slender, black hair and an olive complexion. If two such people came to the Villa they would very probably have the stolen documents with them, and it would be very useful to the bank, at least, if these documents could be apprehended.' She rose. 'That is all.' She made to leave, as expressionless as he— only no blankness of expression could really make Julia look po-faced.

The official remained seated.

'Just one moment, Fräulein; please to sit down again.'

Julia sat down, and the man studied her with a long gaze in which surprise, curiosity, and suspicion were blended with a hint of sterness.

'The Fräulein shows herself remarkably conversant with the personages in an affair which is apparently a crime; and, as you say, you are unknown to me. Have you any documents with you which would throw light on your status? The Fräulein will recognise that the circumstances are a little peculiar.'

'I have nothing but my visiting-card and my passport, both of which you have seen,' Julia said, rather stiffly. 'But if you wish you can telephone to the Pasteur of the Église Nationale at Bellardon; he is the real Herr de Ritter, and knows me well—I have stayed twice at La Cure within the last three weeks. And he is fully conversant with the whole affair.'

The police official made a note, and then asked—'The Fräulein is staying in Merligen?'

'No, at Beatenberg; the Hotel Silberhorn.'

'And do you know the present whereabouts of this young lady?' he asked, touching the police photograph.

'But naturally not! If I did, I should have gone also to the police there—wherever she is,' Julia said, with a chilly smile.

The official reflected.

'Please excuse me for a moment,' he said, and left the room. Julia began to wonder if she was going to be put in the cells, or whether he had merely gone to ring up Bellardon—and, again, if what she had been doing was quite idiotic. She pushed her wooden chair over to the window, opened it—Julia was always opening windows—and sat looking out. Below her were more gardens, white and fragrant with spiraea and syringa; beyond them, across the lake, rose the Niesen, with snowy gleams beyond—probably the Wildstrubel. There is a certain reassurance, for some people,

159

in the mere presence of mountains; Antrobus had not been wrong in his guess that Julia belonged to this fortunate group. She waited quietly in the bare, clean, official little room; she did look at her watch and saw that it was just after twelve; but she had warned Mrs. Hathaway that she might not be back for lunch—which at the Silberhorn, as in most Swiss hotels, occurred at 12.30. She was feeling perfectly tranquil when after a few minutes the greying-blond police officer returned. But the question he instantly put to her was rather upsetting.

'Fräulein Probyn, can you explain to me why you connect Herr Kaufmann with the persons of whom you have been speaking?'

Julia hesitated, and thought. The little 'Corsette-Air' man's remarks about touching *la haute finance* and acting as an intermediary for agencies of foreign powers were far too complicated and tenuous for this blunt intelligent man, with his official limitations. Much better stick to the letter she had read less than two hours ago. She opened her bag and took out what she had scribbled down in the Villa Victoria.

'A certain chemist in Berne,' she said carefully, 'wrote yesterday to Herr Kaufmann to say that "Herr B." might call on him shortly to deposit "A valuable consignment of goods"; he also mentioned that "Herr B." had left his recent address "today"—that is to say yesterday. And yesterday morning Mister Borovali left the Hotel zum Fluss in Interlaken at less than an hour's notice, with that young lady and the young man.' As she spoke she reached out and took the snapshot of Colin and Aglaia, and put it in her bag.

'You require this?' the official asked.

'Yes—it is mine. In any case it is not the likeness of the young man who is Borovali's collaborator.'

'Then of whom?'

'Of quite a different person, well known in English society, whom I happen to know. This photograph will not help you, and you already have an adequate likeness'—she chose her words carefully—'of the young lady in the party.' She paused. 'I am sure you have already been informed that she is impersonating someone else.'

The man turned po-faced again. As Julia took up her passport from the table and put it in her bag—'And the name of this chemist in Berne?' he asked.

'Oh yes'—she opened her bag, read it out, and as he wrote it down, once more closed her bag.

'You return now to Beatenberg?' the man asked.

'Yes, immediately; I'm late already—I shall miss the *Mittagsessen.*' Once more she rose; the official said, *'Adieu',* and opened the door.

'Goodbye,' Julia said blithely, and went out into the sunny little street to find the trolley-bus.

It was nearly a quarter to two when she got back, but Fräulein Hanna had saved her an *assiette anglaise* (a dish of mixed cold meats, in which veal and tongue predominated) and a bowl of salad—the kind woman told her that *die alte Dame* had made a good meal, and was gone to rest. Julia made a good meal too, and then went up to her room and brewed some Nescafé, which she drank on her balcony, idly watching more hay-cutting in the field below, and wondering whether she had really achieved anything by her morning's excursion. Was it all a mares'-nest, and anyhow would the Merligen policeman do anything?

Presently she was summoned to the telephone—it was the Pastor.

'My dear Miss Probyn, what have you been up to? Stealing

edelweiss in a Nature-Reserve? The police have been here to enquire about you.'

'Oh, splendid!' Julia said heartily; he laughed loudly.

'Oh, the English! You really love all police, don't you? But you are all right? You are not being troubled?'

'Not yet.'

'Any news of these individuals?' he asked, with a change of tone.

'Yes, I met two of them, but they've flitted.'

'Please?'

'Gone away—we don't know where to.'

'And you actually saw them? How extraordinary! But what has happened today, to cause this interest?'

'Oh, I had a wild idea, so I went and reported it,' Julia said airily. 'I'm glad they paid some attention—I wasn't sure they would.'

'Our Polizisten do not pay attention to wild ideas as a rule,' the Pastor said, again merry.

'Well I hope you gave me a good character,' Julia said. Like Colin she found that the door of the telephone-box wouldn't latch, and there were two or three people in the small lounge outside, which gave onto the garden—she wanted to cut the conversation short. 'How is Germaine?—and the family?'

'All very well. Your cousin is with you?'

'Not at the moment. Give Germaine my love. Goodbye.'

Julia went upstairs feeling on the whole rather pleased. At least the Merligen police hadn't completely ignored her visit; and if they had been activated to the point of ringing up Bellardon, they might possibly do something about the Villa Victoria. She washed out some stockings and hung them on a string across her tiny balcony; then some handkerchiefs, humming a little tune, happily, as she did so; she was just plastering the hankies on the window-panes to iron them—that invaluable trick of the experienced traveller—when there came a tap on the door.

'*Herein,*' Julia called—and in came Fräulein Hanna, with a distressful face.

'Fräulein Probyn, I am most heartily sorry, but the *Polizei* are here, and ask to speak with you! I tell them that it must be a mistake, but they give your name, and insist that they must see you.'

'Oh never mind, Fräulein Hanna; it's quite all right.' She paused, and thought. 'But I don't want Herr Schaff-hausen upset. Where are they now?'

'They wait *im Bureau.*'

'Then shall I come down to them, or were it better that they come up and see me here? There are people in the *Kleine Saal*, aren't there?' (The *Kleine Saal* was the small hall or lounge containing the telephone-box; the Bureau opened off it.)

'*Jawohl.*'

'Well then bring them up to me here, in the lift—that will be less noticeable. Don't worry,' she said, seeing the big kind woman's troubled expression. 'You will see, there will be no unpleasantness.'

'It is *höchst unangenehm* that they come to the trouble the Fräulein at all,' Hanna said indignantly. 'All this nonsense about passports! But it is perhaps better so—though *das Fräulein* should not have to receive strange men in her bedroom.' She went out, and returned in a couple of minutes with two large, pink-faced, countryfied policemen, whom she ushered into that exceedingly small room, with its single wicker armchair, the two rugs on the waxed floor, and the wooden bed with its white honeycomb quilt. 'Shall I remain?' she asked earnestly of the English girl.

163

'No, dear Fräulein Hanna; I thank you, but do not give your-self this trouble,' Julia said easily. 'Very probably I can help *diese Herren* better by myself.' This was of course said in German, and the two pink faces manifested a simple but evident relief. Hanna, casting a baleful glance at them, went out.

'*Also, meine Herren*, how can I be of service to you?' Julia asked—as she spoke she sat down in the solitary chair. 'I wish I could ask you to be seated, but as you see there is only the bed.'

The Beatenberg police did not fancy sitting on the bed; they stood. It was only a formality, the slightly senior one explained—could they see the Fräulein's passport? Julia produced this, and the man wrote down her name and the passport number, in a black note-book.

'And the Fräulein entered Switzerland when?'

'The date is *gestempelt*,' Julia said patiently. 'Allow me to show you.' She took the passport and showed him the entry stamp, nearly four weeks previously.

'And since then the Fräulein has been where?'

At dictation speed Julia gave him all her movements: Gersau, with her host's name and address; La Cure at Bellardon; the Hotel Bergues at Geneva; Bellardon again, Gersau again; and finally here at Beatenberg. All policemen write incredibly slowly; so did the Beatenberg worthy, poising his note-book on the small bed-table—however, at last he closed it with an elastic band.

'And *das Fräulein* expects to remain here?'

'For the present, yes. But, *mein Herr*, I would like to make one request of you.'

'And that is, Fräulein?' He looked suspicious at once.

'That you do not cause the Polizei in Gersau to disturb Herr Waechter with their enquiries. He is a very old man, and it might upset him to have the police calling at the house and asking him

164

about his guests. This cannot really be necessary—you know that I am here, and since when, and the police at Bellardon have already verified my presence there at La Cure, on the dates I have given you.'

A slow look of surprise gradually disturbed the bland pinkness of the older policeman's face.

'And may I ask how the Fräulein knows this?'

'But because the Herr Pastor himself telephoned, only now, to tell me so!' Julia said merrily. 'He asked if I had been stealing edelweiss on the Niederhorn—he has laughed very much.'

The two policemen grinned a little, though evidently shocked by such levity. '*Die Edelweiss* are not yet in bloom,' the younger one added seriously.

'*Nicht?* But please hear me,' Julia pursued earnestly. 'With the old Herr Waechter it will be otherwise; he will not laugh, he will be greatly distressed. If it is really essential that you verify my presence in Gersau on these dates, can it not be arranged that the *Polizei* there speak only with his servant Anton—Anton Hofer? He is in the house for twenty years. I beg this favour of you.'

Julia's earnestness, and probably also the doves' eyes which she turned on the two bucolic policemen, gained her point. 'It shall be done as the Fräulein desires,' the older one said. 'Have no anxiety. *Schönsten Dank, Fräulein*, for your co-operation.' They bowed themselves out, rather awkwardly, past the end of the bed.

Julia was just wondering whether she ought to ring up Herr Waechter herself, and warn him, when Anni, one of the waitresses, came in to say that *die alte Dame* was about to take tea in the garden, and desired to know if the Fräulein would join her? Julia ran down, and found Mrs. Hathaway and Watkins sitting at a table on the gravel, under clipped chestnuts, which constituted the garden of the Silberhorn.

'I thought we would have tea out here, as it's so fine,' Mrs. Hathaway said, 'but perhaps it was a mistake. The tea Watkins makes for me upstairs is much better than this.'

'Swiss tea is Hell,' Julia said, dispassionately—'it was even at the Bergues. I suppose it's because it isn't their drink—coffee yes, tea no. And hadn't we better have some sandwiches or bread-and-butter instead of these ghastly *Kuchen*?' She had bitten into one of the dismal cakes supplied by the hotel, and as she spoke flung the remainder over the low terrace wall into the hayfield below. 'Shall I go and order?' she asked—she knew that Mrs. Hathaway was now drawing an invalid's allowance, and was not limited to £100.

Mrs. Hathaway, laughing, said Yes; Watkins beamed; Julia ran in to Fräulein Hanna and asked for tongue sandwiches and bread-and-butter and honey to be sent out at once. 'And how went it with the *Polizei*?' the Swiss woman asked.

'Oh, they couldn't have been nicer; just a technicality,' Julia said, reassuringly.

'They should not have come,' Hanna said. 'The older one is my cousin—I shall speak with him at Mass on Sunday. Troubling good, polite, *excellent Herrschaften.*' Julia, laughing, returned to the garden; there she found Antrobus sitting at the table, and the tea-tray littered with botanical specimens. As he rose to greet her, she experienced an almost frightening pang of pleasure.

'Oh, how do you do? Bringing your finds to be identified?' she asked teasingly, to conceal her delight.

'Do look, dear child—Mr. Antrobus has brought me the Astrantia and the red Cephalanthera,' Mrs. Hathaway said exultingly. 'And Sweet Woodruff—you know it grows in the

166

Cotswolds; smell how fragrant it is.' She held up a small flower rather like the common Bedstraw, only larger, with frills of leaves in sixes all up its stalk.

'Yes—delicious,' Julia said, knowingly squeezing the stem as she sniffed.

'They make a drink of it here with white wine,' Antrobus said; 'they call it *Mai-Kop*. And the peasants call the plant itself *Waldmeister*'.

'Master of the Forest is a much more imposing name than Sweet Woodruff,' Julia observed.

'I've sometimes wondered if it mightn't really be the same idea,' Antrobus said—'"Woodruff" merely a corruption of "Wood-Reive", the Warden of the Wood.'

'How charming; that had never occurred to me,' said Mrs. Hathaway. 'I shall look it up when I get home. They make a drink of it in Austria too,' she added, 'only there they call it *Mai-Bohle.*'

Julia again smelled the potent scent of the small flower—she liked to think of two different nations using the delicate, precisely-shaped little plant to make a spring drink, and calling it by two such pretty names as May-cup and May-bowl. 'I wonder if it grows here,' she said—'if I could collect enough I'm sure Fräulein Hanna would make us a *Mai-Kop.*'

'It's rather early for it as high as this,' Antrobus replied—surprising Julia, who had not yet grasped that the seasons in Switzerland depend partly on altitude, and that a difference of three thousand feet may also mean a delay of two or three weeks in the flowering of plants. 'But the woods round Interlaken are full of it,' he went on; 'if I can I'll bring up a good bunch tomorrow.'

'Then you must bring it up in time to have the brew made,

and stay and dine,' Mrs. Hathaway said happily; she was greatly taken with Antrobus.

'I should be delighted to do that, if—if I'm not called away,' the man replied, for once showing a trace of embarrassment.

'Oh, are you leaving?' Mrs. Hathaway asked, a note of chill coming into her voice. She belonged to a generation which was accustomed to having its invitations accepted or refused, but not left hanging in the air.

Antrobus did his best.

'Dear Mrs. Hathaway, I hope very much both to be able to bring you the Sweet Woodruff tomorrow, and to dine with you and drink the product. But I am not altogether my own master.'

'Oh.' A pause. 'Then who is your master?' Mrs. Hathaway asked, implacably. Julia listened enchanted to Mrs. H. turning the heat onto the detective—what would he say? She might learn something.

What he said struck the girl at once as being a cover-story.

'My master is one of these modern Juggernauts, the Press-Barons,' he said. 'They are very arbitrary, and quite unpredictable.' He put this out with a rather graceful aplomb, but Mrs. Hathaway, unmollified, regarded him with a steady look which had all the quelling effect of an Edwardian dowager raising her lorgnette to her face. The very fact that she so liked and approved of this man made her all the more severe, now that his behaviour fell short of her standards.

'Oh, you are a journalist?' she said at length. 'I should never have suspected it.'

Nor should I, and I don't believe it for a moment, Julia thought to herself—if that was all he was, why had Nethersole made such a fuss when she asked what he did, at lunch at the Palais des Nations? But she saw Antrobus, at the old lady's tone, actually blush; the ready unconcealable blush of a fair-skinned man. She intervened.

'Mrs H., dear, what's wrong with being a journalist? Aren't I one?'

'Not very seriously, my dear—and only with a very nice Press Baroness!' She turned to Antrobus. 'Well, if Lord X., or Lord Y., or Lord Z., whichever your so needlessly ennobled "master" is'—she put a sardonic stress on the word master—'leaves you free tomorrow evening, it will be delightful to see you at dinner. 7.30. Won't you have another cup of tea?'

Not unnaturally in the circumstances, Mr. Antrobus declined a second cup of tea; he took his leave rather hastily, striding out of the garden on his long legs, got into a large car which he had parked near the cow-stable across the street, and drove off. Watkins excused herself at the same time.

'I never saw a car like that before,' Julia said, as she watched him go. 'I wonder what on earth it is.'

Mrs. Hathaway was often unexpected—she was now.

'It's a Porsche' she said. 'I've seen them in Vienna. Porsche was the man who designed the Volkswagen, and afterwards he made this car too—on the same principle, but bigger and faster. An Austrian friend was telling me about it. Rather expensive for a journalist, I should have thought—they're practically racing cars.'

'Mrs H., what a lot you know! But I think you were rather hard on that wretched man,' Julia said.

'Mr. Antrobus? Why is he wretched?'

'He wasn't, till you made him so. I expect he has quite a sunny nature really,' Julia said, trying to sound casual.

Mrs. Hathaway studied her young friend with a speculative eye. Why this concern for Mr. Antrobus?' She spoke carefully.

'My dear, I am sorry if I have distressed you on his account. I was taken by surprise—his neither accepting nor refusing an invitation was so unexpected, in him.'

'I daresay he really couldn't help it,' Julia said. In fact she had learned nothing from Mrs. Hathaway's pressure except that Antrobus could lie, but not very well. And would he come to dinner tomorrow, after this? She did want him to.

They sat on for a little while, deliberately talking of other things, while the air cooled, and the white peaks across the lake turned to a richer gold; the pine-forests on the slopes in front of them assumed a quite extraordinary colour—a sort of rosy bronze, but with the deep softness of velvet. The white-and-yellow hotel cat came stalking out and sprang and clawed its way up one of the clipped horse-chestnuts, where it stretched and rolled in a broad fork among the branches; Julia laughed at the cheerful animal, and went over to rub its thick coarse fur—she was doing this when Fräulein Hanna came stumping out across the grey gravel on her thick grey-stockinged legs.

'One demands Fräulein Probyn *am Telefon.*'

Julia abandoned the cat and went to that insecure telephone-box in the *Kleine Saal*. The voice was Colin's; he sounded cross.

'Darling, what are you up to? You seem to have stirred up an absolute hornets' nest among the local polus, just when we wanted to do everything as quietly as possible. What goes on?'

'I don't know for sure if anything goes on at all,' Julia said, not in the least disturbed—Colin was so often cross. 'I just had a hunch, and acted on it. The bobbies have been here too,' she added, gurgling.

'Hell! Whatever for?'

'Just to check on me. They were quite sweet.'

'Why did you send them to see the parson?'

'Oh, as a Swiss "reference as to character"—really the only one I've got except Mrs. H.'s old boy-friend, and I made them promise not to worry him.'

'I think you're *quite* mad,' Colin said angrily.

'Could be. Time will show. But I hope someone is keeping an eye on that chemist's, darling darling—I really think that might pay off. Your colleague with the nice voice seemed to be willing to.'

'Oh yes—that's being taken care of. Another dead end, I expect,' he said irritably. 'I wish to God I knew what all this is about.'

'Well when are you coming back to hear? I'm not going to telephone the whole story, automatic or no.'

'I don't know—as soon as I can. But do try to keep *quiet*, will you? This may be rather a crucial forty-eight hours.' He sounded tired, anxious, and overwrought to Julia, who knew his voice so well.

'Bless you, I'll try to. Oh by the way'—she paused for an instant—'What about the detective?'

A click indicated that Colin had already rung off.

171

Chapter 9

Interlaken—the Clinic and the Golden Bear

Alittle before nine on the following morning Julia was finishing her breakfast in the restaurant, vulgarly scraping up the black-cherry jam off her plate with the delicious Beatenberg bread—the rolls, which come up from Interlaken, don't arrive in time for breakfast—when once again she was called to the telephone. An obviously Swiss voice asked, in uncertain English—'It is Miss Probeen who speaks?'

'Yes.'

'Miss Probeen herself?'

'*Aber ja, unbedingt,*' Julia said reassuringly. 'Who wishes to speak with me?'

'One moment please, Fräulein.' There was a pause, a faint confused noise of voices 'off', and then Julia heard June's unmistakable sub-Cockney tones—'Is that Miss Probyn?'

'Yes, Julia Probyn speaking. Is that June?'

'Yes. Oh, I am glad I've got you. You couldn't come down and see me, could you? I *am* so unhappy!—and my ankle's so swollen, it's terrible. The two gentlemen have gone off, so I thought you might come and see me.'

'Of course I will. Where are you?'

'Oh, in ever such a funny little hotel—not a bit like the Flooss! And it's got such a silly name, the Golden Bear. Whoever heard of a golden bear?' June demanded, with a fretful giggle.

'But where is it? What town, I mean?'

'Oh, poor old Interlarken! I don't know why we had to come here; it's ever so small, and one can't see the steamers—well reely one can't see anything! And we rushed away from the Flooss in such a hurry, I couldn't pack properly; and here there's no room to hang anything. My dresses will be ruined, staying in the cases, and not folded right.'

'I'll fold them for you.'

'Oh you are sweet!—I would be glad. But can you come soon? You see I don't know when they'll get back, but not before dinner-time, I don't think.'

Julia guessed that by 'dinner' June meant what she called luncheon.

'I'll come down at once. Not to worry,' she said, employing an idiotic phrase which she hoped would appeal to June. It did; she was rewarded by a happy giggle, and 'Oh, lovely!' Bye-bye—see you in no time.'

Outside the telephone-box Julia consulted the bus timetable which is such an essential feature of life in Beatenberg. The next bus for Interlaken left in five minutes; she raced upstairs, collected a jacket, looked in on Mrs. Hathaway with—'Flying off—can't stop—back some time—and ran down again, out through the *Kleine Saal* and along the gravelled garden to where the bus pulled

173

up, between the cow-stable and a petrol-pump. She just made it, and got the front seat of all, next to the driver.

This happened to be the blond man whose goings-on had exasperated Watkins on the day they arrived. So early in the morning the passengers were mostly local Swiss; they all referred to the driver as 'der Chrigl', the Swiss-German diminutive for the name Christian—and from him, on the way down, Julia enquired how to find the Golden Bear? In the Cantonal-Platz, he told her: along the main street, and then a turning to the left soon after the Post-Bureau. 'It is a very small hotel; few foreigners go there,' der Chrigl observed, eyeing her a little curiously—and most dangerously—as he swung his vast machine round one of the hairpin bends. 'But the Fräulein cannot miss the big golden bear over the door—it glitters.'

The Cantonal-Platz is in the old indigenous Interlaken, which few tourists ever see. Deep-eaved plastered houses line narrow streets, many of which end at the river—then the vista is closed, not by more houses but by the green wooded slopes of the Harder-Kulm, rising steeply above the farther bank. Local trades are carried on here—timber-yards, warehouses for coke and briquettes or for wine, shops for second-hand clothing; Julia paused before a very small window indeed, in which a splendid pair of climbing-boots was displayed for twelve francs, or roughly one pound. She was tempted to go in and try them on, remembering Antrobus's suggestion that she ought to climb; but June was more important, and she walked on. Presently she found the Cantonal-Platz, a very small square, most of one side of which was occupied by the Hotel zum Goldenen Bären and its garden, as usual shaded by clipped horse-chestnuts; exactly opposite stood a rival hostelry, the Gemsbock, also with a garden. But there was no mistaking the one she sought, for in the strong sunshine a

174

large gilt bear glittered—der Chrigl had been quite right—over the entrance. The small door stood open; Julia tapped on it—a middle-aged woman in black, wearing a grey-and-white flowered apron, emerged from the dark interior of the little hallway.

'*Grüss Gott*,' Julia said. 'Could I speak with Miss Armitage?'

The woman, who had a pleasant kindly face, had smiled at the Swiss salutation 'God greet you'; but at the name 'Armitage' her expression became troubled and hesitant. 'I am not sure that the Fräulein is *zu Hause*,' she said doubtfully.

'*Aber ja*, I know she is. She has spoken with me only a short time ago *am Telefon*, and I wish to see about her foot,' Julia replied firmly.

'*Ach so!*—you are the friend. *Ja, die Arme*, it does not go so well with her foot. Please to enter.'

This interchange confirmed Julia's suspicions about how Borovali and Wright probably dealt with June. She followed the woman along the narrow hall and up two flights of steep stairs; at the top, at the far end of a tiny corridor, the woman in the grisaille apron threw open a door, saying 'Fräulein Armitage, you have a visitor!'

In a little, low-ceilinged room June was sitting in a small cheap armchair by a small window, looking out over the Platz, her injured foot propped on a stool; several pieces of luggage, half-opened, with clothes coming out of them, stood about the floor. Besides the bed and the inevitable commode there was a wash-stand with a ewer and basin, a slop-pail under it; a small chest of drawers on which stood a cheap blurred mirror in a wooden frame, and a row of pegs for clothes along the wall in one corner. That was all—the Golden Bear was clearly a very simple hotel indeed. June greeted her in a way which Julia found quite upsetting.

175

'Oh, you *have* come! Well in a way I knew you would, if you promised—but reelly sitting here, I began to think I'd have to live and die in this room. Oh, I do wish I could go home!' As Julia went over to her the little thing stretched up her arms and gave her an almost passionate hug.

'How is your foot?' Julia asked. 'Has the doctor seen it again?'

'No, and it hurts ever so. I am so worried—if it loses its shape I shall be finished for modelling. But I'm not allowed to go out, and Mr. B. says he doesn't want the doctor coming here just now.'

Julia could well understand Mr. B.'s attitude, wicked as she thought it. She pulled down June's stocking; above and below the strapping the flesh was purplish and unwholesome-looking.

'Dr. Hertz must see this,' she said. 'Just wait—I'll go and arrange it.'

'Mr. B. will be mad,' June said, half-alarmed.

'Let him be!' She heard June giggle as she left the room and ran downstairs. From a tiny office off the dark hall she telephoned; Dr. Hertz was in, but could not leave his clinic.

'Then I bring you one of your patients—Fräulein Armitage, this young English girl from the Fluss.'

'Very good—it is time I see this foot again.'

'Well please see her *sogleich*, when we come,' Julia said firmly. 'I think it is urgent, and we shall not have any time to spare.'

'Agreed. Give her name when you arrive.'

Julia asked the woman in black to send for a taxi. 'I take the Fräulein to the doctor; her foot is very bad.'

'But she should not leave the hotel!—those were the wishes of *der Herr*'

'If you do not let her go, I shall fetch the *Polizei*,' Julia said sharply. 'It is essential that she sees the doctor.'

176

The woman crumbled. 'Heinrich!' she called—from the kitchen regions a rather dirty youth appeared, and was dispatched to fetch a taxi. Julia went upstairs again, pulled a foolish velvet slipper onto June's bad foot, unhooked the pale tweed coat which she had seen at Victoria from one of the pegs, and helped the girl into it. Then an idea struck her.

'Where are your hats?'

'All in the hat-box, over there.'

'Have you one with an eye-veil?'

'Oh yes, a lovely one! I've only worn it once, when we went to a bank in Geneva. I'd love you to see it.'

Julia was already pulling hats out of a vulgar tartan-covered hat-box, doubtless Mr. Borovali's choice, and laying them on the bed. 'This one?' she asked, reluctantly admiring Mr. B.'s astuteness.

'Yes, that's it.' June hobbled over to the dim little mirror on the chest of drawers, powdered her face, added—quite needlessly— to her lipstick, and skilfully arranged her pale hair with smart strokes from a semi-circular nylon brush—as she watched this process Julia noticed that a much darker shade was beginning to show at the roots of the pretty *cendré* hair. H'm!

'Have you always been as fair as this?' she asked casually, while the girl was adjusting the hat to a becoming angle.

'Oh no' June replied, without the slightest hesitation—'lovely brown hair, mine is; sort of chestnut, with goldy lights in it. But for this job Mr. Borovali wanted me a real ash-blonde, so in the end I agreed. Mum simply loathed it!—but he paid me twenty quid, in cash, just for the colour of my hair; and I thought that was worth it.'

'It's frightfully becoming,' Julia said. 'Now stop titivating and come on down; the taxi will be waiting. Pull your veil down.'

177

Slowly, they crept down the dark narrow stairs.

Dr. Hertz's clinic was at the far end of the town, beyond the Bahnhof-Platz; it was clean and functional, with trim nurses in attendance, one of whom ushered them into a waiting-room deplorably full of patients—Julia followed her out into the corridor.

'Please inform the Herr Doktor that Fräulein Armitage is here. He knows that she cannot wait, and will see her quickly; we have spoken on the telephone.'

The nurse put on the face of obstruction common to nurses the world over. 'The Herr Doktor sees his patients strictly in rotation' she said smugly.

'You deceive yourself—and seek to deceive me,' Julia said coldly. 'This patient the Herr Doktor will see next.' She took out a card and wrote June's false name on it. 'Have the goodness to take this to the Herr Doktor immediately.'

'He is with a patient,' the nurse said sulkily, barely glancing at the card.

'Naturally—I do not imagine that he sits alone in his surgery!' Julia said laughingly. 'But you can enter and give the card.' She could hear voices from behind a door a little way off, and moved towards it. 'If you do not, *I* do,' she said.

The nurse gave way, and took in the card; in a moment a short man in a white overall, with grey hair and a pale clever face appeared, her card in his hand.

'You bring Miss Armitage? Good—in five minutes I see her.' He said this in quite good English—then he disappeared again.

In the surgery Dr. Hertz frowned as he removed the strapping from June's foot.

'This has been on too long. I arranged it for less than twenty-four hours, and it is now two days'—glancing at a card on his

178

desk. 'I went to the hotel on Tuesday, as arranged, and you had left, giving no address.' He felt the ankle skilfully while he scolded, his hands more sympathetic than his voice. 'Where have you been?'

'We went to another hotel,' June said feebly.

'Then why not leave an address?' He pressed a bell on his desk, and a young man, also in white, appeared. 'An X-ray, at once; and I want the films promptly.' In a moment another nurse came in with a wheeled chair, and June was propelled out.

'I'll come in a minute,' Julia told her, and turned to the doctor. 'Is it serious?'

'I think not, but it is better to know. The swelling may have been just from the strapping, which should have been renewed. But what is this nonsense of changing hotels and leaving no address?' He spoke in the arbitrary manner of a clever busy professional.

'Just a nonsense, as you say,' Julia replied, looking him straight in the eye.

'So?' He was evidently surprised at her tone. 'And this man de Ritter, her guardian—why is he so careless of her health?'

'Well, he just is. Therefore I should like you to inform *me*, exactly, about her condition, and what treatment she ought to have.'

'You are a relation?' the Doctor asked with a certain incredulity, studying Julia's beautiful calm face, and the indefinable distinction of her clothes and her whole appearance.

'No—just a friend. But quite as much *in loco parentis* as Mr. de Ritter,' Julia allowed herself to say, thinking of 'Mum', and again angry at how June was being treated as utterly expendable.

The Doctor continued to eye her steadily and curiously.

'Then may I have your address?' Julia gave it.

'And hers? She is with you?'

'No.' Julia thought quickly.

'Dr. Hertz, I am going to take you into my confidence; and I beg you for the moment to trust me, and not to ask any more questions, for this girl's sake. I would prefer not to give you her present address, for if you were to call there it might put her, I believe, in actual danger.'

He stared at her. 'This sounds like a detective story!'

'It *is* a detective story,' Julia said coolly. 'But if you will tell me, when you have seen the X-ray, what needs to be done, I will see that it gets done, somehow or other.'

He studied her again. 'You ask a great deal; but for some reason I trust you,' Hertz said, with a faint smile. 'I will come to you when I have seen the X-ray; meanwhile I must attend to my other patients. Will you wait in the *Warte-Saal?*'

'You are very kind,' Julia said as she went out.

It seemed hopeless to track June down to the X-ray department, so she sat in the waiting-room; quite soon the girl was wheeled in, giggling and saying that X-rays were ever so funny— 'all that black glass'. And after very little delay they were summoned back to the surgery to hear the verdict. No, no bones broken, only a severe sprain. The foot should be kept up, mostly, but the patient should use it a little every day to prevent stiffness. Hertz eyed June carefully—in spite of all her make-up she looked pale, and somehow slack.

'Get her *out,*' he said to Julia. 'Let her sit in the sun; let her amuse herself. There is a failure of nervous energy; she is altogether below par.'

'Very well. Thank you.' Julia enquired about the fee, which seemed very small, and paid it.

Out in the street—

'Well now, as he says you're to use it a little, see if you can hobble along till we find a carriage,' Julia said. 'Then we'll go and eat cakes somewhere, and look at the shops.' With Julia's arm June got along quite well—'It doesn't hurt nearly so much now,' she announced. 'You are good, to take me there. Was there much to pay?'

'No, hardly anything.'

'Well I'll pay you back when Mr. B. pays me.'

'Aren't you paid by the week?'

'No—he said he'd give it me in a lump at the end,' June said. 'I wish I had a little cash on me sometimes, I must say. I can't even buy a paper.'

Just then one of the open one-horse victorias came by—Julia hailed it, and they got in. 'Where to?' the driver asked.

'To wherever they have the best cakes,' Julia told him—the man whipped up his horse. 'In Interlaken, if one will eat cakes one goes to Schuhs,' he said.

In fact, though Julia did not know it, the cakes at Schuhs in Interlaken have an international reputation—deservedly. They went in to the comfortable old-fashioned place (now alas pulled down) and sat at a table beside windows giving onto the Hohe Matte, the great grassy open space bordered and intersected by avenues of limes and horse-chestnuts which the municipal authorities, wisely regardless of building values, have preserved right in the centre of the town—across it one looks straight up the Lauterbrunnen Valley to the Jungfrau, framed between dark interfolding pine-clad slopes.

'Which would you like, coffee or chocolate?' Julia asked.

'Coffee, please—I'm quite thirsty, and I don't like cocoa.'

'This isn't cocoa,' Julia said, and ordered two chocolates, with cakes.

June was a wholesome creature with a healthy appreciation of physical pleasures, including food; but of this her experience was rather limited. Cups of foamy creamy chocolate, and Schuhs' melting deliciousnessses in the way of cakes—chestnut, caramel, coffee, nut, or cream, with éclairs and *milles-feuilles*, were something she had never dreamed of; she devoured one kind after another, saying at intervals—'But this is *exquisite!*' Presently, sated, she looked out of the window at the Jungfrau, solitary in her green frame.

'Now I call that a pretty mountain,' she said.

'That's the Jungfrau.'

'No! I saw it once on a poster, and I've always wanted to see it—I told Mr. B. so, and he said we'd see it in Interlarken. But you don't see it like this from the Flooss—and from that old Bear you don't see anything!'

Presently they went out and walked along the main street. June Phillips was just the sort of person at whom the window-displays of the Interlaken shops are aimed: the bracelets of edelweiss in imitation ivory, the carved wooden bears, the handkerchiefs luridly embroidered in blue gentians or pink Alpenrosen—she was ravished by them all; the word '*exquisite?*' was never off her lips.

'Oh, I *should* like to get that! I do wish I had some money,' she said at length, stopping in front of an outsize edelweiss brooch, all by itself in a glass case.

'Isn't it rather big for you?

'Oh, I could never wear it; it's not my type at all. I want it for Mum.'

Julia melted to her. She groped in her purse and found that she had 150 Swiss francs in notes, as well as some silver. She handed June the notes. 'Here you are.'

'Sure you can spare it?'

'Yes, quite sure,' Julia said, liking this nice child more than ever, and more than ever hating beastly Mr. Borovali, who wasn't paying her by the week. In deed and in truth she couldn't spare it very well; she had left so hurriedly that she hadn't bothered to lay on her journalist's allowance, expecting to spend most of her time at Herr Waechter's, all for free, with a brief dash to Bellardon and Geneva. But the Bergues had been very expensive, the Silberhorn was not cheap—and even things like her run to Merligen and this down to Interlaken mounted up. But Mrs. H. would see her through, at a pinch—come to that, Colin could pay for the Merligen trip!

They went in and bought the brooch. June was rather tempted by a carved wooden holder for toilet-paper, which played a tune as one pulled on the roll; she shrieked with laughter when the shop-girl demonstrated it, but decided against it. 'It's ever so comical, but it's a tiny bit vulgar, don't you think? I don't believe Mum would care about it.' For herself she bought nothing but a handkerchief embroidered in gentians of a deplorably violent blue. She took another of these and gave it to Julia.

'There—now we both have a souvenir of how we met! I'm quite thankful now I picked those silly flowers—if I hadn't I'd never have got to know you.'

Julia was more moved by this than she expected. Out in the street June suddenly began to wilt. 'Oh, my foot does hurt again! Is it far to that Bear?' Julia hailed one of the open carriages trotting leisurely by, and they drove off. Glancing at her companion she noticed that she had pushed her eye-veil up to examine the brooch and handkerchiefs.

'Pull your veil down, June,' she said.

The child obeyed at once, but asked, 'Why on earth?'

'Oh, it's so much prettier—and Mr. Borovali didn't want you to be seen much outside, did he?'

'No. Oh mercy, I do hope they aren't back yet. What's the time?'

'Only just twelve. Anyhow I'll deal with him if they are there.'

'I *hate* this job!' June burst out nervously, as the cab turned into a side street. 'I don't know what really goes on; I mean, it's all so peculiar. I believe there's more in it than meets the eye. I do wish I were out of it.'

Julia instantly tried to profit by this frame of mind.

'It must be very worrying for you,' she said. 'But, June, can you tell me one thing? When you were at the bank in Geneva, did Mr. Borovali take anything away with him—papers and so on?'

'Oh, I'd tell you anything! Where should I be without you? Lose my foot, as like as not! Yes, masses of papers was what he took—they were carried in on a sort of tin tray. There was two lots—one whitish papers, some with red stars on them; and then there was a great big envelope with blue papers in it. Ever so funny, they were; Mr. B. had them all out to look at them, and they had white lines, well sort of drawings, on them—he looked ever so pleased when he got those.'

'What did he take them away in? Not the tin tray, surely?'

June giggled.

'No—a black sort of leather bag, like business-men carry. Thin as misery it was when we went in, and stuffed out fat when we came out, like this'—she held up her small beautifully-shaped hands some six inches apart.

'Did you have to sign anything?'

'Aoh no—Mr. B. did all the signing. I just told the old gentleman that Mr. B. was my guardian—of course I called him Mr. de Ritter. That was what they told me to say beforehand, and it seemed all right then; I mean, I know it was telling lies, but that seemed so little to do for a month's keep, and all my outfit—and the pay as well. But now'—she paused.

'Yes?' Julia prompted.

'Well now I'm beginning to think there's something really screwy about the whole thing,' June said worriedly. 'It's partly Mr. B. turning so nasty lately, and keeping me shut up; if there was no harm in it, why doesn't he go on being nice, like he was at first? If people get nasty, it generally means there's something wrong behind it, in my opinion. What do *you* think?'

Julia had been doing a positive *blitz-think* ever since June first burst out about hating the job; wondering, given the child's extreme innocence and bird-wittedness, whether it would help her to give a guarded warning about the character of her two companions, or whether it would be safer to leave ill alone. She hedged.

'It does all seem rather odd,' she said. 'Did Mr. Borovali ever tell you why he wanted to be called Mr. de Ritter, and Mr. Wright to be called Mr. Monro?'

'No, not why. He just said that was the job. But if you ask me the real reason, I haven't a clue,' June replied—so airily that Julia had an impression that the girl might be hedging in her turn. In any case she, Julia, who had such an ample clue, decided not to enlighten her as yet.

'Oh well, I shouldn't worry too much,' she was saying when the cab pulled up before the Golden Bear. In the hallway she asked the woman in the grisaille apron if *die Herren* had returned? They hadn't, and she ordered June's lunch to be served in her room—'The Fräulein is tired, and Dr. Hertz says she must rest.' In fact she put her to bed, and then, as she had promised on the telephone, she unpacked all the suit-cases,

185

shook out the clothes, and repacked them, folding them neatly on the bed across June's knees and feet.

'Goodness, you are a lovely packer! Where did you learn?' June asked.

'Oh, I travel a lot,' Julia said carelessly, going on with her work; June watched her in silence for some time, and then surprised her with a question.

'How did *you* know we went to that bank in Geneva?'

Julia straightened up from a suit-case, startled; to gain time she lit a cigarette. 'Sorry—what did you say?'

'I asked how you knew we'd been to that bank in Geneva?'

'But, June, you told me yourself that you'd worn the hat with the eye-veil when you went to the bank, and what you'd been told to say.'

'Oh yes, so I did. But why did you ask me about the papers Mr. B. picked up? And what he took them away in?' The girl had suddenly turned suspicious, with the ready suspicion of the under-educated and underprivileged. Julia decided that up to a certain point it was no use hedging any more. She went over to the bed.

'Listen, June. You know as well as I do that your real name is June Phillips, and that Mr. Borovali paid you twenty pounds to dye your hair to impersonate a girl called Aglaia Armitage, who really has got ash-blonde hair.'

'So what?' June asked defiantly.

'So nothing. I went to the bank on behalf of the real Miss Armitage, to see about her money, and found that some other people had been there before me and taken it away. That's all— quite enough too, I think, to make me want to know what's become of it.'

'So you're a spy? That's why you've been being nice to me? Oh!—oh my God, what *am* I to do? Now there's no one.' She burst into tears.

Julia waited and let the poor little thing sob herself out, her face buried in the pillow; she was distressed on her behalf, but sooner or later this probably had to come. Presently June stopped crying, and raised a sad and swollen face.

'Oh, I'm sorry I said that. I don't know whether I'm coming or going—and now my foot and all. I do *wish* I could get home.' She began to cry again. Then, with a sudden flash—'But I must have my clothes and my pay!'

At this point a maid brought up June's lunch on a tray; it was ample, and smelt good. Julia arranged it all: poured out the soup, set a chair by the bed and put the other dishes on it, gave her a hanky to dry her eyes, and started her on her meal—to her astonishment, in spite of all those cakes at Schuhs June tucked into it with a will, while Julia finished the packing. Then she looked at her watch, and went over and sat on the bed.

'June, will you listen to me?' she said slowly—'I shall have to go in a minute.'

Her mouth full, the girl nodded.

'When I saw you up on the Niederhorn,' Julia went on, 'I recognised you as the girl who was pretending to be Miss Armitage; and when I went down to help you with the man who wanted to take you up for picking those gentians, I did want to get in touch with you, and find out anything I could. But then you hurt your foot, and we talked, and you told me about yourself; and we've talked again today. And now I want to help *you*. I hope you believe that. I think you're a good girl, really; and though you must have known that it was wrong to tell lies for money, I think perhaps you didn't fully understand what you were being used for.'

June clutched at this—which was letting her out rather liberally.

'Well yes, I did know it was wrong, in a way; but the little they told me, I thought of it as a bit of a fiddle—rather a lark, really, just to show up at that bank and say Mr. B. was my guardian and Wright my fiancé. As if I'd marry *him*! And then to have my lovely outfit. But I am sorry now—I wish I'd never done it. You don't think'—again there was a return of that curious anxiety— 'that it's doing any *real* harm, do you?'

Julia wondered what this odd little being meant by 'real' harm, when another girl's fortune had been stolen.

'I hope it won't,' she said soberly. 'But we must get Miss Armitage's papers back, you know.'

'Oh yes, I see that. And you'll forgive me?—please do. I'd no idea it was a friend of *yours* that the money belonged to.'

Julia could have laughed at this further example of modern morality.

'Yes, of course I forgive you. Now do look after that foot, and if you move anywhere else be sure to let me know—I expect to be at the Silberhorn for another ten days at least.' She looked again at her watch—twenty to one; she didn't want 'Mr. B.' to catch her in June's room.

'Oh, I will,' June said earnestly. 'You've been so sweet. I'm ever so sorry I was nasty just now—all along you've helped me, whatever your reasons.'

'That's all right. Goodbye, dear.'

June held out her arms—awkwardly, over the tray—and gave her a long kiss. 'You will forget what I said?' she muttered.

'Yes. And you'll trust me?'

'Oh, I will. Who else have I to trust *to*, out here?'

'Trust in God,' said Julia, and went out.

Chapter 10

Interlaken—the Golden Bear and the Gemsbock

When Julia left June's room she found herself in that little dark narrow corridor, now feebly lit by a single electric bulb, left on presumably by the maid who had brought up the tray; in its faint glow two glassy eyes shone out at her—startled, she went over to look. A stuffed marmot, rather moth-eaten, occupied the blind end of the passage, standing on a plaster rock; Julia laughed softly to herself—how Swiss!—and then gave a tiny sigh, recalling that happy morning on the Schynige Platte, only three days ago, and how Antrobus showed her and Mrs. Hathaway live marmots on the way up. Turning from the animal, she examined the corridor. It had only four doors, June's and three others. Were Wright's and Borovali's rooms up here too, she wondered? Softly, carefully, she tried the second door on June's side; it was locked. Feeling that she might be taking a foolish risk, but unable to resist the temptation, she went silently back towards the marmot, with its silly seal's face, and tried the last door on the left, opposite June's. To her surprise it opened, and she stepped into a small room exactly like the one she had just left, even to the pegs on the wall in one corner; on these, carefully suspended from a coat-and-trouser hanger, hung a wind-cheater and a pair of pale corduroy slacks. Julia recognised them at once; she was in Wright's room.

Her heart began to beat rather fast. She moved cautiously over to the window, which gave onto a timberyard shaded by an immense walnut-tree; beyond, over a vista of shingled roofs rose the steep wooded ridge of the Harder-Kulm, its pine-toothed crest cutting the sky like a green saw. She looked round the sparsely-furnished apartment and now noticed that there was a door communicating with the next room, which stood ajar; she tiptoed over and looked in. In the ewer on the wash-stand just opposite was a huge bunch of *Waldmeister;* she pushed the door a little farther open—standing at the chest of drawers under the window and methodically going through its contents stood Antrobus.

For a moment Julia paused, undecided whether to advance or retreat; then the fact that he was rummaging through what were almost certainly Mr. Borovali's clothes suddenly gave her, she thought, the answer to the question that had been tormenting her for days, and the relief was so great that she gave a little gasping laugh. The man looked round.

'Well, well, if it isn't Fatima!' This time the name didn't come like a blow at all; his voice was almost caressing as he turned to her. Still utterly taken aback, Julia came in and sank down on what was presumably Mr. Borovali's bed; the only chair was covered with underclothes from the chest of drawers.

'How on earth did you know they were here?' she asked.

'I didn't, till you showed me. I saw you and that pretty little creature, Miss Armitage's stand-in, driving along in a *Fiaker*, and followed you. At Cambridge I used to be a tolerable half-miler, but one doesn't need a great turn of speed to keep up with an Interlaken horse-cab,' he said, grinning, as he came and perched beside her on the bed.

'I think we'd better clear off,' Julia said, suddenly nervous.

'No, we've got lots of time. They took packed lunches with them—I asked the old Frau downstairs.' He was perfectly at ease. As for Julia, a dozen questions were battling for priority in her head—a rather foolish one came out.

'Why on earth do you suppose they leave their doors unlocked?'

'They didn't. But I happen to be rather good at opening doors.' He pulled a bunch of curious-looking metal instruments from his pocket. 'A burglar, you see, rather than a detective,' he said gaily.

Julia was rather irritated by his nonchalance.

'Don't you think it's about time you came clean?' she asked crisply. 'What you said just now about that poor little creature being a 'stand-in' sounds as if we were on the same side; but I have to be sure. Can you give me any proof that you are? Colin doesn't know you.'

'My dear girl, do relax,' Antrobus said gently, putting his hand on hers. 'No, your delightful cousin doesn't know me, and I didn't know him when we met up at Beatenberg. But he and I are on the same job.'

'Then why didn't you know him?' Julia asked suspiciously.

'Oh, the two branches—the same initials, but different numbers, you know. We tackle things on rather separate lines.'

'None of that is proof,' she objected.

'You are perfectly right—it isn't; and you are also quite right

191

to make sure. I see that you are every bit as good as Torrens says.'

Hugh Torrens's name upset Julia afresh; that was still a sore subject.

'How does Major Torrens come into this?' she asked, trying to sound indifferent. 'Do you know him?'

'Of course. He's rather big brass, whereas your cousin is very junior. Look, do stop worrying, Julia, and let me explain. Will you?' He asked this in a very beguiling voice.

'I wish to goodness you *would*—I think we've been fencing about quite long enough,' she said.

'Very well. Let's begin with the birth of the Dragon, like the man who wrote the Life of St. George.' Julia laughed. 'I did rather wonder,' Antrobus pursued, 'what you were up to when we kept on meeting in all the relevant places—Victoria, and Geneva, and so forth. And when you seemed in such close touch with that girl up at Beatenberg, kissing her in the bus and so on, I became definitely suspicious. So naturally I rang up London to make enquiries, and was put on to Torrens; and he told me all about the really splendid job you'd done in getting Dr. Horvath out of Portugal. It was you who arranged the hide-out for him with that duke who breeds sheep up in the North, wasn't it? At Gralleira, or some such name.'

This really was proof, and Julia did at last relax, with infinite relief. But her next question surprised him.

'Do they know your name in Berne?'

'Who? The outfit your cousin works with? Of course. Why?'

'I do wish Colin wasn't such a *clot!*' Julia said. 'I've kept on asking him to check on you there, and he never has. If only he had, I should have known where I was.'

'Well do you know where you are now?' he asked, very kindly.

'Oh *vis-à-vis* you, yes at last, thank goodness!' But the form of

192

the question revived her anxiety on June's account—anything might happen if Borovali caught them in his room. 'Look, have you finished your detection in that chest of drawers?' she asked—'because if so I do think we ought to go. Merligen is no distance away—they might come back quite soon.'

'Why should you think they have gone to Merligen?' the man asked, staring at her.

'Oh, just a hunch—and a little private detection on my part.'

'Goodness, was it you who triggered off the Merligen thing?' He shouted with laughter. 'Do tell me all.'

'I simply won't, here.' She got up off Mr. Borovali's bed; so did he, and she watched with interest the meticulous care with which he rearranged all that worthy's effects in the drawers he had been examining, polishing the knobs and edges with a silk handkerchief as he closed them. He leaned out of the window and studied the timber-yard below—'Easy of access isn't the word,' he muttered—'Even a ladder.' Finally he gathered up the dripping bunch of Sweet Woodruff from the ewer on the wash-stand, and mopped the stalks on the bath-towel. 'That will tell him nothing—he'll just think it's his own feet!' he said, grinning. 'All right—where are you going now?'

'I rather thought I'd like to wait and see Mr. B. and Mr. W. come back,' Julia said. 'But how do you re-lock this door? And don't talk in the passage, or the child will hear. Wait till we get down.'

Again with deep interest she watched him polish the door-handles, and re-lock the door of Wright's room with one of his skeleton keys. Half-way down the stairs—'Where do you propose to conduct this piece of detection?' he asked over her shoulder.

'There's another little pub just across the Platz, and I thought of having a beer or something in the garden there. It has a nice spindly hedge one could see through—I noticed it.'

'All right—I want a beer, anyhow.'

In the hall downstairs Antrobus exchanged some friendly remarks with the woman in the grey-flowered apron, ending with the words '*Auf wiederluoge!*'

'Is that the Berner-Deutsch for *Auf wiedersehen?*' Julia asked, as they went out into the hot sunny little Platz.

'Yes. *"Luoge"* and "Look" are obviously the same root— "Till we look again." Their phrase for "Look here" is like it: *"Luoge-Du"*—"Look thou!" Amusing, isn't it?'

'Yes, charming.'

The other hotel, the Gemsbock, had a small and rather stuffy garden enclosed in the privet hedge already observed by Julia; over its door a wooden chamois, rather dingy, confronted the gilt bear opposite. Julia went and sat down at a table on the extreme left of the entrance, exactly opposite the door of the Bear, and peered through the straggling hedge.

'Perfect,' she said in a satisfied tone. 'We can see everything, but from outside you can't see a thing—I looked as we came across.'

'How thorough you are!' Antrobus said laughing, as he sat down opposite her, and laid his bunch of flowers on the table. 'Now, please tell me why you want to watch these individuals' return?'

'Well really, I should have thought you could guess that! To see if they've been able to drop the papers in Merligen, of course.'

He gave her a long amused stare.

'You evidently know more about Merligen than I have yet been told. However, we can go into that later. But how do you expect to know, simply from looking at them, whether these unpleasing creatures have left the papers there or not?'

At this point a pretty waitress in a short-sleeved cotton frock and a lace-trimmed apron came up and asked what they wished.

'*Bier*,' Julia said.

'*Hell oder dunkel?*'

'*Hell*,' Julia replied. In German 'Hell' merely means light beer; Antrobus also ordered 'Hell', and the pretty maid tripped away.

'Well, go on—how will you know, from seeing them?' Antrobus asked.

'They carried off the papers from the Banque Républicaine in Geneva in a black brief-case, stuffed out fat. If they come back with a thin brief-case, or none, I shall deduce that they unloaded the goods at Merligen; if they bring it back as fat as ever I shall hope that they've been stymied there, and still have what we're after with them.'

'How do you know about the black brief-case? Oh, the little girl, I suppose. You kissed her in the bus to some purpose—no wonder, of course.'

'Don't!' Julia said sharply. Her relations with June were beginning to trouble her, they were so equivocal.

'So sorry. But what put you on to Merligen in the first place?'

'Well really, I don't know what the British Government think they pay you for!' Julia said. 'You say you're functioning out here, and I presume you draw a tolerable salary, since you run a Porsche on it, and yet you never seem to put two and two together. Do you really not know that "Corsette-Air" have their Swiss Agency in Merligen? I told you and Nethersole how I met the little man who runs it in the train, just to make a story—and somehow I got the impression that you did know something about them.'

'Can you tell me why you got that impression?' he asked, rather seriously.

'Oh, you looked so dead-pan,' the girl said. 'People like you and Hugh never seem to realise that that blank expression can be quite as much of a give-away as registering emotion of some sort. Nethersole laughed; you didn't—and that in itself made me begin to wonder. I hadn't given two thoughts to the little man before that.'

Antrobus regarded her across the little table. 'You are slightly alarming,' he said—'especially because your appearance gives so little indication of these gifts. Well, go on—my blank expression at the Palais des Nations focused your suspicions on "Corsette-Air". So then?'

'When B. and Co. left the Fluss, Colin asked me to try to find out where they'd gone, so I went to Merligen to call on Monsieur Kaufmann at his villa.'

'And what did you find?'

Julia told him what she had found, and how she had reported to the local police. 'I was afraid they'd simply take me for a harmless loony; I was absolutely delighted when the Pastor de Ritter rang up and said the police had been to him to check. But Colin was merely furious! Can you tell me one thing?—are they watching that chemist in Berne? Because I do think—' she broke off with a sudden exclamation. 'Hullo! Here they are!'

Peering through the hedge she and Antrobus saw two figures crossing the little Platz towards the Golden Bear—one with a greying beard, the other the young, sinisterly handsome creature whom Antrobus had seen up at Beatenberg; he carried a black brief-case positively distended by its contents. Both men looked hot and out of temper.

'Hooray!' Julia said under her breath. 'They've not been able to unload them.'

'No, it looks as though you'd stopped that earth. But I'd better find out.' He made to rise, as the two men entered the other hotel.

'Oh wait a moment, for goodness' sake! There's something we must settle.'

'What?' he asked rather impatiently.

'We shall have to arrange something about June.'

'June? Oh, is that the little creature? Why do we have to settle anything about her? She's an accessory to a major fraud, and as such liable to quite a long sentence.'

'Oh, accessory my elbow! She's a nice, harmless child whom these horrible crooks have roped in—well, bribed in—for their own ends, and they'd be absolutely merciless to her if she got in their way, or was a hindrance. They've been pretty merciless already'—she recounted their visit to the clinic and the state of June's foot.

'Oh, that's where you took her?'

'Yes, and then to Schuhs to gobble—and after we did some shopping. But look—when you pounce, as I suppose you will in a few hours, can't you do something about her? That ankle of hers needs regular attention—it's her livelihood. And those toads would just pitch her into the Aar as soon as look at you.'

'What a nice person you are,' he said. 'But my dear, I'm not the one to do the actual pouncing—that's up to your cousin and his show.'

'Oh!' Julia was taken aback. 'Why?'

'I told you. I deal with the local people; Colin's lot work with Interpol and the Special Police, who handle international crime. We work in, of course, and that's why I really must go and telephone now.'

'Who to?'

'Well first to Merligen, to find out if B. and K.'—Julia grinned

197

at the familiar phrase—'succeeded in getting into the Villa Victoria or not. Then I shall report to Berne accordingly, telling them the new address, of course.'

'And then will Colin and Co. pounce?'

'I expect so.' He got up, and then sat down again. 'Really, I think I'd better explain the whole set-up, as you seem to be playing these uncontrollable lone hands—and I'm sure no one can stop you! They'd be foolish to try, really, because "the Fatima touch" does seem to produce results.'

'What is the set-up, then?'

'Two-fold. That's what makes it rather complicated. Large sums of money and securities have been extracted by an elaborate fraud, from a Swiss bank, and naturally the Swiss authorities wish to recover that, lay the thieves by the heels, and save the bank's good name. But we'—to her surprise he paused, and looked at her consideringly.

'Well, "we" what?' July asked impatiently.

'You do *know* what your cousin is after?' he asked. 'I don't want to be the one to tell you.'

'Oh really!' Julia exploded. 'No, I know *nothing*! Except that Colin wrote that some vital papers were in the bank along with the cash; and the Pastor spoke of "the oil question"; and June has described seeing "blue papers with white drawings on them" put into that brief-case we saw just now. So I deduce blue-prints for a hidden pipeline, or an atomic-powered submarine oil-tanker, or something. But does it matter?'

'Yes, it does matter,' Antrobus said, rather severely. 'However, I am satisfied; you're so near the mark as makes no difference, anyhow. Well our people, unlike the Swiss, aren't worrying very much about the late Mr. Thalassides' fortune, or whether the real Miss Armitage recovers it or not; but they do want those blue-prints—and they don't want anyone else, not even the good neutral Swiss, to see them. That's why your cousin's outfit must do the pouncing themselves; the Swiss police can have the cash, but the important thing is that Colin and Co. should get what they want first.'

'I see.' She summed it up aloud. 'You find out all you can from your local contacts, and pass the proceeds on to Berne; but after that your main job is to hold off the locals while Berne pounces. Correct?'

'Perfectly correct.' Again he got up.

'No—sit down.' Grinning a little, he obediently sat down once more. 'We still haven't settled about *June*,' the girl said. 'You rode off onto all this stuff about your separate branches. But when Colin's lot do pounce, what will happen to June?'

'My dear, how can I answer that one? I probably shan't be there. Can't you get your cousin to deal with that?'

'No!' Julia said. 'That's absurd, and you know it. As you yourself said, Colin is very junior, and presumably cuts no ice at all. We've got to do something about June.'

He looked at his watch.

'I am so sorry,' he said rather formally, 'but I positively must go and telephone now, or I shall be falling down on my job. Where can I find you? Where shall you lunch?'

'Nowhere!—here; I haven't thought.'

'Well lunch here, or anyhow stay here for the next half-hour. I should be back by then; we might lunch together, and try to plan something for your little stand-in.' Julia agreed to this, and Antrobus went off.

Julia ordered a Cinzano—beer made one so sleepy—and sat on behind the hedge, thinking where June could be stowed, or parked, if it were possible to get her away from the Golden Bear.

The Silberhorn was not much use: it was too close, for one thing, and June's presence wouldn't really help Mrs. Hathaway's convalescence, while Watkins would probably despise her to the point of hatefulness. Then where? Gersau? No—Herr Waechter was too old to have that sort of thing put on him. After a moment it came to her—La Cure would be the ideal place, if Jean-Pierre and Germaine would take the job on; and she believed they might. She went along to the little hotel, which was even humbler than the Bear; the telephone was in the hall, but she had the good fortune to get Jean-Pierre himself, so the conversation could be in English. Julia explained, with calculated vagueness and no names, what her idea was.

'I see,' the Pastor said at the end. 'You wish us to house for an indefinite time a very uneducated English girl, who is connected with criminals. Yes, of course we will; gladly.'

'You're an angel!'

'Not in the least. I am supposed to preach Christianity and what is Christianity about, but things like this? When do you want her to come?'

'I don't know yet. It may be at rather short notice, I'm afraid.'

'Ah well, Germaine always has rooms ready.' He paused, and then said, 'Do not answer if I am being indiscreet, but could this be *la jeune personne* who has recently purported to be my god-daughter?'

'Yes—who else?'

'Then *raison de plus* for my entertaining her!' the Pastor said, with his infectious laugh. 'A god-child is probably still a god-child, even at one remove! *Alors très-bien;* I shall await your *coup de téléphone*'.

Julia went out in to the garden again. This was marvellous. But as she sat looking up at the window on the extreme right of the Bear's front door, which she knew to be June's, she wondered how on earth she was to extract the girl from that innocent-looking little hotel, which was now her prison. Perhaps Antrobus could help—if he would. He wasn't very sympathetic about June.

Before she expected him he reappeared through the garden, and stood beside her.

'Goodness, I never saw you come.'

'No. Back entrance—no need to be seen too often. Now let's go and eat something; you must be starving.'

'Did they leave the papers at Merligen?' Julia asked, as he led her out through another garden gate into a small alley.

'No—you fixed them there. Most useful. The local police were lurking in the next-door garden, and they saw them and cleared off. That was rather inspired of you.'

'Where do we eat?' Julia asked, turning the compliment off.

'Oh, a nice little place, in the main street.'

They did not, however, walk to it along the main street. Antrobus shepherded her down to that delightful hidden feature of Interlaken, the narrow path leading almost from one end of the town to the other along the river-bank, flanked on one side by back-yards, gardens, walls, and orchards, and on the other by the broad viridian-green current of the Aar, twisted into swirling patterns by its own speed. Close above the surface of the great river swifts skimmed to and fro, the bronze of their slender bodies and back-curved wings vivid in the sun, in exquisite contrast with the colour of the water—Julia exclaimed with pleasure. A little farther on, where trees overhung a back-water with a private landing-stage, a loud alarmed chittering of birds' voices brought her to a halt.

'Oh do look! There's a whole family of young redstarts—see?

201

Let's hurry on; Papa and Mamma are in such a fuss, poor sweets.'

'Birds, too?' the man asked.

'No, only the commonest.'

At that moment a train, which had crossed by the bridge across the river from the East-Station, crashed along the farther bank opposite them on its way to recross the Aar farther down to reach the West-Station.

'So like the Swiss to have the intelligence to keep the railway outside the town,' Antrobus said. 'Their sense for the amenities is quite extraordinary.'

'I was thinking that in Schuhs this morning,' Julia replied. 'God knows what they must have sacrificed in ground-rents to keep that lovely open space right in the heart of the town.'

'The Hohe-Matte? Yes, simply inspired. Of course you may say it's an enlightened self-interest, because of the *turismo*—but how unenlightened our own self-interest is! Can you imagine the humblest Swiss municipality allowing Adelphi Terrace to be destroyed, simply to get inflated rents for office buildings? But London allowed it. People sometimes say the Swiss are dull, but at least they aren't idiotic, which in aesthetic matters we are. Up here.'

A small road led from the river to the main street, where Antrobus led Julia into the garden of a small restaurant, as usual with tables set on gravel in the shade of trees. A waitress brought the menu. 'Have you eaten Brienzerli?' he asked.

'No—what's that?'

'A strange little fish from the Lake of Brienz—rather like smelts. They're delicious—care to try them? All right, we'll have those—and Wiener Schnitzel, do you think? They do them quite well here; the chef is a Czech refugee. What for an apéritif?'

Julia asked for White Cinzano.

'How comes it that you know that? It suits this climate so much better than anything else.' He gave the order, insisting in Berner-Deutsch that the Cinzano was to come instantly; the waitress giggled, but in fact brought it within sixty seconds. While they smoked and sipped the fragrant aromatic stuff—'Now,' Antrobus said, 'let us make plans for your little protégée.'

'In fact I've made mine.'

'Already? Oh very well. May I know what your scheme is?'

'Of course. You'll have to help with the preliminaries, but she's to go to La Cure at Bellardon.'

'Good Heavens! Will they have her there?'

'Yes—as soon as I telephone.'

'Do they know she's the fraud?'

'But naturally. Jean-Pierre said a god-child was a godchild, even at one remove,' Julia said, with her slow laugh.

'He must be a remarkable person,' Antrobus said slowly.

'Oh he is. Such a charmer, and absolutely boiling with Kafka and Rilke and all that.'

'Kafka and Rilke don't by themselves necessarily produce actions like this,' he said.

'Not? I've never read them,' Julia confessed. 'But you see he's a Christian, too; when I thanked him he said—"This is what Christianity is about."'

'Extraordinary,' Antrobus muttered broodingly.

'Oh, is it? I don't see why. Don't you know any Christians? I know several, and this sort of thing is really common form with them,' Julia pronounced, thinking of the Duke of Ericeira and other people in Portugal. 'Anyhow, have you never read the New Testament?'

While he was laughing the Brienzerli appeared; crisp little fish fried a golden brown, but with much bigger heads than smelts. Julia tucked into them eagerly. 'Goodness, I am hungry. And these are delicious.' Antrobus was hungry too, and they ate practically in silence; having finished her fish Julia asked—'Did you get Berne?'

'Yes.'

'When do they pounce?'

'Not today.'

'Why not?'

'Because they rather hope that if they wait till "the principals" come—the higher-ups in the organisation that is after the papers—it might be possible to snaffle them too. It's not certain, of course; that's part of the complication.'

'Any idea who these principals are? Sheiks or Emirs, one supposes; but they would be rather noticeable if they turned up in long robes and a silver-plated aeroplane, or a solid gold Cadillac.'

He laughed.

'They won't do that. The principals almost certainly represent a particular financial—and political—interest which supplies the gold Cadillacs to the Sheiks and Emirs.'

'I see.' She paused, frowning. 'Yes, I see. Look, John, we ought to get that child away before all this starts.' She stopped as the little waitress removed the remains of the Brienzerli and put the veal and salad before them.

'Have you a plan for her actual removal?' he asked.

'Not yet. It was no good trying to arrange anything till I had somewhere to put her; which I hadn't, this morning—and anyhow I should be rather frightened of letting her know of a plan in advance.'

'Why? Is she unreliable?' His voice was cold; Julia realised that for Antrobus June was still simply one of a gang of criminals, a willing accessory to a fraud.

'Yes, completely unreliable,' she replied readily. 'Not from vice; it's simply that she's so frightfully silly—she's really almost an institutional case. It's not her character I distrust, it's her I.Q.!'

He accorded the phrase a frosty smile.

'Then what do you propose to do? Just walk in and sweep her off?'

'Not unless those two murky characters are out of the way. I'm sure they'd shoot us both for tuppence. No, I think this is where you come in. You're in touch with the local police, who I presume will now be hovering nonstop in the Gemsbock garden. Can't you arrange for them to give me a ring when B. and K. go out, so that I can hustle down and collect June?'

'No. I'm sorry, but that wouldn't work. You see, for one thing you are now on their list of suspects.' He grinned at her.

'Oh how unfair! They ought to be grateful to me; and so ought you, and Colin and his lot.'

'I am,' he said, suddenly serious. 'And so will your cousin's superiors be when they have digested the facts—which I shall give them. But I don't propose to furnish those facts to the Swiss at this stage.'

Julia munched her veal.

'I don't suppose Chambertin told them, either,' she said, forking salad into her mouth.

'Chambertin of the Banque Républicaine? What might he, or might he not, have told them?'

'Only that it was I who sent him the photograph of the real Aglaia Armitage, from *Paris-Match*, which was reproduced and circulated to all the Swiss police. That's why Borovali and Co. fled from the Fluss to the Bear.'

'How do you know that?—apart from having so usefully

furnished the photograph, a fact I didn't know myself.'

'Oh, the porter at the Fluss told me why they left—Mr. B. came down at the very moment when the photograph was lying on his desk, with the Bumbles enquiring. And the Super or what-ever you call them here at Merligen had a copy too—he showed it to me.'

He shouted with laughter.

'Oh Fatima, Fatima! You don't need to open doors; everyone tells you everything, seemingly. Not that I'm in the least surprised, mind you—if I were a Swiss policeman or a hotel porter I should tell you everything myself!'

'Well I do think it's hard that at least one Swiss policeman can't be organised to let me know when Messrs. B. and W. go on their next little trip, so that I could twitch June away,' Julia persisted. 'But if they can't, can't you? I do think you might.'

'My dear, if I possibly can, I will. Of course I ought not to, and I can't altogether share your affection for the little imper-sonator. Probably I shall be compounding a felony, or some crime like that. But she can always be picked up at the good Pastor's, and I agree that anyone would be better away from B. and K.'

'Well give me all the notice you can,' Julia said, with her usual practicality. 'Bellardon is a long way away.'

A clock struck from one of the towers of the two churches, the Catholic and the Protestant, which stand side by side at the eastern end of the Hohe Matte, the chime ringing out through the sunny hay-scented air.

'Goodness, it's a quarter to three! I must simply race, or I shall miss my bus,' Julia exclaimed.

'But you've had no coffee.'

'Can't be helped,' she said, rising. 'Thank you for the lovely lunch—and be sure to let me know when Mr. B. goes to have his beard trimmed at the coiffeurs, or whatever.'

Antrobus had risen too.

'Would it be a great nuisance to take this with you to Mrs. Hathaway?' he asked, holding out the now rather drooping bunch of *Waldmeister*, which during lunch had lain on the gravel under his chair, in the shade.

A chill of dismay struck Julia.

'No, of course. But does that mean you aren't coming to dine?'

'Yes, please God I am—with this pause I think I can get away all right. But the longer this little herb is steeped in the white wine, the better our *Mai-Kop* will be.' As he spoke an empty horse-carriage came clopping along outside the open garden— Antrobus hailed it, paid the driver, and handed Julia in.

'There—now you won't have to race,' he said. Julia leaned out towards him.

'Why on earth did you tell that frightfully silly story about being a journalist to Mrs. H.?' she asked, rather anxiously.

'To tell you the truth, I lost my head. I do occasionally—in fact quite often!' he said, grinning at her; if a grin can express a *double-entendre*, that one did.

'Well keep it tonight—and think up some corroborative detail,' Julia said urgently. 'You can't fool Mrs. Hathaway at all easily.'

'I'm sure not! I'll do my best.' He spoke to the driver. 'Beatenberg Post-Auto, Bahnhof-Platz.' As she drove off *'Auf wiederluoge!* Sorry about the coffee,' he called after her.

Julia enjoyed the drive, short though it was. Her over-mastering feeling was of relief at the knowledge that Antrobus was on their side; this coloured her own feelings towards him. It would have been impossible to—well, to let oneself go at all with a person who was in league with crooks; but as it was—. She didn't finish that sentence in her head; anyhow, he was coming to dinner tonight.

On the broad sunny Bahnhof-Platz the Interlaken Post-Autos always draw up next to a long set of roofed open-sided platforms, through which trains clank across the street on their way back from the far side of the river. These huge buses carry both mail and passengers to places not served by the railway—hence their name. The Beaten-berg bus was still nearly empty when she drove up; she got in and took the front seat, disposing the soggy bunch of *Waldmeister* on the floor. The blond driver was fussing about at the rear of the great machine, attaching a trailer full of luggage; presently he got in.

'You found the Golden Bear?' he asked, as he clipped her book of vouchers and gave her a ticket.

'Yes. It seems a nice little place.'

'It is very small,' der Chrigl said disparagingly.

'The personnel are very agreeable; in big hotels this is not always the case,' Julia said, faintly irritated by his contempt.

'Oh, the old Frau Göttinger is all right, and she gets good girls to serve her—that is quite true. She is my aunt! I expect you saw her; she is never off duty. Old, and wearing black.'

'With grey flowers on her apron?' Julia asked, instantly intrigued by the possibility of a link with the Golden Bear through der Chrigl; conceivably this might come in useful.

The fair man laughed.

'Oh, those old black aprons with the grey flowers! She will never wear anything else. They aren't made any more, but I believe she has two dozen of them! You have friends staying there?' he asked rather curiously.

'One friend, yes.'

At this point a gaggle of passengers arrived to board the bus;

a train from Berne had just come in. The driver busied himself with their tickets, while Julia looked on idly, wondering how, if at all, she could use him and his aunt for information about Borovali's movements. Suddenly, among the group waiting to get in she caught sight of Colin, most oddly accoutred: shorts, a beret, and a hideous tartan wind-cheater, with an outsize rucksack on his back and heavily-nailed climbing boots—the very picture of the native tourist on holiday. She grinned at the sight, and at that moment he saw her too; he gestured over his shoulder towards the rear of the bus. Julia turned and deliberately looked the other way. Drawn up on one of the further platforms was an empty *Wagons-Lits* coach with black-and-white placards at both ends; these, to her great surprise, read—'Dortmund—Interlaken'.

'Goodness, fancy through sleepers coming here from Germany,' Julia muttered to herself; she regarded Interlaken, though a bewitching little place, as definitely what Americans would call 'up-State'—i.e. at the back of beyond. The Berne train, clanking slowly along towards the river and the Ost-Bahnhof, cut off her view of the surprising Dortmund coach; it gave some treble hoots before it crossed the street. Insular Julia laughed; she still thought trains running about loose in towns funny. But she was relieved by Colin's prudence in not coming to sit with her, especially in view of the driver's connection with the Golden Bear. She was glad that he had come back—and he might be able to help about getting June away, though she doubted it. But as the bus rolled slowly out of the Platz, roared along the flat road through the Interlaken suburbs, and then ground its way up through the woods, hooting its little tune before the hairpin turns, it occurred to Julia that with Colin at the Silberhorn tonight the stroll with Antrobus, on which she had been counting when Mrs. Hathaway had gone early to bed, might not come off as easily, as inevitably, as she had hoped.

This idea upset her to a degree that was rather frightening. Was she really losing her head? She found herself running over in her mind phrases Antrobus had used: 'What a nice person you are!' 'Birds, too'—and what he had said about telling her everything if he were a Swiss policeman or hotel porter. But when you added them up, they really amounted to nothing more than that he enjoyed her, which men in her experience practically always did. She shook herself, mentally; at her age, she was behaving like a schoolgirl!

The bus gradually emptied itself at various hotels and pensions along Beatenberg's interminable village street. It pulled up at the foot of the Sessel-Bahn; here Colin got off, and went striding up the path towards the station, his vast rucksack on his back—Julia wondered what on earth he was up to. However, after she had arrived, handed the now very withered bunch of *Waldmeister* to Fräulein Hanna, looked in on Mrs. Hathaway and reported this, as well as the fact that Antrobus was definitely coming to dine, and was quietly brewing tea in her room to drink out on the balcony, there came a tap on the door, and in walked Colin.

'Hullo! Are you staying here after all?'

'Certainly. Only I didn't want to advertise it, especially with you on the bus too; so I walked along the Parallel-Weg and popped down. Do I see tea preparing? Good—I'm frightfully thirsty.'

'You'll have to have it in the tooth-glass; I've only got one cup.'

'No matter.' Colin held the tooth-glass up to the light and polished it with the fresh face-towel.

'Are some of the others watching the air-ports?' Julia asked in a lowered voice, as they sat rather crampedly on the balcony on two wicker chairs, and she poured out tea.

'No—at least not much. We hear they're probably coming by train now. More unobtrusive, in a way,' he replied, in the same tone.

'Oh.' She reflected, sipping her tea, and was suddenly struck by the recollection of that Dortmund-Interlaken sleeping-car which she had noticed down at the West-Bahnhof. 'From Germany?' she asked.

'Yes, almost certainly. But why on earth should you think so?'

Julia explained what she had seen.

'That could be quite useful,' Colin said. 'I didn't know about those through sleepers. You're a good observer, J. dear—but we knew that before!'

'Who will watch the trains?' she asked. 'Antrobus, I suppose, as he's down in Interlaken.'

'Why Antrobus?' Colin asked, in his most carefully neutral voice.

'Oh, he came clean this morning,' Julia said, with her warm laugh. 'In spite of your total clottery, you silly creature, I do now know that he's in with your lot—but how idiotic that neither he nor you knew about one another. Really, the Secret Service!'

'He had no business to tell you,' the young man said. 'After all, he knows nothing about you.'

'Dear child, he knows everything about me—Morocco, Portugal, and all.'

'How?' he asked sharply.

'Quite simple—rang up London to ask, and was put onto Hugh.' She reddened a little at that name. 'Anyhow he was more or less compromised into telling me, because I caught him red-handed in the Golden Bear, going through Borovali's effects.'

'That's where they've shifted to, is it? In Interlaken?' She

211

nodded. 'How did you find that out?'

Still in a low voice Julia recounted the events of the morning, beginning with June's telephone call; Colin listened attentively.

'How I wish all international crooks and thugs employed such morons!' he muttered fervently at the end. 'This June girl is a piece of cake. Of course they had to use her for her face, but she's God's gift to us.'

Julia proceeded to tell him that God's gift must be got away promptly—'before you start clamping down on those unsavoury characters, B. and W.'

'Where can she go?'

'Oh, they'll take her in at La Cure, at any time.'

'Good Lord! Does that delightful Pastor know what she's been up to?'

'Of course. He and I went to the bank together, you remember, and he heard the whole story there. He doesn't mind a bit—he calls her his "god-daughter at one remove".'

'Good Lord!' Colin said again.

'More tea?' As she refilled the toothglass—'Why the fancy dress?' Julia enquired.

'Ah—well—perhaps slightly less obviously English. You see we think that Borovali and Wright almost certainly won't hand over the papers to their principals in Interlaken itself; much more likely on a sight-seeing tour of some sort. So when I tag along I want to look as Swiss as possible.'

'Oh I see. Very crafty! But how did you get hold of this idea of the excursion meeting?'

To her surprise Colin's dead-white face, a face as utterly white as his sister Edina's, suddenly reddened like a girl's.

'Well—in fact—look here, J., I apologise for ticking you off last night about your goings-on at Merligen. My superiors took a different view, and they were quite right; we got some "bugging" arranged for that chemist's telephone in Berne, and that produced this information about the meeting.'

'And their coming by train?'

'Yes.' Colin's face got redder still.

'Oh ho!' Julia said cheerfully. 'So the chemist, all innocent, rang Mr. Kaufmann at the Villa Victoria, and he, if he's back from Lugano—and if not sour-puss Mrs. K.—rang up Mr. B. at the Bear, I suppose. Did you get any date for this *Ausflug?*'

'Not hard, no. But not before tomorrow, and more likely the day after.'

'Ah—that's why Antrobus felt safe to come to supper tonight.' She felt that Antrobus might have told her some of this himself.

'Is he coming to supper?' Colin asked, looking pleased.

'Yes—Mrs. H. invited him. She rather fell for him, and then fell away again!' Julia said laughing. 'But look, Colin'—she paused.

'Yes?'

'Well, he and I might have something to discuss, rather privately, after Mrs. H. has gone to bed.' Julia as she spoke reddened as deeply as Colin had done a few moments before. 'So if you could contrive not to be too much in evidence, darling—'

He studied her face, more beautiful than ever scorched by the blush, with affectionate curiosity.

'Very well. Is this *it*, Julia my sweet?'

'Oh, how do I know? Clear out now, there's a lamb. I must have a bath.'

Chapter 11

Beatenberg and Interlaken

Dinner that night was rather a success. Julia, who bought clothes so skilfully—and so expensively—that they lasted almost for ever put on the green brocade dress which she had worn at a royal wedding in Lisbon nearly two years before; Antrobus startled everyone, and delighted Mrs. Hathaway, by appearing in a dinner-jacket. He bowed over her hand, apologised for not telephoning, but felt confident that she had received the verbal message he sent by Miss Probyn that he was coming, and expressed his great pleasure at being able to do so—Mrs. Hathaway was mollified. Fräulein Hanna had done wonders with the *Waldmeister*, and the May-cup was delicious; so was the soup, the tiny local trout, and the tender steaks. Small the Silberhorn rooms might be, but the food was admirable, and so was the view—beyond the window the snows of the Blümlisalp turned a tea-rose pink, faded to pale gold, and then to a cold lavender-grey. Within the brightly-lit room the curiosity of the English party was aroused by a table close by, evidently prepared for some celebration: broad mauve-and-white ribbons were stretched across it from corner to corner, mauve-and-white bows were pinned here and there, and posies of mauve flowers lay at each place.

'What can it be?' Antrobus speculated. 'What does one celebrate by half-mourning?' Julia enquired of Fräulein Hanna, who stumped over intermittently to supervise the service of their meal, and learned that it was a Swiss silver-wedding party.

'Oh well, I suppose half-mourning is quite appropriate for that,' Antrobus said. 'The onset of middle age, and so on. After all, what colour could they have? White is bridal; red—well presumably all passion is *nearly* spent; green—oh, perish the thought! And blue is too dismal—so far as I know no one has composed "Silver Wedding Blues". No, I think mauve is very well chosen.'

Mrs. Hathaway, laughing, agreed. She was pleased with Antrobus for taking the trouble to make this sort of civilised conversation; her former approval of him returned. Colin as usual sat rather silent; Julia put in a slightly *cassant* drawled observation from time to time—so as not, as she said later to Antrobus, to have two death's-heads at the feast.

For she got her stroll. After coffee in the *Kleine Saal*—Mrs. Hathaway was still too cautious about evening chills to risk having it on the balcony—Colin offered to escort the older lady to her room; when he came down he asked Antrobus to excuse him, as he had some letters to write.

'You two don't want a little chat about unfinished business?' Julia asked helpfully. Colin scowled at her; Antrobus grinned.

'We can have that tomorrow morning, can't we?' he said to the young man. 'What about 10 a.m. in the Englischer Garten?—you know, by the river, with the superb silver poplars and the monument to the man who built the railway up to the Jungfrau-Joch? I shall be sitting on a bench, reading *The Times* and listening to the blackbirds.'

'I don't know, but I will find it, and be there,' Colin said, not very graciously. 'Good-night. 'Night, Julia.' He took himself off.

'What's upsetting him?' Antrobus asked.

'Just what I'm wondering myself.' She glanced round the small room, where two other parties were sitting, the men smoking cheroots. 'It's stifling in here—let's go into the garden for a minute,' she said.

The garden was empty; the gravelled paths and the now cloth-less tables were clearly illuminated by the big arc-light across the street. Julia went over and leant on the parapet above the hayfield.

'Colin worries,' she said to Antrobus, as he came and leant besides her. 'I expect you've heard about the line-tapping, and that the principals are expected to come by train now, from Germany.'

'Yes, I heard that this afternoon.'

'Personally I fancy those through sleepers from Dortmund to Interlaken,' she said. '*Wagons-Lits* passengers give their tickets and passports to the attendant in order not to be woken up at the frontier; so even if the passport officials were alerted, they'd have a frightful job rousing up all the women with their hair in nets in the upper berths.'

He laughed out loud.

'What a splendid scene! No. I don't think the Swiss would go as far as that—too bad for tourism. But all passengers, even in sleepers, have to tumble out and pass their luggage through the Customs at Berne; and there someone, I hope, will be keeping an open eye tomorrow—improbable—and the day after, and the day after that.'

'And then give you a ring about people booked through to Interlaken?'

'That, roughly, is the idea.'

'And you loiter with intent at one of the Bahnhofs, and tip off Colin, in his incredible hiker's outfit, who to follow?'

'Some arrangement of the sort, if we are lucky.'

'Well can't you tip me off, so that I can go and snatch June while B. and W. are going up to Mürren or the Jungfrau-Joch on Ferien-Billets to hand over the doings?'

He laughed rather grimly.

'Julia, I've told you already that I will if I can. You are so persistent—one would think nothing mattered but your little criminal and her ankle!'

'I'm not sure that anything else does matter quite so much. Certainly not beastly Sheiks and Emirs and their revolting oil for revolting aeroplanes.'

'You're incorrigible!' he said, with an unwilling laugh. 'Anyhow, I think I have a better idea—for once—than yours. How would it be if I could arrange to have B. and K.—well whatever they are; it all comes to the same thing—summoned to the police-station on some excuse about passports or what have you, tomorrow? And meanwhile you nip in and carry off your meretricious little protégée?'

'How long could they be kept at the police-station?' Julia asked, thinking of all June's clothes and make-up, and how slow the limping child was. 'Anyhow she isn't meretricious; that's the last adjective to apply to her.'

He ignored this.

'Say half an hour.'

'Could you make it three-quarters? If you can do that I could work it.'

'Probably—yes.'

'Is this a hard offer? Because if so I ought to ring up the Pastor and lay him on. He's frightfully busy always, and it's quite a drive from Bellardon to Interlaken.'

'Oh do for goodness' sake leave that till later!' the man said impatiently. 'You can't talk from that hopeless box now, with those people sitting just outside. All this is so boring, really, and it's such a divine night. Come for a stroll. Do you want a scarf or something?'

His impatient urgency delighted Julia. It was indeed a divine night; too warm for her to want any sort of wrap, she said. They crossed the street and took the narrow little path up towards the Parallel-Weg, passing the cow-stable where the enormous Emmenthalers, chewing the cud gently but audibly in the darkness, exhaled the sane and sweet smell of cows' breath, delightful to the country-bred—Antrobus paused and looked in through the open half-door, which a shaft of moon-light penetrated, touching some of the huge peaceful hind-quarters. 'Sweet beasts,' he murmured. The moon was near the full, and its light strong; out to their right it illuminated the white-and-yellow hotel cat, sitting watchfully on the verge of the high uncut grass waiting for field-mice. 'I love that cat,' Julia said, pointing it out.

When they reached the Parallel-Weg they turned right along it, in the direction of the Sessel-Bahn; the forest proper was some distance above them, but isolated trees studded the fields here and there, the moonlight throwing their shadows sharply onto the silvery sheen of the high meadow-grass.

'What is this tremendously strong scent?' Antrobus asked suddenly, stopping short.

'Rowan.'

'What?'

'Mountain-ash I suppose to you. It's just coming into flower—the whole place smells of it.'

'Delicious,' he said, walking on. 'Clever of you to know what it is.'

'I think it so odd that you don't know it,' Julia said. 'After all, aren't you supposed to be Scotch? It's such an amusing tree—the great antidote to fairies.'

'What do you mean?'

'Oh yes—in the West Highlands in old days practically every garden had a pair of rowan-trees planted at the gate, with their boughs twisted together to form an arch; the fairies can't go through that, you see.'

'Can't they fly over the hedge, or wall, or whatever?'

'Apparently not—the entrance is the entrance, and if you protect that, you protect all.'

'How charming. Yes, of course it's the same idea as the Chinese putting those short isolated walls at the entrance to their court-yards—the devil-dodgers. Demons can't fly or climb either, it seems; or even make right-angled turns.'

'What fun! You've been in China, then?'

'For a short time—before all this Communist beastliness really got going, thank goodness. I'd sooner have positive swarms of demons than Mao Tse-tung.' He stopped again beside one of the wooden seats which the Swiss so thoughtfully place along their paths. 'Let's sit,' he said, and taking her elbow drew her down beside him.

Julia's heart began to throb a little. She felt shy and nervous, though this was exactly what she had hoped for all day—to walk and sit in the moonlight with John Antrobus. He had chosen their seat well. The meadows sloped away below them, broken to the left by the irregular bends of a small stream which tinkled musically between flowery banks; from other cow-stables down by the village came an occasional note, deeper and even more musical—Swiss cows wear their bells all night, and any movement of the great animals gives off this soothing sound. Away across the darkling lake the Blümlisalp stood up, white in the moonlight, above the dark silvery-velvet shimmer of the forest slopes in front of it. The air was full of smells: a resinous whiff from the pines up the hill-side, the sweet breath of summer in the meadow, and, sharper and more intense, the almost savagely penetrating scent of rowan-blossom. Antrobus looked round; a mountain-ash stood a little way behind the seat.

'There's another of your anti-fairy trees,' he said. 'I shall always know that smell from now on. It *is* strong.'

'It seems to smell stronger out here than at home,' Julia said.

'Practically all flowers smell stronger and are more intense in colour in mountains,' he observed. 'Odd, with their very short blooming season. Or perhaps that is the reason—*carpe diem*, if you know what that means.'

'Gather ye roses while ye may,' Julia replied readily.

'Quite so,' He paused—when he spoke again it was hesitantly. 'I have an idea that there are roses you and I might gather—together. But I don't know how you feel about it.'

'I'm very fond of roses; they're one of my favourite flowers,' Julia said lightly—but a slight breathlessness in her voice belied the flippancy of her words. He turned, and put an arm round her.

'I really do like you very much,' he said. 'Do you like me at all?'

'Yes.'

'Enough for a kiss?'

220

'Well for a litttle one, anyhow.'

He put his free hand on her farther shoulder and drew her round towards him, saying—'A little kiss? A butterfly kiss?' He brushed her cheek with his eye-lashes, as children do. 'A shower of kisses, I think, if they are to be so very little.'

He gave the shower of little kisses in a rather absurd way, all over her face—cheeks, temples, eyelids, even the tip of her nose; but it was done so lightly and gently that Julia was somehow reassured, to the point that presently she twisted her head round and gave him a kiss in return.

'Oh sweetheart, that *is* nice of you. Are you all right? Happy?'

Julia was very much all right, and very happy indeed, but she was irresistibly reminded by his words of a sentence in Harriette Wilson's *Memoirs*, and gave her slow laugh. ' "*Amy, Amy,* does it feel nice?" ' she quoted.

Antrobus gave her a little shake.

'What a monster you are! Am I so like poor Lord Berwick?'

'Well not to the point of being a peer, unless Antrobus is just an alias! You certainly aren't the Duke of Alba, because for one thing he's dead, and for another I knew him in Spain, and you aren't really like him at all.'

He laughed gently, then settled himself more comfortably on the seat, and drew her head down to his shoulder. 'Really, how very pleasant it is to be able to be together like this, at ease and safe, instead of on guard and suspicious the whole time. Don't you agree?'

'Completely. And all totally unnecessary if the Secret Service weren't so inept. How idiotic of them to send Colin out here without either letting you know about him, or telling him about you.'

'Oh don't bind, darling! I told you we're in different branches.

Anyhow it's all right now—for goodness' sake forget it, and look at the Blümlisalp.'

They did this very satisfactorily for some time, talking a little, happily, with an occasional kiss as punctuation—Julia found his lightness of touch and his percipience extraordinarily delightful. But presently through the cool still air the little six-note tune of the Post-Auto came up to them.

'Goodness, that must be the last bus going down!' she exclaimed. 'John dear, we must race back.'

'Why?'

'To ring up the Pastor about fetching June tomorrow. They go to bed early at La Cure.'

'Why?' he asked again.

'Because Jean-Pierre starts saying his prayers in the Church so early; breakfast is at 6.30 or that, to let Marcel catch his train to school at Lausanne. And it will be ten by the time we get down.'

'I wish you weren't so conscientious!' Antrobus said. 'No, I don't really; I see that, however surprisingly, conscientiousness is part of you. Well, one last one, darling.'

But the last one wasn't a little kiss at all, and it left Julia rather shaken. When he let her go she hurried ahead of him, with her light graceful step, along the Parallel-Weg, and practically ran down the narrow stony path between its silvery wooden railings that led past the cowstable.

'That cat's still there,' he called to her.

'Oh, so it is. It's a sweet wussker.' In the hotel garden she paused.

'We'd better say good-night now—when I've finished with the Pastor I must tuck Mrs. H. up, and I can't leave her too late.'

'Goodbye, stern daughter of the Voice of God,' Antrobus said, taking her hand and kissing it. 'Though why a woman with a face like yours should trouble to be *good* as well, I can't think.'

Julia brushed that aside—she knew all about her face.

'What time shall I tell him to come?' she asked. 'We never settled that. When can you have B. and K. dragged round to the police-station?'

'What time would suit you?'

'Oh, late morning. It's a long run from Bellardon, as I told you.'

'Have them there at 11.45, and not released till 12.30?'

'Perfect. Goodbye. Thank you for the *Waldmeister*—I must say it makes a lovely drink.' She ran up the steps into the hotel.

The *Kleine Saal* was fortunately now empty, and she rang up the Pastor at once. '*Jean-Pierre? Ici Julie.* English now, please. It's for tomorrow.'

He made no fuss or protest, merely asked—'At what time?'

'Twenty past twelve—very exactly. Can you manage that? I made it as late as I could.'

'Yes, certainly. Where?'

Julia hadn't thought where. After an instant's hesitation she gave the address of Dr. Hertz's Clinic; it was in a side street, in a quiet part of the town, where the presence of a limping young lady would arouse the least comment. 'Wait outside, would you? I shall be bringing her and her gear in a taxi.'

'*Plaît-il*, "gear?" *Qu'est-ce que c'est?*'

'Luggage.'

'Has she much "gear"?'

'Mountains! Tell Germaine to give her the room with the biggest cupboards of all.'

His rich laugh came ringing over the line.

'*Ma chère*, your criminal friends are very eccentric, or else very unpractical! I thought burglars always travelled light.'

'Not this one,' Julia said, laughing too. 'Bless you for this. See you tomorrow.'

'You will not come with her? We should like that so much—and it might be a help.'

'No, I can't come now. I will later on; I'd love to.'

She gave this answer quite instinctively; after they had rung off she wondered why. Because she didn't want to leave the neighbourhood of Interlaken while Antrobus was there?—or simply because she wanted to see his and Colin's job through? With all the honesty she could muster—and Julia was rather honest—she realised that it had simply never occurred to her to leave before the papers were recovered, quite apart from Mrs. Hathaway and her needs. She went and tucked that good lady up, and then tapped on Colin's door.

Colin seemed to have recovered his temper.

'Nice walk?' he asked, with a puckish grin.

'Very nice,' Julia said, grinning back—then she told him of the plan to evacuate June next day.

'Why you fuss so about that really rather unworthy little crea-ture I can't imagine,' Colin said—'nor why Antrobus gives in to you about it. Well yes, I can imagine that! But honestly, Julia, in this job it's much better to leave sentiment and emotion out of it altogether.'

'Oh really? Like Mata Hari, I suppose?' she responded blithely, at which the young man gave an unwilling laugh.

'That was passion—a very authentic and useful tool. But I can't believe that you have any passion for this June girl—whatever you may feel about Antrobus.'

'Blast you!' Julia said, but without heat. 'Anyhow, though both you men seem to forget it, there is such a thing as charity—which is quite independent of sentiment, or emotion, or even passion.

224

Witness Jean-Pierre having her to stay. Good-night.' She gave him a cool affectionate kiss, and went out.

Colin left on an early bus to make his contact with Antrobus in the English Garden. Soon afterwards June again rang up Julia.

'I've got something to tell you, something I overheard. I think you'd like to know it, and I'd like to do something for you.'

'Splendid. But don't tell me over the telephone. I'm coming down to see you this morning, so you can tell me then.'

'Oh, how lovely! Oh'—there was a drop in the voice, and a pause. 'You'd better not come when they're here. They're out just now.'

'They won't be there when I come,' Julia said. She wondered if she should give a hint about getting packed, but decided against it. 'Is the foot better?' she asked.

'Oh yes, a lot. Thank you ever so.'

'I'm so glad. Be seeing you, soon after half past eleven.' She rang off before June could reply.

Well before 11.30 Julia walked into the garden of the Hotel Gemsbock, carrying a parasol tilted over her shoulder in the direction of the Golden Bear, concealing her face from any observers on that side of the square; she ordered coffee, and sat behind that convenient hedge, watching the small sunny Platz. As usual it was almost empty: a workman wheeled a hand-cart full of briquettes across it from the coal-merchant's establishment opposite the timber-yard, and presently a neatly-dressed man, obviously Swiss, came walking in from the direction of the Bahnhof-Platz. This individual came into the Gemsbock garden and sat down at the table next to hers; he ordered a beer, and then opened a newspaper, but from time to time he too seemed to be looking through the hedge. At precisely 11.35 two figures emerged from the Golden Bear, those of Mr. Borovali and Mr. Wright—they both looked exceedingly out of temper. As they passed the Gemsbock the neatly-dressed man downed the last of his beer, put a couple of coins on the table, and rose and walked out into the sunshine—Julia, peering through the privets, saw that he was casually strolling along behind the pair.

'A flatty!' she muttered gleefully. And she too paid, walked across to the other hotel and up, past the marmot, into June's room.

'How*ever* did you know they'd be out just now? They've only just gone,' the little thing said, after giving Julia a warm kiss. 'They've had to go to see the police about our papers—furious, Mr. B. was. But how did *you* know?' The old ugly suspicion showed signs of reappearing. 'Are you in with the police?'

'The Swiss police? No,' Julia said firmly. 'Does it matter how I knew? Do you want to get out of this show or don't you? You said you did, and so I've come to do it.'

'Go home?'

'Yes—quite soon. Not to London today. Yes or no?'

'Oh, *yes*!'

'Then there's no time to waste. We must pack your things and get you away before they come back.' As she spoke Julia brought the tartan hat-box to June's chair by the window, and began to collect the hats which were perched here and there round the room—on two hideous vases on a shelf, and on the bedposts, and brought them over. 'There—now you be packing those while I do the rest.'

This calm assumption of authority quelled June; obediently, though unskilfully, she began to pack her hats. 'What a mercy you packed all my frocks yesterday! Did you know then?' she asked.

'No, yesterday I hadn't a clue! I just packed them because you wanted them packed. Which case do your night-things go in?' The work went on; after some minutes June asked—'Where am I going? To be with you?' This with eager hopefulness.

'Not just now—my hotel is too near. You're going to stay in the country with some friends of mine, darling people; they'll look after you, and get a doctor to keep an eye on your foot.' As she spoke Julia made a mental note to mention June's ankle to Jean-Pierre.

'English friends?' June enquired, pausing with a hat in one hand and a ball of crumpled-up tissue paper in the other.

'No, Swiss; but they both talk English. You'll love being there, and I shall come over as soon as I can.' She noticed the hat June was holding; it was the one with the eye-veil. 'Don't pack that—you'd better wear it.' She removed the hat and perched it on the ewer. June giggled—but she had another question.

'Will I be able to get a set there? My hair's frightful, with Mr. B. never letting me go out this last week or more.'

Julia suppressed a laugh. Her brief impression of Bellardon had not led her to suppose that it could supply a set of any sort, let alone a rinse, which June would certainly want; the dark line along the roots of her bogus ash-blonde hair was becoming rather marked.

'Oh, Germaine will see to all that,' she said easily.

'Who's Germaine?'

The question brought Julia up with a round turn. Should she say 'Madame de Ritter'?—and reveal that June was actually going to stay in the house of the man whom Borovali had been impersonating? She had never thought of that aspect when she arranged this hide-out for the girl.

'Oh, she's his wife—the wife of the gentleman who's coming

to drive you over,' she said, falling back on June's own ghastly idiom. 'Look, which coat shall you wear? And what case do these shoes go in?' All the time that she coped with these various problems of June's she was packing at high speed. When the job was nearly done, and June was arranging her face and hat, she went downstairs and spoke with Frau Göttinger.

'The little Fräulein is leaving now. Could the valet bring down her luggage? And a taxi be called?'

Frau Göttinger was startled, put about.

'*Die Herren* leave too?'

'So far as I know, not; only *das Fräulein*. Her bill I can pay,' Julia said; she had borrowed a supply of Swiss francs for this express purpose from Colin before he left, greatly to his annoyance.

The old woman drew herself up, a most dignified figure in her shabby black and her curious apron.

'The Herr de Ritter booked the rooms; therefore he shall pay the bill,' she pronounced firmly.

'*Sehr gut*—as you wish,' Julia said, smiling her slow smile. 'But can one fetch a taxi while the *Gepäck* is being brought down? We are a little in haste.'

Frau Göttinger bent on Julia then a glance suddenly full of meaning—comprehension? complicity?—the girl could not be sure. But Heinrich was summoned by an imperative shout to bring down June's luggage, and a girl in an apron stained by cooking was bidden to go and fetch a taxi. *'Aber die Schürze zuerst abnehmen!'* Frau Göttinger said, brusquely pulling off the soiled apron. *'Schnell, Luise.'* And five minutes later Julia, June, and all June's luggage drove away from the Golden Bear, that very ungilded cage; to Julia's surprise the old woman gave the girl a kiss, saying *'Gott geh mit Dir, mein Kind.'*

'What did that mean, what she said?' June enquired, as they

turned out of the square.

'God go with you, my child.'

'Oh. Oh how funny.' A pause. 'Rather nice, wasn't it?' June said thoughtfully.

'Very nice indeed. Now June, we haven't much time; will you tell me what it was you overheard, that you thought I should like to know?'

'Oh, I heard the two of them, Mr. B. and Wright, talking about those papers we got from the bank, that I was telling you about. It seems they want to give them to some people coming from outside, from Germany, I think; and they were discussing where to do it—on the quiet, not here in Interlarken.'

'And did they settle where they would do it?' Julia asked casually, though she was burning with interest.

'Yes. On a bus tour!' June brought out, with her usual giggle. 'Mr. B. said there was a bus that 'does all three passes'—whatever passes are. Not passes at a girl, I don't suppose; not in a bus! Anyhow that's what they said—"the three passes tour". And when these Jerries come—today or tomorrow, so I understood—Mr. B. and Wright will go on the same bus, and give them the papers somewhere on the way.'

'Thank you very much, June.'

'Does that help you? I want to help you.'

'Yes, it helps me a lot.' The taxi, Julia observed, was now approaching the street in which Dr. Hertz's Clinic stood—hastily, she rode at her next fence.

'Listen, June. You know that Mr. Borovali isn't really Monsieur de Ritter, don't you?'

'Yes, of course.'

'Well to get you away from him—Borovali—I had to arrange for you to stay somewhere, and the only nice place I knew of out here was the house of the real Mr. de Ritter, who's Aglaia Armitage's guardian. So I've fixed that up, and we're meeting him now, in a minute, and he will drive you home, and he and his wife will look after you till I can come and take you back to England.'

June was absolutely horrified—her reaction startled Julia by its violence.

'Oh, Miss Probyn, I *can't!* Not go and stay with that man. Oh, this is awful! Let's stop'—she started to hammer on the glass of the taxi; Julia pulled the small hands away and held them.

'June, don't be foolish. He knows all about it.'

'Knows about me? Pretending to be that heiress, and all?'

'Yes, everything. I told him on the telephone when I settled it.'

'And just the same he'll have me in his house? But that other girl that I'm so like, whose money Mr. B. has taken, is his god-child!'

'Of course, but when I told him the trouble you were in, and asked if they could put you up, do you know what he said? He called you his "god-daughter at one remove". Don't worry, June—it will be all right.'

'Well! He must be someone!' June exclaimed. 'I never heard anything like it; really I never did. But are you sure—'

At this point the taxi stopped outside Dr. Hertz's Clinic; across the street she saw with satisfaction the Frégate drawn in to the kerb, and Jean-Pierre himself standing smoking a cigarette in the sun beside his car. She jumped out and went over to him.

'There you are! This is so very good of you. But look, the little creature is in a panic; I had to tell her your name, and that you were the reality which her horrible Middle-Eastern slave-driver has been impersonating, and it has upset her terribly. So can you be tremendously reassuring?'

The Pastor wrung her hand, laughing heartily.

'How nice to see you! I only wish you were coming with us. Of course I will do my best—it is really a main part of my profession to administer reassurance! Is that her, in the taxi?' He started to cross the empty street, but checked mid-way. 'Good heavens, what an extraordinary resemblance! For a moment I thought it was Aglaia herself.'

'That's what those beastly people engaged the poor little wretch *for*,' Julia said, moving on towards the taxi. Jean-Pierre caught her arm and halted her.

'But how could they find her? This is so strange.'

'Oh, she's a model-girl, or whatever they call it; she sits to be photographed for advertisements—in her case mostly her feet and ankles, to display shoes. All they had to do was to ruffle through the files in all the advertising agencies till they came on someone reasonably like Aglaia. In fact this girl, June Phillips, really has brown hair; they had it bleached for this job.'

'This is horrible,' Jean-Pierre said, slowly walking forward again.

'Of course. The modern world is horrible, beyond belief; personally, I regard the atom bomb as one of its more respectable features.'

Jean-Pierre's loud laughter at this observation was still filling the small quiet street as he approached the taxi, and this produced a slightly reassuring effect on June when he went up and opened the door.

'Good-morning, Miss Phillips,' he said, shaking her hand. 'I am so glad that you are coming to pay us a visit, and so is my wife. All our daughters are married, and we miss them; we shall enjoy having a young girl about the house again.' He told the taxi-man to cross over and pull up behind the Frégate to simplify moving the luggage from one car to the other; the man did so. June had made no reply to his welcoming words; when Julia went to help her out she saw that tears were pouring down the pretty foolish little face.

'June, dear, what is the matter? Do stop crying, and come into the other car. You've got to drive quite a long way, you know.'

'He's too good and too kind!' June sobbed out. 'I can't understand it. I don't deserve it.'

'Which of us deserves all the kindness we get? I know I don't,' Julia said. 'The only thing we can do is to give as little trouble as possible to the people who are being kind to us. Come on—hop out.'

During this interchange the Pastor and the taxi-driver had been switching June's luggage from the cab to the car; when the girl got out and hobbled along to the Frégate Jean-Pierre looked at her with concern.

'But she is lame!' he said to Julia, when June had been bestowed in the front seat.

'Yes, she sprained her ankle the other day, up on the Niederhorn. I wanted to tell you about that—Dr. Hertz has been treating her here, but a good doctor ought to see it from time to time, and say what she may and mayn't do. Her feet and ankles are her bread and butter. Hertz said she was to use it a little every day, and she can get up and down stairs all right; but I'm afraid she won't be mobile enough to be much help to Germaine. I am sorry—I ought to have told you about this before, but I was concentrating on getting her away.'

'That aspect is quite unimportant,' he said, brushing aside any possible inconvenience from having a female criminal who was also lame foisted on his household. 'As to her foot, it

232

can easily be seen to; I often have to go to Lausanne, where the doctors are *hors concours*'. He paused.

'I'll get all that paid, of course,' Julia said, thinking that in view of June's information about the bus tour the Secret Service, in the shape of Colin or Antrobus, might well pay for the child's medical expenses.

'Another aspect of no importance,' Jean-Pierre said, quickly though smilingly. 'Many of our doctors do half their work for love, as I believe yours do also.'

'I daresay they did before the Welfare State came in,' Julia replied rather acidly. 'Now I think the National Health Service has spoiled the old easy comfortable family-doctor business, and the all-for-free treatment of the poor. For one thing there are no poor now.'

'So? That is very sad. But I am thinking—should not Dr. Hertz perhaps see her before she leaves? Here we are precisely at his Clinic.'

Julia looked at her watch; it was exactly half past twelve.

'No. There's not time enough to be safe; without an appoint-ment one may have to wait ages. Anyhow he saw her yesterday. No,' she said again—'I'd rather you cleared off at once. Goodbye. I can't thank you enough for doing this. My love to Germaine.' She went and leant in at the door of the Frégate.

'Goodbye, June dear. I shall be coming to pick you up very soon, and meantime the Pastor will get a doctor to keep an eye on your ankle.'

'The what?' June asked—the word 'Pastor' had caught her ear. 'Is the gentleman a minister? Dad was Presbyterian.'

'Really? Yes, I think it's all more or less the same,' Julia said, trying vainly to remember how much Calvin and John Knox had had in common. 'You can ask him. Goodbye.

Thank you very much for what you told me just now; that may be quite a help.'

Once again the little Londoner startled Julia.

'*You* won't go after them on this bus trip, will you? Oh don't, *please!* They both carry revolvers!—and Mr. B., he'd stick at nothing.'

'No, I'm sure I shan't. Don't worry, June dear—bless you.' She gave the girl a quick kiss, and turned and bade Jean-Pierre goodbye. With the utmost satisfaction she watched him manœuvre his car round at the end of the street and drive back past her, waving as he went. Anyhow June was sorted—one job cleared up, and a main one.

The taxi-man was patiently waiting. '*Das Fräulein* desires to return to the Bear?' he asked.

'No, not to the Bear.' Where should she go to try to put a call through to Antrobus? She had his number. 'To Schuhs' she said, getting in. Surely a big place like Schuhs would have a telephone-box?—and please God with a door that shut! Like all English visitors to Switzerland she glanced anxiously at the meter as they drove off; to her surprise it registered only the minimum price. Julia spoke through the front window.

'You have been paid to the Clinic?'

'*Ja. Der Herr* paid me, while *das Fräulein* was consoling *das Mädchen*'.

Julia laughed rather wryly to herself. Switzerland might be the oldest democracy in the world, but even among its taxi-drivers social *nuances* were recognised: she was 'The Small Lady,' poor June only 'the Girl'. As the taxi passed along the main street towards Schuhs she caught sight of two men, one tall and graceful, the other rather stocky and bearded, turning down the little side street that led towards the Cantonal-Platz—Wright

234

and Borovali, both looking as sour as vinegar. What would they say when they found their wretched captive gone? Poor Frau Göttinger! But she was well able to defend herself. At the sight of the two discomfited crooks Julia laughed again, this time with full-hearted pleasure.

Chapter 12

The Passes

There was a telephone-box at Schuhs, and Julia got Antrobus at once. 'I have a little news-item,' she told him.

'Where are you speaking from?'

'Schuhs.'

'Have you had lunch?'

'Goodness no!—I've only just finished off-loading the little party.'

'Then why not come and eat something with me? Where we lunched yesterday? Was that all right?'

'Yes, lovely. I shall have Brienzerli again. When?'

'Now. It's not two minutes from where you are.'

'All right. Only oughtn't I to have an ice or something for the good of the house, after telephoning? No, I know—I'll buy some cakes for Mrs. H.'

She bought her cakes, and then wandered along the walk beside the Hohe Matte, lingering to smell the newlymown hay and to gaze up the valley at the Jungfrau; when she turned into the garden she saw, with a small throb of delight, Antrobus already seated at a table, two misty glasses of iced Cinzano before him. He got up.

'Darling, you've taken rather a time. What have you been doing?'

'Looking at the Jungfrau,' Julia said, sitting down and putting the parcel of cakes under her chair.

'Quite a good excuse, as they go. Now take your drink—has it got hot? No? Well half-way through it I hope you will feel strong enough to pass on your news.'

Julia did this after a couple of sips—she was boiling over with her information.

'On the *Drei Pässe* tour!' Antrobus exclaimed. 'How ingenious!'

'Why?'

'Because on that trip the bus makes five halts: on the top of the Grimsel, on the top of the Furka; a long stop at Andermatt for lunch, a pause again on the top of the Süsten-Pass, and finally all the more energetic passengers get out at the upper end of the Aares-Schlucht, to walk through it and be picked up again at the bottom—after having coffee and buying picture post-cards. So there's a vast choice of places for a brief-case to change hands in.'

'What's the Aares-Schlucht? And why should one walk through it?'

'Oh, it's a "sight". In fact it is rather spectacular. The Aar runs through a very narrow gorge between vertical or even overhanging limestone cliffs three hundred feet high or more, and the water races along between them frighteningly fast—in fact everything about it is rather frightening, especially those unclimbable walls.'

237

'How does one walk, then? Is there a beach?' Julia asked, with her usual practicality.

'No, there's no beach. To exploit the place the ingenious Swiss have built a little sort of gallery-path all through it, fastened to the rock on steel brackets, thirty feet or so above the water; it's barely a yard wide—no place for people who easily get giddy.'

'I think it sounds horrible. Let's hope the other side have bad heads for heights! Not that that would worry Colin—he was always one for peering over the edges of towers, and climbing cliffs.'

The waitress came to take their order; when she had gone Antrobus said—'I must get hold of Colin and pass this on. Your little creature has done us quite a good turn this time.'

'Did he find you all right this morning?'

'Oh yes. But he was fairly sour.'

'Why?'

'That's what I was going to ask you. Is he in love with you?'

Julia laughed out so loudly that heads turned in their direction.

'Don't make so much noise!' Antrobus said, with a hint of irritation. 'What's the joke?'

'Only that he's engaged to Aglaia Armitage! I'm sorry, John— but he really can't be "J." about you and me.'

'Was he never in love with you? That seems unlikely.'

'Yes, I suppose a bit, when he was finishing with Eton and I was a pre-deb. But it was much more that we were tremendous muckers, and did everything together, as we had ever since we were small children. Anyhow all that is as dead as mutton,' the girl said airily. She paused, thinking. 'Listen; June said another thing—that B. and W. always carry revolvers. Has Colin got one?'

238

'I shouldn't think so—no. They're such a nuisance at the Customs; draw attention, and all that.'

'Well when he goes along on this tour I think he ought to have one. Can you supply?'

'Not myself—I don't carry one either. It isn't done, normally. But I can get him one from Berne, I expect.'

'In time? Do you know when this bus starts?'

'Yes. 7.30 a.m. from the Fluss, and then it wanders round the other hotels, picking up passengers. I shouldn't think it would bother with anything as small as the Bear; I expect B. and K. will board it at one of the big places like the Victoria.'

'Then he ought to have it tonight,' Julia said anxiously. 'He'll have to come down to sleep here anyhow, to be in time. Can you fix that?'

'Yes. If you'll excuse me for a moment I'll go and telephone at once—then it should be here by tea-time.'

While he was doing this the Brienzerli arrived, and Julia began on them—no sense in letting them get cold. When Antrobus returned and started on his cold trout he said—'You do fuss about Colin, don't you? Are you still in love with him?'

'Oh don't be such a clot, John. That was practically in our infancy! And would anyone of my age stay in love with someone who wasn't in love with them?' She said this with complete sincerity, but even as she spoke a little pang of anxiety struck at her heart. If Antrobus wasn't in love with her, and she couldn't be sure, would she be able to stop falling more and more in love with him?

His answer was not altogether reassuring.

'It's been known to happen,' he said, with his rather twisted smile. 'Look at the wretched Baron de Charlus and Odette.' Julia nodded—she remembered that agonising infatuation. 'Anyhow I

239

don't know what your age is.'

'Do you want to guess? No, I hate any rubbish about one's age. I'm 28.'

'You're so *posée*, and have so much expertise that I should have given you 30. But clearly you'll be quite as beautiful at 45 as you are now; you have bones and eyes, which don't change, as well as your fantastic colouring.'

This was in a way more open than anything he had said yet, and Julia's colouring promptly showed one of those modifications which so exasperated her. She changed the subject abruptly.

'Couldn't we go too?'

'Where? On the bus-tour?'

'Well not in the bus. In your car, I thought—just follow on and be there at all these halts. You might ring Berne up again and indent for two more revolvers—"One for me, one for Moses, and one for Elias"!' she said irreverently. 'I'd adore to go over those passes—I've read about them in Baedeker, and they sound too lovely.'

'They are—I want very much to take you over them some time. But I'm not sure that tomorrow is quite the moment—we couldn't concentrate on the view and the flowers if we are keeping lynx eyes on B. and W. all the time.'

'Oh.' Her dove's eyes mourned at him. 'Oh, John, couldn't we do some of it?'

'You beguiler! Yes, I think we might do a short run, anyhow; but I shall have to check with Berne and make sure that they don't want me to be here.'

'Oh do do that.' Then another idea struck her. 'How do you think B. and W. will react to June's having flitted? I saw them coming back from the police-station, and they looked frightfully soured—but of course they didn't know about June then. Do you suppose it will make them alter their plans?'

'They can hardly do that at this stage. In their place I should be only too thankful to be relieved of such a liability as that little nitwit! She's served their turn, and ever since she can only have been an embarrassment, even before she started turning King's Evidence to you. But I daresay it will bother Mr. Borovali quite a bit. Did the hotel know that it was you who took her away?'

'But of course. I even offered to pay her bill, because I didn't want her to lose all those frocks that were the main bribe; but Frau Göttinger wouldn't hear of it. She said "Herr de Ritter" had booked the rooms, and he could foot the bill.'

Antrobus laughed.

'Good for her! How do you come to know her name?'

'Oh, der Chrigl, the Beatenberg bus-driver, is her nephew— he told me.'

'There you go again! You really ought to be employed whole-time. Why don't you apply?'

'I don't need money except abroad, and I get quite a good business allowance for my papers, when I remember to put in for it. I was in too much of a hurry this time, racing out to take Watkins to Mrs. H.'

'Watkins being the lady's-maid you mentioned at Geneva?'

'Yes.' Julia was pleased that he should remember this detail from the conversation at the Palais des Nations. 'But here is something else, while I think of it.'

'More information?'

'No.' She paused, considering how to present what she had to say. 'Did you tell Berne about the bus-tour?' she asked.

'Yes.' He looked a little surprised.

'Were they pleased?'

241

'Delighted. I was congratulated warmly on my "local sources"!' he said, smiling at her.

'Fine. However, as you very well know, your local source is not me, but June Phillips,' Julia said, in a rather *cassant* tone.

'My dear, so what? What's biting you?' he said, leaning across the table towards her, plainly upset by her sudden change of manner.

'Money,' Julia said firmly. 'I know your people pay their local sources for "hard" information, and often for information that isn't hard at all—soft as putty, half the time. What is this rather crucial information about the bus-tour worth to Berne? What would they have paid a genuine "local source" for it?'

He stared at her in surprise, his expression slowly stiffening.

'I have no idea,' he said, rather coldly.

'Oh nonsense! Of course it's your business to have a very good idea,' Julia replied brusquely. 'You are such a bad liar, John! Anyhow I want three hundred francs for it. Probably miles below the real tariff, but I think that should be enough for my need.'

'May I know what your need is?' he asked, a little less coldly. 'If you are really short of cash of course we can help you out; you have done a great deal for us. Merligen, and the Bear, and now this.'

'And the photograph the police used,' Julia reminded him. 'Personally I think three thousand francs would be much nearer the mark!'

'I don't disagree. In fact it is hardly possible to put a cash value on what you have done in the last few weeks. Only I didn't realise that you wished it to be on this basis.' His tone was very cold indeed.

'I shall slap you on both sides of your face if you make any more remarks like that,' Julia told him, in her slowest tones. 'I hadn't realised that being offensive was in your repertoire at all.'

He blushed.

'I do apologise. Pray forgive me. If I was offensive—and I see that I must have sounded so—it was because I am so taken by surprise at your raising the question of money.'

'That's simply because you never use your imagination. Look—June Phillips, to whom the unutterable British Secret Service owes most of the information on which they have been, and tomorrow will be, acting, has injured her ankle, which is her livelihood. She has got to see doctors, and they will have to be paid. I've paid Hertz's bill here—quite small—myself. But now she's gone to the de Ritters, who are as poor as the traditional Church mice, and I want three hundred francs—damn it, it's only twenty-five pounds!—to cover her medical expenses while she's with them. Isn't what she's given you worth that?'

'Fully. Only you see she may be involved later in criminal proceedings.'

'Well if you must be hateful, *be* hateful,' Julia said calmly. 'Goodness, what a creature you are! Anyhow I'm not asking you to give it to her, only to me—the so useful intermediary.'

His grin appeared, again oddly accompanied by his fair man's blush.

'How savage you can be! We both seem to be getting revelations about one another today.' He took his wallet from his pocket, counted out five 100-franc notes, and handed them to her across the table. 'Will that cover your little criminal's medical expenses, do you think?'

'Should do. Thank you very much.' She stowed the notes away in her bag, without the smallest embarrassment. 'Well-earned,' she said.

'Oh, Julia, you are fantastic! You appear so sophisticated, and then suddenly you go and behave as naturally as a charwoman!'

'Nature is much better than sophistication, I think,' Julia said, tackling her veal; she was glad to have got the money for June's foot, and even more glad to have triumphed over Antrobus.

Presently this gentleman returned to the subject of Mr. Borovali.

'We have an informant at the Bear,' he said. 'I expect he will let me know what the reaction there is to your little friend's departure.'

'If you mean Heinrich, the valet, he's practically a mental deficient! However, I daresay he'll get his facts from the chambermaid, who's quite bright, and I'm sure like all chambermaids peeps and listens through keyholes.'

Antrobus laughed, but went on considering things from his own angle.

'On the whole I don't think you had better go up to Beatenberg on the bus,' he said presently, as they drank their coffee. 'If this driver happens to have called on his aunt for a free beer while he was down in the town, and hears that you carried that girl off, it might conceivably lead to complications—given the suspicions the Swiss police already entertain of you! And one never knows who is in whose pay.'

'Thank God June is now in yours,' Julia said cheerfully, patting her handbag.

'Oh really! Anyhow, why not take a taxi?'

'To Beatenberg? It would cost the earth! Best of reasons why not. And please don't expect me to start embezzling Miss Phillips's salary, because I won't.'

He laughed again.

'You really are quite monstrous! I can't think why I should like it, but I do. Well, if you can wait fifteen or twenty minutes while I make some telephone calls, I can take you myself. If your cousin has gone up again—I'll ring him too—I could see him about coming down tonight at the same time, and kill two birds with one stone.'

'Poor birds!—me and Colin. Very well.'

'He is a ring-ousel, a mountain bird,' Antrobus said unexpectedly. 'You are a thrush.'

'I don't sing.'

'No, but you are rather thrush-coloured, and your speaking voice is extremely musical.'

While Antrobus telephoned, Julia sat in the shade of the chestnut avenue along the edge of the Hohe Matte; the Porsche, large and low-hung, was parked by the restaurant, but he told her not to sit in it. Presently he came back and they drove off, spinning through the old wood-built town on the Beatenberg side of the Aar, where pear trees, white with blossom, were trained up against the dark timbers of the houses; then across flat open meadows into the forest, where the road began to climb. The Porsche made nothing of the ascent, and took the hairpin bends at a speed that startled Julia. 'Nice car,' she said.

'I like it, yes. It's competent—like you!'

'I'm not fast!'

'Well, you're not slow!' They laughed, once more at ease together; as the car swung up the mountain-side they heard from far below the six notes of the bus's theme-tune coming up, softened by distance.

In Beatenberg Antrobus drew up by the little *épicerie* where Julia and Watkins habitually bought sugar and Nescafé.

'Would you very much mind walking from here to the hotel, and telling your cousin to come down and talk to me? He is in, and I told him I was coming.'

'Not in the least—but why the precautions? We all dined together last night, quite openly.'

'Well everything is rather hotting up now—one can't take too many precautions. Goodbye, my dear, I'll leave word with Colin where you and I are to meet tomorrow.'

'Oh, are we going? Lovely!'

'Yes—but I must concert everything with him first. Up to a point this is his show.'

'Colin won't want me anywhere about,' Julia said. 'I don't think he's ever quite forgiven me for stalling him in Morocco.'

'Well, in the last resort he must do what I say, here. Anyhow there are no Phoenician graves in Switzerland!'

'Goodness, what a long talk you and Hugh must have had! You seem to know every detail. Right—I'll send him along. Thank you for my good lunch.'

Later that afternoon Colin—sure enough with a very ill grace—told Julia that she was to go down on the bus which reached Interlaken soon after half-past nine—'Then you just potter along the main street towards the Ost-Bahnhof, on the right-hand side, till he picks you up. Kerb-crawling, I call it!'

'But you'll have started ages before that.'

'Yes, thank God! Julia, for heaven's sake don't *please* go and do anything silly tomorrow. This is important.'

'Yes—and who found out where this important meeting was to be? Don't be so pomposo, Colin—really you bore me.'

'Sorry, J. dear. I know you've been doing wonders for us. But you see this is my first really big job, and I don't want to bog it.'

'I'm sure you won't, darling.' She planted a forgiving kiss on his dead-white cheek. 'The Lord love you! Oh—' she paused. 'He *is* getting you a revolver, isn't he?'

'Yes. Was that your idea?'

'No, June's. She says B. and W. always carry them, and I didn't want you to be at a disadvantage.'

'It isn't usually done,' Colin said disapprovingly.

'Well I'm glad it's going to be done this time.'

On reflection that evening Julia found herself a little disturbed about the scene at lunch. She was not pleased with the way Antrobus had behaved—why was it necessary to assume the worst, and to put it so offensively? But she was not too pleased with her own behaviour, either: perhaps she ought to have explained at once that she wanted the money for June—and wasn't he being rather charitable when he compared her to a charwoman, rather than to a fishwife? Julia knew from long experience that when people lose their hearts it makes them liable to lose their tempers too; had she reached that stage? The whole thing was on quite a small scale, but still it was disquieting. Why had he used that harsh voice, those unpleasant words, to her? And all right on top of their rose-gathering together on the Parallel-Weg the evening before. Somehow it didn't fit; there was a sense of—ugliness, almost; something wrong somewhere. As she went to bed she hoped fervently that tomorrow's excursion might show her more where he stood; alas for her, she feared she knew her own position only too well! The words 'or crossed in hopeless love' rang in her head as she went to sleep, though she could not recall either the poet or the poem.

Well before ten o'clock on the following morning Julia, idling along the right-hand pavement of Interlaken's pretty innocent main street, was overtaken by the Porsche. In Switzerland traffic drives on the right, hence cars have a left-hand drive; as Antrobus pulled up she got in beside him almost before the car had stopped, and they shot off again, swinging left presently over the road bridge across the Aar at the end of the Englischer Garten, to take the main road to the East along the northern shore of the Lake of Brienz. Julia had never been out of Interlaken on this side before, and looked about her with interest. Across the lake a ridge of limestone cliffs cut into the sky, with steep pastures and pine woods below the crest, on which a rounded turret of rock stood up conspicuously.

'Oh! is that lump sticking up above the Schynige Platte the Turm?'

He leaned across her to look.

'Yes. You must have the beginnings of an eye for mountains to recognise it from this side.'

Julia repressed an inclination to suggest that he was being patronising—she was determined not to be what he called 'savage' today. Instead she asked if they couldn't have the hood down—the Porsche was a model with an adjustable top. 'We should see so much more.'

He pulled in to the side of the road at once; the hood went down practically at a touch. 'Lovely,' Julia said—'much nicer.'

'You may find it cold up on the top.'

'Then we can put it up again. I like this push-button car of yours.'

Between gently-sloping fields studded with great walnut-trees and occasional patches of pines they came to Brienz, a hot little town tucked into an airless cauldron between the hills; on to Meiringen, up the wide trough-like valley which separates the Bernese Oberland proper, with the great peaks of the Finsteraarhorn, Schreckhorn, Wetterhorn, and Jungfrau groups, from the complex of lesser mountains to the north of it. On and on, the slopes to the south of them now clothed with a low growth of curious amorphous bushes which, as Julia rightly said, looked like green crochet; then by several huge and quite ferocious hairpin bends they approached the summit of the Grimsel Pass. Water-filled valleys stretched away on their right, as steep-sided as Norwegian fiords; somehow they had a rather unnatural look, and Julia enquired about them.

'Oh yes, they're artificially drowned,' Antrobus told her. 'It's all part of the hydro-electric system. The Swiss have everything—everything to make life clean, that is to say. Limitless water-power to electrify their railways and factories, wood for building and for burning—no stinking smoke or grimy coal dust anywhere. Limitless limestone for cement, limitless meat and butter and milk and cheese. If they could strike oil they would be almost completely independent of the outside world, except for coffee and chocolate!'

'Are they likely to strike oil?' Julia asked, as the car entered a cutting between high banks of discoloured snow.

'Yes, geologically it's perfectly possible. But they're quite lucky enough as it is.'

The summit of the Grimsel is a rather bare and forbidding place, especially when snow lies, as it did that day, in patches between the grey outcrops of rock rising from the dark and largely barren soil; to Julia it was rendered even more forbidding by the large numbers of parked cars and the swarms of tourists in bright locally-purchased woollen caps and pull-overs. Several huge motor-buses were also drawn up in a lay-by.

'Can one of those be them?' she asked ungrammatically, but to Antrobus comprehensibly.

'Oh no—they'll be over the Furka by now, heading down to Andermatt. Look, there's the road up to the Furka'—he pointed out to her the white loops twining up across a slope above the valley which lay immediately below them, a valley down which another road ran. 'That's the great through route from Eastern

Switzerland into the Valais,' he said.

Julia ignorantly asked what the Valais was?

'The whole district along the Rhône Valley, from the Lake of Geneva up to Brigue and beyond; that road in the valley to our right goes down to Brigue, where the Simplon road—and railway—start for Italy. Surely even you know that?'

'No, I don't—I can't see why I should. I do know that the Simplon is a pass that Byron or Tennyson or someone went over and picked a daisy on, and wrote a poem about, and that there's a railway tunnel under it now. Do you suppose the modern poets, Auden and Spender and so forth, go through in the trains and write poems about the insides of tunnels?'

He shook her elbow, laughing.

'Your shrewd silliness! I don't know what modern poets do on their travels, but if they did pick daisies they wouldn't dare to say so! Shall we have a cup of coffee here? I've brought lunch for later on.'

They had coffee in the small restaurant, with its racks of picture post-cards and steamy windows. Julia was impressed in the 'Ladies' to find a spotless towel and scalding water, practically on a mountain-top; when she returned to the single room where one ate or drank Antrobus was in jocular conversation with the landlord over glasses of Kirsch—another awaited her at their table. She sat sipping it while the incomprehensible syllables of Berner-Deutsch went on at the far side of the room, by the rather primitive bar; presently Antrobus came over to her, followed by the coffee.

'They didn't hand over the stuff here, anyhow,' he said, looking cheerful. 'Borovali and Wright certainly came in and had coffee—they're rather recognisable—and B. was carrying the brief-case, still very fat indeed. The *patron* thinks he saw them just

250

speak in passing to a woman at another table, but he won't swear to that—he's always so rushed when a bus comes in.'

'A woman!—what sort of woman?' Julia asked in surprise.

'Fat; middle-aged; ill-dressed—German, he thought. She had a little man with her.'

'But would they use a woman for this sort of job?'

'Oh yes—and a middle-aged couple of German tourists is an excellent disguise, especially if the woman is the senior partner. So un-German!'

'Had she a *big* handbag? I mean, she'll have to have something to put the papers in.'

'Oh blast!—I never asked about that.'

'Can't you ask him now?'

'The *patron*? No, one mustn't go back over questions. I had to pretend that B. and W. were friends of mine, who might have joined some other people on the trip.'

After their coffee they walked some distance across the bare slopes, beyond the range of most of the tourists, looking for flowers. Little was out at this altitude so early in the season, but Julia exclaimed in delight over some tiny things only three or four inches high, with small veined white chalices, golden hearts, and narrow upright channelled leaves of a blueish silver, three to each stalk—she knelt down on the damp black earth to examine them more closely.

'How lovely! I never saw anything so exquisite. What on earth are they? Some sort of baby lily?'

'No, it's *Ranunculus pyraenaeus*. They are beautiful, aren't they? I'm glad you've seen those—they're not very common.'

Julia, still on her knees, looked up at him with incredulity.

'John, don't be absurd! One of the few things I do know is that a Ranunculus is a buttercup; and they are yellow, and have *round,*

251

green leaves, with dents in the edges.'

He laughed at her delightedly, as she knelt there on the cold sodden ground, her tawny-gold head profiled against the blue ranges beyond the valley, worshipping the little plant.

'All the same it is a Ranunculus, darling.' He stooped and picked one, and as he did so the delicate veined petals fell off, exposing the tiny comical seed-head, still covered with golden stamens. 'There—isn't that exactly like the heart of one of your yellow buttercups with the round green leaves?' And Julia had to admit that it was precisely like.

'Could I pull one up?' she asked. 'Mrs. H. would so love it. But if the flowers fall it's no good.'

'One won't matter—let's find a plant in bud.' He took her hand and pulled her to her feet. 'Look—you've gone and muddied your good skirt!' Presently they came on two plants with closed buds, and with a pocket-knife Antrobus carefully extracted one from the soil—it had three white thong-like roots.

'How extraordinary!—three leaves and three roots,' Julia said.

'I never noticed that before. Amusing.' He took a small polythene bag from his pocket and stowed the small object in it, closing the top with an elastic band. 'Polythene bags are the answer to carrying flowers about,' he observed; 'perfectly airtight; they'll keep unwithered for twenty-four hours or more.' From another pocket he took out a small cardboard box, put bag, flowers and all into it, and replaced it in his pocket.

On returning to the car they doubled back on their tracks, down the valley up which they had come. Julia would have liked to go farther and see more, but Antrobus said No. 'We've sent a man up to Andermatt, where there's the long halt to eat, in case your cousin needs reinforcements there; you and I, I thought, would have lunch up on the Süsten-Pass, where the view is rather good, and then go down and loiter in the Aares-Schlucht, in case they come that way.'

'Would they be likely to do the hand-over in a place like that?'

'You never know. Anyhow there's a bird there that I should like to see if I could.'

'Oh—combine business with pleasure!' Julia said blithely, as the big car hummed gently off down the hairpin bends.

It was a brilliant day in early June; the sun was so hot that in the valley Julia threw off her green nylon windcheater and sat in the open car in her thin pull-over—up near the Süsten-Pass, however, she put it on again when they paused a little below the actual summit to watch the skiers climbing up and spinning down the snowy slopes of the Stein-Gletscher, which at its lower end forms a great white bowl between the mountains.

'Fancy ski-ing now!' Julia said enviously.

'It's a late year. There was a big fall of snow in April, and another about a fortnight ago. Usually it's over down here long before this.'

The top of the pass was crowded with cars. Antrobus with some trouble found a space, turned, and parked facing downhill before they went off to eat their lunch, sitting on an outcrop of rock a considerable distance above the road. A patch of Alpenrosen projected from underneath the grey stone on which they sat; the deep rose-red flowers, just opening, filled the air with their aromatic scent.

'Oh, they are delicious,' Julia said; she stooped and tried to pick a sprig, but the stems were surprisingly tough—Antrobus cut some for her. Up where they sat there was space and peace, but the slopes down by the road were thronged with people: hikers eating modest lunches out of paper bags, car-travellers feasting from elaborate picnic-baskets; several parties had even set up canvas chairs and tables, and were eating at those—meanwhile charabancs came up, paused for five minutes, and passed on, ceaselessly. Julia surveyed this scene with astonished distaste.

'It might be the Portsmouth Road on a Sunday,' she said.

'Well today is Saturday; this is the week-end traffic. At mid-week it's much quieter.'

'You're sure they aren't in any of those buses?' she asked, as two more huge vehicles, coming up from the St. Gotthard and Andermatt side, manœuvred into a parking-space and disgorged a swarm of tourists.

'Quite sure.' He looked at his watch. 'We're at least an hour and a half ahead of them. Have another roll.'

Julia realised that she had been foolish to hope for any manifestation which might make Antrobus's attitude to her more defined on this expedition—the teeming crowds made anything of the sort out of the question. She accepted her disappointment philosophically, and concentrated on two things she could always enjoy, scenery and food. Antrobus had rather surpassed himself over their lunch. Instead of the fairly tough-crusted *Brötchen* with slices of ham in them, hard-boiled eggs, and an apple and orange, normally provided by Swiss hotels, he had brought delicious squashy Bridge rolls lined with smoked salmon, *pâté de foie gras*, and Emmenthaler cheese; there was a polythene bag of fresh lettuce, and a white-wood box of Carlsbad plums.

'You do do yourself well,' Julia said, taking another *pâté* roll.

'Why not? In nice places, eat nice things. This is rather beyond my usual style, I may say—laid on for you, Julia.'

'Thank you, John. I do like food.'

'So I observe—and applaud. I cannot stomach those austere women who subject their guests to what really amounts to garbage! I believe that in reality thinking gets higher in proportion as the living becomes less plain.'

Julia laughed and took a Carlsbad plum, while from a thermos Antrobus poured coffee into two pretty Chinese porcelain bowls.

'Oh, don't I know!' she said. 'Good works and bad food! Thank God Mrs. Hathaway combines her innumerable good works with quite excellent food.'

'Ah, she would. But she is a most exceptional person.'

After they had eaten they drove down again to the main valley, passed through Innertkirchen, and on to the lower entrance of the Aar Gorge. Here a small restaurant was flanked by a large car-park, where Antrobus left the Porsche; the restaurant had a sort of open-air extension roofed over and full of little tables, now, at the week-end, thronged with holiday-makers—Antrobus walked past them towards the ticket-gate.

'There,' he said, pointing to a framed drawing on the wall, 'that's what I should so very much like to see.'

The picture was of a small bird poised, apparently in perfect comfort, against a vertical surface of rock, on which it appeared to maintain its hold by long curved claws; its beak was slender and also curved. Otherwise, apart from rather defined light and dark markings round the head and on the wings, it was thoroughly insignificant.

'It looks rather like a tree-creeper,' Julia said.

'Naturally. It's his first cousin, the wall-creeper—only this fellow has red splashes here, and here.' He touched the drawing with his finger. 'But this particular bird is rather rare; the Aares-Schlucht is one of the few accessible places in Europe where one may hope to see it, because the gorge is so enclosed. And this is unusually low for it; its normal bottom level is seven thousand feet, and here we are not much over two thousand. Come on in—there's a pause between the buses just now, so we might have a chance. He's rather shy.'

While Antrobus got out a handful of coins to buy their tickets, Julia idly looked round at the crowded tables behind them. At one, fairly close to the ticket *guichet*, sat M. Chambertin. She touched Antrobus's arm—'Half a moment.'

'What is it?' He was all impatience for his bird.

'There's Chambertin,' she murmured.

For a moment the name failed to register.

'Who?'

'Chambertin, from the Banque Républicaine—sitting there, reading a newspaper. Do you suppose he's waiting for them too?'

Antrobus frowned, and walked back towards the carpark. 'That wretched von Allmen must have told him,' he muttered vexedly. 'He promised to leave this part to us. Has he seen you?'

'He's reading his paper so hard that I think he must have,' Julia said. 'Shall I thwart him?'

Antrobus thought for a moment. 'Yes, do,' he said then, grinning. 'It may cramp his style. I've never met him.' As they turned back towards the restaurant Julia saw, sitting several tables away from the banker, the man sho had come into the Gemsbock garden the previous day and shadowed Wright and Borovali when they went to the police-station.

'He's got his detective in tow, too,' she said.

'Where?'

'Three tables to the right of the door—the very ordinary-looking little man.'

'By Jove, so he has! Well really that is rather much, to bring Müller along! All right—go and accost him, Julia.'

'Shall you come too?'

'Yes, I think I will. Damn, now we shall miss that bird! There are more buses due soon.'

Antrobus watched with amused satisfaction Julia's manner of accosting the banker.

'Oh, how do you do, Monsieur Chambertin? What a surprise to see you here! But how nice to meet again.' Chambertin rose, quite as embarrassed as the Secret Service man had hoped, and greeted Julia fussily.

'I am on holiday,' he explained needlessly. 'I have a little villa near Spiez.'

'Oh how nice. Are you going to look at the Aares-Schlucht?' Julia pursued. 'So are we. This is my friend Mr. Antrobus'— Chambertin bowed, with noticeable coldness. 'There is a rare bird here which he desires to see. Are you interested in birds?'

'Not birds—no. They are not a subject of mine. I am here simply *en touriste*, sight-seeing.'

Antrobus, still resentful that the Interlaken Chief of Police had obviously betrayed his information about the bus-tour, which he had given him the evening before, to the Bank, now decided to add to the other man's discomfiture.

'Not even interested in birds of prey, Monsieur Chambertin?' he asked, with a sort of deadly relish.

'In no birds, Monsieur.' Chambertin raised his hat—of which the tourist effect was increased by a tuft of chamoistail stuck in the back—to Julia, bowed, and abruptly stumped off into the restaurant with a cold *'Au revoir, Mademoiselle'*

'*Not* pleased to see us,' Julia murmured.

'No—nor I to see him, and his flatty. This may complicate things.' He looked at his watch. 'Their bus is due at the top end in about half an hour. For goodness' sake let's go in and see if we can spot *Tichodroma muraria* meantime.'

'Heavens what a name!' Julia observed.

They went in and walked along that strange little wooden

pathway propped out precariously over the grey-green rushing water. The Aares-Schlucht is both deep and narrow; its cold grey limestone walls limit the sky above to a thin pale line; a deadly chill comes up with the loud sound of the water, racing by so close below—on Julia the whole place produced a highly disagreeable, almost an uncanny impression. 'Why any bird should choose to live here!' she remarked.

'Walk very slowly, and don't make any abrupt movement,' Antrobus said, taking a pair of Zeiss glasses out of the big poacher's pocket of his tweed jacket; he returned the leather case to the pocket, slung the glasses by their narrow strap round his neck, and then focused them carefully on the opposite wall of the gorge. For the moment no tourists seemed to be coming through it, and they walked slowly forward, Julia constantly looking at her watch, her companion incessantly scanning the opposite cliff.

'There it is!' he exclaimed suddenly. 'Look! Oh what luck!'

Julia, standing behind him and following the direction in which his field-glasses pointed saw—a little ahead of them and rather high up—a tiny bird, grey like the rock, but darker and splashed with crimson, with white spots on its tail, fluttering about on the farther rock wall.

'It's not a bit like a tree-creeper,' she said rather resentfully. 'It flits like a butterfly, it doesn't creep.' Her resentment was partly an echo of her disappointment with this whole expedition, as far as her relations with Antrobus were concerned, and partly of the irrational dislike which she felt for the Aares-Schlucht as a place. Once before, in Morocco, she had felt a similar irrational dislike for a house and garden in Marrakesh—but in Marrakesh, within an hour or two, she had been blown up by a terrorist's bomb.

Antrobus ignored her remark. The bird was slowly moving

forward, upstream; he followed it, and Julia followed him. 'I wish it would come down a bit,' he said. 'Oh damn, what's this?'

'This' was that the path now dived into a tunnel hollowed out of the rock; Antrobus hurried through it, Julia still following—when they emerged he eagerly scanned the opposite cliff. The bird, though now abreast of them, had gone higher up than ever.

'Little brute!' Antrobus said, watching the small creature intently pecking at a thread-like crevice in the rock, clasped to the vertical surface by its claws. He looked about him to see if there was any means of reaching a level nearer to that of the bird. The cliff on their side was obviously impossible, but oddly enough behind them, close to the exit from the tunnel, a slender iron ladder, reddish from the remains of oxide paint, rose thirty feet or more against the rock wall, though for what purpose it was impossible to guess.

'Corn in Egypt!' Antrobus exclaimed. He moved stealthily back towards the ladder and began to climb up it with slow, wary movements.

'It may not be properly fixed—do be careful,' Julia said, alarmed at this manœuvre, for the ladder was fastened against a bulge in the cliff which projected out over the racing water below.

'No, it's quite firm,' he called back—the noise of the river was so loud that the sound of their voices could hardly disturb any bird. Julia watched him anxiously as he climbed steadily upwards, pausing now and then to raise his binoculars and peer at the wall-creeper which, having apparently struck a rich vein of grubs or insects in the crevice, clung there absorbed, exactly as in the picture, prodding diligently with its slender beak. The ladder did appear to be quite firm, and one way and another it seemed to Julia that the bird was becoming rather a bore—reassured, she stopped watching Antrobus, and looked about her.

Some hundred yards away, coming downstream towards her along the narrow plank-walk, where two people could barely walk abreast, she saw Mr. Borovali, moving partly behind a stout woman in a hideous tartan coat, with an enormous tartan shoulder-bag slung over her arm; a short distance behind them came Wright and a small man with a broad Teutonic face, who, like Chambertin, wore a green felt hat with a chamois-tail stuck in the back. Wright was carrying the black brief-case, still distended.

'Yes, do the switch-over in the tunnel!—*I* see!' she muttered to herself as she returned to the foot of the ladder; there she called up urgently to Antrobus, who had now reached the top and was staring entranced through his Zeisses at *Tichodroma muraria*.

'John, here they are!'

No response. In her fresh and different anxiety she actually shook the ladder. 'John, they're *here*! Do come down.'

At this moment an immensely loud tune suddenly blared out from somewhere close by, filling the chasm and echoing from wall to wall. This, though Julia could not know it, was produced by a man round a bend in the gorge blowing the *Alpen-horn*, a musical instrument nearly ten feet long whose principal if not its only merit is the enormous volume of sound which it can produce. As these trumpet-notes suddenly echoed and re-echoed between the high walls of the narrow cleft, three things happened more or less at the same moment. The stout lady came to a halt, looked behind her, and started to walk back in the direction whence the sound came, followed by Borovali, who laid a restraining hand on her arm, clearly trying to stop her. Antrobus started, and nearly lost his balance on the ladder; the wall-creeper flew away.

Chapter 13

The Aares-Schlucht

Julia, convulsed with unseasonable laughter, once more called up from the foot of the ladder, again shaking it—'John, do please come down! They're *here!*'

'Why on earth must the municipality cause anyone to make that filthy row? Now it's gone,' he said indignantly, starting to climb down the reddish rungs. Naturally he had to do this backwards, and therefore could not see, as Julia did, what was taking place on the plank-walk some distance upstream. The stout lady, apparently determined to go back and see the Alpenhorn in action, steadily returned on her tracks, ignoring Borovali's imploring gestures, but within twenty yards she came face to face with Wright and his short Germanic-looking companion. The wooden path was so narrow that it was impossible for people to pass one another without goodwill on both sides, including a certain flattening of the person against either the rock wall or the rail overhanging the water—and Wright displayed no such goodwill. On the contrary he stood scowling, effectively blocking the stout woman's path. There was an altercation, diagramatically visible to Julia, though of course inaudible because of the roaring noise of the river; arms were raised in angry gestures, the woman tried to push past, Wright continued to obstruct her, Borovali wrung his hands. While this was still going on Julia saw Colin coming round the bend in the gorge from beyond which the Alpenhorn continued to resound, and approaching the other group.

'Now, what were you shouting about?' Antrobus asked Julia, wiping traces of red paint off his hands with a tuft of grass snatched from the rock-face. 'I couldn't hear a thing.'

'Look,' Julia said, pointing.

The four people now formed a sort of angry knot, completely blocking the cat-walk.

'Which of them has the stuff, Wright or the woman?' Antrobus asked hastily.

'How should *I* know? He's still got the brief-case, but she's got a bag big enough to hold the Treaty of Versailles,' Julia replied.

Antrobus started forward towards the group as Colin bore down on them from behind; they were all so engrossed in their altercation that they never noticed the two Englishmen till they were almost upon them. Colin, saying '*Verzeihung*' and '*Pardon*' very politely, pushed right in among them, and with a swift movement wrenched the black brief-case out of Wright's hand; the next second he was racing away in the direction whence he had come. Wright whipped out a revolver from the pocket of those pale corduroy slacks which Julia had so recently seen hanging up in a bedroom in the Golden Bear; but Antrobus leapt onto the slender rail like a cat, took one step along it past the three solid bodies of Borovali, the German man, and the German woman, and even as he sprang down behind them onto the plank-walk knocked up Wright's wrist—a little pale puff of limestone dust showed where the bullet had hit harmlessly on the cliff overhead.

Wright, furious, instantly tried to turn the revolver onto him; Antrobus struggled to wrest it out of the other's hand—they grappled confusedly on the narrow path. The stout woman now took a hand; raising her enormous tartan bag she bashed at Antrobus's head with it—Antrobus ducked. The bag was one of those open-topped ones, and out of it now fell, not the Treaty of Versailles or any other documents, but a positive shower of packets of chocolate, bags of biscuits—which burst—oranges, bananas, and some knitting; finally a tiny pistol dropped onto the planking among the edibles—this, with a quick movement of one foot, Antrobus kicked off the boards into the river, while he went on wrestling with Wright for the possession of his revolver.

Meanwhile Julia, who had come forward from the foot of the ladder to watch what was going on, saw that Colin's get-away with the black brief-case was hopelessly blocked by some twenty tourists, who came round the bend in the gorge, whence the Alpenhorn continued to blare out its cheerful notes, in a solid block. He checked, looked behind him, saw her, and came running back, right up to the others.

'Over to you, darling,' he shouted above the roar of the river, and pitched the black brief-case clean over all their heads; it fell with a plonk on the boards at Julia's feet.

But there were more than two revolvers in that party—June had been quite right. Mr. Borovali now extracted one, not without trouble, from somewhere about his stout person, and called out—'Please put up your hands, all of you. I am armed.'

Antrobus paid no attention whatever to this; he was entirely concentrated on his struggle with Wright, who was as muscular and elastic as an eel. 'Look out, John!' Julia called to him, snatching up the brief-case as she spoke. But just then a second revolver-shot rang out. For a moment Julia thought that Borovali had fired, but she was wrong; Wright had managed to put a shot through Antrobus's leg. Antrobus lost his temper, and exerting the unnatural strength of fury and self-preservation heaved the younger and lighter man up and pitched him bodily, revolver and all, over the railing into the swirling Aar below—the onlookers saw the dark head sink, rise, sink again, rise again, as he was whirled along between the rocks; he was attempting feebly to swim when the green waters bore him out of sight round the bulge in the cliff against which the ladder stood.

Again several things happened more or less at once. Julia, ignoring Wright in the river, from behind twitched Borovali's revolver from his outstretched hand while he stood staring at his colleague in the water, and slipped it into the pocket of her wind-jacket; Colin hurried up to Antrobus; the group of tourists, hearing revolver-shots and seeing a man thrown into the river recoiled, pressing one another backwards—all but one burly individual, who thrust his way to the front demanding, in the unmistakable tones of an English policeman—'What goes on 'ere?'

No one paid much attention to him. Antrobus had sunk down on one knee; from the trouser on his other leg, which was stuck out awkwardly in front of him, blood was streaming over the plank-walk, soaking into the biscuits and packets of chocolate from the German woman's bag. Julia, in an agony, called out—'Oh, Colin, do see how bad it is.'

Antrobus heard her.

'Clear off, Julia—the key's in the car. Take that thing away—Colin will see to me.'

264

This told Julia that Antrobus, in spite of his struggles with Wright, realised that Colin had passed her the black brief-case. For a moment she hesitated—there was John, pouring with blood before her eyes; could she leave him? It was in fact Borovali who decided her to do what Antrobus asked—he wheeled round on her, saying—'It is you who took my weapon?'

'Goodness no! What weapon?' But Julia was full of a blind instinctive rage—at the injury to Antrobus, and at all these crooks who had brought it about; above all she was furious with the German woman. Even as she spoke she stepped past Borovali and snatched the vast tartan bag off the fat creature's arm, and then turned and ran like a deer down the plank-walk into the tunnel, leaving the others staring after her.

She ran all the way through the tunnel too—only when she was approaching the exit did she slow down. Oh gracious, would the man want her ticket? John had got them. But the official at the gate was busy with a swarm of tourists eager to enter, and when she said, 'Just now I came in with the *Englischer Herr*,' he let her pass.

In the open restaurant the first person she saw was Chambertin, no longer sitting at a table but standing talking with two other men, one of whom she recognised as Müller, the detective who had sat in the Gemsbock garden, and shadowed Wright and Borovali to the police-station. She hurried over to them.

'Monsieur Chambertin, can you get hold of a doctor? Mr. Antrobus has been shot.'

'Shot? Where?'

'In the leg,' Julia said idiotically, thinking only of Antrobus.

'But in what circumstances?' Chambertin asked, looking concerned.

'Oh, by those ruffians in there—in the gorge. And one of

them is in the river,' she added needlessly, with a rather hysterical laugh.

The man who was not Müller rounded sharply on her.

'How came he in the river, Fräulein?'

'Oh, go in and ask! There are dozens of people in there who saw it all.' She turned to Chambertin. 'But do get a doctor quickly, can't you? He may bleed to death,' she said urgently, and started away towards the car-park.

Chambertin followed her, and while she was fiddling with the controls on the dash-board of Antrobus's big Porsche, all completely unfamiliar to her, he poked his head in at the window.

'And you, Mademoiselle? Where do you go now?'

'But to my hotel. I have a friend there, an elderly English lady, who is unwell. I must get back to her.'

'Your hotel is in Interlaken?'

Julia noticed that the man who had asked her how Wright came to be in the river had also come up to the car, and stood beside Chambertin, listening intently. Was this the Swiss police chief, von Allmen or whatever his name was, who had given away the business of the bus-tour to Chambertin? Anyhow she could only speak the truth.

'No, up at Beatenberg—the Silberhorn. Goodbye, Monsieur Chambertin—do *please* get a doctor at once.' She let in the clutch and shot away out of the car-park.

Spinning down the road towards Meiringen, through it, and on towards Brienz Julia, in spite of her anxiety about Antrobus, began to do some hard thinking. Since she had got both the brief-case and the German lady's tartan bag presumably she had got the papers, there on the seat beside her in the car—including the documents which John didn't want the Swiss police to see. And John had entrusted her with the job of taking them away,

266

and 'clearing off'. Well she had cleared off; but she would like to find out as soon as possible if she really had got 'the doings', as she privately phrased it; and then she must think of somewhere to put them. If the third man with Chambertin was the Interlaken Chief of Police, or any form of police, he now knew her address, and nothing could stop him from searching the hotel. Oh dear!

Brienz has a rather narrow street, which on fine weekends is apt to be jammed with cars. Julia was more than once brought to a halt where single-line traffic was coming towards her—and she noticed in her driving-mirror that a small grey Volkswagen, with two men in it, was immediately behind her. Through Brienz, in the open country beyond, she slowed down with the idea of looking at the contents of the two cases, and waved the grey Volkswagen on. But it did not pass her—it slowed down too. 'Oh, bloody police-car, I suppose,' she muttered irritably, and shot on again.

The Porsche, if pressed, had the legs of the Volkswagen; Julia pressed it, and soon left the smaller car behind and out of sight. Then she again thought hard. Where could she go, short of the Hotel Silberhorn, to examine the contents of the two bags without interruption?

A ladies' lavatory is one of the few places where a woman can be certain of being alone and undisturbed, and as Julia drove along the shore of the Lake of Brienz she remembered the large, exquisitely clean 'Ladies' in the Hotel zum Fluss at Interlaken, which she had visited when she brought Mrs. Hathaway down from the Schynige-Platte, and acquired so much useful information from the hotel porter. The very thing!—moreover, it was not on the direct route to Beatenberg, but lay in the opposite direction, involving a double-back on her tracks, so that it might throw those snoopers in the grey car off the scent. Grinning with satisfaction, she swung over the road bridge across the Aar at Interlaken, turned left, and passing the Englischer Garten with its dull statue and its beautiful silver poplars, pulled in to the open car-park where the Brienz steamers have their landing-stage. The 'Ladies' at the Fluss had, she remembered, a separate entrance giving on to this; no need to go through the lounge past the chatty old porter. Grasping both bags, Julia hastened in at the side door, through the outer wash-room, and into one of the actual lavatories; there she bolted the door and began to examine her booty.

She had worried rather on her way as to whether the black brief-case might be locked, but it wasn't; the two clips sprang up at the touch of her fingers. Eagerly she raised the flap and looked in—to see large quantities of old newspapers! Then it occurred to her that the documents might have been wrapped in these, and she hastily unfolded and shook out every single copy of the *Journal de Genève,* the *Gazette de Lausanne,* and the *Continental Daily Mail,* thinking as she did so that these must represent Borovali's and Wright's tastes in newspapers respectively. No—only news-papers. Could everything have gone wrong, and John been wounded for nothing? However, there remained the German lady's tartan bag—she had already noticed as she carried it in from the car that in spite of the loss of all those comestibles which had been poured out in the Aares-Schlucht it did not feel like an empty bag; in fact it was quite heavy. (At the Aares-Schlucht she had been too hurried and upset to notice anything.) Stuffing the useless newspapers behind the lavatory seat, Julia, her fingers actually trembling, tackled the tartan bag.

In it, just below the broad imitation-leather band which bound the open top there was a second compartment with a zip fastener, running the whole length of one side of the bag. The zip was secured with a silly little imitation-gilt padlock, but it was a cheaply-made affair; Julia fished a tiny nail-file out of her handbag, slipped it through the ring of the padlock, and wrapping her handkerchief round her fingers wrenched the thing off, and pulled back the zip.

Inside she found a very large, stiff, shiny envelope, heavily re-sealed with black wax; as well, bundles and bundles of papers, folded narrow and long, some tied with white tape, others not fastened at all. She examined these first, looking them over rapidly. Julia had been left a considerable fortune by her grandmother, and she was perfectly familiar with the appearance of certificates for debentures, stocks, and shares; the only thing which startled her about these was the colossal size of the figures typed or written in—here was Aglaia's fortune, and it must be vast. But that was not what John cared about. She turned to the big envelope, and hastily pulled out her Biro pen from her bag—the slender oval end of a Biro is perfect for opening envelopes without tearing them—rolled it along under the flap, cracking the black wax of the seals, and drew out the contents.

'Blue-prints', a word so casually used in the press for any project for the future, when they are scientific and technical really are blue—blue, with the design for the machine or plan showing up on them in white lines. Such sheets, just as June had described them, Julia, sitting on the lavatory seat in the Hotel zum Fluss, now unfolded—and then most carefully folded up again along their original creases. With things like these she was quite unfamiliar; she had no idea whether she was looking at the plans for a nuclear-powered submarine tanker or for the pumps on an underground pipe-line from Kirkuk to Iskenderun, emerging into the Mediterranean on Turkish soil. The drawings of one or two large bulbous-looking objects reminded her, vaguely, of

Colin's account of the huge under-water containers in which food for man and beast was even now stored in the green depths of the lakes of Thun and Brienz—but this could hardly interest the Swiss. She was faintly intrigued, too, by another set of papers, drawn in ink on bluish paper with a linen pattern; but these seemed merely to be duplicates of the blue-prints. What she did realise was that she had got, here, under her hand, the documents that both John and Colin were so desperately anxious to secure; and she must, absolutely must, somehow contrive to hand them over to one or the other without letting the Swiss police, or anyone else, see them first.

It struck her at once that this might not be so easy. Whether or not the grey Volkswagen was a police-car it had been on her tail, and knew the number of the Porsche; if it was not a police-car, but belonged to some nefarious associates of Borovali or the two Germans, so much the worse. But in any case Chambertin and the man with him knew that she was staying at the Silberhorn, and nothing could stop the Swiss police from—perfectly properly—searching her room for missing property.

Julia considered. The blue-prints were much too big to be stuffed down her bosom, in the good romantic manner, and her own handbag was too small to accommodate them. She did some more thinking. Some people say they think best in their bath; Julia thought to quite good effect, perched on the seat in a ladies' lavatory. What Chambertin—and hence the Swiss police—really wanted was Mr. Thalassides' fortune, entrusted to the Banque Républicaine and, by fraud, stolen. Good—they should have it; sooner or later they would have to hand it over to Aglaia Armitage anyhow. She picked up the certificates representing that fortune from the tesselated floor, where she had left them while she looked at the blue-prints, placed them in the black brief-case, and snapped it to; then she replaced the stiff envelope containing the blue-prints in the inner compartment of the tartan bag.

'One for John, one for the Swiss,' she murmured, gurgling—for an idea had come to her about the disposal of the tartan bag which made her laugh. She looked at her watch—twenty to six. There ought to be time, if Colin got back fairly soon. Carrying her three bags, she went out to the Porsche.

Julia had guessed—rightly, as it happened—that if the grey Volkswagen was a police-car it would go straight on up to Beatenberg, and look for her at the Hotel Silberhorn; its occupants could have no means of knowing that she had doubled back to the Fluss. There was no sign of it on the parking-place by the quay when she left the hotel, nor on the Bahnhof-Platz by the West Station—she looked carefully there as she passed, and then drove on, as fast as the low-hung Porsche could take the hairpin bends, up through the scented woods to Beatenberg.

But she didn't go to the hotel. Instead she drove into the big lay-by at the foot of the Sessel-Bahn, left the car, and went up the zigzag path to the little station. She took a ticket to the Niederhorn itself, and was soon swinging up between the tree-tops, through evening air sweet with scents drawn out from grass and flower and tree during the long warm day—and as she sat swaying she took out the local bus time-table, which had on the back the hours during which the Sessel-Bahn was open. Yes, passenger traffic went on up to 20.30 hours, i.e. till 8.30 p.m.—how tiresome the continental habit was of having no a.m. and p.m.; one always had to do these complicated sums! It was now nearly a quarter to seven—that was cutting it pretty fine; please God Colin did somehow come to the hotel at once. If he didn't, she would just have to come up again alone.

At the mid-way station, where the twin seats are pulled round by hand from the lower steel cable to the upper one Julia, with her three bags, asked to be let out.

'The Fräulein does not go on to the *Gipfel?*' the man in dungarees, who was conducting this manoeuvre, asked in surprise.

'No, not tonight.' While he was slinging two more seats round the curved rails she walked over to the group of milk-churns which stood in a far corner, ready, as she had learned, to carry water up to the hotel on the summit when the passenger traffic was over for the day. Lifting the lid of the remotest churn of all she slightly bent the tartan bag and stuffed it into this odd receptacle; then she replaced the lid, and walked back to the man in dungarees.

'Do you use all the churns now, to carry up the water at night?' she asked casually, when a pause occurred in the traffic.

'Ah, Fräulein, no; not now—this is not the high season. In July and August, yes; sometimes we are loading these vessels till after midnight! But at present it is not so bad.'

'So how many containers do you use now?'

'Oh, it varies—but certainly not all. We fill these nearest ones, and load them up; the hotel sends down word how many they need.'

This satisfied Julia. It was highly unlikely that the blueprints would be soused, even if she and Colin were a little late. She got onto the next seat that came down empty, and was carried away through the bright air, down to the road and the car; then she drove on to the Silberhorn.

There were three cars drawn up on the gravelled space outside the hotel, where normally there were none except at lunch-time— one was a grey Volkswagen. Grinning a little, Julia avoided the main entrance and went in by a little door which led directly into

272

the bar; there she encountered Fräulein Hanna, who left off polishing glasses, took her arm, and led her with a certain urgency out into the long broad corridor which served as a hall.

'Fräulein Probyn, the *Polizei* are here again!' she said agitatedly. 'And another gentleman also.'

'Are they? What are they doing?' Julia asked. As she spoke she hung the black brief-case up on one of the many coat-hooks which adorned the hall on both sides, and slung her wind-cheater over it.

'They speak with Frau Hathaway; but they have asked first for you.'

'Where are they?'

'In the garden.'

'Is the Herr Monro here?'

'No.'

Julia walked quickly through the *Kleine Saal* into the garden. It was nearly half past seven; Mrs. Hathaway ought not to be out too late—and she ought not to be worried.

Mrs. Hathaway, however, did not appear to be in the least worried when Julia reached the garden; she seemed to be having a party. Chambertin and the man Julia had seen with him at the Aares-Schlucht restaurant were sitting by the old lady, drinking Cinzano and laughing; Müller, the detective, and two other men sat at another table, trying to make conversation with Watkins, who was refilling their glasses.

'Oh my dear child, there you are at last! These gentlemen have been wondering what had become of you; they want to see you about something, it seems. I gather you already know Monsieur Chambertin—and this is Herr von Allmen, the Chief of Police in Interlaken.' Nothing could have been easier than her voice and manner.

273

'So I had guessed,' Julia said rather coldly as she returned von Allmen's bow. 'But look, Mrs. H. darling, you don't want to get chilly after your illness—now that I'm here, hadn't you better go in and get some dinner? It's quite late.'

'Oh no—we're having such fun. Aren't we?' she asked of her two guests. 'And I'm sure they won't mind my hearing whatever it is they want to ask you about.'

It was obvious to Julia that both men did mind considerably being forced to interview her in the old lady's presence, and she knew Mrs. Hathaway well enough to be sure that she realised this too, and was doing it on purpose. She rejoiced at Chambertin and von Allmen's evident embarrassment.

'Before anything else,' she said to Chambertin, 'please tell me about Monsieur Antrobus. Where is he? Has a doctor seen him?'

'Yes, Mademoiselle. It so happened that there was an English *infirmière* in a party of toursts who were passing through the gorge when'—he coughed—'when the accident happened;she attended to Monsieur Antrobus at once, and put on a tourniquet. Meanwhile we had telephoned to Meiringen for a doctor and an ambulance, and he was brought out with the least possible delay; he was carried very carefully—our *brancardiers* are excellent.'

Julia was enormously relieved at this news, though the idea of an English hospital-nurse in holiday rig coping with John on the plank-walk struck her as distinctly funny. But the mention of a tourniquet worried her—that sounded as though the bullet had punctured an artery.

'Where is he now?' she asked again.

'In Dr. Hertz's Clinic down in the town, here. He expressed a very strong desire to be in Interlaken rather than at Meiringen.'

'Oh, I'm so glad. He'll be perfectly all right with Hertz,' Julia said happily.

'You know the Herr Doktor Hertz?' von Allmen asked, looking surprised.

'Yes. But now, Monsieur Chambertin, what is it that you and the Chief of Police wish to ask me about? I don't want to keep Madame Hathaway out of doors too long. And oh darling Mrs. H., could *I* have a Cinzano too? It's been such a day.'

'Watkins, you haven't given Miss Julia anything to drink,' Mrs. Hathaway said mildly.

'Oh, I'm so sorry, Madam. I've got some spare glasses here. There, Miss,' the maid said, bustling over from the other table.

'Thank you, Watkins.' Julia took a good gulp of the Cinzano, gratefully, and then turned again to the two Swiss, with an expectant face.

She saw them glance at one another doubtfully—it was Chambertin who spoke.

'Mademoiselle Probyn, when this—this episode—took place in the Aares-Schlucht this afternoon, I understand—from several witnesses—that you picked up a black leather case full of papers, and carried it away.'

'Certainly I did. Didn't you see it lying on the seat of the car, when you and Herr von Allmen came and asked me where I was going?' Julia asked coolly.

'Yes, I did see it,' Chambertin said, irritated by her tone; 'and if you had not driven off in such haste I should have spoken of it at once. But the papers in that case, Mademoiselle, are the property of the Banque Républicaine, which I represent, and I wish them to be returned to me.'

'They're really the property of Miss Armitage's trustees, aren't they, which your poor old Monsieur de Kessler let a lot of impostors steal from him?' Julia replied—eliciting a glance of startled delight from Mrs. Hathaway. 'What have you done with the impostors, by the way? Have you laid the old one, Borovali, by the heels?—and did you fish the young one out of the Aar? I told you he'd been thrown in.'

Von Allmen's face, at this point, would have repaid observation.

'For the moment Herr Borovali is in our hands,' he replied cautiously. 'But it would interest me to know, Fräulein Probyn, how it comes that you are so familiar with the name of this individual?'

Julia took her time over replying to this. If she mentioned June it might lead to more questions, and then trouble at La Cure, and possibly June arrested too.

'Really, I think you'd better ask Monsieur Chambertin about that,' she said. 'He will tell you that it was I who supplied him with the photograph that was circulated all over Switzerland, and enabled you to trace Borovali to the Fluss. And when you lost him there, I found him again at the Golden Bear.'

'Dear Julia, did you really? How entertaining,' Mrs. Hathaway interposed. Julia turned to Chambertin.

'What have you done with the two Boches?' She realised that the local chief of police was still rather at sea where she was concerned, and that she was likely to get more out of the banker.

'Unfortunately, Mademoiselle, technically we have nothing against them; they claim that they were simply tourists, quite unwillingly involved in this affair.'

'Oh I see,' Julia said, thinking of the tiny revolver that had dropped out of the tartan bag, and what its inner pocket still contained, in a churn half-way up the Niederhorn. 'So back to Dortmund on tonight's sleepers, I suppose.'

Once again von Allmen's face would have repaid observation—and got it, from Mrs. Hathaway. But he was a senior police official, and as such kept to his point.

'In any case, Fräulein Probyn, you admit to having obtained possession of these papers. Where are they now?'

'Hanging up in the hall here, with my jacket. I'll show you in a second, but first, do tell me where Mr. Monro is?'

'In the hospital at Meiringen. He has a concussion.'

'Colin? Good heavens! How on earth did that happen?'

'Fräulein, when a person is thrown into the Aares-Schlucht, bones are liable to be broken,' the police chief said repressively. Chambertin looked embarrassed; Julia laughed rather hysterically. Why did von Allmen know Borovali's real name, and not Wright's? Or had he forgotten? Or had someone thrown Colin into the river too? Before she could work out the answers to these questions the Interlaken bus rolled past, and drew up beyond the cow-stable across the road—a moment later Colin himself walked in from the farther end of the garden. The girl got up, and flew to him.

'Have you seen John?'

'Antrobus, do you mean? Yes—I've just come from there. He's perfectly O.K. in that Clinic; he says the nurses are charmers. The doctor's operating this evening.'

'Operating? What for?' Julia was horrified.

'To take out the bullet. It won't be much, that man Hertz says, but they can't leave it in. I say, have you got those papers all right?'

The urgency in his voice caused Julia to look at her cousin more attentively than she had done so far, concentrated as she was on Antrobus; Colin looked battered, almost bruised, by the day's events, and his anxiety about the job.

'Yes rather—both lots. They weren't in the black briefcase, though.'

'Then where?'

'In that tartan bag I snatched from the German Frau.'

'But she emptied that out; all that fruit and stuff!'

'Ah yes, but there was an inner pocket, and all the doings were zipped into that. There was nothing in the brief-case but old newspapers. I expect the eats were just camouflage.'

'Where on earth can they have done the switch?' Colin speculated. 'I never let them out of my sight for a moment.'

'Even in the loos? That's where I'd expect. In lots of these Swiss pubs the *Herren* and *Damen Toiletten* are side by side.'

'So they were, in Andermatt!' he exclaimed. 'And they all went there in a bunch together. The man from Berne went into the Gents, and I was hovering outside, but I didn't see anything— there was a huge crowd, as there always is when a bus-tour makes a halt.'

'Well, I bet the greedy Frau took the brief-case from Wright in the corridor, did the switch inside, and handed it back to him as she came out. They must have had the old newspapers on them somewhere—no, I expect they were in the black case all the time; the real papers aren't all that bulky.'

'You've actually looked at them?' the young man enquired anxiously. 'Is what we want there?'

'Well a great big envelope of those drawing things.'

'Where are they now?' Colin asked, almost trembling with excitement.

'In two places. What you and John want is where no one would ever think of looking; we must fetch them as soon as we can. What the Swiss police and old Chambertin want—Aglaia's good money—is hanging up here in the hotel.' She looked at her watch. 'Goodness, we haven't a minute to lose! Come and get a drink from Watkins, while I satisfy these types and push them off.' She moved across the garden.

'Good God! Are *they* here?' Colin said nervously—he now saw who was sitting with Mrs. Hathaway.

'Oh yes—I was tailed all the way from the Schlucht,' Julia said cheerfully. 'And I did my *triage* in a loo, too. What goings-on the Swiss lavatories have seen today!' She spoke to the maid as she passed. 'Watkins, I know Mrs. Hathaway has some whisky— could you get some for Mr. Colin?'

'Of course, Miss. I'll fetch it. It's not a known brand, but Madam says it's quite all right.' She bustled away.

Von Allmen was looking distinctly restive as Julia returned to Mrs. Hathaway's table after this colloquy, Colin beside her.

'Monsieur Chambertin, I don't think you've properly met my cousin Colin, have you?' She turned to von Allmen. 'And Herr von Allmen, this is really Mr. Monro; the young man in the hospital at Meiringen is a Mr. Wright, though he has a forged passport in the name of Monro.'

The police chief had risen for the introduction and bowed politely to Colin; but he looked thoroughly disconcerted at Julia's last remark, and threw an angry glance in Chambertin's direction. Julia flowed on. 'And now, shall we go and get those papers you want, Monsieur Chambertin?'

They went through the *Kleine Saal* to the lobby, where Julia reached down the black brief-case from under her nylon wind- jacket and handed it to Chambertin.

'You'd better look at the papers, and see that everything is there, hadn't you?' she said.

'Most certainly. But where can we do this?'

The lobby at the Silberhorn leads into a sort of coffee-room adjoining the bar, with French windows opening onto a broad terrace or balcony which commands the view; since dinner was already going on in the restaurant both these places were empty. But a few people were still in the bar; Chambertin went through onto the terrace, followed by von Allmen, and sat down at one of the small tables, on which he placed the brief-case. 'Where is the key?' he asked.

'It isn't locked—I never saw a key.'

'Incroyable!' the Swiss exclaimed. He opened the case, drew out the papers, and then from his pocket-book took a sheet of paper covered with spider-fine hand-writing and figures; this he spread out on the coloured table-cloth and then, taking the papers one by one he began to go through them, ticking off items on the sheet of paper as he did so.

'Oh good—you've got a list,' Julia said. 'Well while you're checking it, will you excuse me? I must take Mrs. Hathaway to get some dinner; she's stayed out far too late as it is.'

'Fräulein, I shall require to get your account of what took place in the Aares-Schlucht, and of other matters,' von Allmen said as she made to leave.

'Yes, of course. But can't that wait till the morning? I shan't run away, and my friend is still a convalescent; I must take care of her.'

'Very good. Will half-past nine tomorrow morning be too early?'

'No, perfect. See you then.' She hastened back to the garden, where Colin was drinking the un-branded whisky—'Wait here,' she told him, and led Mrs. Hathaway through the whole length of the hotel to the restaurant, where the heels of the waitresses were clacking on the parquet as they served the rather sparse guests.

'Dear Julia, what are those men doing? Have they gone?' Mrs. Hathaway asked.

'Not yet—they're checking,' Julia said laughing. 'And the policeman is coming back to interview me tomorrow morning.'

'Well now do sit down and have something to eat, dear child, and Colin too,' Mrs. Hathaway said comfortably, unfolding her napkin and buttering a roll while she waited for the soup.

'No, I can't eat yet; Colin and I have got to go out again,' Julia said, casting a horrified glance at the restaurant clock, which said five minutes to eight. 'Ask Fräulein Hanna to keep something hot for us. I'll come up to see you last thing.'

On her way through the coffee-room she encountered Colin. 'Where do we go?' he asked eagerly.

'Half a moment.' Through the huge windows Julia could see Chambertin and von Allmen talking; neither the list nor the envelope were visible on the table. She went out to them.

'Are the papers in order, Monsieur Chambertin?'

'*Grâce à Dieu, Mademoiselle,* yes,' the Swiss said, deep relief in his voice. 'On the part of the Banque Républicaine I wish to thank you for what you have done to recover them.

'*De rien!*—it was a pleasure,' Julia said. '*Au revoir.* Till tomorrow morning, Herr von Allmen.' She almost ran out to the car, followed by Colin, and shot down the pretty winding road to the foot of the Sessel-Bahn, where she again swung the Porsche into the lay-by.

'Can't help it if they see the car—we must get up there at once,' she said, and darted up the zigzag path to the little station.

Chapter 14

Beatenberg

'We are about to close, Fräulein,' said the man at the entrance who sold tickets, making no move to produce any.

'We only want to go as far as the midway halt,' Julia said pleadingly, making dove's eyes at him. 'And you must send some of the chairs up there to take the water on to the hotel, mustn't you? They've been busy today, *am Week-end.'* (This word has practically become part of most European languages.)

'The Fräulein seems to know a great deal!' the man said with a smile, as he gave her the tickets. 'Is she *einheimisch?'* (native-born).

'No, foreign. But so much I know!' Julia said, smiling too. '*Schönsten Dank.'* The man drew round one of the twin seats, clamped the metal bars across their stomachs, pulled a lever, and launched them on their airborne career up the mountain-side.

'What on earth *is* all this?' Colin asked as they swung through the pine-trees, whose branches were still set with small upright tufts of a brilliant carmine; these are the cones, which later bend over on the branch to droop downwards, turning brown in the process. 'Are the papers up here? If so, why on earth?'

'Simply to have them somewhere where that infernal von Allmen would never think of looking,' Julia said. 'I don't know if Chambertin knows that they were in the same pigeon-hole as all Aglaia's stocks and shares—if he doesn't, he ought to, and I didn't trust him not to put von Allmen onto the fact. John was furious that he'd told him about the bus-tour.'

'But why up here?' Colin persisted.

'You'll see in a moment, if we aren't too late. Oh goodness, I hope I can find the right one again! Anyhow it's no good fussing—we are in time or we aren't, I can or I can't. Tell me, is it true that there was a hospital nurse as *well* as a bobby in that lot of tourists? Chambertin said there was, and that she put a tourniquet on John's leg.'

'Yes—she was a splendid person. She took off Antrobus's trousers to get at the place; he was furious! But she simply ignored him. It really was a damn peculiar scene,' Colin said, grinning at the recollection; 'I wish you'd been there. That nurse kneeling on the planks, completely professional in her rather dim civvy clothes, doing the necessary and ordering me about; the policeman—who came from Wolverhampton, just to add to it—booming on about "culpable homicide in the presence of witnesses"; and the German woman bellowing that her bag had been stolen. Why did you take her bag, by the way?'

'I don't really know. I just felt angry with her. Anyhow it's lucky I did, since that's where everything was. Go on.'

'Oh well, just when I'd gone and cut a bough off a bush to twist the tourniquet with, and another female tourist had contributed her scarf to fasten it, that old Bank Manager comes processing through the tunnel, complete with the Swiss police—who took depositions from everybody on the spot.'

'How? I mean in what language?'

'English. That von Something man speaks it perfectly, and that bus-load of tourists have had the day of their lives—especially the constable from Wolverhampton!' He paused. 'Then the ambulance men arrived with a stretcher and lugged Antrobus out, and the rest of them all came back to Interlaken on the bus, I suppose.'

'And you?' Julia asked.

'I waited to see the ambulance go off, and then got a lift in a car, and somehow persuaded the people in it to tail the ambulance—they were quite amused when I said there'd been an attempt at murder,' Colin said, giggling.

'Ought you to have said that?'

'Oh don't be silly! The whole place was buzzing with it. Do you suppose anything or anyone on earth could keep those tourists' mouths shut? Anyhow they took me to that Clinic place, and I went in and saw Antrobus, and then came on up here.'

At that point they reached the midway halt. The man in dungarees stared in surprise at seeing passengers arriving so late, but grinned amicably at Julia when she called to him to let them out—he was busy shifting churns, but did as she asked. So many churns had been moved to be filled with water—and were even now being loaded by another man onto the seats, by day occupied by tourists, for their trip up to the summit hotel—that Julia rather lost her bearings; she went from one of the tall white-metal vessels to another, lifting off the lids and peering in, while Colin looked on, an expression of delighted comprehension beginning to dawn in his face.

'Ali Baba and the Forty Thieves,' he muttered, just as Julia, with an exclamation of satisfaction, bent down and from at least the twelfth churn pulled out the tartan bag.

'Oh, you clever darling! No—they'd never have thought of looking here,' he said, and dealt her a shattering blow on the back.

'The Fräulein is removing something?' said the man in dungarees, coming over.

'Only something I put in when I was up here earlier this evening,' Julia said, making more dove's eyes at him. 'Now, can we go down?'

'Ah, Fräulein, it is after the hour—I ought not to allow this.'

'Oh, but do allow it! I'm so tired, and we shall lose our way in the forest in the dusk, if we have to walk,' Julia beguiled.

The man lifted a wall-telephone, spoke, and then beckoned them into a seat. 'For the Fräulein,' he said, clamping them in—Julia said, '*Schönsten Dank*' again as they swung out of the shed.

In the air—safest of places—Julia showed Colin the shiny envelope and its contents; he examined them carefully, and replaced the blue sheets.

'That's IT!' he said triumphantly. 'Do you know, I think I'd better take this on to Berne at once.'

'How?' Julia asked. 'There are no more steamers to Spiez tonight I don't think, even if the funicular is still running. I should leave it till tomorrow.'

'I could drive there in Antrobus's car.'

'Have you got a map?'

'Not a road-map—no.'

'I think you'd better come and have something to eat, and take these things on in the morning,' Julia said. 'If Chambertin has put von Allmen on to suspecting something, there'll probably be road-blocks all the way to Berne.'

Colin laughed, but he was overruled—and when they drove up to the hotel the sight of one of the local policemen, lurking near the front door, reinforced Julia's arguments. 'Let's have supper, and then take them up to Mrs. H.—she'll look after them. Trust her!' she said.

Late as it was, Fräulein Hanna had kept them some soup and cold chicken and salad; in the bright lights of the restaurant Colin's youthful face, always white, showed the marks of fatigue and strain. The restaurant was of course empty, and Fräulein Hanna did her watchful hovering from the servery door at the far end; they could talk freely, and did. Colin spoke of his panic when he found his retreat blocked by the tourists in the gorge, and of the worrying day-long watch on Wright and Borovali. 'I spotted the German couple fairly soon, because they were practically the only other non-English people in the bus; but those Post-Autos are so huge, and so crowded, it was hard to be sure that nothing passed from one hand to another. Goodness, I'm thankful we got them in the end! Where's that bag now?' he asked, with a sudden recurrence of nerves.

'Here, under my chair. Not to worry,' Julia said tranquilly.

After supper they went up in the small cramped lift and tapped on Mrs. Hathaway's door. The old lady was already in bed, wearing a very becoming lacy Shetland bed-jacket; she greeted them gaily.

'So there you are at last! But have you had anything to eat?'

'Yes, a lovely supper, just now. Hanna is an angel. But look, Mrs. H. darling, we want you to do a tiny bit of secretion for us.'

'Dear child, don't one's glands do that? I'll do anything I can, but I can't answer for my glands—I believe they get a little sluggish at my age.'

Julia, laughing, opened the zipped pocket of the tartan bag

and drew out the big envelope.

'All we want you and your glands to do is to keep this safe for Colin till tomorrow morning,' she said. 'There's a policeman hanging about downstairs, and we don't want him, or anyone else, to get it.'

Mrs. Hathaway sat upright in her bed. 'Pull out the top three pillows,' she said to Colin—he did so. 'Now put that thing on the bottom one, and put the others back.' The young man did as he was told, and Mrs. Hathaway leant back again, comfortably, against her four pillows.

'That should do,' she said. 'And now, may I know what I am hiding?'

'Just some papers we need, that were stolen,' Colin said. 'Julia got them back, and I'm taking them to Berne tomorrow.'

'Oh, I see. To your organisation, I suppose. Well I hope no one steals them from you on the way. But, Julia, I thought you were handing over some papers to Monsieur Chambertin and that nice police chief?'

'Ah, I was—but these are different ones; they are for Colin's "organisation", as you call it, in Berne. The Swiss aren't to see these—they might be nosy about them,' Julia said.

'I see,' Mrs. Hathaway said again. 'All right—leave them with me.' She glanced at Colin. 'My dear boy, you look quite exhausted. Do go to bed.'

Colin stooped down and gave her a kiss. 'Bless you, Mrs. H.—I think I will. Have you got such a thing as a Soneryl, by any chance?'

'No—Seconal is my bed-fellow. Julia, in that little drawer in the night-table.' Julia got out the bottle. 'These are the small ones; you'll need two,' Mrs. Hathaway said, shaking them into her hand—'or even three. And don't make too early a start—I assure you that I will look after your papers.' Colin blew her another kiss and went out.

'What has he been doing, to make him so worn out?' Mrs. Hathaway asked. 'And is Mr. Antrobus really hurt? If it isn't too secret, I should rather like to know what has been going on, Julia.'

'You look quite tired enough yourself,' Julia said; she had already noticed that her old friend was rather white. 'You stayed out too long. Do you think you got chilled?'

'Oh no, it was quite warm. Only it was a little bit of a strain when those men came and asked for you—you see I was completely in the dark, except for guessing, and I tried just to keep them going.'

'Well now you shall hear it all,' Julia said firmly—'only I think you'd better have some brandy. Where is it?'

'In the hat-cupboard—the key's in my bag. You had better have some too; I think there are glasses.'

There were, charming miniature cut-glass goblets; when these were filled, and being sipped, Julia told Mrs. Hathaway the whole story of the theft from the Banque Républicaine, of her encounter with June on the Niederhorn, and finally of the events of the day itself. 'Poor Colin, you see, has been tailing these crooks since 7.30 this morning, and in an agony of anxiety all the time, because this is his first big job, and he was terrified of falling down on it.'

'Yes, I do see. Poor boy! And quite an agitating *dénouement*; the shooting, and those tourists in the way, and then Mr. Antrobus throwing that man into the river! Rather unexpected from such a civilised person.'

'Oh, do you think so?' Julia enquired with interest.

'Superficially, yes. Though mind you, I think he is probably *capable de tout,* in every respect.'

288

Julia laughed, a little uneasily, at that last remark.

'And you have bestowed the poor girl, June or whatever her name is, in a safe place?'

'Yes. With Aglaia's godfather, Monsieur de Ritter—the people I went to stay with. He fetched her yesterday.'

'Ah, that is what you were doing! Well now, my dear child, I should like to know a little more about these papers that are in my care. Colin spoke of taking them to Berne tomorrow. To the Secret Service? Have we got people there?'

'Yes. I believe we have them more or less everywhere.'

For the third or fourth time that evening Mrs. Hathaway said 'I see'—thoughtfully. Then Julia rinsed out the brandy-glasses in the basin, kissed her old friend goodnight, and went downstairs and rang up the Clinic.

A nurse answered. '*Justus-Klinik. Hier spricht Schwester Berta*'— and of the Sister Julia made her enquiries. Yes, the operation had gone well, and the patient was sleeping; the Herr Doktor was very satisfied. No cause whatever for *Angst*. Could one see Herr Antrobus tomorrow? Julia asked. Very probably—but better to ring up the Herr Doktor about ten to make sure that visitors were allowed. Relieved, Julia went to bed.

She too was tired, and slept late; it was not far off nine when she hurried into the restaurant, where sun was pouring in through the plate-glass windows. Colin was already seated at their table, tucking into bread and black-cherry jam—he looked a different being from the exhausted creature of the night before.

'Sleep well?' Julia enquired.

'Far too well—that's most wonderful stuff of Mrs. H.'s; no back-lash either. But I must get off as soon as I can.'

'That policeman is still on the door, or a relief—I looked on the way down.'

'I know—so did I. But if I put the envelope in my rucksack he'd hardly search that, would you say? And I've decided not to take the car; I shall go down by the funicular, take the boat to Spiez, and on by train.'

'That's a much better idea,' Julia said, buttering bread and pouring out her coffee. 'Unobtrusiveness is the ticket, every time. You'd better get off before von Allmen comes to interview me, though.'

Colin ate such a vast breakfast that Julia finished nearly as soon as he did; nevertheless he hustled her over her last half-slice, in his impatience to be off. 'You ought to think of *la ligne*,' he said.

'Bother my line!' Julia replied.

Colin raced upstairs ahead of her to collect his rucksack; they met outside Mrs. Hathaway's door, and went in together—like Colin, Mrs. Hathaway looked much better for a night's rest, and greeted them gaily.

'Good-morning, dear children. Colin, I see you have had a good night; I'm very glad.'

'Wonderful, Mrs. H. And now I'll just relieve you of that envelope, and push off to Berne.'

'It's gone,' Mrs. Hathaway said.

'Gone? Gone where?' Colin asked, in an agonised voice. 'Did they get in after all? I thought—'

'Colin, you must learn not to get into such a fuss about nothing,' Mrs. Hathaway said, interrupting him peremptorily but calmly. '*I* sent it off, by post—that is to say, Watkins has taken it to the Post Office.'

'But where have you sent it?' Colin tried to control the anxiety in his voice.

'To the Embassy in Berne. No one ever dares to interfere with

Embassy mail; and with all these police about, and you known by sight, I thought it much the safest way.'

Julia began to gurgle. 'Oh, splendid, Mrs. H.' But Colin was not pacified.

'But this has nothing to do with the Embassy,' he said agitatedly.

'Of course not. So I marked the inner envelope "NOT TO BE OPENED. TO BE CALLED FOR'—and now you can either telephone to your superiors and let them know where to collect it, or go and tell them in person. But in the post, I think it can't be held up.'

There was a tap on the door, and Watkins came in.

'There you are, Madam—the receipt for the registered letter,' she said, tendering a minute and rather grubby piece of paper to her mistress. 'Good-morning, Mr. Colin. Miss Julia, the police are downstairs; they want to see you again, that Hanna says.'

Julia rose resignedly from her seat on the foot of the bed. 'Oh very well,' she said. 'I'll come up when I'm through, Mrs. H.'

'Do. And Colin, in your place I should wait up here till Julia comes back. You can sit on the balcony. Watkins, find yesterday's *Times* for Mr. Colin.'

During her talk with Herr von Allmen Julia was mainly preoccupied with getting the thing over in time to ring up Dr. Hertz at ten. They sat out on the long balcony, at that hour in the morning normally unoccupied; one old lady with a deaf-aid at the farther end was hardly a threat to confidential conversation. The police chief opened his enquiries by asking why she, Julia, came to be in the Aares-Schlucht with Herr Antrobus the previous afternoon.

'We were looking for a bird,' Julia said.

'*Um Himmel's Willen!* What bird?'

291

'It's called *Tichodroma muraria,*' Julia said briskly. 'It lives there. It's very rare. We saw it, too—such luck! We watched it for ages—it's very pretty.' She began to describe the wall-creeper.

Von Allmen, exasperated—as Julia had wickedly hoped and expected—interrupted her description, and passed on to another point.

'A German lady who was present said that her bag was stolen—by someone resembling you, from her description.'

'Does that trouble you? Julia asked coolly. 'Surely you know that she was the receiving end of the fraud on the bank? I don't think receivers of stolen goods deserve much consideration.'

Von Allmen would not let himself be outfaced. 'Do you admit to taking her bag?' he asked.

'Of course—I'll get it.' She walked into the lobby, and returned with the tartan bag. 'She had it full of things to eat, chocolate and so on,' she remarked, laying it on the table between them.

'Why did you take it?' he pursued suspiciously.

'Because she hit Herr Antrobus with it—that's when all the food came tumbling out,' Julia replied readily. 'And because she was a nasty, fat, greedy woman, and I wanted to annoy her! So I just snatched it.'

Von Allmen gave a short unwilling laugh at this.

'Give it back to her, if she hasn't gone off to Dortmund, and you mind about her so much,' Julia added, encouraged by the laugh. 'I don't want it—it's hideous.'

But von Allmen was too astute to be deflected from the purpose of his enquiries.

'In any case I retain the bag,' he said. 'And now, Fräulein, I return to a question that I asked you yesterday evening, to which you evaded giving a direct answer. How comes it that you know the real names of these two fraudulent gentlemen, Mister

Borovali and Mister Wright, so well?'

Julia was disconcerted, but she determined not to show any hesitation.

'Last night I referred you to Monsieur Chambertin for the answer to that,' she said. 'I do so again now.'

'Why are you unwilling to tell me?'

'Because really I don't see what this has got to do with you at all,' the girl said rather haughtily. 'You are questioning me as if I were a suspected criminal, when in fact—again as I mentioned last night—it was I who supplied the photograph which enabled you to trace the real criminals in the first place, and when you lost them, I found them again for you. What have *I* done wrong?'

'Except for a little bag-snatching, nothing that I know of,' the police chief said, with a small placatory smile. (Good police at some point always try to placate the subjects of their interrogations.) 'Where did you get the photograph?' he asked smartly, with a quick change of subject.

'Out of *Paris-Match.*' She paused to watch the effect of this—it seemed to be satisfactory; von Allmen looked rather nonplussed for a moment. Only for a moment, however; then he resumed his questioning, ploughing doggedly on.

'This photograph was of the young lady in Mister Borovali's party, who impersonated the heiress?'

'Look, Herr von Allmen, don't treat me as a fool,' Julia said, now rather irritably. 'Would *Paris-Match* bother with the photograph of an impersonator? Of course it was of the real heiress, Miss Armitage, who left for South America not long ago.'

'Then how did you know that the resemblance would help us?'

'Because I saw all the impersonators on the platform at Victoria, when I was coming out here,' Julia replied fearlessly. 'I

293

was struck by the girl's resemblance to Miss Armitage, and looked at them all carefully. That is why I was able to describe them at the bank, and establish the fact of the fraud. You heard Monsieur Chambertin thank me for this—are the Swiss Police not also grateful?'

'Undoubtedly, Fräulein.' Von Allmen sketched a bow. But he was still not to be deflected from his enquiries.

'This young lady, who played the part of the heiress at the bank, has disappeared. Do you know where she has gone?'

Julia was frightened—this was *it*. Playing for time—she must think—'Why do you ask me that?' she said. But she guessed the answer before it came; that bloody Müller had probably seen her drive June off in the taxi from the Golden Bear. Had he been quick enough to tail them to the Clinic? Or questioned the snobbish taxi-driver? She decided simply to stall completely.

Von Allmen duly gave the answer she expected. 'You were seen to drive her away, with her luggage, from the hotel.'

'Why not? Is there a law in Switzerland against rescuing innocent young girls from the hands of international crooks? I know you don't allow women the vote,' Julia said nastily, 'but is what I did a crime?'

She was pleased to see that the police chief looked annoyed when she spoke of the vote, but he kept his temper admirably.

'My question is, where did you take her? And a second one— where is she now?'

They stared at one another, both stubborn and remorseless, across the table with its red-and-white checked cloth for a long moment. Then:

'I am not going to answer either of your questions,' Julia said, very slowly and deliberately. 'I am alone with you, without a lawyer; I know nothing of Swiss law, so I don't know whether you are even entitled to cross-question a foreign national like this. I can ring up our Embassy and find out, of course; probably I shall.' Again she stared at the police chief across the table; her dove's eyes could become as hard as onyx when Julia was determined. Suddenly, at something she half-saw in the man's face, her own expression altered completely.

'Herr von Allmen, need we oppose each other?' she asked, in quite a gentle voice. 'I know you must do your duty, but are we not really on the same side?—the side of right and justice?' Surprised, the man's face also relaxed; he half-nodded. 'I have seen quite a lot of this wretched little girl,' Julia went on. 'She is an ignorant child, hardly out of her teens, who works for an advertisement agency to support her mother, a widow.'

'Ah, this is how they found her?' von Allmen interjected.

'Precisely. And she took on the job because those brutes bribed her with a lot of pretty clothes! She's vain, and silly, and as stupid as a rabbit,' Julia said candidly—'but she's fundamentally a good honest girl, who had really no idea of the use to which she was to be put. And because I was a little kind to her— quite by accident—she determined to help me, rather than her beastly employers, and rang me up to tell me that the papers were to be handed over on the *Drei-Pässe* tour.'

'*Unmöglich!*' von Allmen exclaimed, thoroughly startled.

'But certainly. So she, not I, is the person you and the Banque Républicaine ought to be thanking for their recovery.'

'But Herr Antrobus knew this,' the police chief said, still incredulous.

'Only because I told him, after she had told me. She warned me that they were armed, too. Now, do you still want to harry and pursue her? Or arrest her, and frighten her out of her wits?' She paused—the man was silent. Julia leaned across the table, her eyes again dove's eyes.

'Look, Herr von Allmen, I have sent her away to good kind people, who will look after her until I can take her back to England. Can't you just lose her, like you lost the others last week? You've got back the papers, you've caught the real criminals—can't you forget about her, and allow her to disappear?'

He laughed a little at this outrageously barefaced request.

'Fräulein, she cannot cross the frontier. All posts have been told to look out for her passport.'

'Yes of course; I'd thought of that. But that was a bogus passport anyway—your frontier officials won't be looking out for one in the name of Phillips.'

'This is her real name?' He drew out a note-book.

'No, don't write it down,' Julia said, stretching a long, faintly tanned hand across the table, and laying it on the note-book and on von Allmen's hand together. 'Please! This is off the record— aren't we working together, now?'

The police chief, rather slowly, withdrew his hand from under Julia's, and put the note-book back in his pocket. Instead of answering directly—

'It was she who told you their names?' he asked.

'Not told—she's so frightfully stupid that she kept on letting them slip out,' Julia said, half-laughing at the recollection. 'But I can easily get her a fresh passport, in her real name.'

'Is this so easy?' the Swiss official asked, looking rather shocked.

'Goodness yes! I'm always letting my passport run out, or losing it, and having to get a new one. Any Consulate can do it.'

He looked more shocked than ever.

'Actually I expect horrible Mr. Borovali has got hers,' Julia pursued blithely. 'If she has it, I shall burn it—and if he has, you can burn it!'

Von Allmen laughed out loud.

'And we are told that the English are so law-abiding!' he said.

'So we are—only we realise that laws, like the Sabbath, are made for man, and not man for the Law. Also'—the tone of her voice changed—'we are a merciful people. I believe you are, too; who invented the Red Cross? Be merciful, Herr von Allmen— and you shall obtain mercy.'

There was a long pause. Julia forced herself not to look at her watch, though surely it must be ten o'clock by now? But June was the first thing. At last von Allmen spoke.

'Fräulein, I have had a long experience in administering the Law, which you treat so lightly; but I have never yet encountered a person who appeared to be at the same time completely unscrupulous, and also good. This is very curious.'

'Oh, I'm not good—only merciful on occasion!' Julia said lightly. She did not press her appeal—this rather oblique response was probably as much as she could expect; at least he had not refused outright. Better finish now—and at last she did look at her watch; it was five past ten. 'Herr von Allmen, have we done? Because if so I ought just to go up and see my old friend before I go down to the town—she got rather over-tired last night.'

'I am sorry for this. Please convey my compliments to Frau Hathaway—that is a most gracious lady,' von Allmen said.

'Yes, isn't she? She liked you so much too,' Julia said. She held out her hand. 'Goodbye—thank you for being kind.'

'Have I been kind?'

'Well, I rather think you're going to be. *Auf-wiederluoge!*' she said, laughing, and ran away to the telephone-box.

She was too late for Dr. Hertz, who was on his rounds, but the *Schwester* with whom she spoke said that certainly it would be possible to visit Herr Antrobus; he had slept well, taken a good breakfast, and had very little pain. Relieved, Julia went up to Mrs. Hathaway's room, ascertaining on the way from Fräulein Hanna that the *Polizei-Chef* had driven off.

'All serene,' she said as she entered—at the sound of the door opening Colin came in off the balcony. 'I'm not in prison, and von Allmen has gone. He sent you his respects, Mrs. H.—you've made a hit.'

'What did he want to know?' Colin asked.

'Why I was in the gorge yesterday, and what I'd done with the little stooge, June. I told him that Herr Antrobus and I were looking for a bird in the gorge, and gave him its name—he hated that,' Julia said, laughing reminiscently. 'And I refused flat out to tell him where June was. But it all went very well—we parted friends.'

'How extraordinary!' Colin said, beginning to jerk his double-jointed thumb in and out, with a horrible clicking sound. 'He didn't ask about the papers?'

'Not a word. He said the Hun Frau had accused me of snatching her bag, and I said of course I did, because she was using it as a weapon on John. I gave it to him, and he's taken it off. I shouldn't worry, Colin—either Chambertin didn't know about the prints, or if he did, he didn't tell von Allmen.'

'That all sounds very satisfactory,' Mrs. Hathaway said. 'The police in most countries are quite reasonable as a rule, if one treats them sensibly.'

'Now, Colin, are you going to Berne?' Julia asked. 'Because if so you'd better drive down to Interlaken with me and get a train from the West-Bahnhof—much less hanging about than with the steamer.'

'Yes, I think I'd better go and report,' Colin said. 'There are bound to be repercussions from the Swiss end, and I hope to

Heaven there won't be a fuss with the Embassy.'

'Colin, I am quite sure there won't,' Mrs. Hathaway said. 'Letters quite often are sent to Embassies to be called for. Anyhow if you go with Julia you will be in Berne as soon as the package. Dear boy, do keep that thumb of yours quiet; it makes such a disagreeable sound.'

'Yes, go and pack your ghastly great rucksack quickly,' his cousin adjured him. 'I want to be off in ten minutes.'

Colin got up—at the door he paused. 'I ought to see Antrobus, and let him know what's happened.'

'I'll tell him; I shall be seeing him. Do go and pack,' Julia said impatiently.

When Colin had gone—'Have you heard how Mr. Antrobus is?' Mrs. Hathaway asked.

'Yes, I rang up just now. The operation went all right, and he slept well, and ate a huge breakfast.'

'The operation?'

'Oh, didn't you hear that part? That revolting Wright shot him through the leg in the Schlucht, and they had to take the bullet out, and stitch up the artery. That was why he threw Master Wright into the Aar—he felt a little cross with him.'

'No wonder,' said Mrs. Hathaway.

Chapter 15

Interlaken—The Clinic

'Ah, there you are at last. I expected one of you before this,' Antrobus said, when a nurse ushered Julia into his small austere room at the Clinic next morning.

'Couldn't get away any earlier—I was stuck with von Allmen. He turned up at 9.30 to cross-examine me about the goings-on in the Schlucht,' Julia said, seating herself in the single wicker chair, with its bright cretonne cushions. The sight of Antrobus lying rather flat in bed, in pyjamas, a cradle over his right leg, brought about in her a set of emotions so strong that she spoke even more slowly and casually than usual.

'Why didn't Colin come?'

'He's gone to Berne to report.'

'I think he might have reported to me first,' Antrobus said.

'There wasn't time. Anyhow I can tell you all he can, and a good bit more,' Julia replied, rather chilled by his tone.

'I don't see why the rush to get to Berne. However, as you're reporting you'd better report. Is everything all right?

Did you get the papers?'

'Yes, I got them. They weren't in the black brief-case, though.'

'Good gracious! Then where were they, and how did you get them?'

'They were in the Hun woman's tartan bag.'

'And where are they now?'

'Well, all old Thalassides' stocks and shares I gave to Chambertin; the drawings—'

'Yes, what about them?' he interrupted sharply.

'They're in the post, on the way to the Embassy in Berne. That's why Colin's raced off—he wants to be in time for his people to ring up the Embassy to say they'll call for them.'

'Why on earth did you do anything so idiotic as to post them to the Embassy?' he asked, quite irritably.

'I didn't. Mrs. Hathaway did. Look,' the girl said, becoming irritated in her turn by his carping manner—'if you want to hear my report, I'll report, but I don't see why I should be scolded by anyone. If I hadn't snatched that bag, by now your papers would be safely on their way to East Germany or wherever, and you'd have got nothing but a brief-case full of old newspapers.' She was upset that this meeting was turning out so disagreeably.

'Not really? So they did manage to switch after all. I wonder where—your cousin swore he'd never taken his eyes off the black case.'

'He had to take them off Frau Dortmund when she went into the lav at Andermatt, which is almost certainly where it happened,' Julia said, and rehearsed what Colin had told her.

'And when did you find out that this had been done? I still don't understand about the need for posting to the Embassy,' Antrobus said.

'Of course not, till you're told,' Julia said, trying not to upset him further. 'Do let me tell you what happened; but I don't want to be bullied until you know the facts.'

'How tough we are!' he said. 'All right, my dear—tell me your story in your own way.'

'I'm afraid your leg must be hurting you,' Julia said. 'I believe pain does make people bloody-minded.' The patronising tone of his last remark had hurt her very much.

He held out a placatory hand.

'I can't reach you—come nearer.' She kept her seat. 'Oh very well—I'm sorry. Will that do? Now tell me.'

Julia told—of her encounter with Chambertin and von Allmen at the Schlucht restaurant, of finding herself tailed by the grey Volkswagen, and how she had examined the contents of the two bags in the ladies' lavatory at the Fluss; Antrobus laughed at that.

'An excellent idea—very neat. So then what did you do?'

'Divided them. Lolly in the black case for Chambertin, the blue-prints in the other bag for you. John, such an odd thing'—his praise had restored her equanimity.

'What?'

'Some of the drawings looked rather like Colin's description of those under-water food-containers that are sunk in the lakes here; I mean there was a line that looked like water-level at the top, and measurements in metres up to it. Only there were pipes and things going out of the containers as well, as far as I could see—of course I was on a hurry.'

'Have you mentioned that resemblance to anyone else?—Mrs. Hathaway, for instance?' he asked sharply.

'No. Why?'

'Well don't—don't speak of it to anyone.'

'All right. Am I ever to know what they are?'

'Some time, perhaps, Fatima!—as a reward for saving them. Now go on telling me about your complications.'

'Well sure enough when I got back to the pub, there was von Allmen with Chambertin, and the grey Volkswagen, and spare police, and all.'

Antrobus laughed.

'What were Chambertin and von Allmen doing when you got to the Silberhorn?'

'Being beguiled by Mrs. Hathaway!' She continued to recount her and Colin's doings, including handing over the blue-prints to repose under Mrs. Hathaway's pillows. 'I thought that a rather safe place,' she concluded.

'So do I,' Antrobus said, laughing again. 'But why post to Berne?'

'That was her idea. When Colin and I went up this morning she told us she'd sent Watkins to post it to the Embassy. Things are pretty safe in the post,' Julia said. 'Personally I think it was a sound notion. If Colin had taken it in by hand anyone could have slugged him on the way—as it is he'll be there by the time it's delivered, and his people can ring up, or go round in false beards and collect it, or whatever you all do.'

'The Ambassador won't like it,' Antrobus said, looking dissatisfied.

'Well he won't have to lump it for more than an hour, if that,' Julia replied cheerfully. 'That is, if no one does slug Colin. If they do I don't know what happens—I go in with a chit from you, I suppose, to the anonymous office.' She was laughing.

Antrobus didn't laugh. He reached out and pressed a bell. When the nurse appeared—'*Telefon, Schwester, bitte,*' he said; the nurse nodded, and disappeared.

'Goodness, can you telephone from your bed?' Julia asked.

'Yes—there are plug-ins in two or three of the rooms here, like in American military hospitals; there's one in this. But they're rather slow. Meantime, tell me what von Allmen asked you.'

'How I knew Borovali's real name, mostly. And if I'd stolen Frau Dortmund's bag, and why?'

'I should rather like to know that too. What moved you to snatch the bag? It seems almost like direct inspiration, since you'd got the brief-case. Why did you?'

'Well really because she'd tried to cosh you with it, I think,' the girl said rather slowly, the ripe-apricot stain beginning to appear in her cheeks. 'And she was so fat!' she added, rather hurriedly.

He studied her face, with its betraying blush, with remorseless steadiness. Julia had expected him to laugh, or at least grin, at her last words, but he did neither. 'I *see*,' he said slowly, still looking at her; Julia became uncomfortable under that steady, non-committal scrutiny. She lit a cigarette, got up, and went over to the window, which looked out on a trim plot with the usual Swiss town-garden mixture of espalier fruit-trees, vegetables in soldierly rows, and narrow edgings of bright flowers.

'And how did you answer the one about Borovali?' Antrobus's voice from the bed recalled her. 'That involved your little friend, of course. Did you tell von Allmen where you had stowed her? I'm sure he wanted to know.'

'Yes, he did—and I didn't tell him,' she said, turning round.

'Oh! How did he take that?'

'Poorly, till I told him that it was she who had provided the information that the papers would be handed over on the bus-tour. That shook him quite a lot—and I suggested that in view of the service she had rendered the Swiss police, he should leave her alone.'

'Did he agree?'

'Not in so many words. It must be awful to be police or lawyers, and never be able to say anything straight out,' Julia said. 'But I don't think he will make any trouble—or let anyone else make any. I told him I should take her home myself, when Mrs. H. is quite fit again.'

Now Antrobus was laughing.

'In fact you got away with it? What a getter-away with things you are, aren't you?'

Again Julia was hurt by the detached amusement in his voice—it was so unlike his former frequent praise of her skill, his warmth towards her.

'It's just as well, for other people, that I do sometimes get away with things,' she said, turning back to the window.

Before Antrobus could answer there was a tap on the door, and the nurse trotted in with a telephone which she set down on the bed-table; she plugged it in at floor-level, saying—'Now the Herr can get his connection. I return'—and trotted out again.

Antrobus reached out and set the instrument down in front of him on the honeycombed coverlet; the movement hurt his leg, and he gave a grunt of pain—'Ough!' This upset Julia still more. 'Shall I go out?' she asked, while he twiddled the dial.

'No, it doesn't matter.' He lifted the receiver to his ear—his intent expression showed her that she was completely out of the picture for the moment.

'Hullo? Oh, Philip—John here. ... Yes, everything's fine. ... No, not according to plan in the least, but perfectly successful. ... No, I shan't be coming for a few days yet. ... Because I'm in hospital. ... No, nothing much. ... Yes, there was a bit of a fracas. ... Exactly—young Colin is on his way in to you now; he'll tell you everything. ... No, but as good as. ... He'll *tell* you, I say. Don't fuss, Philip—it's cast-iron. ... News for me, did you

305

say? … Yes, I got the letter you forwarded, this morning; the hotel sent it round by hand, but it didn't say where to … Having *Tommy* as a colleague! Oh, how perfect!—I've always longed to get out there. … Well really, Philip, I can't say exactly how soon; "the undertaking is completed" all right—in their tedious phraseology—but I've had a bullet through an artery, and the doctor won't commit himself about dates just yet—he only stitched it up last night. … Yes, of course—tell them I shall report the moment I can move. I can't wait to get out there!— I've wanted to see those mosaics all my life. … Of course I shall look in on you on the way—there will be one or two points to tidy up. … What?—this thing's started to buzz; say it again. … Oh yes, the two main ones, who are what matter. I expect you'll get the Interpol report tomorrow, or later today possibly. Not the ones from outside. … No, technically impossible. … No, lay off the third; that's of no importance. I'll tell you when I see you. … Listen, Philip, did you hear me tell you to *lay off?* Well do what I say. … No, I won't explain anything now. You can give me a ring after you've actually laid hands on the things; my number is'— he gave it. 'And don't get impatient when you ring up—the machine has to be lugged upstairs to my room. Goodbye.'

Listening to one end of a telephone conversation is always a tantalising business, but a shrewd and attentive listener can usually pick up a certain amount of the drift. Julia was fairly shrewd, and had listened with the most concentrated attention; she gathered quite clearly two points: that Antrobus had been insistent with his colleague in Berne not to pursue June, and that he was being transferred to another assignment as soon as he was fit to move, in a place where there were mosaics. Where would that be? She thought at once of Ravenna, but that was hardly likely; too unimportant, and too near—he had said 'out

306

there'. Then probably Istanbul—she remembered about an old American restoring famous mosaics in Santa Sofia, the great church that had become a mosque. But what struck her with painful force as she listened was that he was longing to go; there was no hint of regret or reluctance in his words or, more important, in his voice—he was all happy eagerness. In fact—she swallowed a little as she faced and digested the wretched knowledge—he didn't mind leaving her in the least. He had just been enjoying himself, but he didn't care—he didn't care at all.

The last few moments of the conversation gave her a chance to pull herself together, nor did she stop paying attention even after she heard her new-found happiness being knocked from under her feet by a few words—she continued to listen carefully, and so heard that Antrobus was safeguarding June. That was something; indeed it was vital. But while she went on listening, her mind was at work. So he'd had the letter announcing his transfer this very morning, before she came; that would account for his being so different—if anything could decently account for the alteration between his attitude today and his behaviour up on the seat under the rowan-tree. 'Write it off—a lost option,' Julia said to herself. She took out her compact and began to powder her nose, as Antrobus replaced the receiver.

'Well, I expect you heard that I've done my best to prevent your little friend from being chased,' he said.

'Yes, I did. I heard everything. Thank you.'

'I think that what with you mopping up von Allmen, and the fact that she did really turn King's Evidence, it ought to be all right,' he said. 'But she'll have to have a fresh passport, you know.'

'Of course. We can get that from the Consulate in Berne.'

'How?'

'I shall say she's lost it—that's what I always do when I lose mine. But if your Philip has the Passport Control Officer in Berne on a string, you might get a word passed to smooth our path when the time comes.'

He laughed. 'Very well—I'll do that. You both deserve it.'

'Yes, don't we? Where would the poor old Secret Service be without us?' Julia said. Talking about concrete things like getting June home had done her good, taking her mind off her private misery—she cracked back at Antrobus almost without effort. But it was not without effort that she now said—'And you're being transferred, I gather?'

'Yes. I was only laid on here temporarily, for this bank affair, because I know the people and the language.'

'But did they know in London beforehand that Wright and Borovali were going to rob Mr. Thalassides' numbered till?' Julia asked, so startled that she again forgot her own unhappiness.

'Not *who*, or *how*—no. But there was a hint that an attempt would be made to get hold of the blue-prints; that's why I came out; and why you were able to accost me at Victoria!' he said smiling.

Julia didn't smile—she could no longer bear to recall that light-hearted moment. But her curiosity mastered her pain.

'How on earth did Borovali come to know the account number? That seems so extraordinary.'

'We don't know. He comes from the Middle East, as Thalassides did, and practically everyone there is as crooked as a dog's hind leg! There was certainly a leak somewhere—more likely east of the Piraeus than in London. But he did know the account number, and the lawyers' names, and got hold of a faked death-certificate, and of writing-paper with their letter-head, and forged the signatures.'

'Must have been a minor leak in London too, mustn't there?

Some trumpery underpaid clerk with a pregnant wife or a girl-friend with extravagant ideas, I expect,' Julia said. 'Poor toad! He was exploited just like June, no doubt. How I do hate and *loathe* the way international crookery plays on these silly ignorant creatures.'

He looked at her rather earnestly. 'You really are always on the side of the angels, aren't you? I like that,' he said, with more warmth than she had yet heard in his voice that morning. But what good was it for him to like this or that about her, if he didn't like her enough to mind going two thousand, or whatever it was, miles away?

'Oh, I hope I am,' she said, in her most casual voice. 'No point in being on the side of the devils, that I can see, unless one's a commie.' And as he laughed—'Where are all these mosaics? Istanbul?'

'Yes. I've always longed to be there,' he said, with the same eagerness that she had heard while he was telephoning.

'I thought Ankara was the capital nowadays,' Julia said, still using this protective disguise to her feelings. 'Why won't you be up there?'

'Oh, so many things really go on in Istanbul still,' he said, 'in spite of the Cabinet and the Embassies being stuck up on the plateau. Of course one will be going to and fro—I believe the wild-flowers round Ankara are amazing: they say one of our Ambassadors, between the wars, found a new species, unknown to science, within a hundred yards of his newly-built Embassy.'

'How nice,' Julia said, rather tepidly.

'Don't publicise this,' he added.

'Oh don't be absurd, John! Really!'

'I apologise,' he said at once. 'That was stupid of me. What can I do by way of reparations?'

'Well, as I don't suppose I shall be seeing you again, you might tell me what those blue-prints are of,' the girl said. 'And don't call me Fatima,' she added hastily.

'Do you dislike that? I didn't realise. I suppose it was rather a silly joke.'

She couldn't tell him that in fact she had greatly enjoyed his calling her Fatima, and that that was just why, now, the name had become unendurable.

'Rather a moderate one,' was all she said.

'But why shan't you be seeing me again? I shall be in this bed for at least a fortnight, that man Hertz says. I hoped you would be coming to bring me flowers, and cheer my loneliness.'

'Hopes are nearly always dupes, whether fears are liars or not,' Julia said. (Really, this was a little much.) 'My pan is over-full of fishes as it is, and now that Colin's job's done, I must start frying away.'

'What fish?'

'Mrs. Hathaway, who overdid herself last night coping with bankers and policemen. I must concentrate on looking after her till she's fit for the journey to England. And then of course shep-herding June home. Goodness, I suppose we shall all have to travel in a bunch! Watkins will hate June,' Julia said, suddenly visualising this very ill-assorted party. As Antrobus laughed, and before he could reply she said—'Don't ride off on side-issues, John. Pay me my reparations!'

'I wonder why you want to know so much,' he said, looking at her speculatively.

'Never mind. I just do. Come on—tell. What are those container things?'

'You do really realise that I've no business to tell you this at all, and that you must keep it a deadly secret?' he said.

'Oh yes—and I do really realise that but for me they'd be in enemy hands by now, and therefore that much deadlier. You seem to have forgotten that.'

'I shall never forget that,' Antrobus said. 'Neither your hunch or inspiration or whatever it was in snatching that bag, nor your resource in securing the papers afterwards.' He paused. 'Couldn't you bring that chair a little nearer?'

'No—it has lead in its legs,' Julia said, making no attempt to move the light wicker construction. 'No one can overhear you—don't stall. Tell.'

'Well, old Thalassides was a bit of a genius in his way; at least he had the gift of looking farther ahead than most people. And with the Middle East the way it's going, he thought that nuclear-powered submarine tankers would be a much better way of moving oil about than over-land pipe-lines, with grasping little oil-less States demanding exorbitant transit dues, or blowing up the pumping stations if they happened to lose their tempers.'

'Sound enough,' Julia commented.

'So he conceived the idea of having submarine pumping stations on the sea-bed, off-shore from these coastal oil-producing places like Bahrein or Kuwait, with underwater pipe-lines leading into them from the land, and nozzles and so on to make the connection with the in-take tubes from the tankers. I'm not an expert in these things, but roughly, that's the idea. Just a junction, you see.'

'Oh yes—and then frog-men with aqua-lungs go down and operate it when the nuclear tanker has anchored itself alongside. How ingenious.'

'Exactly. I believe they're to be made of Perspex, to let in as much natural light as possible—though I fancy there will be electric lighting too. But of course the whole thing is immensely complicated: the doors and valves for ingress and egress, and so on.'

'Oh, like the Schnorkel thing in submarines?'

'*No*, dear; that's the mistake everyone makes. Like the Davis Escape Hatch is what you mean. But you've got the general idea. Anyhow old Thalassides and his experts got the whole thing worked out, and drawn out; I believe they even experimented with one in the Mediterranean, where there are next to no tides, of course, to pull things crooked. And if Russia gets too much of an ascendancy in the Middle East, as she shows every sign of doing, it might save the life—or at least the mobility—of the free world if these things were in operation. That's why you really must keep all this completely dark.'

'And that's why Frau Dortmund, and all our other enemies, wanted the blue-prints so much. Well, I think I ought to have the D.B.E.,' Julia said briskly. 'Which of all these old Dames, Civil Servants or professional do-gooders or what have you, have done anything more useful than June and I have?'

'None of them; nothing like so important. You've rendered a major service. But you won't get it, and I shan't recommend you for it.'

'Why not? "For Services rendered Abroad" sounds very like the Honours List, to me.'

'No. It's all much too serious. Anyhow, what on earth do you want to be a Dame for? "Dame Julia Probyn"—at your age, you'd look a fool!'

'Yes, I suppose I should,' Julia agreed candidly. 'Still, I think I might have something. What about the Order of Merit? "Julia Probyn, O.M."—I don't think that sounds at all bad. Surely I measure up to some of the people who get it?' She rose as she spoke. 'I ought to be getting back to Mrs. H. Do you need soap or gaspers?—or some paper-backs? And do you want anything fetched from your hotel?'

'As a matter of fact I do—I made a list, hoping that someone would be a ministering angel.' He reached for his wallet on the bed-table, grunting again with the pain of the movement, and took out a sheet of paper. 'There—it's rather a lot, I'm afraid.'

Julia scanned the list.

'Oh, I can do that quite fast—I'll have the things from the shops sent in. But are you going to keep on your room at the hotel, or do you want everything packed and brought round? I can't do all that today.'

'No, I'm keeping the room—if you could just throw what I've listed into one of the suit-cases and get it round here it would be a great help. I should like to be able to shave!'

'Right, I can manage that. But telephone to the hotel to authorise them to let me take away your property.'

'I'll do that, of course.'

'And what shall I do with the car? Leave it outside the door here, or what?'

'I think you'd better keep it while I'm laid up,' he said, after a moment's consideration.

'Oh, that's absurd,' Julia said, thoroughly taken aback.

'Why? I can't use it, and I should have thought you might like to take Mrs. Hathaway for some nice drives.'

Julia was silent, considering in her turn. It would of course be absolutely lovely to be able to drive Mrs. H. up the passes and round the two lakes in the Porsche, so swift and smooth—but as things were, she couldn't be under any obligation to John.

'You might even slip down occasionally to cheer me up,' Antrobus added, before she had spoken.

'No, I don't expect to have time for that. I think "No" all

313

round—though thanking you for the kind thought,' Julia said, as lightly as she could. 'Tell me where to leave it, and when I've brought your things round here I'll go back on the bus.'

'I think you are making the wrong decision,' he said, after studying her face. 'In fact it would be very useful for you to have a car, not only to get about here, but to go over to Bellardon to collect your wretched little June and take her to the train at Berne. You could turn it in there; it's where I hired it. I shan't be able to drive a car myself till long after I've gone home, Hertz says. Personally I think you've earned a free car for two or three weeks, just as we both think you deserve a D.B.E. You can't have that—you can have this. I wish you'd take it.'

Again she was silent, thinking. How quick he was to guess her reason for refusing—disconcertingly so. But then he was quick. She stood irresolute, torn between the delightful prospect of driving Mrs. Hathaway about—and it would be madly convenient for fetching June, of course—and her reluctance to accept anything from John, now. On the other hand she didn't mind what she accepted from the Government, if it was on them—certainly she had earned something from the Welfare State, which lived, or rather moved, on oil, if she had helped to secure its future supplies. And was it much good trying to safeguard her personal position, with someone as astute as John, by standing on her dignity? Was it ever, really, all that important to safeguard one's personal position, even if it were possible?—which in this case it almost certainly wasn't.

She moved over again to the window, and stood looking out on the military array of vegetables while she wrestled with this new idea. Men didn't worry about their personal position: Geoffrey Consett hadn't, Steve hadn't, Hugh Torrens hadn't; they had all simply thrown their personal positions away, thrown

314

them at her, openly imploring. She suddenly remembered, with a curious twisted pang, how Colin up at Glentoran—was it really only five weeks ago?—had remonstrated with her for leading men on and then rubbing them off—especially Torrens, to whom he was devoted. And now she had been led on and rubbed off herself! Oh, but for women it was different, at least by convention; very few Englishwomen, at any rate, were Clare Clairmonts, shamelessly pursuing their Byrons to the point of running from one villa beside Lac Leman to the other in their nightgowns, across the dew-grey meadows. She giggled a little at the picture; she had always thought Clare a funny phoney. And accepting the use of a Government car for a fortnight was hardly on all fours with running about in one's nightgown to pursue a lover.

'What are you laughing at?' Antrobus asked from the bed.

'I thought of something funny.'

'May I know what?'

'No.' Suddenly she found that she had taken her decision. 'And it's "No" to the car, too,' she said, quite gently—' though it was sweet of you to suggest it. Must I drive it to Berne, or can I leave it at the garage of your hotel here, after I've brought your things round, and let them cope?'

He looked at her rather fixedly.

'My dear, why not use it?'

'You must answer my question before I answer yours. Can your hotel cope?'

'Yes, of course. But I still don't see why not.'

Julia went over towards the bed.

'You'll have to learn to understand a lot of things before you're through,' she said lightly. 'Goodbye. Don't forget about June's passport.' And ignoring his outstretched hand she walked out of the room.

315

Chapter 16

Interlaken—Bellardon

It was a good thing for Julia that after taking this knock there was so much to be done as to leave little time for thought. On the other hand going into Antrobus's room at his hotel, and collecting and packing his more intimate accessories, like sponges and pyjamas and shaving-things, was strangely painful. All this might have become part of a common life with him; now it wasn't going to. Nevertheless, his list in hand, methodically, she went through the job, and then rang for the valet to take the suit-case down and put it into the car. In the hall she told the porter that she was shortly bringing the Porsche back to be garaged—'Herr Antrobus will give further directions himself.'

'How goes it with *der Herr*' the porter enquired solicitously. 'I hear that he was wounded in an affray in the Aares-Schlucht. What an affair!

'He is going on well,' Julia said.

'The Fräulein has seen him?'

'Yes, just now. He is recovering. Quite soon I bring back the car.' She hurried away from the kindly man, who obviously doted on Antrobus—well, didn't she?—made the purchases of books, cigarettes, and lighter-fuel that were also on his list, and took everything round to the Clinic. The nurse who answered the bell said—'*Der englische Herr* wished to see the Fräulein when she brought his luggage. He asked this most urgently.'

'Tell Herr Antrobus that I regret it very much, but it is too late,' Julia said, looking at her watch. It *was* late; she would barely have time to get the Porsche back to the hotel and catch her bus—but everything between her and John was too late now. She helped the woman to carry in the suit-case, dumped her purchases on the small table in the hall, and drove away very fast.

At the hotel there was a further delay. The manager came out, washing his hands in the traditional *hôtelier* manner, and asked if Herr Antrobus desired to keep on his room? And what was to be done with the rest of his *Gepäck?* And with the car?

Julia was suddenly exasperated by all this.

'In God's name, ask *him!*' she exclaimed. 'He has the telephone by his bed in the Justus-Klinik.' Really, John might have tele-phoned before now to save her this final worry.

'*Verzeihung!*' the manager said, with a polite bow. 'But as *der Herr* is ill, and as *das Fräulein* came to pack some of his effects, I thought it right to ask her.'

'No; ask Herr Antrobus himself. And can you get me a cab or a taxi? I am afraid I shall miss the Beatenberg bus.'

'Ah, the Fräulein is at Beatenberg? A charming spot. My chauffeur is here—allow me to let him take you to the Bahnhof-Platz.'

The drive up to Beatenberg was long, hot, and wearisome. Julia found a seat at the back—she didn't want to talk to der Chrigl, who, as so often, was at the wheel; even the little tune on the horn was a burden, like King Solomon's grasshopper. In fact between her various exertions—beginning with von Allmen at breakfast-time—and her private misery she was tired to a degree most unusual for her. But there was no respite; she had hardly sat down to lunch with Mrs. Hathaway—late, anyhow—when the good Hanna came to summon her to the telephone. Dreading Antrobus's voice, she walked along to the *Kleine Saal*, but it was Colin who spoke.

'I thought I'd just let you know that everything is perfectly all right. I got in so soon that we were on the doorstep at H.M.'s Personal Representative's as the postman walked up!—so no fuss at all. Everyone here is delighted, naturally.'

'Good—I'm very glad.' At once she thought of June and her passport. 'Look, could you talk to "Philip", whoever he is, and arrange about a passport for our little friend?' (Could she count on Antrobus for anything, now? Not with any confidence.) 'He can check with John,' she nevertheless added.

'That will hardly be necessary. They're all so madly pleased with what you've done—I told them everything—that I rather fancy it will be "ask and have", where you are concerned.'

'Splendid. Well do ask—I'll ring Jean-Pierre and get her home address, date of birth, and so on, and send it. Can she sign the form? She's only 18.'

'I must look that up—hold on.'

Julia held on. Quite soon Colin was on the line again.

'Here you are—between the ages of 16 and 21 "children" must have individual passports, but the application must be signed by "a parent or guardian", it says.'

'Oh, that's all right,' Julia said easily. 'I'm sure Jean-Pierre will sign as her guardian like a shot—after all, she's been posing as his ward for weeks! Post the form to him at La Cure, will you?—and I'll ring up and do the rest.'

'The Pastor isn't a British subject,' Colin reminded her.

'Oh, so won't that do? Well then send me the form, and ring John at the Clinic and tell him to sign as her guardian!—he promised he'd see that it was arranged. I should have thought that there was so much on your files about Jean-Pierre that his signature would be accepted. But if you run into any snags ring me—Mrs. H. would sign, I'm sure. Now I really must go and eat—I'm fainting!'

Over their delayed meal she told Mrs. Hathaway that the vital papers had reached the Embassy safely, and been retrieved by Colin's people; she replied cheerfully to the good lady's enquiries about Antrobus, and reported favourably on his condition. But it was with infinite relief that she at last slipped away to her cell-like room; there she had a good cry, and then lay down on her narrow bed and slept for a couple of hours.

Later on she had plenty of time for thinking, and did a lot of it, reviewing her acquaintance with Antrobus from beginning to end. It was an unhappy process. Julia was as remorseless with herself as she frequently was with other people, and at one point she recalled that she had once made use of poor Geoffrey Consett and his infatuation for her own ends, in the Morocco business. Had John perhaps just been doing the same thing with her? No—honesty and common sense alike recoiled from the idea; that cock wouldn't fight. From the moment of their encounter below the Sessel-Bahn he had known that Colin was her cousin, and hence must have assumed that she was committed to helping him; he had been at pains—and vast official expense—to get her whole record on the telephone from Hugh Torrens in London. Alas, she had to face it—in the common but all too accurate phrase, John Antrobus had simply been 'amusing himself' with her, and she had lost her heart and her head and been had for a mug.

For the time being Julia was too fully occupied to mope. She had to write to the Pastor, asking him to get and send to her the essential facts for June's fresh passport in her proper name; she told Mrs. Hathaway the girl's story, far more fully than she had yet done, and explained that June would have to travel home with them. 'I mean, I've got to take her, and I should so much like to go with you and act as courier—I could save you all trouble. But I'm afraid Watkins will be terribly despisey about her; servants are such frightful snobs! And precious June is just the lower middle-class type that good servants do despise. She'll amuse you, I think, but I'm worried about Watkins.'

'I will deal with Watkins,' Mrs. Hathaway said, in a most convincing voice. 'Yes, do let us all travel together, dear child; you will be the greatest help.'

Nothing ever put Mrs. Hathaway about, and she willingly further agreed to sign a passport application form as June's 'guardian', if necessary. 'Poor child, I'm sure she needs a guardian, if ever a young creature did.'

The application form arrived from Berne, and the facts as to June's birth and parentage from Bellardon, by the same post. 'We have decided to put "blonde" for her hair,' the Pastor wrote, 'though she has confessed to Germaine, as she did to you, that the present shade is artificial. Dr. Lavalle is treating her foot; he says there will be no permanent disfigurement, *grâce à Dieu*. This is a good child, as you said; she sits in the kitchen and slices the beans and peels the potatoes and shells the peas—Germaine finds her a great help. When do you come to us? We await you eagerly. Please make as long a stay as you can.'

Colin's covering letter was less helpful; he had changed his tune since that enthusiastic telephone call.

'Here you are—but please don't try on any funny-business about forged signatures of guardians! We don't want to run into trouble.'

Julia, anyhow overwrought, was infuriated by this. Here was Colin, like almost all junior officials, just making difficulties for their own sake. She filled in the form with everything except the signature of the 'parent or guardian', and then rang up her cousin's number.

'Oh, is that you? I want to speak to Philip.'

'Philip Jamieson? Do you know him?' He sounded astonished.

'I want to speak to him,' Julia repeated. At least she had now got the man's surname—but was he a Major or a Colonel, like so many of them?

'But look here,' Colin was protesting, 'you can't bother him unless it's urgent. If it's just about that infernal girl's papers, tell *me* what you want.'

'What I want is to speak to Philip Jamieson. Do please get him.'

'Well, hold on—I'll see if he's free.'

Of course he was free; in a few moments Julia recognised the cheerful voice she had heard when she rang up from Merligen, saying—'Is that Miss Probyn? What can we do for you? We're prepared to do almost anything after what you've done for us! May I congratulate you on at least three separate excellent performances?'

'Oh good. Yes, there is something you can do. I want the P.C.O. to give a passport to a British subject, to whom you really owe much more than you do to me. Colin is being rather tatty about it, and John A. is in hospital, flat on his back, as you know, so I don't want to worry him. It's this tedious "parent or guardian" business, as she's technically "an infant". Can I sign for her? Her only parent is her mother in London, an old widowed prole.'

A jolly laugh came down the line.

'Don't worry. Have you got the date and place of birth, and the parents' names, and so on?'

'Yes, I've got all that.'

'How is she going to get home?'

'I'm taking her myself, in ten days' or a fortnight's time.'

'Where's the other document? The one she came out with?'

'I should think in the Super's safe in Interlaken,' Julia said. 'I think horrible Mr. B. had it; and as he's now "inside", I presume the Swiss are keeping it as Exhibit A.'

Again that jolly laugh.

'Highly probable! But just check, will you?—and if she's got it, turn it in here. Meanwhile shove in the form, and I'll see that she gets a travel document to take her home without any "parent or guardian" trouble.'

'Oh thank you so much.'

'Shall you be coming to Berne yourself?—if so, we might meet.'

'Possibly. We board our sleepers there,' Julia said, rather cautiously.

'Well let your cousin know if you do make any sort of stop-over. Goodbye.'

In fact when they came to make their plans a stop-over in Berne was inevitable. Julia wanted to spend three or four days at La Cure when she went to fetch June, so when they had found a date on which they could book four sleepers from Berne to Calais it was arranged that Mrs. Hathaway and Watkins should travel to Berne four days earlier, under Julia's escort, and stay in an hotel there to break the journey. Julia, arranging all this in Cook's hot office in Interlaken, found it hard to resist the temptation to go round to the Justus-Klinik and see how John was, but she did resist it—that most terrible of all temptations, of knowing the beloved object a bare half a mile away. Partly at Mrs. Hathaway's suggestion, partly to occupy her mind, she wrote an article on the economic self-dependence of Switzerland for *Ebb and Flow;* this didn't help her much, since all through it recalled John's remarks on the subject, and the places in which he had made them—the views, and tiny details of rocks and small groups of flowers. She wrote to Jean-Pierre about June's bogus passport—had she got it or not? Then Mrs. Hathaway said they must write to June's mother, who lived at Malden, in a road horribly called Something 'Way', and tell her the day and hour of her child's return; of course Julia did this too.

It was gradually borne in on the girl that these various sugges-tions of Mrs. Hathaway's were made with a purpose—the purpose of affording her, Julia, distraction. On the first two days after that disastrous interview in the Clinic her old friend had asked her how Mr. Antrobus was?—Julia said that she hadn't heard. After that Mrs. Hathaway rang up the Clinic herself and made her own enquiries, the results of which she passed on, casually, to Julia. Quite evidently Mrs. H. had seen that some-thing was up, and now had guessed that it had gone wrong; but she was the one person whose perspicacity Julia did not dread. Some time she would tell her all about it—had not Mrs. H. said that Antrobus was *capable de tout?* But not just now.

Colin embarrassed and bothered her by ringing up several times to ask how John was? She gave rather vague replies, based on the reports given by the *Schwester* to Mrs. Hathaway.

'But haven't you seen him yourself?' Colin asked at last, surprised.

'No. Let it alone, will you?' She rang off abruptly—to Julia it was really a relief when they heard that the young man was returning to London. She speculated occasionally as to whether John himself would attempt any further approach or farewell, even if it was only a note of thanks for packing and bringing round his things; she guessed that he would not, and he didn't. This rather raised him in her estimation; he had had the quickness and tact to recognise the double import of the message she sent by the Sister when she dropped his luggage—'Tell him it is too late.' It was too late for anything more—even for the casual kindnesses of taking flowers or cigarettes. It was over.

Colonel Jamieson—'Philip' proved to be a Colonel—in due course sent a travel-document for June. 'The other one was where you supposed,' he wrote laconically, and added—'Here are your protegee's tickets. I know how tiresome the travel-allowance is.' An inner envelope contained a first-class ticket from Berne to London, a sleeper-ticket, and vouchers for meals.

Armed with all these, Julia was ready to go to Bellardon; Mrs. Hathaway was beginning to feel that she had really exhausted the resources of Beatenberg, and to the girl's infinite relief they left the torturing neighbourhood of John Antrobus two days earlier than they had planned, after a telephone call to La Cure. It was raining when der Chrigl drove them down in the Post-Auto, sounding his musical horn; the upper forests were shrouded in mist, and they splashed through puddles crossing the Bahnhof-Platz, where the cab-horses stood with dismally drooping heads, their coats streaked and dark with moisture. Apart from Mrs. Hathaway getting her feet wet, Julia was quite glad that the skies should weep as she left darling Interlaken, the sweet, beautiful little town where she had been so exquisitely happy and so miserably unhappy.

In Berne she insisted on going with Mrs. Hathaway to her hotel and seeing her installed in good comfortable rooms; then she drove back to the Haupt-Bahnhof, where for the third time the same tall grey-blond porter took her luggage to the train for Lausanne. Just before it pulled out another passenger came into her carriage—with something like horror Julia recognised M. Kaufmann, of 'Corsette-Air'.

He recognised her too—Julia's was a face that men remembered—but nothing could have been more genial than his manner.

'Ah, Mademoiselle, *quelle chance!* Once more we travel together! Mademoiselle goes again to Geneva?'

'This time only to Lausanne,' Julia said. It was positively uncanny, sitting opposite this cheerful little man, with his natty summer suit and his brief-case, to think that she had penetrated into his house, spoken with his wife, heard his child screaming, and burgled his desk for vital information—while he now greeted her so warmly. Had the sour-faced Frau Kaufmann suppressed all mention of her morning visitor?—or had he heard, and failed to put two and two together? She enquired politely how his business was going?

'Oh, very well indeed.' Julia expressed satisfaction; he offered her a cigarette, and lit it for her.

'Of course from time to time there arrive *des embêtements*', he pursued, confidentially. 'One expects to bring off a *coup*, and behold, something goes wrong at the last moment.' (Like Hell it does! Julia thought to herself. But obviously the Frau had at least not described her.) She spoke sympathetically, and ventured the hope that he had experienced no serious contretemps?—she was burning with curiosity to hear what else he would say. Herr Kaufmann shrugged philosophically. These things were all in the day's work—only one did not like to disappoint clients.

Julia, who had so successfully caused two of his clients to be disappointed, made appropriate sounds—again, it seemed uncanny that he should be telling her this. The little man then asked politely how she was enjoying her *séjour* in Switzerland?—and added 'Now this time, Mademoiselle really *must* see Mont Blanc! It is a perfect day—all the peaks are clear.'

In fact it was a perfect day. The weather had lifted, and the Lake of Geneva shone a brilliant blue in the sun; at the right spot, this time, the little 'Corsette-Air' man pointed out to Julia Europe's highest mountain, standing up like a vast pearl, projecting into the blue sky above the blue water. She looked at it with delight.

At Lausanne she got a porter and was making her way to the platform for Bellardon when suddenly Jean-Pierre appeared, waving his black felt hat above his so un-clerical grey flannel suit.

'Ah, there you are! I came on the chance; I had to be in Lausanne this morning, but I could not meet the earlier train, which we thought you might take.' Julia explained about taking Mrs. Hathaway to her hotel, and apologised for not having telephoned—'I really didn't know exactly when I should arrive; and when I found out, there wasn't time to ring up. I am so sorry.'

'Do not torment yourself! Germaine is an adept at keeping late lunches for me—cold, or in casseroles. Do you call these hot-pots?'

'No—a hot-pot is a special kind of food: we call those dishes with lids casseroles too.' As they sped through the green fruitful countryside she asked after all the family; Jean-Pierre in his turn informed her that the Banque Républicaine had formally announced to him the recovery of the whole of Aglaia Armitage's fortune.

'The old de Kessler signed the letter, but it was not very informative, so I rang up Maurice Chambertin; like all bankers he was extremely cautious, but he allowed me to gain the impression that you had played a considerable rôle in this affair; and when I told him that you were coming to visit us, he said—"Ask of her." So now I do ask you.'

'Well really June played a much larger rôle than me,' Julia said. 'However, this is how it was'—and she gave him the whole story.

'Made the exchange in the *toilette*! That was very *rusé!*' the Pastor exclaimed on hearing about Andermatt; he bellowed with laughter when Julia recounted her *triage* of the papers in the ladies' lavatory at the Fluss, and laughed more loudly still when she described how she had hidden the documents in a churn half-way up the Niederhorn. 'Really, you should have one of the English decorations for this! You have earned it.'

Julia couldn't bear to go into the subject of decorations, because she and John had laughed about them together. Instead, she asked if the police had been after June in any way? 'Of course she is involved, up to a point; she did impersonate Aglaia, and made false statements at the bank—but I tried to keep her out of trouble.'

No, there had been no difficulties, he told her. 'As La Cure is not registered as an hotel—though often it very much resembles one—I do not have to show the passports of my guests to the police, who in any case know me well. But I must say I feared trouble of some sort, since she was known to have been associated with that gang. How did you manage to avert it?'

'Oh well, one way and another,' Julia said, with studied

vagueness. 'Your police are really very nice, I think.' She wanted to keep the Berne office out of it.

'I expect they also think you very nice,' he said slyly.

They stopped in the nearest town to Bellardon for Jean-Pierre to make some household purchases for Germaine; Julia got out too, and stood in the little street in the hot sunshine, looking at the windows of the small shops, so curiously full of very up-to-date things. When the Pastor returned he threw his parcels into the back of the car; as he held open the door for her to get in he saw her face in the strong light.

'You look exhausted!' he exclaimed—'no, overstrained, rather. This whole affair must have worn on your nerves, I think?'

Julia agreed that it had been rather anxious work. She had not realised that her unhappiness actually showed in her face, and was upset.

'Well, with us you shall rest, and restore yourself. At La Cure there is, thank God, always peace. Oh—have you the new passport for *la petite?*' he added, as they drove off.

'Yes—its equivalent, anyhow. She can get home.'

When they arrived Germaine and June met them on the doorstep; Julia noticed the surprise in her host's face when the young girl threw her arms round her neck and kissed her, saying—'Oh, it's simply *lovely* to see you again! And thank you for sending me here; I am so happy,' she added, with a grateful glance at her hostess. Germaine and June had already eaten, but they sat with Julia and the Pastor while they consumed the soup, the cold veal with salad, and the cheese which awaited them. Germaine too commented on how tired Julia looked, and after coffee dispatched her to her room to rest.

'No, June; you are not to go up now—you can talk with Miss Probyn later.'

'I thought I might unpack for her,' June said. She was hobbling about quite actively with the aid of an ebonised stick shod with rubber, known as a *Kranken-Stock*, but she spoke perfectly unresentfully.

'You shall help me with that when I've had a shut-eye, June,' Julia said. She went up to her old room, and before lying down looked out of the window. Washing still hung along the lines beside the lawn, little apples were beginning to swell in the orchard-trees; the lilacs and peonies were over, but the familiar benign sense of peace and kindness reigned. She threw open a suit-case, took out a wrapper, and removed her pretty linen suit; as she lay down to rest she murmured—'Blessed place!'

She got an even stronger sense of the blessedness of La Cure from seeing June there. The little ill-educated English suburbanite, so many of her values completely shoddy, was the oddest possible inmate of that household; yet there she was, perfectly at home and as happy as a bird, with no sense of strain on any side—and moreover making herself quite useful. Germaine exercised on her the quiet discipline normal in those fortunate families where tradition is still strong; and June did as she was told, obviously with great contentment.

The child duly came up after tea to help Julia unpack, which she did briskly—Julia was again struck by her ease of movement on her bad foot. 'How is your ankle? It seems much better,' she said.

'Oh, it's wonderful! That surgeon or whatever he is, in Lawsanne, pulled it about—oh it did hurt!—and then he said I was to have massarge for it, every other day.'

'But can you get massage here?' Julia asked.

'No, but there's a very good massoose in that little town where Mrs. de Ritter does her shopping, so they've been taking me in—I haven't missed a single day. They *are* kind! And the swelling's nearly all gone—look.'

Julia looked, as the girl held out her foot—the injured ankle had almost returned to the delicate perfection of the other one.

'How excellent—I am so glad,' she said.

'Yes, but how's it all to be paid for?' June asked, with her usual directness. 'That surgeon!—and an English girl who came and stayed a night here told me that Swiss massooses charge the earth, in our money. And these people are *poor*, reelly,' June said, staring at Julia with wide eyes. 'Look at Mrs. de Ritter!—up before six, and doing all the housework, as well as the cooking. I asked her why she didn't have a girl in to help, and she said she couldn't afford it. I don't want them to spend money on me.'

'I've been given the cash to pay for all your medical expenses,' Julia said. 'So you needn't worry.'

'Who by?' June, true to type, was incredulous.

'The bank,' Julia lied swiftly. 'You gave me that tip about the bus-tour, and the papers were all recovered; and the bank people were so pleased that when I said your ankle needed treatment, they gave me the money I asked for. Everything's covered.'

'Oh, I am glad. And that girl, the proper Miss Armitage, will have her money back all right?'

'Yes.'

'I can't think now how I ever came to do a thing like that,' June said thoughtfully, smoothing and folding sheets of tissue paper on the polished top of the heavy old walnut chest of drawers. 'Mum said I was a silly to go in for it; but it was worse than silly, it was downright wicked, helping to steal another girl's money. Oh'—with one of her bird-like hops to a different subject—'what's happened to Mr. B., and that nasty Wright?'

'Mr. Borovali is in prison,' Julia replied deliberately.

330

'What, for stealing the papers and the money?' June turned pale. 'What about Wright? Is he in prison too?'

'Not yet—he's in hospital with concussion,' Julia said—still, in spite of everything, relishing the recollected picture of Antrobus hurling that disagreeable young man into the Aar. 'But he'll be put in prison too, as soon as he's well enough.'

'Out here?'

'Yes. The crime was committed here.

'Oh!' June, still very pale, again stared at Julia, her brown eyes wide. 'And what about me?' she asked. 'Shall I have to go to prison too?'

'I hope not—I've tried to prevent it. You see you did something that's called "turning King's Evidence", and when a person does that—'

'Oh, I *never!*' June interrupted indignantly. 'That's when a wide boy gives away his pals! I never did anything like that.'

'No, I don't suppose you would call Wright and Borovali your pals, exactly,' Julia said calmly. 'But in fact you did, didn't you, at one point decide to help me instead of them—and told me about the bus-tour? That's what is letting you out.'

June began to cry.

'Oh, I never thought I'd be called King's Evidence! That's a nasty thing!'

Julia was startled afresh by June's highly peculiar moral code— for clearly she had one, of a sort.

'Which do you think is worst—to let down two crooks like Wright and Borovali, or to steal another girl's money?' she asked. 'You did let them down, granted; but what you were helping them to do before you changed your mind was plain theft. Which is worst? *Think*, June—you don't think enough.'

June sniffed and dabbed at her eyes with, Julia noticed, the gentian-embroidered handerchief bought in Interlaken.

'Oh yes—"Thou shalt not steal"—Dad was always saying that. Yes, the stealing was the worst, and I'm glad I helped to stop it. But "King's Evidence" is a nasty word to have tacked onto one!'

'Do try to make up your own mind, June,' Julia said rather impatiently; 'don't be fooled by words.' June's attitude to the phrase 'King's Evidence' was, she thought, an astonishing example of the frightening power of certain words among the ill-educated—purely emotive, bearing no relation to morals or conduct. It was like the Trades Unions' idiotic use of the word 'black', which is really only short for 'blackmail'—of the public at large.

The girl's reply, when it came—after more sniffing and eye-dabbing—surprised Julia.

'These people here, the de Ritters I mean, don't care a thing about money. I never knew anything like it! And they're good, and *enjoy* being good. Can you beat that? She's so beautiful, and she dresses quite well; but she does her hair in that fearfully old-fashioned way, and never uses lip-stick—she says the Pastor's congregation wouldn't like it. I will say, they make you think!'

'Well have they made you think whether you did right or wrong to help me to recover Miss Armitage's fortune, which you set out to steal?' Julia asked remorselessly.

'Oh yes, I'm sure now that that was right. Only "King's Evidence" *is* a nasty word.'

'Well it's the word that will keep you out of prison, please God—nothing else will,' Julia said.

June said nothing more, but continued to unpack; in the bright light from the high window Julia noticed that the dark line at the roots of the girl's hair was now very marked.

'You didn't do anything about a rinse?' she asked. 'Wasn't it possible?'

'Yes, I found I could have had one in Lawsanne, but I didn't like to ask for it,' June replied. 'I was worrying about them paying, of course; but even if I'd had the money, I should have felt funny, suggesting a rinse to them! It's not their sort of thing at all. But one of the daughters, Hahnriette they call her—she brings her wash for her Mum to do; as if she hadn't enough work!—said she'd set my hair if I washed it, so I did. Washed my hair in Lux, imagine!—but it came out lovely, as a matter of fact. And Hahnriette set it a treat, don't you think?' She turned her small head this way and that, to display Henriette's set. Julia duly admired it.

'Hahnriette has the sweetest kiddies,' June pursued. 'They run round after me, though I can't speak a word of French. I do like them—I teach them English words, and they love it.' She paused, seeking for words to express a meaning new and unfamiliar to her. 'This is the queerest set-up ever! They're all poor, and they're all good, and yet they're *happier* than any people I've ever known. It makes you think, doesn't it?' she repeated.

After supper that evening June went out to the kitchen to help Germaine put the plates in the washing-up machine, polish the spoons and forks, and generally tidy up; Julia sat with Jean-Pierre in his study. She began by again thanking him for having June, and then brought out the five hundred francs which Antrobus had given her. 'Will this cover her doctor's fees, and all this massage, which is having such a wonderful effect? And then there is the petrol for taking her to and fro; I'm positive Germaine wouldn't have sent the car to Guyardon for groceries every other day!—she's far too good a housekeeper.'

He smiled a little, and sat looking at the notes on his desk, but

333

made no move to touch them.

'Where does this money come from?' he asked at length.

'From my cousin's colleagues. As I told you, the child rendered them an important service by giving me certain information which helped in the recovery of the documents; so when I asked for money on her behalf, I was given it.' She blushed a little, remembering that uncomfortable scene at lunch. 'But I told June a lie about it,' she added rather hurriedly—'I said the bank had given me the money.'

'Why?'

'Oh, do you ask that? How could I let her know that the Secret Service was connected with this? She's so fearfully silly.'

'You do not like her? We have received the impression that she is devoted to you. Most understandably—you have been very good to her.'

'Not all that good—and I've made use of her for my own purposes, or rather for Colin's. I've been rather bothered about that—I was practically trading on her affection. But what was at stake was so vitally important, and at least I did her no harm—in fact getting her here (thanks to your kindness) has conferred a major benefit on her.'

'Why do you say that?' he asked. There was sometimes a refreshing innocence—or was it humility?—about the Pastor.

Julia told him, at some length, about her conversation with June, and the revolution beginning to be effected in the child's muddled values by her stay at La Cure; Jean-Pierre laughed a great deal about the girl's dismay over the words 'King's Evidence'.

'Yes, this is how they think now,' he said. 'Crime is fairly reputable, but to report a criminal to authority is unutterably shameful! The whole moral outlook is becoming completely distorted.'

Julia presently returned to practicalities.

'Well is this enough for her massage, and the surgeon, and the petrol?' she asked, touching the notes on his desk. 'I suppose she's due for two or three more treatments by the masseuse while I'm here, isn't she?' (She had a moment's regret that she had not got the Porsche to run June about in, and to be parked by the Frégate at the edge of the village green outside La Cure.)

Now, at last, Jean-Pierre looked at the money.

'In fact this will be exact,' he said—'even covering the extra petrol, which I would gladly have given. You have begun a good work on this child, and if we really have, as you say, contributed to it, that is a privilege for us.'

'Of course you have—you've done far more than me.'

'Will you be able to keep in touch with her?' the Pastor asked.

Julia was greatly taken aback by this question. The idea of visiting the house in What's-it Way at Malden had never occurred to her, and was distinctly dismaying. She was kind by nature, but it was a casual, spontaneous kindness, lightly given and soon forgotten.

'Do you think I ought to?' she asked.

'But obviously. Any redemptive work needs to be followed up, followed through. What future do you envisage for her?'

Julia was positively horrified. It had never occurred to her for a single second that she was doing a 'redemptive work' for June, and the future she had envisaged for the girl was the same as her past—going on having her feet photographed in pretty shoes for advertisements. She had taken a certain amount of trouble to ensure that this employment could continue, but she had never looked any farther, and she told de Ritter so frankly.

'I could see her from time to time, of course,' she said at the end. 'But this job seems to suit her very well.'

'You really think so? A job that simply involves advertising her body, or parts of it? If she is as foolish as you seem to think, I should have thought it rather dangerous for her.'

'I haven't thought about it at all,' Julia said, flatly. 'I'm not a do-gooder. She makes her living from her feet, and I've tried to help her to go on doing that—and to keep her out of prison!' She rather resented these problems suddenly being thrust upon her. 'Have you got other ideas for her?' she asked.

'Yes. But you are tired tonight—we can discuss them later. I will call Germaine; she shall take you up to bed. Here you shall rest.'

Chapter 17

Bellardon—Berne

Those six days at Bellardon did Julia a lot of good. As the Pastor had said, there was peace at La Cure; but almost more useful to her state at the time was the being immersed in the life and concerns of a quite different set of people, who knew nothing of her private trouble, and attributed any lack of spirits on her part to the nervous strain of rescuing Aglaia's fortune from a gang of desperate criminals, armed with revolvers. The affair in the Aares-Schlucht had of course got into the papers, though not its real background; and to Henriette and Armand's wife, when they came over with their children to get their washing done, Julia was a heroine to be admired and cosseted, merely because she had been present. 'You saw the shots! But this is extraordinary!' Henriette exclaimed—'To see people shooting with intent to kill!' (Julia had some rather unenthusiastic thoughts about neutral nations, which she suppressed.)

But the presence of Germaine's grandchildren introduced a new idea in connection with June.

'This young girl really has a great gift for children,' Germaine exclaimed one day, looking from the kitchen window into the garden, where Gisèle sat tranquilly sewing in the arbour while her infants swarmed round June, who was folding paper caps for them out of an old copy of the *Gazette de Lausanne*. With Julia, Gisèle had just hung out a line of newly-washed sheets along the lawn, and, as her mother watched, one of the children went and fingered them, leaving muddy marks.

'*No,* 'Toinette! Naughty!' June said, and slapped the fat little hand; ' Toinette pouted and cried a little, but two minutes later she was cuddling up to the English girl as confidingly as ever— '*Meess June, faites-moi un papper-cap.*' Julia had already noticed with surprise that June, herself half a child, not only enjoyed playing with the children but in fact kept them in order with the flat, matter-of-fact competence of working-class people, untroubled by psychological theories; if a child did wrong it was slapped, promptest and least troubling of punishments.

'It is really a pity that she could not take a position as *bonne d'enfants* out here,' Germaine pursued, returning to the window after a careful glance at the various saucepans on her big stove. 'There is such a demand for English nurses and governesses, and they are very well paid, especially with the rate of exchange. Would not this be a more wholesome employment for June than being photographed for advertisements?'

Julia hesitated before replying. On the night of her arrival she had resented the Pastor's attempt to saddle her with the respon-sibility for June's moral welfare—partly from sheer fatigue. But earlier she had also resented, fiercely, the use to which a harmless child like June had been put. The Modern Face Agency had let her in for Mr. Borovali—what would they let her in for next time? Being a *bonne* in some respectable Swiss family was obviously a much more wholesome—*sain* was the word Germaine had used—form of employment for the girl. But Julia was always practical—and now wished to be noncommittal.

'She'd teach any little Swiss she was with an appalling accent,' she said. 'And no grammar at all. She's completely uneducated.'

'So? All the same they would learn some English—and she is a person who can rule children easily, which is the essential.' She turned away to her cooking, and Julia went out with a basket to pick peas.

She left Bellardon three days later not only with regret, but with a strong sense of privilege that Fate and Colin between them should have sent her there; it would have been a real loss not to have met Jean-Pierre and Germaine and seen the calm beauty of their lives. As for June, when the Pastor had driven their luggage down to the hot little station—June's ill-gotten trousseau of clothes was too much for the hand-cart—she burst into tears, and threw herself into Germaine's arms.

'Oh, you have been so good! I'll never forget it. And I've been so happy. Give my love to the kiddies when they come over—I shall miss them like anything.'

Jean-Pierre wrung Julia's hand.

'Come back! *Ne manquez pas!* We shall expect you.' He lowered his voice and spoke in English. 'Thank you for what you have done for my godchild—I think at some cost to yourself! See her when she returns to England.'

'Of course I will—I want to.'

The long train from the frontier drew in, the stationmaster and Jean-Pierre put the luggage aboard, Julia kissed Germaine, June pulled herself up the high steps and nipped along to their carriage; she and Julia both leaned from the window—lowered

339

to get the luggage in—as the train pulled out.

'Bye-bye! Thanks again!' June shouted, waving. The Pastor had removed his black hat and also waved it in farewell. 'Remember that he who has put his hand to the plough must not look back,' he called, his resonant preacher's voice carrying above the noise of the train.

'What on earth did he mean by that?' June asked, when a curve in the line hid Bellardon, and they sat down on the soft grey-green seats.

'I can't imagine,' Julia said carelessly; she could in fact imagine only too well, and was still a little reluctant.

June had some ideas of her own about her future, very concrete ones, and as the train rolled through the rich country-side she put one to Julia.

'Miss Probyn, you said Mr. Borovali was in prison. How long will he be there?'

'Oh, seven or eight years, I should think, at the very least. It was a big robbery, with forgery and all sorts of other things as well.'

'Can he pay me my screw from prison?'

'No, certainly not. And for your own sake you'd better forget that you ever knew him,' Julia said sharply. 'You don't want seven years in prison yourself, do you?'

June's face puckered with dismay.

'Oh no!—that would kill Mum! But who will pay my salary? Six pounds a week I was to get, and it's just on six weeks now since I came out. I can't afford to lose my pay'.

'No one will pay you anything, and you mustn't ask for it.' Julia foresaw the silly child possibly tackling the Agency on this head. 'Don't you realise that you will be tremendously lucky if you escape going to prison yourself? Don't be a fool, June.'

'But I ought to have my pay!'

'No you oughtn't—not for helping to commit a crime. Anyhow the bank gave me something over £40 for you, because you turned King's Evidence'—Julia deliberately used the distasteful phrase. 'That is more than your six weeks' pay, and it has put your foot right, or nearly. Let it go.'

'Well if you say so, I will,' the young girl said. 'Only I meant to repay you the money you lent me in Interlarken out of what Mr. B. was to give me. Never mind—I'll save up and pay you back. £12 it was, wasn't it?' She glanced up at the broad racks above their heads, loaded with her luggage. 'At least I've got my outfit,' she said, in a satisfied tone. She paused. 'Anyhow I don't feel now that one ought to worry so much about money—I mean not after staying with the de Ritters. Rich or poor, they couldn't care less! But one can't get out of the habit all at once, and every-one else I know does. Except Dad—he was always talking about not serving Mammon.'

Mrs. Hathaway had arranged to bring her luggage in early to the Haupt-Bahnhof, and that they should all dine together at an hotel only a short distance from the station before boarding their sleepers. On arriving in Berne Julia put her and June's luggage in the *consigne* too; then they walked across through the warm bright evening towards the hotel.

'There wouldn't be time to see the bears, I s'pose?' June asked. 'This is Berne, isn't it? Mr. B. said there were real bears here, in a sort of sunk place they can't get out of, and that they'll eat buns if you give them to them on a stick. He said he'd bring me to see them before we left. I *would* like to see a real bear—not like that silly old Golden Bear!'

'No, there isn't time now,' Julia said, thinking how well the hatefully astute Borovali had taken June's measure, and offered

341

the appropriate lure and bribe to every facet of her character: her vanity, her cupidity, even her childishness. 'But some time when I'm in London I might take you to the Zoo,' she said recklessly. 'There are bears there. I expect you've been, though?'

'No, never. It's such a long way from Malden. Oh. I should love that.'

A tall dark man was sitting with Mrs. Hathaway in the lounge of the hotel when they went in; after June had been introduced to Mrs. Hathaway he was presented in his turn—'Dear Julia, let me introduce Colonel Jamieson, who is longing to meet you.'

'I have really gate-crashed this party with that object,' the Colonel said. 'I met Mrs. Hathaway at lunch at the Embassy three days ago, and when I overheard her telling the Ambassador that you would be coming through tonight, I forced myself on her. Didn't I?' he said, turning to his hostess.

'Well yes!—but I was delighted at the opportunity of seeing you again.'

Watkins, seated at a table a short distance away, now came bustling up.

'Good-evening, Miss Julia—I'm glad to see you looking so much better! Now, Madam, is this the young lady who's travelling with us?' She shook hands cordially with June. 'Would you like to come and have a nice lemon-squash with me? As we shall be sleeping together tonight we might as well get to know one another.'

Julia saw, without surprise, that Mrs. Hathaway had dealt with Watkins to some purpose concerning June; she also noticed the keen appraising glance with which the Secret Service man followed the small, slightly limping figure to the other table, after he too had shaken hands with her.

'So that is Miss Phillips?' he said. 'How pretty she is—and

342

what an extraordinary resemblance.'

'Oh, do you know Miss Armitage?'

'No, but of course when this thing broke we got every possible photograph of her—though you were ahead of us in turning in that one from *Paris-Match*'.

'Miss Probyn so often seems to be ahead of people,' Mrs. Hathaway said blandly.

'You *are* kind; you mean ahead of Us! Yes, invariably; that is one reason why I wanted so much to meet Miss Probyn.' He turned to Julia. 'And to say Thank you. You retrieved the whole situation. May I ask you one question?'

'Yes, ask away—I won't promise to answer,' Julia said.

'What prompted you to snatch the German lady's bag with the papers in it, in the Aares-Schlucht?'

'No real reason. I simply thought the owner was a vulgar fat woman, who'd stuffed her bag with eatables—and a revolver; such an odd combination. So I just snatched it,' Julia said. She was not going to admit to a stranger the other reason.

'Oh, when did you find the revolver? I hadn't heard about that.'

'I didn't find it—it fell out with the biscuits and chocolate and all the rest.'

'What happened to it?' the Colonel asked, interested.

'It went the way of Mr. Wright, into the Aar,' Julia said, with her slow grin. 'Mr. Antrobus kicked it in. How is he, by the way?' she asked, as casually as she could.

'He came through yesterday; he isn't allowed to walk much yet, but the wound has healed very well,' Colonel Jamieson said.

'And what about Wright? Is he still in hospital?' This was a useful cover-question—first John, then Wright.

'No, he soon got over his concussion; he's in prison, along with his detestable superior.'

Julia glanced across at June, sucking lemon-squash through a straw at Watkins's table, in cheerful conversation with the lady's-maid.

'What about the little creature?' she asked. 'Will she be all right?'

'Oh yes. She was our main source—through you. Any-how you're taking her out of Swiss jurisdiction tonight.'

'How soon could she come back into Swiss jurisdiction?' Julia asked, thinking of Germaine's suggestion.

'Oh, as soon as her hair has returned to its natural colour!' Philip Jamieson said—'and with a proper passport in the name of Phillips. Naturally you realise that this is all a frightful wangle' he went on; 'but she did produce crucial information at a crucial moment, and the one thing the Swiss do really worry about is the reputation of their banks. Of course we fell down on that infor-mation, and you saved us—but I have tried to underplay that part, and to put her up as the saviour of the Banque Républicaine.'

'Very wise,' Mrs. Hathaway put in. 'Miss Probyn does not really need the approbation of Swiss banks, where as it has obvi-ously been of assistance to Miss Phillips.'

Colonel Jamieson gave her an appreciative grin. 'Nothing could please me more than to have your approval, Mrs. Hathaway,' he said.

Julia had a question to put too.

'What about Monsieur Kaufmann of "Corsette-Air"?' she asked. 'I met him in the train the other day on the way to Bellardon, and he seemed as merry as a grig.'

'No!—did you really? How amusing. Did he show any signs of distress?'

'All he said was that it was *"embêtant"* sometimes to have to disappoint one's clients. But the Swiss police must know quite well who his clients were; will they get after him—for the bank's sake?'

'I rather think he may be advised to restrict his activities to his lawful business of selling surgical stays,' the Secret Service man said guardedly. 'But however much he may have wished to oblige these particular clients, in fact he did nothing except receive a telephone call. One might say that he is the second person your activities have kept out of prison,' he added, with a glance at the neighbouring table.

Colonel Jamieson soon afterwards took his leave, and they all went in to have dinner. June had evidently got onto quite comfortable terms with Watkins, but she was a good deal overawed by Mrs. Hathaway, with her height, her grey hair, her assured manner, and clear incisive way of speaking. In fact the older lady went out of her way to be nice to the young girl, enquiring about her foot, her advertising work, and her mother; but June was too abashed to give more than brief answers—there was none of the giddy outpouring to which Julia was accustomed, though a direct question as to whether her mother was not lonely while she was away at work elicited the fact that 'Mum' belonged to a whist-club, which occupied all her spare time.

'She's like a real dowager on the films, isn't she?' June observed to Julia in the Ladies as they were washing and tidying-up before going to the train. 'One can just see her wearing a tiara at some grand ball!' Julia, who took the dimmest view of the utterly phoney dowagers usually displayed on films said Yes, but the thing about Mrs. Hathaway was that she was kind.

'Oh I'm sure she is—only I mean she doesn't look it,' June said. 'Dowagers don't, do they?'

Julia went on ahead to get all the luggage out of the *consigne* and register the big pieces through to Victoria; she met the rest of the party at the station entrance, and with their small luggage they boarded the *Wagons-Lits* coach to Calais. This was very hot, after standing all day in a siding in the sun; the gleaming mahogany panels, the green plush, everything was warm to the touch; the windows were closed and the slatted shutters drawn up. Mrs. Hathaway sank down on her bunk—the beds were already made, but even the fresh sheets were not cool, as sheets should be—opened her bag, and handed Julia a fifty-franc note.

'Do give that to the attendant, and tell him to come and open the windows.'

'But that's four pounds!' Julia said, rather shocked.

'Yes, but there are four of us. In any case I want a bottle of Vichy Water, and so do you, I expect—and what is four pounds compared to being asphyxiated?'

Julia went and did as she was told. The note produced a deep bow and instant attention; the bottles of Vichy-Water were brought—with corks; their tickets and passports were taken over; the shutters were lowered, and the windows, in both compartments—when Julia went to supervise this operation in the one next door, occupied by June and Watkins, she found the girl screaming with laughter, half-way up the little carpeted ladder leading to the top berth.

'I told her I'd sleep on top, Miss, because of her foot,' Watkins said; 'but she says she has a fancy for the steps.'

'There was none of this when we came out,' June observed, climbing down after the man had left. 'Sat up all night, we did. I call these beds lovely—and this.' She patted the little ladder. 'And the wash-basin is ever so clever, folding up like that.'

'Now, shall you be all right, Watkins?' Julia asked.

'Oh yes, Miss. It's much better with a bit of air.'

'Well if you get cold in the night just ring that bell and tell the man to put the window up a little.'

'I can't tell him anything, Miss,' Watkins said, smirking complacently.

'I can work the window myself,' June put in. 'See?' She raised first the window and then the shutter, and lowered them again.

'There's a smart girl! Yes, Miss Probyn; I shall be all right with her.'

'Good-night, then'—she returned to Mrs. Hathaway.

'Yes, they're fine,' she said in answer to a question. 'June's taking the top bunk, because she has what Watkins calls "a fancy for the steps"; and she can work the window too,' she added, with her gurgling laugh. 'I wish this tedious train would leave, so that we could undress and go to sleep. Are you very tired, Mrs. H.?'

'No, not in the least. But I think I will unpack, and get out my sleeping-pills and so on.'

'I'll curl up on top while you do,' Julia said, and climbed a little ladder like that which so pleased June.

'Do smoke,' Mrs. Hathaway said, quickly and expertly taking what she required from her small dressing-case. 'Here's something for you,' she said after a moment; 'something I'm sure you'll need tonight'—and she handed up a small pewter saucer with delicate but rather florid ornamentation. 'The worst feature of top bunks in sleepers is no ash-tray,' Mrs. Hathaway pursued. 'I thought you could carry this in your hand-bag for journeys. Don't lose it—it's an old one.'

Julia was examining the small object delightedly.

'It's quite beautiful,' she said. 'Darling Mrs. H., how very good of you. It's the perfect thing. Where did you find it?'

347

'In an antique shop here. Rudolf Waechter came over a couple of days ago to have lunch and say Goodbye, so I asked him to help me to get it—all the *antiquaires* here know him too well ever to try to swindle him. He thinks that it's not Swiss, or it would be plainer; possibly South German, or perhaps from the Low Countries. But it is quite a good piece—probably seventeenth century.'

Julia climbed down the ladder and gave her old friend a hug. 'Mrs H., it's too darling of you! Why should you give me an antique ash-tray?'

'Why not?' Mrs. Hathaway replied, kissing her in return. 'But do go up aloft again, or I shan't have room to move.' When Julia had obediently re-climbed the ladder, pewter ash-tray in hand, Mrs. Hathaway spoke again, measuredly.

'Apart from the fact that I wanted to give you a pretty ash-tray to travel with—instead of that horrible tin lid that I have so often seen you carrying about—I felt that you ought to have some tangible reward or memento, however small, of what you have done. Our officials can't do it, and for June's sake, as you heard, they have wisely prevented the Swiss authorities from understanding the true position; I didn't really understand it myself till Colonel Jamieson and I had a little talk at the Embassy, and he did what I believe they now call "put you in perspective" for me. So I thought *I* would give you something.'

Julia didn't venture to climb down again for fear of being in the way, so she spoke her thanks over the edge of the bunk. She was almost ready to cry, touched by the charming present and by Mrs. Hathaway's feeling that she deserved a reward, but tormented by the fact that she so little wanted any reminder of this Swiss trip. The up-and-down conversation went on.

'Rudolf Waechter sent you his best wishes—he said he was

too old to send you his love,' Mrs. Hathaway remarked from below. Julia said that Herr Waechter was a lamb, and she wished she'd seen him again. Then, with a smart switch of subject—'What are you going to do about this child June?' Mrs. Hathaway asked.

Julia, touched a moment before, felt a little impatient even with her beloved Mrs. H.

'Why should I do anything about her?' she asked, knocking ash from her cigarette into the little pewter dish, perched on the green blanket of the upper berth.

'Oh, surely you can't get out of it?' Mrs. Hathaway said, opening the wash-basin and preparing to brush her teeth. 'Is there any real difference between the slopes of the Niederhorn and the road from Jerusalem to Jericho? And if ever anyone fell among thieves, she did.'

Julia was silent, at last rather ashamed of her reluctance to 'take on' June. When the tooth-brushing was over she told Mrs. Hathaway of Germaine's suggestion that June might take a post as a *bonne d'enfants* in Switzerland.

'Oh, that was why you asked Colonel Jamieson how soon she could re-enter Swiss jurisdiction? I think it an excellent idea; if it was arranged through the de Ritters, as of course it would have to be, one could be sure of her being sent to a suitable family. Yes, obviously that is the perfect solution,' Mrs. Hathaway said, rinsing out her tooth-glass and beginning to wash her face in soap and water; her generation did not use creams and cotton-wool to clean their faultless skins. 'But what is she to do till her hair grows brown again?' she asked, as she dried her face.

'Oh, go on with modelling her feet—she doesn't need her hair for that, and she can wear one of those full smothering French berets that cover everything,' Julia said. 'Pity we aren't going by Paris, or I could have got her one; but Fanny de Purefoi is always coming over—I'll make her bring one.' She paused. 'Someone ought to call on the "Model Face" and hint to the manager not to give her any more outside jobs, don't you think? You'd do that much more impressively than me, Mrs. H.— could that be your share in this Good Samaritan effort?' She stubbed out her cigarette, gratefully, on the pewter saucer, so much firmer and more solid than the tin lid which—Mrs. Hathaway was quite right—she usually carried in her bag for use as an ash-tray on journeys.

Mrs. Hathaway laughed. 'Very well.' As she spoke the train at last pulled out; the blessed air came in at the window as the express began to roar across a darkened Europe, in fact soon Julia had to climb down and raise the shutter so that Mrs. Hathaway should not get chilled as she undressed. 'Are you coming to bed?' that lady asked, when she herself was comfortably installed.

'Not just yet, if you don't mind; I thought I'd stay up till the frontier, in case there's any bother over June's travel-paper—that attendant man pulled rather a face when I gave it to him. But are you dying to have the lights out and go to sleep? If so I'll undress now; I don't a bit mind confronting officials in my nightgown.'

Mrs. Hathaway laughed again.

'No, I'm not at all sleepy; I'd like to talk for a little.'

'Good.' Julia climbed down from her bunk and perched on the little pull-down snap-up seat attached to the wall; there she lit another cigarette.

'I had a letter from Edina in Berne,' Mrs. Hathaway said. 'She asks us both to Glentoran—she was dreadfully disappointed that I dragged you away the moment you arrived, and so was Philip. So you will come up with me, my dear child, as soon as we have resettled your protégée in her detestable employment—where she must remain while her hair grows—I see that. But I think you need a rest,' the older woman said firmly.

Julia began to feel nervous.

'I've just been having a holiday', she protested.

'No, dear child; not a holiday at all. First you were nursing me, and then having some very wearing experiences. Now you ought to have a change; and one can really rest at Glentoran. It is so peaceful there.'

Julia nodded. There was always peace at Glentoran, as there was at La Cure; a different *ambience*, but the same peace. Only what did Mrs. H. mean by 'wearing experiences'? She looked at her old friend's wise, kind face, framed between the white pillows and the mahogany panels, and saw there what made any attempt at concealment useless. Suddenly she burst into tears. Mrs. Hathaway leaned out and stroked her hand.

'You had every excuse, but I am sorry that it should have happened,' she said presently. 'A most charming man, but a *coureur*'.

'Was that why you said he was *capable de tout?*' Julia asked, wiping her eyes.

'Yes. I mean that I said it because I thought it; I wasn't warning you—one doesn't warn people of your age, it wouldn't be any good if one did. But I did recognise both his quality—which is great—and his charm, and I became rather alarmed on your account.'

This speech was immensely comforting to Julia; it made her feel less of a fool.

'There really *is* good in him, don't you think?' she asked. 'As well as all his gifts and his interests, like birds and flowers and climbing?'

'Yes, I think so. Only at his age he should be less self-indulgent and more scrupulous,' Mrs. Hathaway pronounced. 'His fatal weakness is that he hasn't realised this. But you may have taught him something.'

'I felt such a beast, not going to see him, or taking him flowers or anything,' Julia said, immensely relieved at getting all this secret trouble at last presented before the incorruptible tribunal of Mrs. Hathaway's standards.

'Oh no, you were quite right. When I telephoned from Beatenberg he was always begging to see you, but I said that you were too busy. I think he took it in, in the end,' the old lady said.

The train slowed to a halt; from the darkness outside, farther down the platform, came the demand '*Les passeports, s'il vous plaît,*' addressed to the non-*Wagons-Lits* passengers. Julia got up, her little seat flipping up behind her.

'I think I'll just go and lurk,' she said.

'Leave it to the man, unless there is trouble—but I feel sure there won't be,' Mrs. Hathaway said.

In the corridor Julia found Watkins lurking too, but for a different reason.

'I said I'd just let her get undressed and into bed,' the maid said, with a nod towards her and June's compartment. 'Is Madam in bed? She ought to be.'

'Yes, all tucked up some time ago,' Julia replied.

'That's right. I didn't like to come in and disturb you. Has she got her Fishy Water?' Watkins asked, with an old servant's jealous interest in her mistress's welfare.

'Yes—and with a cork in the bottle, so it won't spill. Would you like some Vichy, Watkins?' Julia asked.

'Oh no thank you, Miss. I only tried it once, and fishy it tasted to me! There's a water-jug in that wash-stand affair, if we're thirsty.' She tried to peer out of the window. 'Why are we stopping? Is this a town?'

'Not really—it's the frontier, where they do the passports.'

'Ah. Will *she* be all right?' Watkins asked, with another nod in the direction of the sleeper door. 'She seemed a bit worried about her passport—something wrong with it, I gathered.'

'She's got a new one,' Julia said. Oh, dear foolish gabbling June!—how much else had she told Watkins? She soon learned some of it.

'You know, Miss, she's really a very decent little girl, if she is a bit flighty and silly,' the maid pursued. 'She gives a lot of her pay to her mother, to help her out—a widow's pension isn't much. But I don't fancy the idea of her going on doing all this modelling, or whatever they call it. It's my belief that these agencies lead young girls astray, as often as not—I mean I think they're often agencies for other things than adverts! And she's silly enough, in a way, to be taken in by anyone. Couldn't you get her into some decent job, where she'd be safe? She'll take anything *you* say, that I'm positive of; she thinks the world of you.'

Julia, glancing down the corridor, saw the frontier officials in a huddle outside the *Wagons-Lits* man's little cubby-hole, going through the passports of the sleeper passengers—she watched them, and was immensely relieved when they went out to by-pass the sleeping-car on their way to the next coach.

'Good!' she muttered. 'Yes, Watkins, I think there is a chance that I might find quite a nice job for Miss Phillips, and I mean to try, presently. Good-night.'

'Good-night, Miss,' the maid said, and after a tap on the door re-entered her compartment.

Julia stood a moment longer in the corridor. First the Pastor; then Mrs.H.; now Watkins! Undoubtedly June was her

353

neighbour; there was no escaping that fact. But June's pretty, silly face was not the memory that she must carry home from this journey, whether she would or no; it was the memory of a gothic face, with triangular eyelids and a twisted smile. Tears smarted again behind her eyes; she brushed them away angrily—goodness, what a fool she was! Anyhow there would be peace at darling Glentoran, and in time she would forget. Like Watkins she tapped on a polished wooden door, and went in and rejoined Mrs. Hathaway.

Ann Bridge was born in 1889 in Hertfordshire. Bridge's novels concern her experiences of the British Foreign Office community in Peking in China, where she lived for two years with her diplomat husband; her works combine courtship plots with vividly-realized settings and demure social satire.

Bridge went on to write novels based around a serious investigation of modern historical developments. In the 1970s Bridge began to write thrillers centred on a female amateur detective, Julia Probyn, as well as writing travel books and family memoirs. Her books were praised for their faithful representation of foreign countries which was down to personal experience and thorough research. Ann Bridge died in 1974.

Lightning Source UK Ltd.
Milton Keynes UK
UKHW022247281119
354412UK00005B/1145/P